I0452628

Time and Chance

A Novel

Tom Blackburn

<u>Time and Chance</u> is a work of fiction. All characters and situations herein are fictional, and any resemblance to actual persons and events is purely coincidental.

Copyright © 2016 Thomas R. Blackburn, and Tom Blackburn Books. All rights, including the right to reproduce this book or any portion of it in any form, material or electronic, are reserved to Tom Blackburn Books of Washington, DC.
ISBN 978-0-9826576-7-6.

Cover design: Bofers Studios

By Tom Blackburn:
<u>Fiction:</u>
The Cello Francesca, or, Balderdash

The Hap Maryland Series:
Surviving Mozart
Thanks to Mister Merrydown
Roots of Evil
On Honeyman Bald
Dancing With Granny
Assisted Living

Time and Chance

<u>Nonfiction:</u>
Equilibrium: A Chemistry of Solutions
Getting Science Grants

Tom Blackburn Books

Time and Chance

I looked around and saw under the sun, that the race is not to the swift, nor the battle to the strong, neither yet bread to the wise, nor riches to men of understanding, nor yet favor to men of skill; but time and chance happen to them all.

- Ecclesiastes 9:11

Time and Chance

1.

F AYE BYNUM, recent graduate of Mount St. Anne High School, Class of 1947, stands before a mirror on the top floor of a rooming house – *L. Merrill, Transients and Long-Term* – on Mecklenburg Street in Charlotte, North Carolina. Faye is not Long-Term; nor is she exactly Transient, how that sounds. She is here for the summer. She is dizzy. Sleepy and wide awake, and thus dizzy. Looking back at her is a Depression refugee with a sober face hung in a frame of straight, not exactly stringy, black hair that crowds forward on her temples, giving her an exotic air; Levantine or gypsy maybe, though she is 100% black Irish.

Face: pale, intelligent, not plain, but no knockout; level black eyebrows, eyes so brown as to be pretty much black too. Chin solid, romantic, 19th-Century; mouth wide, considering, unsure. Nose, well, generous. Shoulders: slumpy, with funny bumps on top. Belly: flat but soft-looking from neglecting her situps. She will go back to them tomorrow. Hips: narrow but, she must admit, kind of graceful. She bends a knee to cock them slantwise, streetwise, provocative; then straightens up. Legs: long, muscular. Kind of bowlegged, or just skinny? Toes wiggle on skinny feet that have always been kind of big. Grandpa said once it would take a strong wind to blow her off them.

In the mirror, the reflection of a half-unpacked suitcase, a cigarette balanced on the hinge, smoke rising blue and lithe into the lampshade, emerging from the top jumbled and grey. She hates cigarettes, but look here, a Room of Her Own in the attic of Mrs. Merrill's Transients. She finished the Virginia Woolf piece on the endless haul across Illinois, clutching it to herself as she dozed into Ohio. No parents, no Gordon to nag or tease about it. Under the lamp, a letter from Gordon, mailed two days before she left St. Louis, so it would be here when she arrived. She has not opened it because she already knows what it will say.

A song bumps and grinds through her brain, *You've come a long way from St. Louie* - which she had - with insistent ragtime alternating major and minor sevenths: On the one hand, on the other. A long way from Saint *Looie*, but *bay*by, you *sti-ill* gotta *long*. Faye recognizes it as heartbeats, rendered too abrupt by lack of sleep, by the hallucinatory ride from St. Louis to Charlotte that, long before its end, became a matter of doggedness, leaning forward, pushing, watching the flat prairie roll back as the old smooth mountains swallowed her, hid her away from Gordon. Gordon's letter. Postmark Fort Leonard Wood, Missouri. Baby, we'll have a house of our own. Baby, we'll have all the time in the world. Baby, we'll have a *bay*by.

"A house of our own," is something Gordon started plugging not long after she granted him a first kiss, sort of playing house, sort of seriously, not very, on Faye's part. The fun of kissing startled Faye, whose upbringing by nuns and a devout Mama would have militated in other directions - any other direction - if consulted, which it was not. The thing is, Gordon - or kissing Gordon, Faye never bothers to think much about the difference - is so pleasant that Faye sometimes has a hard time focusing on her writing, which is the other thing at which Faye is precociously excellent.

A year before Faye finished at MSA, Gordon graduated from Northside, having excelled in nothing but football and foolishness. But he had been fun to dance with, and he went straight into the Army, before Faye began to realize - at the prompting of a dry stick of a nun named Sister Rose Penitentia - that she, Faye Bynum, was cut out for bigger things than playing house with any Protestant Private Gordon Simmons. A teaching career, maybe writing of some kind. Probably not holy orders. Probably not journalism either, but that is the part of the University of Missouri in which Faye is pre-registered, and in fact what has drawn her to Charlotte in the broiling summer of 1947.

Time and Chance

Faye doesn't want a house or a baby, at least not soon enough to think about. Faye has a gift with words, or so the guy at the Charlotte Star-Dispatch claimed. Come on out, take this internship, we'll show you the ropes. Faye suspects that means, we'll let you make our coffee and sharpen our pencils. But there would be hope of better. Hope of becoming a writer, being published, of making people sit up and draw breath at beauty and power. If Faye has any gift, it is nothing much yet, she knows that. But the speed and cleverness of words, the sensuous admiration of her own work, stitching and tweaking to make it better – these are what hope is made of.

Some of Faye's gift is just that, a hand-me-down from older, better writers, real stuff like Leaves of Grass, Gatsby, and Sweet Thursday that led in their turn a certain distance along the road that even Gordon sees when he looks at her. Faye's finger circles a hickey Gordon's nibbling mouth put under her chin, that has still not faded after four days. For a time, Gordon and writing were parts of the same thing, a thing as sinuous and lovely as the smoke that rises into the glow of the lamp. Now, Gordon has gone to be a soldier, and writing means North Carolina, vast absence from him that will either be temporary or not; more likely not. Heartbeats alternate. Charlotte, *Gordon;* writing, *Gordon;* hope, *Gordon.* On the other hand, on the one, or the other.

Faye picks up the cigarette an instant before it burns the edge of the suitcase, flicks ash to the floor, draws on it, faces the mirror and holds the glowing tip under her chin, close enough that she can feel the heat on the skin of her throat, where it could burn off the hickey that Gordon made. Closer, until it starts to burn. Here it is. A movement of my hand, a nod of my head, like the tiny nod that will be all it takes to put me on the train to Fort Leonard Wood, I'll have a scar for life. I'll have to wear a scarf. *Wonder if that's where it comes from. I'll have a scarf, or life.*

Time and Chance

The rising smoke carries a faint burden of scorch. Miz Merrill's gonna kill me, I smoke up this room. Faye draws a breath and opens the screen to throw the cigarette out the window, a shower of sparks through the chuckle of Southern bugs. Sister Penitentia nods approval from behind the mirror. This isn't the end of the world. I'll write to him.

About the trip. About Mrs. Merrill, her barely functional hearing aid, and her cat that looks like her hairdo; about the mountains and the heat and the steam locomotive from Raleigh down to Charlotte. Not about the ferocity of Gordon's wooing – if such it was.

Wooing. Pitching woo. Faye can't help laughing at the silly, sad word, a word like a dog would sing, but wouldn't give your Aunt Mabel a hickey on her little finger. There's nothing *woo* about Gordon, he comes at you like a truck, like he's mad about something, and all the time he's whispering about love, you can feel his engine, steaming away. Being married to Gordon would be about as much pain as pleasure, and not a very pleasant sort of pain at that, it seems to Faye.

On the other hand, it's not like they'll be in bed all the time. Gordon is the kind of fellow who will do what he says. The House of Their Own might, though probably would not, contain a Room of Faye's Own, but there will at least *be* a house, banks are falling all over vets these days. And really, look at that lanky dame in the glass. How many other men had come along, or would be likely to in the time she will spend here, working her fingers off and trying not to look like "wife material," which is what Gordon calls her to his buddies, talking about how true-hearted she is.

There it is, isn't it? She has no illusions about true-heartedness. She is far from home. You'd think, she thinks, that would make home things more dear to her; it makes them less demanding instead, already a time left behind, along with the iffyness of Journalism school, Daddy's penchants for fast cars, weak budgets and frequent absences, and Gordon's daunting charm. Every mile the Southern's rickety railroad carried her, she could feel her heart lightening, plunging her into dark Southland that in its turn knew nothing of her except - in one place - that she had the ability to write a decent English sentence. No Sister Penitentiary, no Gordon, even no Mama, whom Faye loved dearly above all others, including Gordon.

This summer is her time. If other chances come along, she'll have the choice of breaking Gordon's heart, or her own. Either way, no hope. If hope is what she wants, she will have to stay here - not here on the third floor of Mrs. Merrill's Transients, but in some place like it; stay by herself her whole life. That will have its own kind of pain, but it will be small on any one day. A nickel a week, say, out of her wages; the wages of having a career, of being herself and not Mrs. Gordon Anything. And the hope could make up for it. Most of the time.

Faye puts on a cotton nightie, and sits on the bed. The bed is lumpier than she noticed when she tried it at Mrs. Merrill's garrulous invitation, Faye's daddy's check for two months' rent in her hand. Before Faye can turn out the light, she has picked up the letter and opened it. It looks like Gordon wrote it with a two-inch pencil that he sharpened with his teeth. Every loving, wooing, hound-dog word confirms what she'd known would be there. She drops the letter to the floor and turns off the lamp. Hope, she thinks, has got to be about the lonesomest thing there is.

2.

L EN BIGGS said, "Welcome to the Charlotte <u>Star-Dispatch</u>." Len had a speech impediment that rendered the name of the paper almost impossible to hear without giggling. Faye didn't giggle, but the other intern snorted a little bit, which could have been a boy's version of a giggle. Len Biggs looked like he was used to it. He sent the guy a stony look, and kept talking. Faye was glad of the snort, because it took Len's attention off her.

The other intern looked like a dope. Cowlick, vee-neck sleeveless Argyle sweater, little bow-tie like Jimmy the office boy in Superman. Soft look to him, like somebody that didn't miss meals, and slept in of a morning. Big funny near-sighted blue eyes that seemed to miss a lot of what was going on, or maybe they were just fastened on something else – Faye wanted to be fair – that she, nor anybody else in the room, couldn't see. Faye got out the steno pad that she bought at Kress Drug, and started taking notes.

Forget this television baloney, Len Biggs told them. Edward R. Murrow coming on with a haircut and a way of talking. Folks will never trust what they can't hold in their own hands and read for themselves. And they won't trust some magazine, either, that comes four or five days after the shouting is all over, and tries to pretend it's news. No, it is newspapers that folks trust, and afternoon papers like the <u>Star-Dispatch</u>, that bring a thoughtful, settled view of developments, more than the morning papers with their fat headlines and their travel contests and silly gimmicks. Young Mr. Morgan and Miss Faye – Len took the trouble to learn their names, Faye noticed, a little embarrassed – were right at the heart of journalism, a vital, almost sacred profession in an up-and-coming city, and Len Biggs, for one, envied them the wonderful careers that lay before them. Appropriate, of course, to a fella and a young lady, respectively.

Len Biggs went on to say a good deal more in his Daffy Duck diction about trust and duty and mutual respect between a newspaper and its community, with its "family of readers," before he finally walked them through the pressroom, the plummy ink smell of the reception area now magnified a hundred-fold, along with the roar and the heat. They watched the enormous stripe of newsprint racing along and magicking itself into a line of newspapers, potbellied guys with newspaper hats and giant wrenches smoking and watching slit-eyed for trouble. A little bald guy with scarred fingers and an eyeshade, hunched under the blazing menace of a linotype machine, made them each a slug with their names on it in mirror-writing. Faye admired hers, tossing it from hand to hand while it cooled off, and decided she would get herself an ink pad, and stamp her name on things with it. Maybe sign her next letter home with it, Mama would get a kick out of that.

"Downstairs is where they sell the ads, that keeps us going," Len Biggs said, with pious dismissiveness. "But this here," he pronounced, swinging open worn double doors, "this here's your newsroom. This is what makes the difference between a newspaper and a phone book. Them offices over there are the editors – they ever stick their noses out, you be sure they catch you with your nose stuck in your work. Rest of us get desks out here in the bullpen, helps us stay in touch with what-all everybody else is up to. Editors set policy, write editorials about the UNO, Harry Truman, and God, and figger out what amounts to news and what don't, each day. Reporters and feature writers check the assignment board, and then go out and get the facts and write the paper, whether it's who pitched for the Hornets, or what young ladies come out in the Cotillion, or whose house got burnt down. This here's where you two young folks'll be learning your ropes."

Time and Chance

Faye looked around the room. There was a mild bustle, not exactly the stop-the-presses atmosphere you'd see in a movie. About everyone there was a man. The air was rich with ink, sweat, smoke, and something a little smoother, that Faye thought might be bourbon, the time of day being a little past noon by now. In a far corner, an angular woman sat with a phone jammed between her shoulder and her ear, nodding, scribbling, blowing smoke from a crimson downturned mouth. Len Biggs smiled at Faye, looking a bit like an unfriendly fish, not necessarily a shark.

"Alma Brackett," he said, a little cryptically. "We figgered you for her, Miss Faye. What Miz Alma don't know about the social life in this town ... well, frankly, who'd care?"

"Frankly, not me, sir," Faye said. "I was kind of hoping - "

"That's exactly right, little lady. Social life is society, and society is civilization, some fella says. The rest's just riff-raff. Now, young Forde, as for you."

Forde Morgan, Faye thought. Sounds like a car dealer, got twisted backwards in a tornado. Kind of looks like one, too. She looked across the room at Alma Brackett, now scratching her head, tapping a pencil on a notepad. The phone was back in its cradle, but her shoulder was still hunched against the side of her head. Faye could see the dandruff snowfall all the way from here, where she stood poker-faced while Len Biggs talked to Forde Morgan about his assignment. Obits to start with, then sports, City Council by the time the summer's over.

"And what," Faye asked, "will I graduate to, after I finish with Miz Brackett?"

Len Biggs looked at her, an eyebrow up. "Y'all had your lunch yet?" he asked.

*

Time and Chance

"Star-Dispatch, thiz Alma Brackett ... Why, Clara Thatcher, as I live and breathe, you know you needn't to worry about us on top of all your other planning. You just tell little Evvy not to worry herself, we've had her Introduction on our calendar since March, dear ... Of course. We'll have a photographer there the day you call us, you just count on it. And not some football fella, our very top fashion ... Yes, Ma'am. All righty. 'Bye."

Alma Brackett's smile faded as she turned back to Faye. "OK, Hon," she said. We'll set you up a table next to me for now, you can put your things in the coat closet, or stick 'em under the table, I guess. There's a card table in the breakroom closet you could use."

She tapped Faye's carefully typed resumé, grunted, and shook the last cigarette out of a grey pack. "Now. It's a lovely fine thing you won this internship, I bet they're just like to bust their buttons back there in ... mm ... in St. Louis. But honestly, there's hardly any way I can keep a helper busy a whole summer. This beat almost writes itself, given experienced supervision of course. I can do that with both hands behind my back. How am I supposed to use a kid from way Missouri somewhere, when you don't even know the people we write about?"

"I don't know," Faye said. "Maybe I ought to talk to Mr. Biggs and work for somebody else."

Alma Brackett looked thoughtful, and shook her head. "No. If he thinks I'm not cooperating, I'll never hear the end of it. No, I'm stuck with you, honey. We'll just have to make the best of it."

Other way around, Faye thought. Do me no favors. "Yes, ma'am. Is there some errand I could run for you, help out that way?" *Sure, run down to the City Hall and see who's like to be a corrupt boss, write me a thousand-word exposé.*

"Sure, Hon." Alma Brackett handed her the crumpled cigarette pack. "I'm out of smokes. Spuds."

"Yes, ma'am. Pack or carton?"

"Carton. Menthol." She dug in a drawer and came up with a $2 bill. "Keep the change."

"Yes, ma'am. Is there a place nearby?"

"Kress, down the corner. Don't be all day at it."

Faye left the newsroom, face burning, extra gentle with the swinging door so she wouldn't make a fool of herself trying to slam it. On the sidewalk, Forde Morgan, his stupid bow-tie bobbling, laughed at a joke from the middle of a little knot of men who seemed to be coming back from lunch. White shirts and fedoras and ties swam in her vision, and she turned her face away and headed for the Kress's at the corner. They'd have chips and a coke, which was about all Faye could afford anyhow.

When she got back to the newsroom with the cigarettes, Alma Brackett was settling a hat on the back of her head. It was kind of an orange skullcap, with a pheasant's tail feather rising from the back. She looked, Faye thought, like if Sacagawea converted to Judaism.

"Gimme a pack and put the rest in the drawer, Hon," Alma Brackett said. "I got an appointment with Mrs. McCrae, her girl Joan Rae is fixing to come out in August. Be back around three, maybe four."

Faye found courage, picking at the end of the carton. "Couldn't I go along with you? Watch how you work?"

"You want to meet Mrs. Millington McCrae, dressed like a waitress?"

Faye looked down at the corduroy jumper that was about the best clothes she owned. She held out a pack of Spuds, a little out of easy reach. "You could pass me off as your, um. Your personal assistant. Personal assistants don't have to dress so smart, do they?"

Alma Brackett grimaced, looking like she was trying not to grin. Or maybe trying to burp, Faye thought. "Scrub the grease off your chin, Hon. We'll give it a shot."

3.

Dear Mama -

I miss you something awful, but I am settled into a nice place, you would like Mrs. Merrill who is deaf as a doorpost and has a cat who is friendly but standoffish, something like Mr. Pickles. My room has lots of space for things. It is on the third floor, so very hot just now, but cozy toward morning when things cool down.

I am working for now with the lady who writes the Society page at the Star-Dispatch, and have tried to make myself useful. Today we interviewed Mrs. Millington McCrae, la-dee-da, whose daughter is to be presented to Charlotte society next month. (Did we forget to present me to society? How will they know which one is me the next time I'm home in a crowd of young ladies?) Anyways, Miss Alma Brackett, who is the lady I work for, drives a Packard, no less, though it has seen many better days. I think it must be from before the War. Miss Alma Brackett told me always to drive Packards when I have my own car, because it is foolish penny-pinching to settle for anything cheaper, and causes more trouble in the end. I hope you will please keep that in mind when you get tired of taking the trolley downtown.

Alma Brackett (I'm sorry, I can't call her just Miss Brackett, since everyone here always uses both her names. It is possible that her name comes in two inseparable parts like Piers Plowman or Pius XII. You would never hear _him_ spoken of as just Pius, or Mr.

XII.) Anyways, she says that the Millington McCraes and people in their circle are the indispensable warp and woof of civilization, and that without folks of their quality American society would be nothing but flotsam and jetsam on the river of humanity. I am hoping to learn flotsam from jetsam while I am here, as well as warp from woof and many other useful distinctions that professors at Mizzou will surely expect of me.

There is another intern working at the Star-Dispatch, a chubby fellow from somewhere East of Charlotte, which I understand from Miss Alma Brackett as well as from Mrs. Merrill, is the land of sand farmers, mill towns, and dirt ignorance. He did not, as I did, win his internship through merit, pluck, and the moral instruction of Sister Penitentiary. Rather, his Daddy owns a little newspaper out there in the sand, and young Mr. Morgan (Mr. Forde Morgan, doesn't that just tell you all you need to know right there?) is being groomed, as they say, for taking it over. So far, he is taking peaceably to his grooming, and not kicking or banging around in his stall. I somewhat fear that Mr. Morgan will have a more interesting time of it than I, learning all the facets of the news business while I strive to understand the difference between the McCraes and the MacRays, the second being a family of neither warp nor woof, but at most flotsam, if they aren't downright jetsam. Mr. Millington McCrae knows warp from woof because he owns nine textile mills, as well as a dimwitted but very woofy daughter; Mr. Verlin MacRay owns nine daughters and a Chevy.

Well, it is late, and I did not sleep very much last night, being too excited and tired from the train ride. Please give a special hug to Mr. Pickles (bandaids are in the kitchen drawer), give one also to Daddy the next time he comes through, and keep me in your kind thoughts.

Your loving and only daughter –

MISS FAYE BYNUM

(Don't you _love_ that? A compositor made it for me on a linotype machine. Oh, Mama, just saying that makes me feel so professional !)

4.

W HEN FAYE came downstairs in the morning, Mrs. Merrill was out, and a good-sized Negro lady was washing dishes. "Oh," Faye said. "Good morning."

"Ma'am," the lady said, without turning from the sink.

"I was wondering … is Miz Merrill around?"

"Wen'day Miz Merrill's hair day," the other said. "She don't be here while I do for her."

"I see. I'm Faye Bynum, by the way."

"She tole me."

"Well," Faye said, opening cupboard doors. "Then you're one up on me. I didn't know she had a, a maid." She found the bowls and got down the box of Post Toasties she'd bought yesterday.

"She do, for a fact. You fixin to get that dish dirty?"

"No. Yes. I'll wash it up." Faye waved her letter to Mama. "Is there a post office near here?"

"No'm. Leave it in the do'."

"Well, it needs a stamp, though. May I ask your name?"

"Junie. Leave three cent caish with it."

"Hello, Junie. I'm F – I'm working down at the Star-Dispatch." Faye poured milk on her cereal.

"Yes'm. When you fixin to leave?"

"Well, I just got here."

"Yes'm, I means this morning, I can do your room."

Faye put her Toasties on the table with a touch of briskness. "Well, my goodness, Junie. You don't have to do my room."

Junie smiled and nodded. "That a fact? What you think Miz Merrill say to me, she come home and find your room not done, still a tangle?"

Faye was silent, chewing for a moment. "First place," she said, finally, "it's not a tangle to start with. Second place, I can keep my things straight for myself, thanks." She took another bite, chewed, and spoke suddenly around the milky wreckage on her tongue. "And third place, why would she be poking into my room in the first place? I understood that I was renting a space with some privacy." *A room of my own.*

Junie laughed, more or less the way Jesus might have laughed at some of Saint Peter's sillier ideas. "What time you fixin to leave?"

*

Alma Brackett was in a bad mood. It was not easy to see that at first; her face was clenched and sour, good times and bad. What tipped Faye to it was the eerie, extra-mile politeness with which Alma Brackett greeted her.

"Good morning, Miss Bynum. Please be seated. Would you care for some gum?"

"No, thank you." Faye put her lunch bag on the table and smoothed her other dress under herself to sit. "What - "

"I have been considering the question – or the problem, I suppose – of your time here. It would be a shame to send you to college ignorant of some of the real inner workings of a big-time newspaper like the Star-Dispatch. There is a good deal more to it than talking to people and writing down what they say."

"Yes, Ma'am. I'm sure that's - "

"For example, how do you suppose I am able to drive a Packard automobile, even an old one, on a reporter's salary?"

"I don't know. I reckon it's really none of my business."

Alma Brackett showed Faye a face of long-suffering. "Right, and at the same time sadly wrong, Miss Bynum. Right, in that my personal life would ordinarily be none of the business of a young person like yourself, and a stranger at that. Wrong, doubly wrong, in that ... " Alma Brackett paused to marshal her line of thought.

"Ma'am, are you upset with me? Did I do something?"

"Don't interrupt when I'm instructing you, be so good. We'll get to your question in due course, but the short answer is, Yes. Doubly wrong, I say, in that to a real newspaper woman, there is virtually nothing that is not her business. Do you understand?"

"Yes." Sober face, narrowed eyes.

"And further, it is your business because it evidences something fundamental about newspaper work. Do you know what my base salary is at this newspaper? Don't even think of saying it's none of your business."

"No."

"Well, I'll tell you, honey. It is forty dollars a week."

"Yes, Ma'am?"

"Can you do simple arithmetic?"

"Yes."

"Good. Don't go sullen on me, by the way. Never show emotion to someone who is giving you information, they'll shut up like a nun at Mardi Gras. Now, then. forty a week, that's the income, week in and week out. How's it sound to you?"

It sounded pretty big to Faye, whose last job, shelver in the St. Louis public library, paid her $14.40 a week in the summer when she could work at it full time. "OK, I guess."

Alma Brackett sniffed. "More than you ever saw at one time, would be my guess. Never mind. Look at the outlay side, bear with me here. Income tax takes the first $3.87 from every paycheck. I pay rent of fifteen dollars a week for a house that I occupy with my mother. Groceries for the two of us cost ten a week. Where are we so far?"

"$28.87 a week."

"Correct. How much do I have left for other things?"

Time and Chance

"Um, $11.13 a week. Ma'am, Miz Brackett, I - "

"Mother's doctor visits and medicine run us another five a week on the average. Miscellaneous, including gas, oil, insurance, and repairs for the Packard – I just calculated this for last year – averages seven fifty a week. Cigarettes, dollar ninety a week. Once in a while, I buy myself a hat or go to a movie. The boy who mows my lawn Saturdays charges a dollar, the little pirate. Now where are we?"

"In the hole $4.27, plus whatever your hats and movies cost."

"Good for you. You have a quick mind, evidently. Do I appear to you to be worried about the poorhouse?"

"No, but I expect you're not showing your emotions."

"That will start any second now. Why not, do you think?"

"You have other money, I guess. I appreciate your telling me all this."

"I'm glad to hear it. It would be none of your business if you had not taken ten dollars of that other money out of my pocket yesterday."

It felt to Faye like Alma Brackett had stabbed her with an icicle. "Ma'am? I did nothing of the sort!"

"Did you not? Do you recall how our visit to Mrs. Millington McCrea ended yesterday?"

"Ma'am? She asked her butler to bring your coat, after you finished getting her to sign the form."

"The form."

Faye shook her head dizzily. "Yes ma'am. Where she signed up for extra pictures and all."

"Mm-hm. Where she _might_ have signed up for an eighteen by 24 portrait of little Joanie Rae in her ball gown, the eight by ten soft-focus in the candlewood frame, and the pack of wallets."

"Well, didn't she?"

"No, Miss, she did not. You saw fit, at the exact instant she was _about_ to sign – against her better judgment but carried away with the excitement of her daughter's debut and anxious to be sure she was handling this important social occasion acceptably – to ask her if you could use the bathroom. Do you remember?"

"She never signed?"

"She did not. Possibly without realizing it, she was looking for any reason in the world not to spend the money without dear Millington's permission, but she was afraid of looking chintzy in front of the society reporter and her personal assistant. At that point the mousy little assistant introduced the subject of toilet functions. What did she do, Miss Quick-Mind?"

"Well," Faye said. "She asked Joan Rae to show me to the ladies."

"Irrelevant, Miss. No, she regained her footing. She straightened up, she smiled, and became the gracious hostess, and not the worried little housewife. She relaxed like somebody had given her dope. After she sent you off on your mission, she was a different woman. She looked straight at me and saw me for what I am. A woman who God forbid works for a living, an inferior hustler scrounging a few extra dollars. She folded up the form and said she would speak to Mister McCrea about it. She never will, of course."

Faye sat back. "And you missed a ten-dollar cut, is that it?"

"That is it. Or, using your arithmetic, I missed being $5.73 to the good this week instead of $4.27 down. Ask Mr. Micawber what the difference is."

" 'Result: Misery,' " Faye quoted. "I see. I truly am sorry, Ma'am. I suppose it doesn't help if I say that as far as I can see, Mrs. Millington McCrae is a ninny, and little Joan Rae is a spoiled dimwit?"

Alma Brackett drew back like the Pope from a snake-handler. "Ninnies and dimwits are our bread and butter, Miss, and don't you forget it. You owe me ten dollars."

Faye sighed. "All right. I can give you part of it now, and the rest when – well, as soon as I can."

"Mm. What part, and how soon?"

Faye pulled a red leatherette wallet out of her purse. "Two dollars. That's half what I got to live on until the end of next week. My folks will send me ten dollars then, and you can have part of that."

"Fine. Let's have the two."

Faye handed Alma Brackett the folding money with shaking fingers, and then raised her head. "Just a second. You had me keep the change from your cigarettes yesterday, which amounted to nine cents. I wasn't figuring on that, so here it is back. Please put that toward my debt. I owe you $7.91."

After work, Faye walked through bug-clamorous sundown to the Piggly Wiggly and bought a box of dry milk for 59¢, a loaf of bread for a dime, and a jar of apple jelly – after hesitating over mint jelly, which cost the same and might be more tasty, but would probably wear thin – for 11¢. It put a prodigious hole in one of her two dollars, but Faye figured she'd taken care of lunch for the next ten days. The Post Toasties and milk she'd already bought could be stretched that far, leaving supper, which might have to be apple-jelly sandwiches and dry milk. If Miz Merrill saw that, maybe she'd share some leftovers once in a while. Or maybe not, but Faye didn't care in any case; she was still mortified and furious at Alma Brackett. When she got to the checkout, Forde Morgan was there.

"Oh," Forde said. "H'lo."

"Hello." Faye put her things on the counter and gave her attention to a Reader's Digest. *Czechoslovakia: Red Mayhem on the Moldau; Can a Negro Play Major League Baseball?*

Forde Morgan plunked a quart of cream soda, orange juice, ice cream, six cans of Dinty Moore, a dozen doughnuts, a Little Debbie and a bag of potato chips next to Faye's rations. "How was your day?"

"Lovely, thanks. And yours?"

"Well," Forde said. "They are nice enough fellas, Mister Biggs an' all." Faye sniffed and used the box of milk powder to push the other things up to the cashier, the rumpled penultimate dollar riding along on the bread. "Still and all," Forde said. "I'm not convinced they take these internships real seriously, are you? I was hoping for a real apprenticeship, like the old guilds used to have. In Medieval times and all."

Faye narrowed her eyes a little, to keep from widening them. The oaf had not said "Mid-evil," but had pronounced it as if he had some idea what it meant. "I'm still hoping for the best," she said. "I'm not too impressed yet." She granted Forde a thin smile in recognition of his articulate little blurt, and tucked her two dimes change in the snap pocket of the red wallet. Forde glanced at the wallet, blushed, and looked out the window, past the newsprint bargain posters to the tranquil street. A streetcar passed, clangor and fogged pale windows in the dusk.

"Shoot, there goes my trolley," he said. "Well, then. Um, would you permit me to walk you home? Folks here are good folk and all, but it's getting toward dark, maybe not a perfectly safe time for a lady – "

"That's nice of you, but I'm sure I will be perfectly safe. It's not far." Faye picked up her bag and walked out, leaving Forde to contemplate the cashier's hand looking for cash.

"Four seventy eight," she said. "Keep trying."

*

The Charlotte <u>Star-Dispatch</u> afforded its staff a "break room" at the far end of the basement, next to the pressroom. There was a table, some unmatched chairs, lockers, and a circular fluorescent light that gave everyone the complexion of a teenager. Here staffers who didn't expect to be summoned by an editor – for example, because the daily editorial conference had just begun and would surely run another half-hour, or because all the editors were out to lunch, as happened regularly on Fridays – could eat lunch, hit the bottle, or get a nap. Here Faye Bynum fled to escape Alma Brackett and to eat her lunch, and here Forde Morgan found her on Friday at the end of the second week of Faye's and Forde's internships.

"Oh," he said, closing the door on the clamor of the presses. "Hey."

"Hey, Forde." Faye was tired and discouraged, and looked it.

"Payday," Forde offered, waving a blue envelope. "Man, feels like it's been a month."

Faye put down her jelly sandwich. "You're getting paid?"

"Well, a course. You doing this for free?"

Faye shrugged, and said nothing. Forde blushed furiously, and walked to the end of the room, where a drink box held a selection long on mixers. He put in a nickel, buying the freedom to open the lid and take out as many ginger ales, Nehi's, or six-ounce Cokes as he cared to. He selected a pair of Grapettes and popped the tops off. When he turned back, Faye was stuffing waxed paper into a brown bag.

"Hey," he called. "You're a quick eater, you know that? Here I got you a Grapette to have with your san'wich, and you already done finished it."

"I decided I wasn't hungry. Thanks, though. You have it."

"I already got one. Listen, um? Faye? That was a pretty good piece you did on the D a' C rummage sale."

Faye gnawed the corner of her mouth. "Thanks. We don't have many Daughters of the Confederacy in Missouri, so I worked hard on it. It's going in for a Pulitzer, Alma Brackett told me."

Forde took that seriously for a second, and Faye kind of admired how he handled it, the dope. "Aw," he said, then. "You know there's no fun in kidding me. I believe everything anybody tells me."

Time and Chance

"You should be working for Alma Brackett, then, in place of me. That's what makes things woof and warp along, is folks willing to suspend disbelief."

Faye watched Forde work at that for a while, and just clearly put it aside to think about later. "I came down here," he said, "looking for you. See if you wanted to help me blow some pay and go out to dinner tonight. How about it?"

His face was shiny, and his voice shook. Faye didn't think it had much to do with the heat and vibration of the pressroom. "I have a regular boyfriend back home," she said, and immediately hated herself for it.

Forde blinked, as if she'd recited from the Koran. "Oh, that's OK," he said. He laughed with, seemed to Faye, something like relief. "Me too. Well, a girl friend, I meant of course. But she's back home, and I expect your fella's even farther away than that. Not implying that we'd be up to anything sneaky or, you know, dishonorable, but I'm kind of lonesome for friends here. This here's the biggest town I ever been in in my life, and I get tired of seeing faces I don't know. This'd just be friends, to sit back and compare notes, like. And, well, there's the new Bob Hope at the Meck Palace that Mr. Len's letting me write the review for. I get my way paid, so I could split with you."

Faye laughed. "Oh, good. Let's see, it's 40¢, so half of that leaves me three cents. I can still mail a letter."

"Leaves you three cents out of what? You really are working for free?"

Faye opened her mouth, closed it, and turned to the door. "Not exactly. I'll be just fine, thank you."

Forde watched her open the door and walk out. She was wearing her hair in a pair of forward-slanting, Judy Garland-ish braids that cruelly, he felt, exposed the pale double ridge of tendons at the back of her neck. Her second-best dress was as loose on her as Dorothy's pinafore had been in Oz. Forde was stunned.

"Wait," he said, to the unslammed door. He yanked it open and caught up with Faye by the compositor's desk.

"Faye," he said. She turned fractionally, smiled, kept walking.

"Listen," he said.

The compositor winked at him. "Keep trying," the compositor said.

5.

THE CHARLOTTE STAR-DISPATCH
INTEROFFICE MEMORANDUM

TO: Miss Faye Bynum   Date: Friday, June 20, 1947

FROM: Forde Morgan, Editorial Assistant

SUBJECT: Strangers' Faces

It has come to my attention that 100% of the persons I encounter outside the confines of this newspaper is a perfect stranger, not known to me, nor even related to anyone known to me. Scientists at Duke University have shown that mice exposed to populations consisting entirely of other mice not related or otherwise known to the subject mice develop anxiety symptoms, compulsive behavior, loss of fur, failure to thrive, and either aggression or withdrawal, with a 14% decrease in life expectancy. This morning, as I was working on the Reverend Max Reilley's obituary, a hair fell off my head, I swear it, and landed across the "L" and "O" keys of my typewriter. I think it was trying to spell out "lonesome." I am, in short, experiencing loss of fur and failure to thrive. A 14% decrease in life expectancy is nearly ten years; years that you could easily restore by providing me a known face to contemplate this evening. I would be most sincerely grateful if you could see your way to granting this boon.

*

Time and Chance

THE CHARLOTTE STAR-DISPATCH
INTEROFFICE MEMORANDUM

TO: Forde Morgan   Date: Friday, June 20, 1947

FROM: Faye Bynum, Intern

SUBJECT: Strangers' fur and loss of face.

Given that my face is probably one of the strangest you will ever encounter, extra contemplation of it can only aggravate your problem. I do have a soft place for thriveless mice, though, so I have done some research of my own. Bus Number 276 leaves the Trailways terminal at Fourth and Brevard Streets at 6:04 this evening, with a scheduled stop in Gabbro, NC at 10:17. Though that is probably a late hour for Gabbro, NC, there may well be a crony or two around the terminal yet, yawning and scratching while a porter mops under the buzz of fluorescents. And of course, you will have all of Saturday and most of Sunday to nibble cheese and revel in hometown faces, including, of course, that of your Gabbro girl friend. Bus Number 275 passes through Gabbro westbound at 4:24 on Sunday afternoon and arrives in Charlotte at 8:50. I look forward to seeing you on Monday, at least as hairy as ever and restored to normal life expectancy.

*

Faye kicked herself all weekend about saying "of course" twice in one sentence. And there was something wrong with "thriveless," too, but no alternative sounded any better. That's what comes of writing when you're hungry and irritated, she thought. Last week's hoped-for letter from Mama brought not the promised ten dollars, but five, along with an oblique reference to another speeding ticket, closing with a promise of better times to come when payday rolled around. Daddy, who had toured the Midwest as Barnstormin'

Bill Bynum in a Gilmore monoplane racer while Faye was growing up, and flown even faster planes in the War, had trouble slowing down afterwards.

Faye figured to see if she could get away with giving $2 and a promise to Alma Brackett. The residue would buy her another ten days of bread and jelly, and the dry milk was still over half full. She wondered if she would have to somehow trick Forde Morgan into asking her out to dinner again. She wouldn't turn him down a second time. But it would be just like him not to ask.

On Sunday afternoon, she took a walk around the neighborhood, seeing mostly husbands and wives, some of them walking dogs and others pushing strollers. Once in a while, a bunch of kids about her age would roar past in an ancient Ford coupe, grinning and intent on scaring themselves. At the far corner from Mrs. Merrill's Transients and Long-Term, a diagonal street, shaded and cool, offered relief from the square blocks and orthogonal glare of a dead-west sun. It was lined with cottages well tucked under live oaks and loblollies, with sparse and peaked grass struggling against the shade and biochemical defenses of the trees, who apparently did not brook the least competition for rainwater and nutrients.

Faye walked on, trying to appear busy and belonging, but unable to bustle convincingly. She identified with the grass. The street rounded a corner and terminated abruptly at a weathered barrier, around which the sidewalk continued through a screen of saplings and across a footbridge that spanned a minor creek. Evidently, auto traffic was not encouraged to penetrate from Mrs. Merrill's neighborhood to what lay beyond. Faye pressed on, and saw that the creek delineated an abrupt up-tick in affluence. The first house beyond the screen of trees looked to be adequate for a family of fifteen, though unlikely to shelter nearly that number. Its address was spelled out in custom-forged black iron lettering. Faye, rather than stand gaping at it, returned to sit on the little bridge and watch the minnows cruising over the pebbles on the bed of the creek, envying their secure occupation of even a subaqueous place of their own in this town. After a mindless time, she rose to return to her stifling garret. Half-way up the shady diagonal, she encountered a pair of families walking a brace of boisterous dogs. They were all strangers, and every last one of the them made eye contact, smiled, and offered her a good afternoon. *Warp, you good folk*, Faye thought, smiling back. *Woof, you doggies*.

When she came in, Mrs. Merrill told her she looked pale and skinny, and gave her a slice of peach pie. She took it upstairs, gloating over its weight and shine, and ate half of it while she wrote a newsy, noncommittal letter to Gordon. It was pretty much a replica of her letter to Mama, except that she skipped the flotsam-jetsam part. It only would fret Gordon, and make him write awkward letters about was she sure she was doing the right sort of thing.

The heavy, sweet pie made poor company for the apple jelly sandwich that was already in her stomach. It made her a little dizzy and nauseous so she lay down, wondering if it was time to leak more salt onto the altar of hope and lonesomeness, or if not, why did she feel so restless and sad. She dreamed of snow, vast heights, and railroad tracks, and woke at dusk with the sharp taste of fear in her mouth, to find Mrs. Merrill's cat on the desk, nibbling at the rest of the pie.

6.

A T THE Star-Dispatch the next morning, Faye found an oblong box on her card table, next to her blue pencil and list of proofreaders' marks. It was most of a pound of Velveeta. Under it was a little card: *Nibbled all weekend, couldn't finish this. Take what you like, and put the rest in the trash.* Faye looked around, saw no sign of Forde Morgan, and put the box aside to wait until he could see her throw it out.

But Forde was not to be seen. By skimming past, not lingering over, the assignment board, Faye gathered that he was probably interviewing a football coach about spring practice. She could picture it, the coach avuncular and tubby, a bunch of lunks behind him on the field sweating and trying to cripple each other. Forde's vague eyes squinting at the sun and the weirdness of it.

Faye picked up the Velveeta and juggled it in her hand over Alma Brackett's wastebasket, and didn't drop it. *Who am I kidding?* She wrapped it in yesterday's Classifieds and tucked it in her bag. It would give her two new sandwich options to go with the apple jelly: Velveeta, and Velveeta and apple jelly. There might be enough there to make the difference between making it, or not, to Daddy's paycheck. And speaking of that ... Faye sorted through the six dollar bills in her wallet to find the two most rumpled, and tucked them into the corner of Alma Brackett's desk blotter with a note, *I owe you $5.91.*

She was proofing Alma Brackett's blood drive story, *Chairman Bettye Blessing Milford vows to surrpass 1944's high-water mark of 547 pints*, when Miss Alma Brackett arrived, unpinning the Indo-Talmudic hat. Faye let her get settled, find the $2, and start clattering drawers open and shut before she opened the dictionary, found "surpass," and turned to Alma Brackett. "I finished proofing the blood drive story," she said. "It's quite – "

"Five ninety five," Alma Brackett said.

"No," Faye said. "It was $7.91, and I gave you two dollars."

"Interest," Alma Brackett said. "You think I lend money for free? Nobody in this town does that. Half a percent a week is what it'd cost you downtown, and believe me, I know. Go down to Miller's Pawn if you think you can get a better rate there. Half a percent of almost eight dollars is four cents. $7.91 and four is $7.95. At that, I'm giving you the first part week at no interest."

Faye stared at the wall, swallowed, and nodded. "All right," she said. "I'll get you the rest of it as quick as I can."

"Good, Hon," Alma Brackett nodded. "That's what interest's supposed to do, keep you interested in paying off. Let's see if you found all my typos in the blood drive piece."

"I found one," Faye said. "Surpass."

"All right," Alma Brackett said. "What else?"

"That was all. But I'm not sure – "

"Really? Come on, now."

Faye picked up the typescript, but Alma Brackett plucked it out of her hand. "Ah-ah," she honked. "When you put it down, it's gone to press, for better or worse. The reputation of the Star-Dispatch is riding on your getting it right before it leaves your hands."

"Yes, Ma'am. Well, then, if you want to know, I don't think 'high water mark' is a very good expression to use in a story about blood."

"Don't mm? What's wrong with it?"

Faye stared at her. "Well," she said. "Meaning no offense, but why don't you say donations have slowed to a trickle? Bettye Blessing Milford is sanguine? Gore takes a bath? Wait, how's this, Chairman says drop in donations is par for the curse."

Time and Chance

Alma Brackett stared back at her. "You are a smart little brat, aren't you?"

Faye shrugged and began to sort through the manuscripts Alma Brackett had piled there for proofing. The card table vibrated with the shaking of her arms. Ooze and Ahs at Success of Drive, damn.

"Miss Bynum."

Faye stared at the top manuscript on the pile. Junior League sets rush season. "Yes?"

"Has it occurred to you yet that newspaper work demands smart brats no less than the debutante season demands ninnies and dimwits? That both would die without a constantly replenished supply?"

"No."

"Did I ask you not to go sullen on me?"

"You did. I was not aware that my behavior answered to that description." Damn. Stupid, stupid. Faye saw that she had dripped on Alma Brackett's manuscript, the Palmer-method loops of Quink now bearing a splatter of pale blue. She put aside the manuscript and rose. "Will you excuse me for just a moment, please?"

"I will not. Sit down this instant. Think about what I said."

"Miss Brackett, you said that I was a smart little brat. I didn't mean to – "

"Stop blubbering, and don't call me Miss Brackett, be so good. My name is Alma Brackett. What else did I say?" Alma Brackett glared at a few faces turned their direction, and the faces swiveled away. One of them, Faye saw, was Forde Morgan's. What about the coach, Forde?

Faye blushed and wiped her cheeks. "Newspaper work requires smart brats. I don't think I qualify on either count."

"I will be the judge of that, for as long as you are assigned to my instruction. In my judgment, you are exactly wrong on both counts. Now, then. I do find merit in your criticism of my choice of words. I even find a certain <u>value</u> in it, and in the wit with which you pressed your case. Not a lot, mind you. A dollar's worth, maybe, stretching a point. Your debt is down to $4.95. That's less than half of what you started with, so you're doing well."

Faye sat back in her chair and looked at the ceiling, giving tears a chance to run backwards into her sinuses if they wanted to. "I did not ask to be assigned to you," she said. "And I was disappointed when I was. I don't think much of your part of the paper, or of you yourself, if you must know. But I will respect your ideas, including the one about the stupid debt. It is $5.91 or, fine, $5.95, if that pleases you. In two weeks, I suppose it will be $6.01, and so forth. It will continue to grow at compound interest until Judgment Day, at which point I certainly hope you will take it to the Devil, and that I'll be there to watch. I guess it will amount to about a million dollars by then, but you're not getting another penny from me on it. Will there be anything else this morning?"

"Yes, there will," Alma Brackett said. "There's a whole stack of manuscripts right under your nose. I put a number of typos in them, some quite subtle. I'll expect to see them carefully and fully proofed by lunch time. However, if you want to go off for a few minutes and collect yourself, be my guest." She picked up the phone book, licked her thumb, and looked at Faye over the top. "You'll get no bravos from me, by the way, for your plucky little speech. Pluck is another word for brat, and it's a reporter's tool that, if you didn't have it, I'd send you back to Daddy tomorrow."

Faye had no intention of going off to collect herself – where would she look for the pieces? But the mention of Daddy was too much. She rose and stumbled with as much dignity as possible through the swinging doors. Going down the stairs to the pressroom, she suspected that Forde Morgan was trying to decide whether to follow her. Well, he could go to hell, along with Alma Brackett, The Charlotte <u>Star-Dispatch</u>, and with hope itself.

Time and Chance

The break room was deserted, by a miracle; the Monday editorial conference was in full swing. Faye figured that the early drinkers were probably all home with hangovers from the weekend. She slammed the door behind her, sat at a corner table, and put her head in her arms to muffle a bit the undignified and un-newsworthy gasps and whuffles that she couldn't hold back any longer.

After a few minutes, she realized that Forde Morgan had in fact not followed her, that he was still up in the newsroom, snorting at jokes about Len Biggs and kissing asses and thinking about lunch. Good, she thought, that's one thing I don't have to deal with. And found the thought as bad as that of Alma Brackett. Or worse, in that it was newer, and unexpected. She gave up on muffling her noise; the warning honker had started up and the presses would be running, and that would cover a Mormon Choir of blubbering brats. If I cry loud and long enough, Faye thought, maybe I'll get to a place where nothing can ever make me cry again.

When she had replayed the horrors of the past weeks, the loneliness, the ungodly distance between herself and home, the problems that waited for her there, and added on the mean, stingy, vicious, prejudiced, greedy, nasty unfairness of Alma Brackett, Len Biggs, Forde Morgan, the Charlotte <u>Star-Dispatch</u>, and Mrs. Merrill's cat, and of the stupid, hopeless, make-believe life of the brat Faye Bynum until their edges lost the ability to hurt – which took a good quarter hour – she drew a shaky sigh and sat up. She was mottled, soggy, and smeared with mucus, her face was sore and her hair was a wreck, and she was grateful that she'd had the presence of mind to come down here. She pulled some paper napkins from the table dispenser, mopped her face and blew her nose.

The thing would be to show Alma Brackett a thing or two. Showing people a thing or two – admittedly, people like Gordon or Mama and Daddy, who were susceptible – had worked pretty well up to now. She'd been close to missing out on this internship three days before the entry deadline, with writer's block and Gordon pestering her, Mama wringing her hands and Sister Rose Penitentia telling her she was letting the whole school down. She'd showed them a thing or two then, leaving a note on the kitchen table, taking the Interurban to Rolla and swearing Grandma to secrecy, and knocking out a thousand words on "America the Pitiful," about Negro schools in St. Louis, that embarrassed everybody and about made the American Legion piss blue, but it was so by God head and shoulders over all the mewling World Peace and My Favorite Teacher and My Little Dog Spot crap that the judges the Legion had hauled in from Mizzou Journalism School told them they had no choice, it was Faye Bynum or nobody, and they'd already got folks from KMOX there to broadcast the big announcement live.

Faye had to laugh; the Legion announcer had given her title as "America the *Bittiful*," kind of coughing it into his hand like it was something regrettable he'd picked out of his teeth. But she told him a thing or two, too, after the mike was off and nobody was watching. "Faye Bynum or nobody," damn it, and don't you forget it.

She stood, feeling in the pockets of the corduroy jumper for bobby pins so she could walk presentably through the clatter and bellow of the pressroom, and jumped in alarm. In the middle of the break room, leaning on a chair and peering at her like a mortuary trainee, was Forde Morgan.

"Are you OK?"

"Why ... certainly I'm OK. Do I look not OK?"

Forde blushed. "Oh, sure. You always look OK to me. I just sort of had the idea you were upset."

"Really. How long have you been here?"

"Not too long. Five, ten minutes, I reckon." He shrugged. "Or so."

"Yes? How loud was I when you came in?"

"Aw. Not that loud. What's wrong, Faye?"

34

Time and Chance

Faye shook her head and laughed. "Oh, really, it's nothing. I was kicking myself that I turned down your kind invitation to dinner last week. If I could go back there and had any sense, I would have said, Sure, heck yes."

Forde blushed again, on top of the fading pinkness from last time. "No, now don't tease me, OK? It's none of my business anyways. Just, you ... well. That's all. I'm sorry if I caught you at a bad time."

"Oh, think nothing of it. You'd have to be pretty lucky not to, the way things have been going." She caught herself. "Oh, listen to that. Poor me. I'm sorry I can't stay and chat, but I have a whole stack of proofing to do by lunch time." She blew her nose again on a new napkin, and smiled at Forde. "Thank you for being worried, Forde. I'm fine."

"Well," Forde said. "Well, good, then. You want to have dinner tonight?"

Faye pivoted in the doorway. Her black eyebrows danced a little. "On Monday night?"

"We could pretend it was Friday, and you didn't say no."

"That sounds kind of risky. Let's call it what it is, Monday, and make the best of it."

He nodded. "Make the best of Monday."

"And I'll turn you down on Tuesday."

He grinned then, and didn't look quite so dopey to Faye. "And on Wednesday they were – "

Faye held up a hand. "Wait and see on Wednesday. Thank you for cheering me up, but kindly don't walk out this door with me. Bye."

Faye closed the door behind herself and all but ran up the steps to the newsroom, the eyebrows that had annihilated Forde Morgan locked in a vee of disgust. *"Bayeee," the little intern cooed.* What on God's Earth was that for, stupid?

35

Time and Chance

Faye spent the afternoon at her card table, proofing and making notes about the Free Library Bake Sale. When she finished, everyone but Forde Morgan and Alma Brackett had left for the day, and the newsroom was quiet except for Alma Brackett's honeyed cosseting of some late-calling ninny or dimwit. Long before Alma Brackett finished, Forde rose and sent Faye a beseeching look, tapping his watch, tilting his head freedom-wards. Faye held up a finger, tilting her own head toward Alma Brackett. Forde shrugged and moseyed to the swinging doors as Alma wound it up.

"Now, Miz Fleming," she said. "You know June is the month of brides, dear. We just have to give them top treatment ... Because, Hon, this is <u>it</u> for them, understand. They've had their coming-out and their engagement and most cases, we'll never hear ... Yes, Ma'am, Emily Perry certainly was below the fold. What's more, she didn't get but twenty-point agate, and you look, we used 24 for your Lolly. Would that make her feel better, if you were to point that out to her? ...Now, don't you breathe a word of that to Miz Perry. ...All righty. 'Bye."

Alma Brackett cradled the phone and sent Faye a look. Faye recognized her moment, and took it. "Ma'am." Her voice sounded loud in the silence of the deserted room.

"Yes, dear."

"Is this what you hoped for? When you were starting out, I mean, did you dream of being a society editor some day? Reporting on the social doings of dimwits?"

Alma Brackett pursed her lips and considered Faye. "When I was your age, for example?"

Faye bit her lip. "Well ... yes, I guess."

"How old are you?"

"Nineteen. I'll be twenty in July."

"Hm. I understood you to be entering your first year in college."

Time and Chance

"Daddy barnstormed airplanes when I was little, so we moved around a lot. I missed a whole year of school, twice, before we settled down."

Alma Brackett nodded. "When I was approaching twenty I dreamed, as you put it, of remaining alive long enough to marry a fellow named Chet Bracken. We met in Sunday School where, if you can believe it, we were seated alphabetically and required to share copies of the Weekly Messenger. One Sunday morning, his hand happened to brush mine while we were opening it, as requested, to the reading. We were on a two-year curriculum to read the entire Bible, and there had already been a number of things it was a little hard for old Miss Emberley to account for – murders and fooling around with wives and all. It being springtime of the first year of it, we had got to The Song of Solomon. I remember it very clearly."

Alma Brackett threw her head back, opened the crimson rectangle of her mouth and honked, " 'Let him kiss me with the kisses of his mouth! For your love is better than wine.' She always had us read out loud – we'd plowed through all that Numbers and Deuteronomy crap that way. It came around to Chet Bracken to read Chapter 4, which as you no doubt have no idea, has the part about 'Your breasts are like twin fawns,' and so forth. Miss Emberley of course wanted us to believe that this load of erotica was just a big old metaphor, celebrating the love of Jesus – if you will, who wouldn't be born for centuries yet – for His church. Chet stumbled through it, blushing as red as the flag, and I, with my accidentally brushed hand still tingling, whispered something to let him know I doubted Miss Emberley's interpretation.

"Well, one thing led to another, and by the time we were of courting age, I couldn't see straight. But then the World War came along. Chet enlisted in the army, which every fellow with any grit was doing. He got a medal for being shot at Chateau-Thierry. He survived it, though, and came home handsome and brown and skinny, ready to take up where we'd left off in 1917. I vowed I would feed him up and make him the happiest man in Bozlee, North Carolina. But somebody in his regiment brought Spanish influenza home on the ship, gave it to Chet, and he to me. In a week, we were both in the hospital, hoping we'd either both live or both die. We got half the loaf. I've never believed old sayings to this day."

Faye stared at Alma Brackett, feeling tears start again. So much for never crying. "You ... And you never..."

"I passed my twentieth birthday in that hospital; Chet had already died by then. I expect it was the wound weakened him more than it showed; they didn't tell me at the time, because they didn't want to upset me, and besides, they didn't expect me to live in any case. I did, as you see. When I got out of the hospital, I went to work for an advertising printer, and eventually that led to a job at the Star-Dispatch. I have been recording the social doings of a few dimwitted young ladies for more than 25 years, and training others to do the same. May I see your copy editing, please?"

Faye handed Alma Brackett the sheaf of manuscript. "Ma'am," she said. "I feel so terrible. I was ... I wasn't ..."

Alma Brackett looked at her over the stack of paper. "Indeed. Not an easy position to maintain, one would think. Particularly with a young man pacing outside the door. Kindly go and tell him that you will be free for social doings in another ..." She riffled through the stack. "Oh, quarter-hour or so."

7.

I S THERE a town in your part of the state named ..." Faye hesitated, strategically. "Bosley, Boswell, something like that?"

Forde smirked a little around his apple pie. "Bozzhee?"

"What?"

Forde held up a finger, blushing, and swallowed. He took a pull on his malt and wiped his mouth. "If you mean Bozlee, it's a one-horse mill town up the road from Gabbro. Bunch of rednecks, pretty much. Public library's in a old cotton gin, books still get covered with fluff. The football team wears uniforms from 1918. They got a railroad shop and about seventy churches. Why?"

Faye shrugged, unsurprised. She'd located Bozlee on the North Carolina map that hung by the newsroom door, and noted its proximity to Gabbro before she left to meet Forde for supper at the Home Kitchen. "Nothing, I guess. Alma Brackett comes from there."

"Alma Brackett comes from someplace? I thought they found her in that corner and built the rest of the place around her."

Faye shifted restlessly on her side of the wooden booth. She wasn't sure, away from the Star-Dispatch, cried-out, tired, and stuffed with food, how much of the day's disasters had been real, how much were the creations of loneliness and a guilty conscience about allowing pretty much a date with Forde Morgan to happen.

"Is there a family there by the name of Bracken?"

"Bracken? Not Brackett? I don't think Bozlee's big enough to have two families that close together in the alphabet. Anyway, I don't know much about the place. What's on your mind?"

"Oh. I just heard the saddest story about ... about somebody there. I guess I thought maybe you might know them."

"Come to think, there's a Negro family named Bracken in Gabbro. Sure it wasn't Gabbro?"

"Yes, and anyhow, this story was not about Negroes."

"What was the story?"

Faye told him the story of Alma Brackett and Chet Bracken. Forde looked perplexed.

"Funny. That's almost exactly the story I saw in a movie last week. 'They Gave Their All.' Except, no, I'm wrong. It was World War II, not I."

Faye's eyebrows went still and straight, making Forde Morgan notice them again, their kinship to the dark down on her arms. And ... he cursed his wanton imagination, and missed Faye's next question.

"Sorry. Did they what?"

"Did they meet in Sunday School?" Patient, eyebrows neutral, voice quiet.

"Lemme think. No, high school, I guess. They sat next to each other 'cause they had near the same last name. Are you on the track of something?"

"Never mind. Do you work a lot with Len Biggs?"

"Len Biggsch the Schunday Editor of the Schtar-Dischpatsch?"

"Don't be mean. He can't help it."

Forde blushed, annoying Faye. "You're right. People can't help how they talk, right? Anyhow, Mr. Biggs gives me the assignments, and I do them, best I can. He doesn't say much about what I do. He marks it up and either gives it to the copy boy or throws it in the trash and writes it himself. How's Miss Brackett? Pretty awful, looks like to me."

Faye resisted the bait. "She's all right. What I meant was, do you trust him?"

"Trust him? Mister Len?" Forde looked like it was something that had never crossed his mind. "I guess. With what?"

"Nothing. With the truth, I guess. He was coming in the building when I was leaving tonight, and he asked me if I was upset about something. I just said I'd heard Alma Brackett's sad story about her dead boyfriend, and he said, 'Oh, that's a real sad story all right.' Just like that, like he'd heard it a thousand times before. Like it was some kind of a joke that wasn't funny any more. Something just seemed a little funny about how he said it, I guess is what I mean. And then you tell me the very same story was made into a movie that's showing this week? What would you think?"

Forde blinked. It seemed to him that Faye had skipped some steps somewhere, but he couldn't be sure where.

"What would I?"

Faye made an exasperated face. "Think, for Pete's sake. Is Alma Brackett really a tragic war bride, supposed-to-be, or was she just making it all up?"

"Why would she do that?"

"How do I know? I'll tell you something, though, if she was telling me that just to put me in my place and make me cry, I'll ..." Faye waved a hand. "I don't know. I'll fix her good."

"Well, whoa, now. If it was an old story to Len Biggs, then it couldn't have come from 'They Gave Their All.' That just opened last week."

Faye raised an eyebrow and brushed a loop of hair away from it. Forde could have, if he wanted, interpreted her look as approving. He plunged on. "But look here, Faye, you don't have to wonder about things like that, like we're in the Dark Ages. It's 1947, you have all kinds of ways to find things out. Call up the Gabbro County clerk and ask about death records in Bozlee. Tell him you're calling from the Star-Dispatch, he'll fall all over himself. Look, I'll be glad to, to help out."

Faye yawned and shook her head. "That's nice of you, Forde, really. And you made some good ... some helpful suggestions just now. But this is my, my ..." *My what, stupid?* "My problem, and I guess I'll have to decide whether I'm going to do anything about it or not. Or let it go."

Mostly, she thought, I cannot imagine some kind of Nancy Drew, Hardy Boys sidekick business with this boy. I'll be calling him Biff or Buzz next thing, and getting rides to The Malt Shop in his roadster. But she didn't say that.

She didn't say much, in fact. She had not eaten so much food since her farewell dinner in St. Louis, and she was tipsy with nourishment. She stared at her fork, nonplussed. The Home Kitchen was as alien as a Balinese squid shop, its denizens grotesque and its cuisine incomprehensible. She was too tired now to hold her head up, exhausted by the labor of digestion and the heavy work of holding Charlotte and Alma Brackett, Len Biggs and Mrs. Merrill and Gordon and, yes, Forde Morgan, holding all of them overhead so she could find just a little space of her own, inside which the suffocating strangeness that crowded in on her would be powerless to make her cry. She wondered if she was coming down with something.

Forde peered at her, biting his lip. "You feeling OK? 'Scuse a remark, but you're a little pale."

"I'm always pale."

"Well. OK. I was going to ask if you wanted to go to a movie. Do you? 'Life With Father' is on at the Indian Head."

Faye's head fell forward, black wings of hair falling across her vision like the narrowing perspective of one sinking rapidly into a depthless ocean. "That's a nice idea, but I think I better get home. Thank you for a lovely evening, Forde. I'm afraid you didn't get much of a chance to compare notes, I think it was you said, wasn't it? Ask me again some time, I'll try to be a little more wide awake."

Forde smiled. "Faye, you seem just perfectly fine to me. Thank you for keeping me company. Can I walk you home?"

Time and Chance

He'll want to kiss me. Well, … "All right. Thank you. If somebody didn't, I'm afraid they'd find me curled up under a bush in the morning. Sleeping, I mean. I don't know what's the matter with me." *Faye, you seem jes' puffickly fahn ta me. Roaming Reader Rattles Redneck Romeo.*

Charlotte had enlisted with enthusiasm in a hot spell that rose from the Gulf like bathwater, slopping and dripping and wilting the afternoons with heat that soaked into the bricks and slicked the tar in the street. Even now, late in dusk, it showed little sign of letting go; Faye and Forde walked with minimal effort, trying not to exert, followed by night air that matched their pace exactly and enclosed them in a bubble of their own making. Faye smelled sweat, and could not have said if it were Forde's or her own.

"Hot," Forde noted.

"Beastly. Will it be like this all summer?"

"We'll get some relief from time to time. Yankee air down from Michigan, Indiana, give us a thunderstorm. Then it'll build back up again. Fall is just lovely."

"Too bad for me. I'll have to cut my hair." Faye raised an arm to lift hair off her neck, became aware of dampness below her armpit, and lowered the arm.

"I thought those pigtails you had the other day were sort of cool looking." Forde's scent of hot-and-botheredness reinforced itself. "Sort of cute, too, really."

"That's how I plan to get ahead, Forde. Get the Pulitzer for cuteness." Smart brat. "I'm sorry, I didn't mean – "

Forde took her hand and began to deny offense taken, but stopped in mid-stammer, jerking Faye to a stop beside him.

"What?"

"Shh." The sweat smell was definitely Forde's now, with an element that Faye knew as the tang of fear that hovered when she woke from nightmares. Forde backed into shadow, and pulled Faye with him, putting his mouth close to her ear. "Klan," he said, almost inaudibly. "Don't stare at them."

"Don't <u>stare</u> at them? What, I'll turn to stone?" Faye twisted away from Forde to peer at a murmuring knot of ghosts walking up Mecklenburg Street. Their feet scraped and stammered, their voices swelled a little on the heat of the night, and one broke into thin, bubbling laughter.

Faye laughed too and said, a little loudly, "Look here! A whole crew of dunce - " And found Forde's hand across her mouth, his other arm turning her roughly away from the street.

Faye squirmed and freed her mouth. "Stop it, Forde! Damn it, let go."

"Stawppit, Fo'd," the bubbling voice wheedled. "Better get in yore damn ol' Fo'd, honeh, 'fore he gets yore knickers off."

Forde took Faye's face between his hands and he glared at her. "Faye," he whispered. "If you don't want a very bad time, you're going to have to kiss me right now, understand? I apologize. Don't answer." And he mashed his mouth against Faye's while she mumbled in shock and pushed away from him, from the salt sweat of his lips. It was the saltiness that she would remember, she thought. If she lived through this.

Bubble-voice started yelling about things that didn't even make English sense to Faye, and a deeper, rougher voice rode over his. "Shut your damn mouth and fall in, Ev'ett," it said. "Niggatown a ways off yet."

"Oh, Jesus," Forde breathed. "Don't turn around, don't turn around. Pretend, can't you? That fella yelling at you, that's Everett Bassler. He killed a Negro lady last week, and he don't care who knows it. The other one's rougher yet. You don't have to mean it, but pretend for your life. I mean that."

Time and Chance

Faye hesitated, thought about Gordon and Mama, and put her arms around Forde's neck. She still wasn't kissing anybody she didn't want to, though. She tucked in her lips like a child at a spoon of medicine, and stiffened her body. But ... well, hell. She stood on tiptoe and lifted one foot from the pavement as she'd seen June Alyson do with Jimmy Stewart. The troop of Klansmen gave that a couple of whoops and a string of handclaps, and the rough-voiced leader ordered them onward into the night. When they were gone, Faye and Forde sprang apart like a pair of north poles. Faye's hair crossed her face in furious diagonals, and she swept it aside to glare at Forde.

"Forde Morgan," she hissed. "The was the feeblest, sneakiest cliché I ever suffered through in my life, up to now. You think I never read a cheap novel? Every spy story that never should have been has a scene like that, where the hero hides the girl from Nazis by kissing her while she mumbles and struggles. Really, how dumb do you think I am? Big disappointment, I guess, I didn't melt in your manly embrace, huh? I believe that's what's supposed to happen next." Faye was wide awake now, blazing with anger, ready to slap Forde Morgan's sweaty lips off.

"I told you I apologized before I did it," Forde said, trying to be reasonable. "Maybe it's an old trick, but it was the only one I could think of. Those guys kill people."

"Racist jerks and drunks. Let them try and, and ..." Faye blinked and shivered. "What?"

Forde nodded. "Try and kill you and me? They wouldn't do that, we're white. But they'd be more than glad to give us a half hour of hell and a week with no sleep, and they'd do it the minute you said anything that let on we were some kind of liberal pinkos, Faye. Sure, they're racists and thugs. Decent folks got nothing to do with them. But when they're out on the street, it doesn't pay to be there with them. You ask anybody on this street if they saw anything tonight, not one in fifty would say they got near a window. And that'd be somebody from up north, hadn't caught on yet."

"Like me, you mean?"

"Yes, like you, or anybody else that didn't grow up here. Don't misunderstand, Faye. Most folks here are decent Christians, and lots go out of their way to do nice things for Negroes. But there's a bunch that's down at the other end of the line, and if it's nighttime, and you don't have about a hundred marines behind you, the smart thing is to stay out of their way."

Faye stared at him. "That's the cowardliest claptrap I ever heard in my life, Forde Morgan. That's the kind of mousy damn weakness that puts that kind of thug on the street in the first place. 'All that's necessary for the triumph of evil is – ' "

"Yeah, yeah. For good men to do nothing. Well, you'd be seeing a triumph of evil right this minute, if I'd of done nothing, and close up, too. Bunch of these same fellas, last month they jumped a Davidson fella and his girlfriend that yelled something sarcastic at a rally down York County, beat the fella up within an inch of his life, and shaved the girl bald. I couldn't of protected you from that." He shrugged. "Except with my feeble cliché."

Faye sat on the curb and looked down Mecklenburg Street. "Where did you learn all that? You're not from here either."

"Not that far away that I didn't hear about it, though. Not to mention, Gabbro's got a Klavern too, six – eight sad cases from the dumb side of town." Forde sat on the curb, not crowding Faye.

"First thing I got here, I went in the morgue files and read it up. There's a lot there, though not much of it ever got published in the Star-Dispatch. You look down the way, where them jimbos went. You see anybody at all on the street? Seems like there was quite a few when we left the Home Kitchen."

Faye looked where his head tilted. The sheeted men flickered in the far-off headlights of a car, quickly extinguished. "Well," she said. She laid her chin on her knees and contemplated her skinny feet. "All right. Thank you, Forde. I still never melted in your manly embrace."

"No, you never. But I did appreciate the little business with your foot. All the more for that, come to think of it. Let's get you safe home."

Faye forestalled the awkward business of a good-night kiss – something that Forde Morgan might have considered fairly earned, taking into account his successful semi-heroism in the face of the Klan, and Faye's steely non-acquiescence in any real kissing under the guise of fake kissing – by a preëmptive sisterly buss on the cheek. And Forde was glad to get it, the redneck oaf. Faye recognized instantly that she had answered his underhanded cliché with one of her own, less heroic and further from any useful feeling than Forde's had been.

Nor, when she had stumbled up the inquisitive stairs of Mrs. Merrill's house, had stripped, scrubbed away sweat and tears, be-nightie'd herself and fallen at last into the lumpy and longed-for bed, was she betrayed by dreams of knights, swords, salt shakers, or any psychic equivalent. No, she found herself in the nonexistent attic of her own house in St. Louis, a place of light and precision, of dovetail drawers full of rulers and sharp pencils, and of clean, straight carpentry. The walls gleamed with well-bound books; the one she chose proved to be, when opened, a treatise of blank pages.

8.

M ECKLENBURG *Street was the scene last night of a gathering of social activists in handsome linen outfits, seeking through example, deed, and persuasion to improve warp and, if possible, woof in Charlotte and its surroundings. Mr. Everett Bassler of Rozelle's Ferry, whose ministries to the unfortunate of Mecklenburg County, while widely known, are too little mentioned, offered the* Star-Dispatch *commentary that, while cast in the robust Anglo-Saxon of his heritage, was felt by this reporter to be a true and fair representation of his mind and heart. Not one word in three of Mr. Bassler's remarks can be reproduced here.*

A higher source, who must remain nameless, reminded Mr. Bassler that the group had much yet to accomplish, and that the gathering and the evening were charged with more than mere social pleasure and public relations. He remarked, in words paraphrased by this reporter, that duty called, that there was a great distance between the present merriment and the wretched lives of the intended targets of the group's mercies, and that immediate attention to the recipient community, offering them the blazing light of the Cross of Our Savior, must take first place over social intercourse. The meeting adjourned and went out from that place, leaving this reporter deeply impressed with a city that, as Holy Scripture admonishes, lets not its right hand see the charities of its left.

-30-

Alma Brackett tossed the manuscript on the card table. "Hilarious," she said. "Burn it before somebody sees it."

Faye smiled. "That's the big crime around here, isn't it? Seeing things."

"I beg your pardon."

"Was I not clear? I mean everything would stay just peachy if folks would keep their eyes where they belong. Don't see the worker trying to make ten dollars on the side, see the gentlewoman society reporter. Don't see the Klan when they walk down the street, don't see the filthy, nasty, miserable so-called schools the Negroes get stuck in so there'll be money enough for cotillions and 24-point agate for the white girls."

Alma Brackett shook her head. "So simple, isn't it? I can hardly remember when things were so clear and easy. Around 1918, I guess it was."

"No, ma'am, I didn't say that. If you'll think back, I was saying things are a lot messier and harder than looks like folks want to pretend. And speaking of 1918 - "

"Yes?" Head cocked back, mouth menacing.

"Yes. Did that really happen?"

"That." Alma Brackett's eyes warned of sorrow to come, if Faye persisted.

Faye persisted. "That story you told me about this Chet Bracken."

Alma Brackett looked around the newsroom. The hour was early, one or two reporters were slumped over the morning paper, slurping coffee, reading passages aloud, cackling. Otherwise, the newsroom was empty. "You have reason to doubt it?"

Faye thought about that, shrugged, picked up her Klan story. "Either it's a very poignant story, or a way to make a kid cry instead of answering her questions. Either way, admirable, I guess. In its own way."

Alma Brackett smiled and seemed to relax. "You're a dilly. I don't know when I've seen a cleaner case of bright adolescent self-centeredness. It's pronounced 'poin-yant', dear. Not like Elmer Fudd saying 'pregnant.' "

Time and Chance

Faye blushed, paused, and tossed a hand. "All right. Never mind, then. I guess nothing I say amounts to anything, if I don't pronounce it right."

Alma Brackett, riding the headlong momentum of amusement, leaned in and patted Faye's wrist. "Run and go potty, dear. We're interviewing Alice Weston and her daughter this morning, and we don't want to queer the pitch at the last second again, do we?"

Alma Brackett's expansive mood lasted most of the way to the Weston villa on Seven Lakes Lane. Tales of Charlotte in the Twenties, when she, Alma Brackett, was in what she called her salad years; of the consolidation of fortunes like the Weston's in the Thirties, when tracts of busted-out farmland along US 74 came up for sale at a dollar an acre, and could be sprinkled with auto dealerships, motels, trailer courts, and fish camps at costs so tiny as to be almost undetectable to people like the Westons. Of the feeling that nothing but profit was likely to come from the new World War, a huge market for cotton and cloth, for tobacco and produce and all the things that Charlotte and the counties for miles around could provide as well as anywhere and better and cheaper than most.

Faye sat next to Alma Brackett in the cigarette reek of the polished but decidedly elderly Packard with her hands folded, suspicious of the scenery – which of the bungalows they passed harbored Klansmen, which vacant lots had witnessed unspeakable cross-lit ceremonies, terror and pain? Why do these streets, which resemble her home's to a hair, never lead to a familiar neighborhood? Trying not to appear interested, humble, or dependant.

"Tell me about the new little debutante," she said at last.

"Courtenay Weston is neither new nor all that little," Alma Brackett said. "We're not in for a re-play here of Joanie Rae McCrea. Courtenay is about to enter her senior year at Radcliffe, if you please, where she is majoring in Modern Languages. She is beautiful, and a superior horsewoman who stands a good sixteen hands herself. She was scheduled to come out two years ago, but she was in Provence as a guest of the French government. Last year was her friend Darby Lambeth's year, and Courtenay arranged to be away for the season in Cambridge, so as not to spoil it for Darby."

Faye looked out the window. They were passing through a rag end of downtown, an abandoned apartment block surrounded by asphalt and weeds; windows boarded except for one, at the top of a fire escape, that had been ripped open by squatters. A slant of sunlight in the hole showed green paint. Faye smelled the dry pine rafters under the roof, the damp silence of summer morning in the room. She had no idea where Provence might be, but it sounded like a place where poignant things might happen, and go unremarked.

"That's not so tall."

"At the withers. It goes without saying that her grooming is immaculate and adorns an already stunning face and figure. She will probably announce her engagement in September."

"Land."

Alma Brackett shot Faye a glance. "You will sit quietly and observe. You may wish to take notes. You will not introduce extranea."

"Goodness. Extranea? You'll be working her for the full package, I suppose. I can't afford more phantom debt than I already carry."

"Do you need to stop at a gas station?"

In fact, Faye could have used a rest stop; to admit as much would have yielded the day to Alma Brackett before it was well begun. "It's tempting, of course. Southern gas stations are just the place I surely love to park my bare behind. No, I'll pass. I expect I can hold it without disgracing myself. I think."

Time and Chance

Courtenay Weston lived up to Alma Brackett's sketch. A gracile maiden of tawny, rarefied air with a Maxfield Parrish face that could have launched either a thousand ships or, Faye supposed, about a million brand-new Packards; a girl of remarkable altitude, who wore exquisite breeding as lightly as breath. Her mother Alice, a formidable woman in her own right, seemed a fluttery afterthought beside her, though she did most of the talking. Courtenay greeted them calmly and led them to a handsome conservatory where tea had been prepared by the servant whose heel showed for an instant through a closing rear doorway as they entered. Faye took a cup, not wanting to offend, but planning to drink as little as possible.

"Now, then," said Alice Weston.

Alma Brackett took not so much notes on Courtenay's long-anticipated début, as dictation. The setting (country club), the chef (the Weston's own), the food and drink (from Charleston by motor express the afternoon of the début), the photograph (not by the Star-Dispatch's photographer or any in North Carolina, but from a Paris studio); the length and wording of the story ("One of the most accomplished and well-favored young ladies of this or any other season in North Carolina, and so forth, I'm sure you can fill it out, dear. I think a minimum of thirty, no more than fifty column inches."). Its placement (emphatically above the fold; indeed Alma Brackett would be lucky to keep it on the page at all, and not hovering a foot above) and the type size, font, and style.

"A parallel story will, you will understand, Miss Brackett, run in the New York Times the day before, and yours in the … what is it, Courtenay? Yes, the Star-Dispatch, following. We are speaking here of a major – "

"Oh, Mother, really." Courtenay lifted a single brow at Faye in graceful mockery. Faye was glad to be able to lift one in return, having practiced and mastered the skill as early as eighth grade. Though, of course, Courtenay's brow was honey-colored and shapely, Faye's black and linear.

Alice bridled. "Be still, Courtenay. This flinty reticence that they seem to encourage in New England simply will not do in the present context. Now, as to the musicians..."

Matters progressed, Faye sipped, put down the cup, took notes, and began to think of the murmur of gentle waters, of restrooms at the Esso, then of anything else. Courtenay too seemed content to let her mother talk, to be poised, learned, slightly amused. Simply, Faye thought, to be content with being what she was; and why not? But maybe that was a skill that even the poor, big-footed and black of hair could learn, though it might take more practice than when you were stunning, rich, and brainy.

It was not very long before Faye saw that what was amusing Courtenay was not the conversation, not her mother's puffery and not even, thank God, Faye herself, but Alma Brackett. Alma's persistent struggles to dominate; how she swallowed annoyance when Alice launched into another long specification.

"Ça suffira, Maman," Courtenay said at last. "The poor woman wants to get to the money part." She turned to Alma Brackett, all graceful attention. "There will be bargains in photo packages, frames, mats, all that. You have samples, I am sure." Alma Brackett looked about as insulted as it is possible to look, Faye thought, while you're still trying to get to the money part.

"We wish to do what we can in assisting the debutante and her family to preserve this special time. Our photographer – "

Alice Weston elevated a hand. "It was understood, I believe, that we shall supply the photograph. There will be no photography from the, the Star."

"Well... well, yes. But duplicate prints ... do you have the negative?"

"We will arrange to have it sent from Paris."

Time and Chance

Alma Brackett took a small breath. "Of course. Many of our debutantes have selected a package of smaller photographs for friends and relatives, and a nicely framed portrait as a permanent addition to the home."

Courtenay retook the reins. "And you offer a choice of frames?" Again, the attentive smile, the entomologist's interest.

Alma Brackett smiled back, knowing what was coming. "The frame will, of course, be the choice of the debutante and her family."

"But you do happen to have samples with you, I am sure. In a range of prices."

Faye had never thought to see Alma Brackett blush. And maybe what she now saw was not so much a blush as the color of rage.

"Yes, miss. Yes, I do." She opened a massive purse and drew out frame samples that she slapped onto the tea cart. "The choices are candlewood at $20 *(slap)*, sterling at $50 *(clatter)*, and chased gold at $150 *(thud)*." She looked into Courtenay's amused eyes as Courtenay reached for the candlewood. "Or, of course, Woolworth's offers a nice selection, much less – "

Faye choked on tea, muffled a sneeze, and nearly paid the price in dampness; but she acted on impulse. "Mama an' Daddy sprung f' th' silver, when I come out," she offered, wiping her nose. "It's ever so gay, an' sort of la-di-da."

*

Alma Brackett slammed the Packard into second gear and rounded the one of Seven Lakes Lane's many curves; Faye lurched against the door.

"You keep slamming me around like that, I'm liable to wet your upholstery."

"Wet away," Alma Brackett snarled. "And be damned to you. You couldn't keep your mouth shut, could you?"

"Not while you were in the process of throwing away a perfectly good commission, no. I'd think you'd thank me for it."

"Thank you? For playing the hick in front of the debutante of the century, while she was having such fun laughing at us already?"

"Laughing at you, more like. Tell me, what do you expect the deb of the century was about to say when I opened my mouth?"

"I haven't the least idea. She was already – "

"She was having fun making you mad. She didn't give a damn for any of your photo packages, a girl that gets her picture taken in Paris and flown over here any time she needs a copy. She was ready to take the candlewood frame, just because she knew it would make you mad."

"Fine," Alma Brackett said, and she honked a little boy into tears as he hovered at the curb, watching his baseball roll toward a sewer. "Let her take the damn candlewood, and be damned to her, too."

"Certainly. But just remind me, now, did she buy a frame?"

"Yes. Who cares?"

"You do, I think. Which frame did she buy?"

Alma Brackett was silent for a block. Faye looked, saw that the sunlight had left the open window of the squatters' slum. Heat, smell, flies. Faye heard a snort from Alma Brackett, turned, and saw that she was biting the inside of her cheek to keep from laughing.

"You owe me a hundred and fifty dollars," Faye said.

Alma Brackett hooted and slapped the steering wheel. "Don't be ridiculous. My whole commission on the gold frame is no more than fifty."

"All right. Fifty, then."

"What makes you think you get the whole thing?"

"What were you set to get, the way you were going at it?"

" … Twenty."

"You get a $20 commission on a $20 frame?"

"I am offering you $20 for your part of the commission on the gold frame. Take it or leave it."

"Forty. That leaves you exactly the ten you were about to get."

The car swerved to the side of the street, accompanied by screeching brakes and a horn from the rear. "Twenty-five," Alma Brackett said. "Don't push me, little girl, or you can walk home from here."

Faye gave her a smile, all cheekbones and shining dark eyes. "All right, then." she said. "Let's have it."

Alma Brackett's good-sport amusement at Faye's slickering of Courtenay Weston did not survive the bargaining session. The actual payout, with Faye's existing debt of course subtracted, was carried out in fuming silence. Faye didn't care. Nineteen dollars looked like a lot of money to her and, since Alma Brackett slammed it down in dollar bills, nickels, and dimes, it made a pretty good heap on the card table.

"Pick it up and get out of my sight," Alma Brackett told her.

"Yes, ma'am, Faye said. "Ever so gladly."

Still, Alma Brackett took Faye along on four more debutante visits, and Faye was able to work her redneck magic on two of them. Julianne Hagen's mother allowed herself to be enticed from silver to gold by Faye's "Ever so gay and sort of la-di-da," and the Morrissey twins from candlewood to silver which, since it was two of them, was another $7.50 each for Faye. Alma Brackett tried to niggle down Faye's cut on the Hagen deal, since the jump was only from silver to gold, and not from candlewood like Courtenay Weston's; but Faye gave her a level stare and a shake of the head, and Alma Brackett sighed, and paid up.

But then the debutante season began to fade – everything, Alma Brackett said, was a comedown after the Courtenay Weston affair at the Bonne Brae Country Club – and Faye to chafe at the silliness, superficiality, and guile needed to extract pittances from dimwits. She went to Len Biggs.

"Mr. Biggs, I reckon I got it figured out, on the Society desk," she said. "Miss Alma Brackett couldn't find a thing to say against with my piece on the Cotillion, nor the Jaycee light-bulb and jelly drive, nor the Summer Serenade. And you know – "

"Yesch," Len Biggs nodded. "I know. She doesn't hold back, except for praise."

"Yes, sir. Couldn't you find me something else to do? Forde Morgan's changed assignments twice since we started."

"Mr. Morgan changed from the obits to the sports desk, and he's now working the County Council. Obits is normally where we put the rookies, and there's one coming in next week. You think you're going on Sports, think again. You gotta go in the locker rooms after your stories, and no young lady from our paper or any other will ever go into a locker room full of half-dressed men."

"Give me the obits, then, and put the rookie with Alma Brackett."

Len Biggs snorted. "He's six four, two hundred pounds, and otherwise unsuitable."

Faye considered that. "The ladies would just swoon over him, don't you reckon? Some kind of he-man like that, Alma Brackett can sell them picture frames and wallet sets they don't even have pictures for."

"Forget it. He's our Outreach Intern."

Faye giggled. "That makes him sound like a pretzel. What does it mean?"

Len Biggs didn't smile. "He comes to us from B.T. Washington High School, because our Managing Editor got a case of the do-goods. Do I got to draw you a map?"

Faye shrugged. "I guess so. What does all _that_ mean?"

Time and Chance

Len rolled his eyes, and walked to the swinging doors, where he turned and sent Faye a patient look. "He'sch a nigger, honey."

9.

T HE NEW intern arrived at the <u>Star-Dispatch</u> the next Monday. He was as massive as Len Biggs had promised, and he wore a tan plaid belt-back suit of shiny serge, a tight-neck "business" shirt with rounded collar tabs framing a tan-and-gold tie in a bolt-of-lightning pattern. Leather briefcase, big nervous hands spinning a mahogany pork-pie hat. Skin a blemished tan-pink, hair a spray of copper wire plastered against a skull the size of a beach ball. He smiled uncertainly into a room full of blank faces and turned backs.

"Folksch," Len Biggs said, "I like to innerduce Horace Hanes. He gone be our Outreach project for the next couple months, be working for Elaine on obits."

"Haney, sir."

Len Biggs grunted. "Sorry. Horace's name is Haney, folksch. Not Hanes. That suit you, Horace?"

"Horatio," Horatio Haney said. "You could call me Horace, though."

On Tuesday, Forde Morgan occupied a seat next to Faye in the staff break room. "So, you met the new intern yet?" He sounded so amused that Faye glanced around the room to be sure Horatio Haney was not within earshot.

"Hush, Forde," Faye said. "What if he was sitting right behind you?"

"Not likely," Forde said. "He got the idea he could come in here, everybody else would walk off the job till he got straightened out."

"Yes? So where does he take his breaks? You can't tell me the <u>Star-Dispatch</u> keeps a colored break room."

Forde tipped his head westerly and dipped a fry in his puddle of catsup. "Out on the loading dock, I reckon. Long as they ain't shipping out the papers, something."

"Well, you sound like that suits you fine, Forde."

Forde frowned a little. "Doesn't suit me or otherwise," he said. "Kid's lucky they took him on at all. Mr. Biggs told me he's the first Nigra they've hired since Reconstruction."

"The first what?"

"Nigra they've had here. Since about 1880. What?"

Faye said nothing, opened her lunch – a good thick sandwich of meatloaf and prickly pear jelly she'd bargained from Mrs. Merrill's Junie for the price of a free advance copy of the first Star-Dispatch that carried an article by Horatio Haney – Horatio being Junie's neighbor's nephew. Faye's studious chewing might have been seen as caution in the face of a new taste, though it was not. She was silent through the rest of her lunch, silent in standing and folding her brown paper bag, and as good as silent in wishing Forde Morgan a pleasant afternoon and exiting the break room.

"Faye?" Forde asked, and was answered by the closing door.

Faye made her fuming way to the newsroom and found Alma Brackett gone, leaving a couple of half-hearted proofreading chores and a note that said, "Miss Weston has further news for us. This one is all mine."

Faye didn't much care. She had earned 65 extra dollars on picture frames, Daddy had come through with a check at last, and she calculated she could just survive the summer and never touch dry milk or apple jelly again, if she was careful. She looked up at a tap on the swinging door, the one door at which no one ever knocked, and saw Horatio Haney enter with a sheet of paper and approach Elaine Barnes at the Community News desk.

Time and Chance

Elaine did not look up until Horatio had placed the paper next to her elbow. She glanced at it, shaking her head, and stood, smiling sadly, and addressed not so much Horatio as the room at large.

"Mister Haney, as Jesus is my sweet Redeemer, what <u>do</u> they teach y'all over there at B.T. Washington?"

Faye didn't catch Horatio's answer; his back was to her, and he managed a deferential mutter that, Faye supposed, might have been something like *(Nothing much, Ma'am.)*

"I'll tell the world that. You call this a piece of English journalism?"

(Yes ma'am. I don't know.)

"Well," Elaine said, loud as a noon whistle, "I'll help you out, boy. No, it ain't journalism, not by a mile. This wouldn't publish on the back page of the Jigaboo Daily Journal. You get yourself out of this newsroom, and you rewrite this so it reads like a white man wrote it. Hear me?"

(Yes'm. Thank you.)

When the door swung shut, there was general applause. Hoo-Wee, somebody acknowledged. You done told him, Elaine. Elaine sniffed and picked up a piece of copy, smiling with something, Faye guessed, like the pleasure one feels at a disagreeable task put behind one.

Faye sat at her card table, staring at a piece of proofing, waiting for her color to come back to normal. Normal, she thought, for a real white, white girl. When things settled down, she rose and went through the swinging doors, trying to figure where Len Biggs might have put Horatio Haney. There wasn't, that she recalled, slave quarters or a stable attached to the <u>Star-Dispatch</u> building. What would be the equivalent?

She found him in a corridor off the pressroom, seated at a splintered wooden desk, picking at the keys of a typewriter so ancient as to resemble some kind of steam-driven farm implement. He seemed unfazed at his recent telling-off.

"Horatio?" Faye asked, unsure how else to start.

Horatio Haney looked up from his typing. "Yes, Miss?"

"My name is Faye Bynum. I'm an intern, too."

"Is that so? Think of that. I believe Mr. Len did mention your name, and look, here you stand before me."

Faye smiled and shrugged. "I guess I wanted to say, don't let those folks get you down. That was sort of rough treatment, back there."

Horatio gave her a look. His eyes, Faye saw, were of an odd, muddy color, at this point cold and as expressionless as mud. "That seem rough to you, did it?"

"Well." Faye shifted her feet, making her jumper sway slightly. "Yes, it did. Insulting, I would think."

Horatio smiled, not warmly. "Jigaboos," he said, "get used to that talk. Don't bother us none. Was there something else?"

"I reckon not. How bad was it?"

Horatio turned to his antique typewriter. "Told you, didn't bother me none. Scuse me, I got to get this piece rewritten."

Faye snorted. "I meant, how bad was the piece you wrote?"

Horatio said nothing, focused on the copy before him, punched a couple of keys. The typewriter made a sound like a tiny tambourine at each keystroke. The ribbon was ragged, actually holed through in places. Faye shook her head.

"Well. If it's anything to you, I have found that if you stand up to these people and don't take their guff, they will often be more reasonable."

Horatio punched keys. "I'm sure that is very valuable advice, Miss. Thank you for your insight."

Faye wheeled and started for the pressroom, and then turned back. "Is it that I'm a girl?"

Horatio turned and gave her the muddy look. "Is what?"

"That you're being so, so ... stubborn and impenetrable?"

"No," Horatio said. "It is because you are a white girl. Don't let it bother you none."

Faye considered sticking out her tongue, decided against it, and settled for a relatively feeble, "Well, then I reckon I can write like ... like Miss Elaine is looking for. You look me up if you decide you want to accept some help, to get you started."

Horatio Haney gave that a half-smile and turned back to his machine. As she left the hallway, Faye heard a staccato jangle that sounded like a midget Salvation Army, Horatio pounding his antique typewriter. Faye would have bet he was just hitting random keys. When she re-entered the pressroom, Forde Morgan was heading into the break room. Faye vowed that she would never enter the place again.

On Friday, the text of Horatio Haney's obituary of Miss Caroline Wentworthy, spinster organist at Mary Queen of Peace, circulated in the newsroom to a traveling accolade of snorts and chuckles:

Wentworthy Caroline: Organest and Lady of the Nights

Miss Caroline Wentworthy of 412 Eulalia Street, Charlotte, pass away last week of a ladys complaint after a long and fruitful even though single life. Miss Wentworthy, was a lifetime ressident of Mecklenburg County, served Merry Queen of Piece Cathlic Church for many years as Organest and Sun. School teacher. She got named Lady of the Year by the Nights of Columbus just last year in recognition of her long service to the perish.

Miss Wentworthy, who certainly live up to her name, is survived by her sister Mrs. Edward Shawnessy of Charlotte, a niece, Miss Alexa Shaughnessy of Indian Trail, and a lot of

Nephews. Services - which will be the poorer for the lack of her touch on the Organ - will be hell at Merry Queen of Piece this Friday.

There were corrections scattered over the first two lines; the rest of it was slashed through and terminated with a question mark and exclamation point. Faye supposed that Elaine Barnes was responsible for its premature publication. At the bottom of the newsroom hierarchy, it came to her last, and she glanced at it, suppressed a giggle, and put it on the absent Alma Brackett's desk. When attention had drifted elsewhere, she took it back, folded it into the pocket of her jumper, and went in search of Horatio Haney.

She found him at his desk, feet up, reading. After a less than momentary glance at her, he went back to <u>Huckleberry Finn</u>. Faye stood before him, outwaiting him. When he looked up again, she said nothing but pulled the Wentworthy obituary from her pocket and showed it to him, its corrections and slash and punctuation.

"You have about three minutes to be away from your desk before Elaine Barnes gets down here and gives you more hell. I'll be at the lunch counter at Kress's."

"I can't go in there."

Faye stamped her foot. "Fine, then you tell me."

Shrug. "Tolley barn, Trade an' Brevard. Where we going?"

"Nowhere. You, for sure. I just hate to see the waste."

"We got to be going somewheres. I can't just stand around and talk to you. What you got I could be totin'?"

"I...nothing, I guess. I don't know."

"Go to Kress, get a cheap picnic hamper. You get to the car barn, act like it's heavy. I'll be there. G'on, now, think I hear Miz Barnes cloppin' down the steps. I go this way, you go that."

*

Time and Chance

Horatio Haney put the picnic basket on a bench at the southeast corner of the Johnson C. Smith University campus. "This be okay," he said. "I'm tired carryin' that thing, heavy as you made it look. What you got in it?"

Faye sat on the bench next to the hamper. "Let's have a look. A box of jujyfruits. Six copies of the Mecklenburg Advertiser. Want one?"

"Take a jujyfruit, I guess. Way you was heftin that thing, I expected a anvil samwich. I bout threw it through the roof, you give it to me."

Faye held out the box of jujyfruits; Horatio held out his hand so she'd have to shake one into it. Faye looked at him.

"Is that so nobody will see you reach into the box?"

Horatio nodded. "Don' want to get lynched, thass it. Somebody think I messin with your box, why, I mightn' live out the day."

Faye shrugged, choosing not to acknowledge a double-entendre. "All right. So, do you want to be a writer, or not?"

Muddy look. "This something you need to know personally, Missy? Or somebody tell you ax me?"

"Neither one. I'm assuming you're good, or you'd never have gotten the internship. I hear you're the first Negro since Reconstruction."

"Heh. Don't they wish. I'm just the first one they had to mess with in their sacred newsroom, though not too much, you notice."

Faye shook her head. "I did notice." She started to extend a hand, saw Horatio's alarm, and withdrew it. "I can't do anything about that. Maybe I can help with your writing." She pulled Horatio's obit from her pocket and handed it to him. "I mean, there's some room for improvement here, don't you think?"

Time and Chance

Horatio glanced at the obit, sighed, and pulled a folded paper from his jacket. "Course, what you see there, that's the second draft. Why don't we start from the top, first draft, just like I handed in. Here. You look at this, tell me how you think I can improve. I would be pleased and honored by your lightest suggestion."

Wentworthy, Caroline: Organist and KC Lady of the Year

Miss Caroline Wentworthy of 412 Eulalia Street, Charlotte, passed away last week after a long illness. Hers was a long and fruitful life of service and art. A lifetime resident of Mecklenburg County, Miss Wentworthy served Mary Queen of Peace Catholic Church for many years as organist and teacher in the Christian Education program. She was named Teacher of the Year by the Knights of Columbus just last year in recognition of her many years of selfless service to the children of the parish.

Miss Wentworthy is survived by her sister Mrs. Edward Shawnessy of Charlotte, a niece, Miss Alexa Shaughnessy of Matthews, and several more distant relatives in South Carolina, Kansas, and California. Services will be held at Mary Queen of Peace this Friday. Donations to the church.

Faye blinked, looked at Horatio, and at the two texts. "What?"

Horatio gave her wide eyes and a minstrel's cackle. "Thass right, Miz Faye. What you lookin at there in yo' lef' hand, thass a carbon of what I give Miz Barnes, that she give me such hell over. I never seen that other one. Got niggered down some, don't you think, li'l Misseh?"

"Oh, stop that," Faye said. "But..." Faye shook her head, breathless at the treachery that lay before her. "But ... God." She clutched her head. "How could she <u>do</u> such a low-down ... Aren't you even mad about it?"

Time and Chance

"Mad? Course I'm <u>mad</u>, you think I made out of road tar? Think I'm some chuckle-haid darkie, give this a laugh and let it go? But I ain't <u>surprised</u>, that what you axin. How many times you think this kind of thing happen to me, comin up in Charlotte, North Carolina? 'Fit ain't white folks doin it, it's other coloreds, cause I ain't as black as them." He snorted and shook his head to ease the tightness of his collar and tie. "You get me yellin, some white man hear and think I forget my place."

Faye stared at Horatio's story, and then couldn't stop herself from saying,. "Well, here. You did spell the sister's name two different ways here. You might want to fix that before you take this to Len Biggs."

Horatio grinned at her. "Good eye. But fact is, the daughter spell it different from the rest of the family. She is some kind of Irish nut, looked it up and all, had it changed legally, but she never could get her mama to go along. I called the funeral parlor and the lady, Miz Alexa, to check."

"Oh." Faye tossed a hand at Elaine Barnes' corrupt text. "Oh, I can't <u>stand</u> this! But, surely she doesn't think she can get away with it, she knows she'll get caught. Or..." Faye fell against the back of the bench, while Horatio smiled and nodded. "It doesn't matter," she said. "Does it?"

Horatio looked around, saw no one within a block, and patted Faye's hand. "Very good for you, Miss Faye. You are a right quick learner, for a white girl. That's right, who's gonna catch her? Mist' Len? I expect it was Mist' Len's idea, don't you? Mist' Len a good manager. Give everybody a laugh at the Outreach Nigra, eases off any little discomfort they might be feeling about it."

"And all the discomfort goes on you. Oh, God, I guess so. I just had no idea it was as bad as this."

Horatio Haney's eyes widened and, in the sunshine, looked less muddy to Faye. "Oh, yes, Ma'am. It is fully as bad as this, and it got room to get a great deal worse, easy. For example, if you and me were to spend another minute in what appears to be an emotional conversation, wavin your arms, tears in your eyes, what all. Next thing you know, you get you a reputation, people yell nigger-lover. Go on, get up, I bring the basket."

When they returned to the Star-Dispatch, Faye took Horatio Haney's carbon-copy manuscript to Elaine Barnes, and placed it beside her elbow, as Horatio had. She decided that she could afford that much of a dig.

"Miz Bawns? I kind of took it upown mahse'f to set down with ... Horace? That his name? The culla' boy? Anyways, and hepped him clean up his prose some. He axed me see if you thought this might would be aw right."

Elaine Barnes looked up at Faye, and saw Horatio standing behind her, smiling humbly. She opened her mouth to say something, looked at the Wentworthy obit, and closed her mouth. Opened it again, turned pink, and closed it to shoot Faye a look of stubborn hatred.

"I'm not sure Mr. Hanes is like to learn much, he gets other folks to do his work for him," she said at last. "Copy!" She tossed the obit in a wire basket on the corner of her desk.

"Forde Morgan, you cannot sit there and tell me you're not shocked."

"OK," Forde shrugged. "I won't. But shoot, Faye. I'm not surprised. I bet half the people in that room knew what was going on. Naw, more than half."

"All but me, in fact. Is that it?"

"Well..."

"So when Horatio took me out and set me down so I could 'help him with his writing,' he was just doing it to teach me something. A lesson."

"You could look at it that way, I guess. Thing is, though, see, folks were just ragging him a little."

"About being a Negro? You can 'rag' somebody about that, and they just have to take it?"

"Aw. They don't mind."

"Really. They don't <u>mind</u>? Well, shut mah mouth, who'd of guessed? And they don't <u>mind</u> their crappy schools and their menial jobs, and they *don't mind* mumbling and shuffling to moron Elaine Barnes? They <u>*don't mind*</u> never having a chance at a decent job or a decent education? I don't know that I've heard anything more positively, affirmatively *stupid* than this stupid notion that human beings *don't mind* being treated like, like ... " Faye threw her hands in the air and gave up. "Or don't you think they are human beings?"

"Aw, Faye ..." Forde looked around the break room. Wil Cosgrove and Shanky Mercer, a couple of his pals from the sports desk, looked down at their coffees. "Listen, you know, you could ..." Forde skidded to a stop.

"Yes?" Eyebrows like the edge of a cliff.

Forde took a bite of his Baby Ruth and chewed, frowning, casting about for an escape. "You could," he said, brightening, "do a lot of good, with how you bring kind of a fresh perspective on things we've all prob'ly gotten too used to. But, just, you'll do more good if you try not to get so mad. Go at things a little slantways, that's how you make progress. You're real smart and real... your heart's in the right place. Folks don't like to be told they're a bunch of racists, is all."

Faye snorted, softened microscopically. "Even when they are?"

"Well," Forde said. "Do you think I am?"

Faye hesitated, smiled, and Forde about fainted with relief. "I guess you're a product of your time and place. That slantways enough for you?"

"Heh. Makes me sound like a bale of cotton."

"Not you, Forde. A pack of Spuds, maybe."

"A pack of Spuds. You know, I'll stay awake all night thinking if that's good or bad."

"Oh ..." Faye stood and folded her lunch bag. "It's not so bad. Maybe you'll grow up to be a whole carton some day."

Forde stood too, and turned his back to the sportswriters. "Faye, listen. I think you're just ..." He shook his head, and slanted it toward the door to the pressroom, where the Thursday shopping bargain supplement was running. "C'mon."

Faye followed him out, knowing what was coming, not sure yet how she felt about it. When they were on the stairs to the newsroom, the thunder of the presses a little muted, Forde turned to her and said, talking as if the words had to be pushed from his mouth like reluctant children, "Faye, you're the smartest, sweetest girl I ever known. Knew. I'd be so honored if you thought I might amount to something." He grinned, and Faye had to admit, it was a pretty good grin. "Even a carton of Spuds. Can we take that as some kind of a basis?"

Faye blinked at him. "Basis?"

"Uh huh. For, well. You know. I mean, I know you got a regular boyfriend back home and all. Just, he's there and you're here." Forde straightened, and looked up the stairs at the doorway above. "I would never go behind another man's back. But I'd be right honored if I could be your substitute boyfriend. Or escort, I guess. In Charlotte, you know. This summer."

"What happened to the girl back in Gabbro?"

Forde blushed. "That was just something I felt like I had to say, right then. There's no girl in Gabbro. Not that I'm attached to, anyways."

"Well." Faye twisted a heel on the cement stair, and listed to the gritty sound. Here it was. What now? "You're a boy, all right; and you're a friend. I guess I can't stop you from saying you're a boy friend. Is that what you mean by a basis?"

Forde uttered a sigh just wavery enough to let Faye understand at last that he was terrified. It softened her to allow this thing to continue, which she did not regret because she was bored, and Gordon was in Missouri, and she was here, and anyway, she also didn't know exactly how she felt about Gordon.

"No," Forde said. "This is what I meant." He put a hand on her shoulder. "There's no Klan around or anything, so this is not meant as a feeble cliché. I just wont to ..." He groaned and ground his teeth.

"Oh," Faye said. "That kind of a basis? Okay, then, here." And she put a tender hand behind his head, looked him in the eye from about five inches away, closed hers, kissed the living bejesus out of him, and ran up the steps to the newsroom. That would hold the redneck Romeo. And, indeed, Forde's neck was still bright red when he came through the swinging doors five minutes later.

At a quarter to ten that night, Faye stood at the mirror in her slowly cooling oven of a room, pinning up her hair, postponing the smothering lumps of bed. And entertaining the notion of a far-from-home, finite-duration summer fling. She wondered about Forde and sex; he had made no very ambitious moves, but he must be motivated by something. He did follow her to the staff room, back when she had her breakdown about Alma. That was kind of sweet, really, she supposed she had to admit, that and his "basis."

Faye grinned, flinging herself into the freedom of her isolation from her former life. Had there been a twitch against her belly during the Klan kiss or the one in the stairwell off the pressroom? She didn't recall, though of course the one on the stairs had occasioned a gasp and a sneezing fit from Forde that she supposed had pre-empted anything much going on below his diaphragm. He was a sweet boy and a lot smarter than he looked, and still, he would worship Faye and do everything he could think of to make her life pleasant. He could be taught to kiss satisfactorily, and that would be pleasant right there, and would certainly stand him in good stead later in life. She was confident that Forde could easily be discouraged from going beyond that to the kind of intense necking that she allowed Gordon. She imagined shady picnics at the end of the trolley line, somewhere innocent in the piney uplands of North Carolina, scratchy soft forests of pine straw overlooking meadows full of southern cattle. She did not hear the tapping behind her for a long few seconds.

"Oh," she said at last. "What?"

Mrs. Merrill stood in the hall, a slant lamplight transecting her housedress. "A young man is here to visit you. Please understand that I do not permit my guests to entertain gentlemen in their rooms, nor do I encourage social calls at this hour. You and he may use the living room this evening, if you wish, but I do ask that in the future you inform me in advance of such visits. It might well not have been convenient."

"It's certainly not convenient for me. Is it Forde Morgan? I didn't invite him. You can tell him I am not receiving visitors this evening."

Mrs. Merrill adjusted her hearing aid and smiled, as at a dim but diligent pupil. "Very well. I think you have made a correct and proper choice. It is, after all, nearly - "

"But it was Forde?"

"He did not introduce himself."

Time and Chance

"That's Forde to a T, excuse the pun. Don't bother yourself with it. I'll tell him to go away."

Faye put a sweater over her nightie, and stuffed the rest of it into a pair of shorts. Stupid Goddamn Forde, what in God's name would bring him here at night? She didn't bother with shoes, but pattered down the stairs like a cloudburst, breath whistling through nostrils flared with irritation, excusing herself past fat-ankle Mrs. Merrill on the landing, wheeling about the first-floor newel post into the front hall.

"Forde, for crying out loud," she said. She was reflecting with satisfaction on the steely depth of her voice, even as she gasped, gripped the newel, and sat on the bottom step.

"Oh, my God," she said then. "Huh ... Hi, Gordon."

10.

F AYE, Honey," Corporal Gordon Simmons said. "Who's Forde?"
"Gordon," Faye said again. "Oh, my God." She sounded shaky,
even to herself. What in God's name was Gordon doing here? Gordon
was a distant memory, a series of painfully created, impatiently read
letters. What was this about, this spiffed and shoe-shined apparition,
bigger than life, hair slicked, cheeks shaved, soldierly and cute?

Faye stood and went to Gordon, trying to smile, achieving at
least a kind of shocked dewiness. She put her hands against him, and
laid her head on his chest, heard his heart and felt his arms claiming
her.

"Gordon, my God," she said, and forced herself to think of
something else to say. "I can't believe this. I can't believe you're here."
Deciding against, for now, also telling Gordon that he had broken into
a part of her life that had been hers alone, the first she'd ever owned
free and clear of the heavy liens held by parents, teachers, and by
Gordon himself. This moment, she realized, divided the summer of
1947 into times before and times after, and ended the time that was of
her own creating. Already the tearful hungry days were gone, and the
strangeness of finding her own way. She was not ready to let them go,
and she felt trespassed upon. Realizing, as she heard his uneven
breathing, that Gordon was as scared as Forde had been this afternoon
didn't help. It was not his fault that she had come to this, but he would
have to bear the blame.

Faye pushed back from Gordon's chest as she heard Mrs.
Merrill's mules clacking on the steps. "Would you like to sit down,
Gordon? Mrs. Merrill, I would like to introduce my... my friend,
Private Gordon Simmons of the United States Army. Gordon, Mrs.

Merrill is ... this is her house. And this is her cat, Butterball. Sometimes I call her hairball."

"How do you do, Private Clemons," Mrs. Merrill supposed.

"Very well, thank you, Ma'am," Gordon said. "Now that I found Faye again. But it's Corporal now. You never noticed, Faye, I got a promotion."

Faye allowed herself to sparkle. "That's wonderful, Honey," she said, and wondered who it was, calling Gordon 'Honey' like that. Thing was, she'd completely forgot how big and cute he was. It seemed to her that there was no way not to call him some kind of pet name.

"Yep," Gordon said. "An' I got some other great news too. I'm gonna - "

"Do you have time to sit for a moment, Captain? Faye, dear, I was about to tell you, my sister called from Rock Hill, not doing at all well. I hate to rush you, but I need to bring her some things. I will be gone for the evening, and of course you will not wish to be alone here with Captain, ehm, Simkins. I do not wish to be inhospitable, but I'm afraid I will have to ask - "

"Oh, of course. Gordon and I are going to take a little walk, aren't we? You just go right along, and I'll let myself in. Gordon is staying with, with some friends, didn't you say, Honey?"

"Sure, that's right. I'm here on a 48-hour."

Faye frowned, struggling for a grip on things. "Well, when do you have to leave, then? You'll hardly have any time at all to get back to Missouri."

"See, that was my other news. I didn't say nothing in my letters, cause I wanted to surprise you. My transfer come through, and I'm in the paratroops now, over't Fort Bragg. I left Fayetteville at four this afternoon, and I don't got to be back till Sunday. Don't take but four hours on the bus. I can see you every weekend, I get a pass."

Mrs. Merrill dimpled at the very thought. "Well, then, Faye dear, I really must be changing to get over to Rock Hill. You'll - "

"Oh, yes. Do, please, don't let us keep you. Gordon, wait two seconds while I get some shoes and my key. I want to show you the neighborhood."

"Don't worry about the key," Mrs. Merrill said. "I'll leave the door on the latch. You're sure you'll be safe outdoors at night, dear?"

Faye smiled and took Gordon's arm. "Now, you look at this big lug, Mrs. Merrill. You think anybody is going to bother me while he's around?"

Mrs. Merrill looked, and so did Faye, gawping up at him like a little kid by the Washington Monument. As different from Forde Morgan and Len Biggs as could be. And Horatio Haney for that matter, who was a big lug all right, but whose pitted face - of dubious color in the first place - was not shaved to a fare-thee-well, who did not wear a jaunty uniform full of ribbons and little brassy things, did not regard Faye with fondness. And had better not.

Still, Faye was puzzled by the sight. In the hungry time, Gordon had been no more than a nuisance, without whose dogged letters Faye would gladly have done. Now, here he was, not looking half as dumb as his letters sounded. What kind of good-looking is it that you can just forget, and then it turns around and clubs you over the head?

In her room, Faye laid out a blouse and a pair of slacks. Taking off the nightie to change, she caught her own eye in the mirror. She looked a little flushed, and she didn't think it was running up the steps. She had just washed out her supply of bras, and there was not one that wasn't wet. She pouted and stretched and considered. And, smiling, she pulled a pair of panties from a drawer, put them on, and the slacks and blouse. *Caveat emptor*, she thought. That's a non sequitur, but I don't know enough Latin for *Christ, what do I do now?*

Time and Chance

The night was warm. Gordon didn't seem to have any agenda beyond just being who he was and where he was. Like, Faye thought, … like who? Any other lug, content within his skin. Not Forde Morgan, by a mile. Like Courtenay Weston, maybe, in her easy, bigger-than-life way. Little folks like Forde and me, she thought, we can never relax. We dart around between the legs of giants who saunter along, beautiful and smiling.

"Faye," Gordon said.

"What?"

"Oh. I don't know. I just like to say your name when you're right here with me, and not a thousand miles away. Isn't this just fine? I'm so glad to be with you again, I could about scream, except I got nothing to scream about. You just make me so … s'darn happy and proud."

Faye looked up at him. "That …?"

"Nothing. Just darn happy and proud, period. That's all."

"Proud?"

"Uh huh. I kep' all your letters." Faye blushed invisibly in the night. She didn't keep Gordon's. She didn't want Junie reading them, for one thing; and for another, really, what was in them to go back to?"

"Mm hm?"

"Yep. I read 'em over, an' I try to see how you write so darn interesting and well. How you do that, when it's all I can do to tell you if it's raining or not. I feel like I know all these folks you work with here, that Miz Alma Brackett, it's so funny when you write about her, I bust out laughing about every time. All I could <u>do</u> not to laugh just now, when you called that cat 'Hairball,' and looked at your landlady's hairdo. You got a wicked tongue on you, girl."

"Well," Faye said. "Well, shoot, Gordon, you know what? You're the first person ever told me my writing was any good."

"Naw, that can't be right. Look at all them folks here, and your teachers and all."

"That I cared about, I mean." Faye's stomach lurched. Saying it, she realized that - God, what a mess - she <u>did</u> care about Gordon. Next to him, Forde Morgan was a boy carved from a banana. She could foresee a time when she might say things like that, about caring for Gordon, and mean them in a way that she couldn't control.

But if she did care about Gordon, did she care enough to give up writing and live in a trailer court with the other Army wives in Fayetteville North Carolina, have babies, wait tables to earn enough to feed them? God, no. I will turn into a slattern with bad teeth and a hairdo a mile across.

Faye put an arm around Gordon's waist and let a medal scratch her cheek while they walked. It was familiar to her, the solidity of his body, the easy working of muscle inside the khaki uniform, the gentleness with which he laid a massive arm across her shoulders. She felt comforted, protected. Her knees wobbled, and she raged at them, even as she fitted herself against him. This beautiful, gentle thing shambling along next to my head might as well be a grizzly bear, she thought. He can cripple me as easy as falling in a ditch. Get a handle on yourself, you fool, or die. While you still have your summer and a life to live.

"Honey," she says, when she sees a way - the only way she can think of - to take things. Her voice in the warm night is tentative, shy as a puppy.

"Mmm?"

"You want to go back to Mrs. Merrill's? I bet she's gone by now."

"Is that what you want?" His voice is thick with longing.

"Yes," Faye says. "Yes, it is."

11.

B EFORE GORDON left, he had given Faye a smallish diamond ring, a picture of himself and Faye on the Comet at Forest Park Highlands in St. Louis (which Faye promised to cherish, though it made him look like Captain Marvel and her like an idiot), and forty hours, day and night, of relentless *woo*-ing. Faye was exhausted by Saturday evening, desperate by the dawn of the Sunday. Only Mrs. Merrill's return from Rock Hill Saturday saved her from another night of evasion, appeasement, diversion, and technical retention of a virginity that seemed no more than an outgrown fossil of girlhood, like a limp-neck doll or lucky underwear.

She lay awake on the lumps through Saturday night, her belly and knees longing for the same Gordon she had firmly booked into the YMCA, brain still planning an hour-by-hour campaign of activity for Sunday. Late rise. Church, which might settle Gordon a bit. Lunch in the park, let him handle me a little. Before he gets too urgent, go to the restroom, come out and suggest a visit to the Star-Dispatch. See if the Hornets were playing. From the ball park straight to the bus.

It worked pretty well, though there were a couple of blushing moments, the first when she lost control of things in the park and they were poked in the ribs and told to break it up by a groundskeeper, and the second when they walked into the Star-Dispatch to find Forde Morgan at his desk, surrounded by pictures of football players.

"Oh. Hello, Faye. Hi, uh … there."

"Hi."

"Forde, I'd like to introduce my friend, Pri – Corporal Gordon Simmons of the 82nd Airborne. Gordon, this is Forde Morgan." Faye thought she sounded like the train announcer at Union Station: *Corporal Gordon, Forde Morgan. Gorp, Gorp.*

Forde turned a color he'd not yet achieved in his talks with Faye, past crimson into a zone whose heat Faye could feel on her cheeks. Or maybe she was supplying part of the heat. Gordon – damn his magnanimous lug ass – just smiled and radiated relief that this unexplained slip-of-the-tongue Forde was so clearly nothing to worry about.

"Hey there, Forde," he said. "I'm glad to meet you. Faye's told me a lot about you."

*

Ten days elapsed in relative peace. The Wentworthy obit and two others by Horatio were passed in fastidious silence by Elaine Barnes, as Faye was by chronically red-faced Forde Morgan. The following Wednesday, Faye gave Junie two copies of the July 7th Star-Dispatch, along with two more copies of the News of Charlotte section, the back page of which carried Horatio Haney's first published lines.

"My," Junie said. "There it is. Horatio wrote that?"

"Every bit of it," Faye said. "I think it reads very nicely. He's had two more since then, but this is the very first. I'll bring you the first one they put his name on a story."

Junie smiled at her. "Horatio tell his momma, and his momma tell me, what you done for him down there."

"Me? He wrote this whole thing, just like you see it there."

"Naw, I talkin about how you made those folks set up straight down there. But listen here to me, Missy. You are a good girl, smart as rain, and truly a lady, but sometimes you worry me. You sure you know what you getting yourself into?"

"Trying to help Horatio? That's the whole point of the outreach business, isn't it?"

Junie nodded, as if Faye had made an inane remark about the weather. "Fine, good for you. Maybe I'm talkin here about this soldier-boy you keepin company with this las' week." She frowned out the kitchen window toward the alley while Faye gritted her teeth over her oatmeal. "What that scamp doin, jumping Miz Merrill's back fence? She find out, she bring the police down our chimbleys quicker than - "

"Excuse me," Faye said. "I didn't know that my friendship with Corporal Simmons was a matter of - "

Junie walked to the back door and opened it. Faye heard panting and scuffling, and a boy's voice. "Miss Junie, you gotta come quick. Miz - " The voice cut off in a muffled, meaningless glub, and Junie went through the door and slammed it behind her. Her voice, scolding and urgent, came through the wall, bringing no information.

I'm a reporter. I should be listening. Faye stood, and hesitated. What would Junie say or do when she opened the door and eavesdropping Faye lurched across the sill? Faye carried her oatmeal bowl to the sink, tarrying as much as she dared, and learned nothing from the subdued sounds that came from the back stoop. When she saw the boy leap into view, she hustled back to the kitchen table and picked up one of the papers. The back door opened and Junie entered, wiping her face.

"I got to leave, Miss Faye. Tell Miz Merrill I come back tomorrow, next day."

Faye looked up, concerned, trying for startled. "Is something wrong?"

Junie sniffed. "Lot of things wrong, Miss. Nothing you got to worry about."

"Well," Faye said. "Well, thank you for your concern about Gordon. Don't forget your papers."

Time and Chance

Junie came to the table and picked up one of the newspapers and exited, shaking her head.

Faye walked to the Star-Dispatch, wondering if she did know for sure what she was getting herself into. After his visit, Gordon called every evening, Faye waiting out the jangle of small change in a pay phone, the occasional complaints and arguments in the background about hogging the phone, and primarily Gordon's longing to repeat the experience that she had counted on being a one-time tactic that would leave him more or less satisfied, and her at least not pregnant. She should have known that the breathless hours of resistance and partial surrender would lead not to satisfaction but to escalation of a demand she no longer wanted to deny.

Though Gordon had been fine about it at the time, and had praised her gentleness and generosity, and joked about her "wicked tongue." But no day had passed since then without a request in some form that Faye get herself to Fayetteville, pending Gordon's next leave, and find some way to carve out enough privacy to "do things," as Gordon put it, "right." Faye could feel the ground sliding under her, a muddy crumbling avalanche that would skid her into a Fayetteville trailer park and the checkout counter of the Piggly Wiggly before she was thirty, and long before she made a name for herself as a writer, which would never happen.

She had been over this ground every hour since she kissed Gordon onto the Fayetteville bus over a week ago, and it never ended anywhere but there. Since many of those hours had been embedded in rumpled nights in which she could not seem to banish the smell of Gordon from her bed, or his taste from her mouth, she was beginning to feel and look haunted. She walked unseeing past a cop twirling his nightstick outside the door of the Star-Dispatch, with the dragging step of a prisoner to the rock pile. Forde Morgan, aloof since the morning after Gordon's visit, met her at the door to the newsroom, looking solemn.

"You hear what happened?"

"No."

"Horatio - Gosh, Faye, you look awful. I guess you did hear."

"Thank you. You look about as usual. What about Horatio?"

"I'm sorry, Faye. You really didn't hear?"

"For God's sake, hear what?" Faye was less emphatic than her words; she was just too depressed to summon the force to match them.

"Horatio. He got beat up something awful."

Faye fell into her chair. "Oh," she said. "Oh, my God. Who did it? Why him?"

Forde sighed and looked out the window. "Nobody knows who, though it wouldn't be hard to guess. Somebody took it wrong that a Nigra - a colored fella wrote personal information about a white lady in the paper. They expect maybe they'll have to keep a police guard on the building the next couple days."

"Miss Wentworthy? What personal information?" Faye was too fogged to focus on anything but this objective question. "Many years of selfless service? That's too personal for anybody but a white man to say about a white lady?"

Forde shook his head. "Long and fruitful life," he said. "They took it as a dig at her because she died a spinster."

"Oh, for - Oh, that's just so stupid ... Oh, poor Horatio!" Faye jumped up, adrenalin taking the place of a week's sleep. "Oh, I can't believe this. How can you stand there so calm and say that? Where is he? The hospital?"

"No, I think he's at home. A neighbor's taking care of him, what I hear."

"What?"

Forde shrugged, "Well, she's some kind of nurse, and I guess they figure he'll do better that way than at the county clinic."

"Yes, no doubt. I can just imagine the wonderful care he'd get at a county clinic. For Coloreds only, of course. Do they have bandaids, do you suppose?" Her eyes drilled Forde's. "How'd you know that?"

She held up a hand against his inevitable Know what? "You know what I mean. That about the long and fruitful life."

Forde pushed out his lips and shrugged. "Somebody in the newsroom said it. Everybody was talking about it."

"When did this happen?"

"I think somebody found him this morning. Dumped him on the doorstep some time in the night. Now, Faye, I know what you're going to say. But this is not the whole South, or even everybody in North Carolina. Klan are outcasts. It's just the few bad apples - "

"No," Faye said. "It is not, and I'm amazed that you can keep saying that kind of thing. But let me recall to you the rest of the saying about bad apples: they spoil the whole barrel. This whole town is a racist ... cesspool, if you ask me. But in fact, that's not what I was going to say."

Forde flipped a hand. "What, then?"

"Horatio gets beat up some time overnight, and dumped on his doorstep, for writing an unsigned obituary. Early the same morning, somebody in the Star-Dispatch newsroom already knows why. That tells you what? Come on, it's not so mysterious."

Forde shook his head. "Not his doorstep. Ours, the paper's. That's why we got that cop out there. It was meant as a warning."

Faye sat at her card table and put her palms against her eyes. She could feel her arms shaking, the card table jiggling along with them. "So Negroes count for something here, I guess. You can use them to send messages; like pigeons, sort of. Except you take better care of pigeons."

She was answered by a rustling and a sniff. When Faye took her palms out of her eye sockets, Forde was across the room, and Alma Brackett sat beside her.

Time and Chance

"I believe you have been neglecting your sleep, Miss Bynum," Alma Brackett said. "You are not making good sense, and your eyes are red. However, if I may have your attention for a moment. You will recall that I had an appointment with Miss Courtenay Weston recently."

"Yes."

"Well. When I presented myself at the Weston home, I was, if you can believe it, accosted by Courtenay and quizzed as to your whereabouts."

"Really?"

"I could not possibly invent this. 'Where,' she wanted to know, 'is that fun girl you had with you last time?' Well, you can imagine that it took me some time to connect this description with yourself. 'Miss Bynum?' I asked her at last, as there seemed no other possible interpretation. 'That's the name,' says Courtenay. 'Faye, was it? Didn't you bring her along?' I was quite at a loss. Courtenay insists that you were, as she put it, 'a million laughs, a very cute girl,' and someone she wanted to know better. She is hoping that you will join her for … tea, was it? Or possibly tennis, this afternoon."

"Courtenay Weston invited me more than a week ago for either tea or tennis this afternoon, and you're just telling me now?"

"It did slip my mind, I admit. Things that are difficult to understand often do."

"Well, I have other plans, in any case. I am going to visit a sick friend."

Alma Brackett smiled ruefully. "You cannot have a friend so sick that you will turn down an invitation from Courtenay Weston."

"No? Excuse me. May I use the telephone?" Faye flittered through the Charlotte phone book for a few minutes, ran a finger down a column, and shut the book. "I can't even call her to turn her down. Evidently the Westons can't afford a telephone."

"The Westons do not list their telephone." Alma Brackett picked up the telephone and tucked it under her ear to fish for a cigarette. "Woodbridge 3370, please, dear," she said. She handed the receiver to Faye. "It's ringing."

Faye took the receiver.

"The Weston residence."

"Courtenay?"

"I will see if Miss Weston can speak to you. May I tell her who is calling?"

"My name is Faye Bynum. I am calling from the Charlotte Star-Dispatch."

After a reasonable interval, Courtenay Weston was on the line. "Faye," she said, sounding like she and Faye were snuggled in pajamas and curlers. "You can't imagine how devastated I was when that pretentious hag showed up here without you the other day."

Faye bit her lip, not entirely to keep from laughing. She didn't think she'd describe Alma Brackett that way, to a stranger at least. Courtenay Weston, it appeared, did not mess around weighing words.

"Really," Faye said. "Well, I did enjoy meeting you on our first visit."

"Yes," Courtenay said, brushing that aside. "I was wondering if you had the time for a little visit, just the two of us. Do you play tennis?"

"I'm afraid I didn't bring tennis things to Charlotte with me," Faye said, not lying about this. "And besides, I'm sure you're much better than I am. I'd just bore you."

"Not at all. Actually, I hate tennis. It's just the way one is expected to begin a conversation in this town, between Memorial Day and going back to school. Would you be at all ... " She paused, seeming a little flustered to Faye.

"Yes?"

"Well, honestly, Faye, I have very little chance, here at home, to talk to women who have actually accomplished anything, or have any ambition beyond how much coverage their coming-out will get in the paper. I'd be very grateful if you would do me the great favor of just dropping by some time and talking to me about what it's like. Being a woman in a man's world, you know. Maybe we could compare notes on college, too."

"I'd be pleased, of course." Faye glanced at Alma Brackett, rooting in her purse, radiating indifference. "Of course, that's also something Alma Brackett could tell you a great deal about."

Faye pressed the receiver to her ear, too late, she thought, to muffle the peal of laughter that brought. "Oh, my, Faye. I just know we're going to get along wonderfully. None of the Charlotte girls, and damn few of the ones I know at Radcliffe have that dry humor of yours. Are you free this afternoon?"

No, Faye thought, I work. "Well, that's what I have to tell you. A good friend of mine is … is quite ill. I want to visit him and see how he's doing."

"Oh, of course. Well, can you make it for a late dessert, do you think? Mother and Daddy are at the beach, it would be just us."

And enough staff, Faye thought, to keep her from having to break a sweat. "What time?"

"Nine-ish, shall we say? Shall I send a car?"

"That would be lovely. The address is - "

"No, no, don't tell me, I'll never remember. I'll put Thompson on. He's quite reliable."

*

Horatio Haney lay on a sofa in his front parlor, surrounded by grieving relatives and a brace or two of neighbors. Faye tiptoed in, gasped a little at the sight, and introduced herself to a handsome dark woman in a folding chair by the sofa who proved to be Horatio's mother. The room smelled of casseroles and iodine. Horatio himself was bandaged to immobility, with splints on his left leg and both arms. One eye was covered with white linen that wrapped the global rotundity of his head. The other was swollen almost shut, but showed a familiar muddy slit and a segment of pupil no larger than birdshot, that regarded Faye without much enthusiasm.

"Look like we not careful enough," he whispered.

Faye leaned over him. "Don't try to talk. I am going to find out who did this to you."

Horatio wheezed and spasmed, making his mother draw in a breath and put a hand on his head. His cheek wrinkled, evidently with merriment. "You thank that's the question, Miss Faye? You thank this some kind of mystery story? Klan done it, bunch a white boys with ball bats. Your job ..." He fell silent, and his visible eye rolled up, showing yellow. Faye turned to his mother, who held a damp cloth to his unbandaged cheek.

"He been doin this all day," she said. "Fade in and out like that."

"Mrs. Haney," Faye said. "I feel just terrible about this. Horatio has a future as a writer, I just know it. He should get out of this town, go somewhere he can be what he's able to be without getting beaten up."

Mrs. Haney said nothing, beyond registering mild surprise that Faye thought there might be such a place under heaven.

Faye turned back to Horatio. He was breathing softly, and his eye fluttered open. "What?"

"Just rest," Faye said. "Your mother is taking good care of you."

Horatio scowled, remembering. "Man. My head hurts. I was saying something."

"You said you know who did this to you. Tell me."

Time and Chance

Horatio closed the eye. "Keep your nose out, Miss. Make some kind stink, what you think happen next?"

Someone by the front door stirred and spoke sharply. "Big ol' cah movin down the street. Look like he checkin' for numbers."

Horatio's mother stood up. "Klan scout. Git away from that door," she snapped. "Cut off the lights. Rosette, you run round the side. You see fire, you sing out. Ahfur, I might need help with Horatio. Rest of you, git on out of here."

There was a quick stampede of feet toward the kitchen, and the room was dark and empty except for Mrs. Haney, Horatio's uncle Arthur, and the dark bulk of the sofa. And Faye.

Mrs. Haney took Faye's arm. "Missy, you best get on out of here. Klan gonna give us a show, next thing. They fine you here, I cain't answer for you getting off safe."

"You watch me, Mrs. Haney. If those cowards see a white girl here that stands up to them, they'll wet their pants."

Faye went to the door. A dark sedan whispered in the shadows of a remote street light. Its door opened and a man stood behind it, peering against the glare of its dome light. He shut the door and began to walk toward Faye, head hunched forward, but not hesitating. When he was halfway up the walk, he stopped and fumbled in his pocket. Faye heard a click, saw a spark. From the side of the house, a girl's voice called "Fahr! Fahr!" and Horatio's mother screamed behind Faye.

Faye ran through the front door, furious, scared enough that she missed the top step and blundered off the edge of the porch into a sumac bush.

"Ow! Jesus, Mary and Joseph!" Faye sprawled on the sparse grass and dirt of the Haney's yard while the man bent over her with a flaring Zippo.

"Miss Bynum?"

"What?" Faye got to her feet, brushing at her skirt, ready to decapitate the bastard. "You forget your bedsheet or something?"

"Er ... "

"Well, just go on home, spook, and take your burning cross and shove it up your stovepipe. You and your cretin friends let these people be, hear me?"

"Are you Miss Faye Bynum?"

His deference infuriated Faye. She put her fists on her hips and stuck out her chin. "Good for you, Sherlock. They tell you to look out for me? I'm not scared of you, either."

"My name is Thompson. Miss Weston sent me to convey you to her residence. Do you need to collect your things?"

12.

C OURTENAY Weston lit a Gauloise with a brushed-silver lighter and leaned against the head of her bed. "More cream?" She held a bottle of Harvey's Bristol Cream toward Faye, slumped parallel to her, a couple of feet away on a vast sea of pink pima.

"What the heck," Faye said. She had rarely taken alcohol in her life, and never in such a gentle form.

"Faye," Courtenay said, "I simply cannot fathom how you had the guts to come all the way out here and jump into this internship business sight unseen. You never met any of those people at the Star-Dispatch, you had no idea where you would live, you had no social base in Charlotte. You just came here and went to work. That's just an amazing amount of ... " She flicked ashes onto the windowsill. "Of balls." Trying out some Radcliffe talk.

"Well." Faye balanced some Bristol Cream on her tongue and inhaled past it as Courtenay had shown her. Twin plumes of warmth invaded her lungs. "All those things you mention would come under the heading of luss ... lugshuries. Luck-shuries. It was this, or back to White Castle for the summer." She gazed, a little blurrily, at the four-poster canopy overhead. *Luxxurries. Silly word. 'Cream,' my foot. Bristol butt-buster.*

Courtenay picked up a stuffed panda and hugged it to her tummy. "And your boyfriend didn't make a stink about it?"

Make some kind stink, what you think happen next? Faye smiled, not as elegantly as Courtenay Weston could do with one hand behind her back. But she lied, probably about as well as Courtenay could. "Gordon? That kind thing doesn't bother me."

"Gordon. That's his name? How ..." Courtenay gestured with her Gauloise. "How <u>elemental</u>. I don't suppose you have a picture."

Faye retrieved her wallet from the jacket she'd slung over a chair, and opened it to reveal the Comet picture. Courtenay snatched it.

"My stars, Faye, what a horse! And cute enough to eat him with a knife and fork! How can you stand being away from him? Oh, and look at you, sitting there with an empty glass. Am I a bad hostess or what?"

"What the heck." Faye did not remember having said that before. "Wh'about you? Lovely girl like you, you muss have all the top boys in North Carolina on your door. Step."

"North Carolina. Honestly, Faye. If it wasn't for Daddy's business, we'd <u>never</u> live here. You can't imagine what a dumpy place this is to spend your life. It's hot, there's no culture at all, just one redneck after another, and the boys in Charlotte are the worst, 'cause the ones out in the hills don't know better."

"So, back in Boston?"

"Boston." Courtenay held the panda up by its ears, and snuggled it again between her breasts. "There are a few men in Boston. Not the Harvard boys, God forefend. A few of the younger faculty are of some interest ... Tell me, what does Gordon <u>do</u>?"

"Jumps outa - out of airplanes."

Courtenay drew a breath and put exquisite fingers to her mouth. "You don't mean it. Why does he do that?"

"Paratooper." Faye squinted at Courtenay to see if that seemed to be the right word. It sounded, suddenly, like a malapropism or a salacious trip of the tongue. What did I say?

"You don't <u>mean</u> it! Faye, he must have all the balls there <u>are</u>. Oh, you must bring him to Charlotte, you lucky thing."

Faye licked a sticky spill of Bristol Cream from her fingers. Having a boyfriend with balls had not struck her as a particularly lucky situation. She watched Courtenay from behind a death mask of drunkenness, shaking her head, thinking of Horatio Haney's mother. There's balls for you.

"Let me tell you so'thing, Court." Faye drew a breath in through her nose, trying to blow away the fumes of Gauloise and sherry. She leaned forward, swaying. "Tell you where I was tonight."

"Thompson told me. Mill Street? Isn't that a Negro neighborhood?"

Faye nodded deeply, grimacing. "Bingo," she said. "What I guess you call a Nigra neighborhood, wouldn't it? I want master the local puh - patois." Pa-twa. Take that, Alma Brackett.

"Faye, darling," Courtenay said. "I am a beast. I have kept you up long, long past your bedtime, and I know you have to rise and shine in the morning, not so? Let's tuck you in, shall we?"

"Tuck me in?" It sounded great to Faye.

"Wouldn't you like a little nap? You look so tired, poor thing." Courtenay twinkled at Faye. "Listen, I've got such a fun idea. Wouldn't it be fun to sleep over here?"

"I din bring anything," was all Faye could think of to say.

"What do you need? Just slip out of your clothes, you can borrow a nightie from me. I've got some you'd look just fantastic in. And look at this ridiculous big bed. There's room for fifteen girls our size. We'd be like twin sisters. I always wanted a twin sister, didn't you?"

Faye looked at the acres of floofy pink, not a lump in a mile of it, she bet. Fifteen twin sisters, tangled and cozy. It sounded warm and horrible.

"Oh," she said. "Truly. It does, sounds like fun, but not tonight. Not ruling it out, mind, some other time. D'you think your fellow, whozit, would mind taking me home?"

"Thompson?" Courtenay pouted and looked at her tiny, sparkling watch. "Faye, darling. You're so tired." Faye only shook her head, smiling, trying for cozy politeness, not trusting her Bristol-slippy tongue. Courtenay shrugged.

"Well. I'll see if he's still up. Wait here, have a little nightcap. After all, you're not driving." She kissed Faye's ear moistly, and padded out.

Faye woke when Thompson opened the door and gently spilled her head and shoulders into the cool night and the whisper of the Lincoln.

"Here we are, Miss. Do you need some help? Give me your key."

"Miz Merrill leave the door open."

Thompson negotiated her to Mrs. Merrill's door, got it open, and handed her through. She made it upstairs by crawling, stopping at the landings to nap and rest up. She didn't remember opening her own door or getting into bed, but she sat up in grey dawn to find herself there.

She woke again at eight with a foul mouth and a sick stomach. She stumbled through a day at the Star-Dispatch that was notable only for the number of stupid mistakes she made, and for the almost supernatural forbearance that Alma Brackett demonstrated about them. It was the end of the day before she opened her wallet and saw that the Forest Park Highlands picture was gone.

13.

F AYE managed not to think about Gordon for days on end - not because there was nothing there to think about, but because there was nothing that she could stand to think about for more than a few seconds. She may have dealt in sleep with Gordon, with the passion that had permitted her to offer him the remote comfort of pseudosex and with the dread of Army wife-and-motherhood that forbade her to surrender and comfort herself in his arms.

But there were no dreams that she could remember, only the night-struggle of lying awake, stripping off a sweaty nightgown to tangle herself in sweaty sheets, and waking drugged and reluctant to another day's work. She recognized her Bristol binge with Courtenay Weston as a momentary escape from Gordon, even as Courtenay prattled about what a "horse" he was. If only he were. Horses can be bridled, locked away, shot. She ate almost nothing the day after the session with Courtenay, and began to slide again toward the gauntness of early summer after her short prosperous fattening in late June.

While she avoided thinking about Gordon, she worried about Horatio Haney, and how she could find a way for him to escape to a writing life somewhere away from here. She wondered whether there were Negro paratroopers. She remembered, she thought, President Truman doing something about that. Goodness, there were even Negro baseball players. Faye did not think Horatio was likely to excel in either field.

*

Horatio Haney died of his injuries – specifically, of a slow hemorrhage that even his roomy skull could not accommodate indefinitely – the following Monday. Faye learned of it from Junie the next morning.

"Oh, Junie! Oh, my God, I never went back to see him again, I just thought he was doing all right. Oh, his poor mother!" A grenade of rage and guilt exploded in Faye's stomach, and she had to sit at the kitchen table, Post Toasties skittering across her plate onto the floor.

"Funeral be this aft'noon, if you was of a mind."

"Do you think they might let me say something?"

"<u>They</u> might. I won't. You be there, that's enough sayin'."

Faye lifted a haggard and tearful face to Junie. "It really is horrible, isn't it, Junie? How do you stand it?"

Junie didn't answer, and when she left the kitchen to attend to other duties, Faye swept together the scattered Toasties and dumped them in the trash.

When Faye walked into the deserted newsroom at the <u>Star-Dispatch</u>, a small fan on Elaine Barnes' desk hummed into silence that only Faye's footsteps and breathing broke. There was a note on her card table:

ALL STAFF MEETING 9 AM, BREAK ROOM

Faye looked at the clock above the swinging doors. Five after 9. When she walked into the break room, she found the whole payroll of the <u>Star-Dispatch</u>, from beer-gut press mechanics through Alma Brackett and Len Biggs and beyond to a couple of formal-looking guys that Faye thought she might have had an introduction to on the first day. Early arrivals, including Wil Cosgrove and Shanky Mercer from the sports desk, who were probably here all along, were seated in booths, facing the higher-ups; all the rest, including glancing, lip-biting Forde Morgan, stood against the other three walls. Faye eased the door shut behind her, not so silently that Len Biggs didn't give her a neutral look, cough, and nod toward the head table.

One of the suited-up men whispered something to Len, who shrugged and stood.

"I have," he said, "the schad duty of informing you that our intern Mister Horace Haney is no longer with us, having expired Monday night. Mr. Claiborne has a few words for us."

Faye found that Forde had moved to stand beside her. "Who's Mr. Claiborne?"

Forde shook his head in mock surprise. "Harold Claiborne? Just the publisher, is all," he whispered.

"Oh."

"Rich as the Pope."

"You don't say."

Harold Claiborne raised a gentle brow at the whispering, and a hand at the multitude. "Death is never an easy thing to understand," he said. "Particularly when a promising young life is cut off before its time. Even a Negro one, as we are all equal in death. Mr. Haney gained his position at the Star-Dispatch on the strength of glowing recommendations from elders of his community, and of a very creditable achievement in the essay contest, titled 'What America Means to Me.' Ownership and Management alike considered it a wonderful opportunity to reach out to the Negro community of Charlotte, to offer one of them the means by which to elevate himself into a useful and productive career in service to his own. It is galling to stand by and watch such promise cut short by a foolish, preventable accident."

"What?!"

Faye felt Forde's grip on her elbow. "Shh."

"Accident, nothing."

"Shh."

"Therefore, Ownership and Management have concurred in declaring a day of mourning at the Star-Dispatch. Of course, we still have to put out a paper, so mourning will be observed at our various workplaces. The Editor will save four inches for a picture and a brief obit in the News of Charlotte. Do we have a volunteer to write it?"

Faye stepped forward into silence. "Yes, sir. I'd be glad to. But it wasn't an accident."

"Yes, Miss? And I believe you are our other Outreach for this summer, are you not? That might be highly - "

"Outreach? I hardly think so. Do you have an 'outreach' program for the Midwest?"

Faye felt Forde's cheeks radiating on the back of her neck. She held up a hand in his direction. "Excuse me. I will be glad to write Horatio's obituary. But you must admit, sir, that his death was no accident. He was beaten to death by Klansmen."

Harold Claiborne looked unperturbed. "Perhaps you know better than I, Miss. And better than the police medical examiner. His report states that Mr. Haney's injuries were consistent with a car accident. Evidently, he was struck sometime in the night in this neighborhood, and managed to make his way to the steps of the Star-Dispatch before collapsing. There was nothing on his person that would explain why he should have been out of his own neighborhood after dark, but it is ludicrous to suggest that he would have crawled from there, in his condition."

"I didn't suggest any such thing. The Klan - "

"Really, Miss ..." Claiborne leaned toward Len Biggs, who slipped a pair of syllables behind his hand.

"... Miss Bynum. You are a stranger in our midst, and of course a welcome one. But you surely have lived among us long enough to discount these invidious myths about Charlotte. There has been no Klan activity in Charlotte for more than twenty years. The Klan is a spent force in a city that prides itself on its progressiveness.

Mr. Haney's regrettable death was an accident according to the Medical Examiner, and so it will be considered by this newspaper until such time as evidence proves otherwise. Miss Barnes, I believe Mr. Haney worked under your supervision. Would you be so good as to provide the obit?"

"Yes, sir." Elaine Barnes shot Faye a venomous smile. "Perhaps Miss Bynum would be willing to assist, since she seems to have struck up a remarkably close friendship with the late Mr. Hanes."

"That would be most appropriate," Claiborne said. "With the understanding that this unsubstantiated business about Klan involvement will play no role. Is that understood, Miss Bynum?"

Faye sighed. *Make some kind stink, what you think happen next?* She felt tears crowding at the corners of her eyes, spilling, flowing, pushed now from behind by the realization that this was the end of hope.

"No, sir, respectfully," she said. Harold Claiborne's face went blank, and Faye's heart began to pound. "I suppose it is possible that Horatio Haney mistook the car that struck him for a group of men in sheets, swinging baseball bats. No doubt it was dark at the time. But I went to visit him the evening after he was hurt. He told me, clearly and unmistakably, that it was Klansmen. Surely you do not want this fine newspaper to publish false information."

"I see." Claiborne turned to Len Biggs, who shook his head, and back to Faye. "I think we are finished here. Let's all get back to our real jobs, after a brief moment of silence in memory of Mr. Haney … Miss Bynum, if I could see you for a moment, please. And Mrs. Brackett as well."

"Good golly, Faye," Forde muttered, while the staff left the break room, sympathetic smiles toward Faye entirely absent. "Now you done it. What happened to slantways and all?"

" 'Slantways' was your way, Forde, not mine. If you think I'm going to - "

"Aw right, fine. Just, I hope I don't see you cleaning out your desk this afternoon."

"As if I ever had one. You can't clean out a card table."

"Please sit down, Alma. I would appreciate having your input on this matter. Miss Bynum, I would like you to take an important lesson from this experience, and never forget it."

"Yes sir?" Faye had availed herself of a wad of toilet paper from the Ladies' on the way to Harold Claiborne's office, and dabbed now at her uncontrollably flowing eyes.

"Miss Bynum." Claiborne held a finger aloft, transecting the line between his eyes and Faye's. "Never, ever contradict one of your superiors in the presence of your co-workers. That is a firing offense at any organization in this country, including the Star-Dispatch. It shows a want of judgment and maturity in any case, but particularly so when that superior is one of the ..." He tossed aside the admonishing finger and chuckled at the thought. "One of the owners of the organization. What can you have been thinking?"

Faye shook her head. The world had become a pair of millstones. "I apologize, Mr. Claiborne. I had no intention of offending you. I hope you will not fire me. Since you ask, though, I was thinking of Horatio lying on a couch, passing in and out of consciousness, and telling me not to raise a stink about it."

Claiborne rubbed his face. "You would have done well to have listened to him. He knew better than you. Alma, I take it you can manage the rest of the summer without Miss Bynum's assistance?"

Alma Brackett – who evidently permitted this powerful man to address her otherwise than in the canonical form – tossed a hand. "I was not given a voice in Miss Bynum's assignment, and I never needed her in the first place."

Time and Chance

Her voice seemed to be coming over a telephone line; Faye looked toward it, and saw that Alma Brackett was somehow a full city block away, though still sitting inside this spacious office. Faye raised a hand to her forehead, and found it cold and wet. She looked at Alma Brackett, wanting to remember this moment, knowing that she would carry it to her grave, if she didn't faint before it was over. *The day I got fired from a no-pay internship.*

"This incident," Alma said, from a mile away, "is by no means the first of its kind in Miss Bynum's brief time with us. She can be a self-centered and insubordinate girl who has been a trial to me in many ways. I should welcome her quick departure." She shot Faye a glance, and plucked a white lace hankie from her purse. "For God's sake, child, control yourself. Blubbering is not going to improve anything."

Faye shook her head and blew her nose on the toilet paper. Alma Brackett returned to the middle distance, shrugged, and turned back to Claiborne.

"However, there are other considerations. Miss Bynum has shown herself a quick and perceptive mind, a fine writer – for someone of her age, mind, but already well above the average at this playpen – and a person of substantial and unshakeable integrity. A day may come when those qualities will be permitted or even, God knows, admired in women. It is even possible that some day the Star-Dispatch will boast of having given her her start in journalism. It would be remarkably unwise of you to fire her over this matter. Kindly do not do so."

Harold Claiborne gazed steadily at Alma Brackett, then at Faye. "Mm. Sit down, Miss Bynum. If you faint, you could hurt yourself, and the next thing you'll be saying I hit you with a baseball bat."

"Yes sir." Faye looked around, found no chair, and leaned a hip against Harold Claiborne's lowboy, evoking a rattle of glass.

Time and Chance

"Miss Bynum, if you ever contradict me in public again ... no, wait. If I ever even hear of you contradicting <u>any</u> of us. Alma, Len Biggs, Elaine Barnes, or ... who's that weedy little chap from Gabbro?"

"Forde Morgan?" Faye found speaking nearly impossible.

"That's it. Knew his daddy at Chapel Hill.... So. If I so much as hear of you correcting young Mr. Morgan's damn punctuation in public, unasked, you will be fired so fast you won't have time to cloud up and blow your nose. And it won't save you that you're right and he's wrong; this is a team, and we don't embarrass each other, am I clear? Yes? Get out of here. No, wait."

Faye straightened, found her knees unequal to it, and sagged against the lowboy again. Something inside it fell over and rolled against something else. Harold Claiborne ignored it.

"Alma, you say you can manage the hellish flurry of engagements and comings-out by yourself for a while?"

Alma Brackett sniffed. "Of course."

"All right, then." He turned to Faye. "Miss Bynum, you are rewarded for your substantial and unshakeable goddamn integrity by being transferred to the police beat, under the supervision of Len Biggs. Maybe you'll learn to respect the kind of work cops do in this town. It goes without saying that I will expect substantial early evidence of the quick mind, fine writing, all that stuff we just heard from Alma. And a complete minimum of tears, if you please. Absence, if possible."

"Yes, sir." Faye blotted her nose with the soggy toilet paper.

"I hope I do not need to say that you are not to take this as any kind of license to play detective in regard to the Haney matter." He leaned back and scowled out the window. "On the other hand, he was another one with a quick mind and all that crap. He may well have seen the difference, as you so quick-mindedly perceived, between a Chevy and a moron in a bedsheet. So, I guess it's possible that, even

102

strictly minding your own and this paper's business, you might run across something about what happened to young Haney."

Claiborne spun back toward Faye and Alma Brackett and slapped his desk, making the contents of the lowboy jangle. "Now, listen to me. If that should happen; if you get the faintest inkling, or for that matter the most blatant evidence of Klan, or any other criminal involvement in Haney's death, you are to shut your mouth, depart the setting or situation in which you inkled it, and bring it to me. Is that understood?"

Faye nodded.

"Feel free to speak."

"Yes, sir," Faye husked. "Thank you, Mr. Claiborne."

As they walked back to the newsroom, Faye turned to Alma Brackett.

"How did you do that?"

"Don't preen yourself, be so good. I said the most I could for you."

"I know that. I'm not asking why you did it, though it was sure a surprise. I'm asking how you got away with contradicting your boss in the presence of a co-worker. According to his rule, he should have fired you."

"Heavens, child. Possibly I oversold your quick mind. Think back; I didn't contradict him once. He said it was a firing offense, and without ever denying that, I pointed out that it would not be a wise choice to do so, that's all."

"Well, but ..."

Alma Brackett said nothing until they reached the swinging doors of the newsroom. She stopped then, and turned to Faye. "You are puzzled that he allowed himself to be guided by a lowly Society writer, and a woman at that. Shall we give Mr. Claiborne credit for recognizing the force of the better argument, and leave it at that? I believe we shall."

14.

Crime This Week

Charlotte Police Chief Ivar Olerud reports the following crime statistics for the week ending July 10:

Forcible entry: 3, resulting in two arrests.

Theft: 15, resulting in one arrest.

Issuing forged paper: 12, resulting in no arrests.

Simple Assault: 35, resulting in 27 arrests, three protective detentions, and one involuntary deportation by bus to Memphis.

Murder: None.

Other disturbances: Mrs. Terrence Plenty of Tryon Street reported that an unknown attacker mauled her dachshund Sparkle, inflicting severe lacerations to the head, throat, and hindquarters. Animal Safety Officer Vardell Shields reported that the unfortunate dog had to be put to sleep at Fell's Veterinary Hospital.

Two boys were apprehended attempting unpaid entry to the sideshow at Macklin's Traveling Circus and remanded to the custody of their parents. Macklin's Traveling Circus reported that vandals released an ocelot from its cage some time during the night of July 4. Offering a reward for information leading to the recovery of the animal, ringmaster Ben Barney advises the Star-Dispatch that ocelots look like a cross between a leopard and a house cat. Animal safety officer Shields cautions the public that the fugitive animal should not be approached, as ocelots are dangerous and unpredictable. They prey on birds, amphibians and domestic pets. (Hmm.)

Chief Olerud Lauds Longtime Officer on Retirement

Charlotte Police Chief Ivar Olerud presented retiring Deputy Cleavis Penn with a gold watch and certificate of appreciation at the annual Policemen's Banquet last night. "Ol' Cleavis," Chief Olerud said. "My land, what'll we do without him?" Deputy Penn, who joined the force in 1912, rising from Patrolman to his retirement rank of Senior Deputy Sergeant, thanked the Chief, and revealed plans to apply his decades of law enforcement savvy in policing perch and cuffing catfish. "Crime any more," he explained. "Got so it's a full-time occupation. I'm ready to wet a line."

Faye made what career fodder she could out of the police beat which, in a town like Charlotte, at the same time rife with crime and determined not to notice it, was not a lot. Len Biggs passed her offerings on to Copy with a minimum of correction and of praise. One evening, she wrote in tiny letters on the trim from a sheet of 3¢ stamps,

"Some day the Star-Dispatch will boast of having given her her start in journalism."

And stuck it to the headboard of her bed, imagining some new intern finding it there, and wondering what hopeful, sweating legend had preceded her. In that bed, she slept restlessly but - as time accrued since Gordon's visit - with the resilience of the young; she wrote cheerful, dutiful letters to her parents, including the "Some day" quote without mentioning its context. She tossed, gnashed, and wept the agonies of Corporal love, with a young woman's intensity and powers of healing. She wrote carefully affectionate letters to base-bound Gordon, whose phone calls continued, though without much new material, and to the increasing annoyance of Mrs. Merrill, which Faye ignored.

Also on that bed, late at night and to keep from thinking about Gordon, she composed two poems about Horatio Haney and one about herself that so revolted her that she scratched them out, wadded them up, unwadded them again at dawn to re-read in consternation what had seemed poignant and true in the writing, and tore the crumpled paper into tiny pieces to flush them down the toilet. Poetry, clearly, would never make anybody boast of giving her a start, and in any case missed by ten miles saying anything that she really believed.

With that, and with the publication of Elaine Barnes' grudging, noncommittal obituary, the name and fate of Horatio Haney disappeared from public commentary and newsroom gossip, if not from Faye's sleep. There, he reappeared in various forms that the dreamer would penetrate only in the last seconds before waking, whether at dawn or in heart-pounding blackness. After a few repetitions, she began to recognize and dread the impostor, who might take the form of a cop, a new editor, her father, or harmless Forde Morgan, only to turn and show her the ruin that lay patiently in the open casket at Horatio's funeral, waiting for the noise and singing to die down so someone could come along and avenge his death. On Thursday, July 26, Gordon's nightly call brought the news that he had at long last obtained a 48-hour pass for the coming weekend.

"And listen, Faye honey, I got another nice surprise for you."

"Uh huh? What?" Faye chewed at the end of one of her braids.

"Naw, if I told you, then where would the surprise be? You'll see. Aw, Faye, I just can't wait to see you again. I feel like I might could jump right out of my skin."

Faye spat out a little tuft of hair ends. "Ewck. Who's supposed to clean up after that?"

"Heh. I love it, you make me laugh like that, Faye. You're just … just the funniest, sexiest woman I ever heard of, let alone met. Man, honey, I just can't wait."

"Is this surprise something I need to get ready for?"

"Naw, I'll take care of that. You'll love it, though. I think."

*

"Lynch? We don't lynch folks in North Carolina. Never have. That's your deep South folks. Alabama, Mississippi, down there."

Faye gaped incredulity. "What are you saying? What do you call what happened to Horatio?"

Forde shrugged. "Either he got beat up, or got hit by a car in the night. You heard what Mr. Claiborne said."

"Yes, and I also heard what Horatio said, and you didn't, Forde Morgan."

"You'd ought to be careful about going over that neighborhood at night. Anyhow, you ever saw a real lynching, you'd say it was something else from what happened to Horatio."

"Murder," Faye flattened a hand on her new desk in unconscious imitation of Harold Claiborne. "Is murder."

Time and Chance

Forde looked around the deserted newsroom, the clock over the door reading almost a quarter to six, and wondered whether he oughtn't just walk the hell out of there. But he couldn't let her have it.

"That's right hard to argue with of course, but it don't get us anywhere to have you say it. Listen, Faye - "

Faye slapped the desk. "You listen. Just because nobody put a rope around his neck, that we know of, doesn't mean he wasn't lynched."

"That's not what I meant. He - "

"Oh, of course, ignorant me. Tell me, Mr. New South, how <u>do</u> you lynch Nigras back there in Gabbro? I expect roasting is probably involved, chains and such."

Forde got as far as the door this time, then turned back and approached Faye. "Faye, that's not fair, now come on."

But Faye was past gentling. "Back home, when a gang of thugs beats a man to death, we often call that murder. Not all the time, of course, we have our own limitations. And I do want to be fair. How's this, Forde? Next time you get word of a real Southern lynching coming off, why don't you bring me along, so I can see what it amounts to, more than what Horatio got. Let's see ... I'm tied up over the weekend, but I'm free most of next week. How's Tuesday, mm? Around midnight, two in the morning be good for you?"

"That'sch a little early. Gen'ly, it'll be nearer dawn. Four, five, in there."

Faye and Forde jumped as Len Biggs let the newsroom door swing to behind him. "Misch Bynum, I thought I heard Mr. Claiborne tell you to let that matter alone."

Not unless you can hear through solid walls. "Yes sir. Forde and I are right sad about Horatio, and we were just, just discussing whether it represents part of a pattern, so to speak, or whether ..." Faye ran out of words lifted a hand, slumped in her chair.

"A pattern of traffic accidentsch? There have been an awful jump since the War, people making money, buying a car, traffic jamming up, even nighttime. Lot of crazy people out drinking then too, not driving too careful. Generally, come to that, I'd recommend careful over dumb and headlong any day, don't you think? Whether you're a newschpaper, or nothing more than schome rookie who'll be gone in a month or two."

Faye squinted at Len Biggs, looking for more than was there to be seen.

"Yes, sir," she said. "I expect you're right. Come on, Forde. You want to keep me safe on the way home?"

Forde jumped to his feet, occasioning a curl of Len Biggs' lip, and they exited. Faye found a pressing need for the Ladies' as they descended the main stair, and let Forde cool down in the marble lobby. As she entered the pebble-glass sanctuary past the dowdy old wicker couch in the anteroom, Elaine Barnes emerged, glanced at Faye, sniffed, and walked out with no further intercourse.

*

"This here's it, I reckon." Gordon Simmons' buddy Calvin said.

Faye leaned across Gordon to peer out as Calvin's daddy's Chevy pulled through a pair of stone pillars that - OK, last time it was dark and strange, and on the way out she was unconscious - still looked awfully familiar. Faye put a hand on Gordon's knee and addressed Calvin as he shifted into second.

"What's your girlfriend's name? I don't want to get it wrong."

"Not so much a girlfriend," Calvin grunted. "Just somebody I knowed in grade school. Lost track when she went off to some prep school up north. Coulda knocked me flat when her fella called th'other day."

"But anyways?" Gordon asked, trying to be helpful.

"Anyways what? Oh, yeah, Cortney. Always thought it was kind of a stuck-up name for a little skinny thing in teeth braces."

And sure enough, by God, there she was, a-skippity down the front steps, past the lion planters and up to the car. A leonine something within Faye lifted its head and sniffed the air; something more primitive in her limbic system stirred and hissed. And neither beast was calmed when Courtenay Weston, dismissing boggled Calvin with a sisterly hug, turned to Faye and smote her flawless brow.

"Faye Bynum, as I live and breathe! Why, my stars, when Calvin asked if he could bring along a buddy and his girlfriend, how in the world did it turn out to be you? So then, this must be the fabled Gordon, n'est-ce pas?"

Gordon blushed and shrugged. "Don't know about the fable part. Gordon Simmons, 82nd Airborne, yes, Ma'am." He extended a massive hand to shake Courtenay's.

Faye took Gordon's arm. "Courtenay, for heaven's sake. Are you asking me to believe this is some kind of coincidence? Out of all the soldiers in the USA, you just happened to pick Gordon's buddy to house-sit for you?"

Courtenay smiled, unruffled. "Faye, darn it, you gimlet-eyed girl reporter. No, I have to admit, I put Thompson on it, and he asked a fella he knew that tracks people down. I just had such fun with you the other night, and I admire your, your enterprise so much, taking on a writing career, I just wanted to see more of you." Courtenay made a little Parisian gesture of wrist and eyebrow. "And, of course, I admit too, I absolutely had to see the fab- the, your friend for myself. Was I a bad girl?"

Faye shrugged, a little disarmed. "No, of course not. But you could have just asked."

"Yes," Courtenay said, tasting the idea. "I suppose I could. Well, you're here now, in any case, and I want you both to have a lovely time, because I do <u>so</u> appreciate your watching the house while I'm gone. Calvin is going to escort me to a godforsaken charity business in Charleston, that Mother and Daddy would have taken care of if they weren't in Majorca. Will you two be all right here by yourselves?"

"You're gone? Ourselves? Well … what about Thompson?"

Courtenay raised an eyebrow. "Thompson? All the staff are on vacation this week. I suppose I could call him and bring him back if you wanted. You're <u>sure</u> you want a lot of servants underfoot, dear?"

"No," Gordon said. "We'll be fine."

"I thought so. Who wouldn't be fine, a big lug like you around? Calvin, the train leaves in less than an hour. Let me just get my case, and we'll have to run right along now."

"Yes, Ma'am," Calvin said.

Gordon tipped the last of the champagne into Faye's glass. "Aw, Honey, OK. So she pulled a little bit of a fast one, with this house-sitting deal. She likes you, and she wanted to give you a chance for a nice time, that's all."

"I can't stand being tricked, no matter why. And she can keep her 'big lug' talk to herself, too."

"Faye, Honey, everybody and their cousin calls me that. She didn't mean nothing by it, I can tell."

"Yes? You have long experience with shades of meaning when people call you a big lug? So when has it happened that somebody did mean something by it?"

Gordon smiled. "Well, a couple weeks ago, you called me that to your landlady. Seemed like there was some shady meaning going on then."

Faye laughed. Wit from Gordon was like rain in the desert. "All right, then, ya big lug. I guess it's not a hanging matter." *Just because nobody put a rope around his neck.*

"Not if it gives us a weekend in a great house by ourselves, no landlady or guys with sticks poking us in the ribs, seems to me."

Faye smiled and watched bubbles rise. "I still have a bruise from that."

"Show Daddy. I'll give it a kiss and make it all better."

Faye lifted her blouse a showed Gordon a rib. "It's about faded out by now. It was right there."

Gordon knelt and nuzzled the indicated spot. When he showed a tendency to widen the area of concern, Faye whacked his nose and pulled down the blouse.

"You just keep your shirt on, Corporal. Come on, let's have a look at the place. I guess we're responsible for it."

Gordon rose with the face of one willing to indulge whims. "Sure."

They were a little constrained at first, peeking into rooms, walking softly; hand-holding adolescent explorers penetrating grownups' space. Some of the rooms were dazzling, some stuffily old-fashioned, some utilitarian, and one or two, like the unused conservatory, a little baffling as to their purpose. There was a cool, musty air to the back and dampness in the kitchen, but four lunches and four dinners under waxed paper in the refrigerator, a plentiful supply of drinks, vast fluffy towels in the bathrooms, and a strange console in the library that proved to be a television set that offered a choice of test patterns. Upstairs, a sitting-room or two, and hallways of bedrooms smelling of past sunlight and undisturbed dust, each with some distinctive and inviting piece of furniture that, by unspoken consent, they no more than glanced at.

"More bedrooms, I reckon," Gordon said at the foot of the stairs that led to a third floor, and they did not go further. Faye recognized this as kindness or Gordon's part, and bit her lip. But at some point, the champagne uncorking itself in their bloodstreams, they stopped whispering, and began making up explanations for things that were puzzling.

"Look here, a silver tray, but too small for breakfast. It's for the mail, I bet. And you reckon that's one of those bell-ropes to call the servants?"

"Nuh-uh," Faye said. "You pull and it lets the dogs out of their kennels to chase off burglars."

"Well, let's remember where it is, then, if we get broke into in the night."

Mention of the night brought renewed constraint, and an offer, accepted, to return to the kitchen, open another bottle, and sit down to supper. And when that was done, partly in silence, partly in laughter at the watercress, the little panties on the lamb chops, and the size of the napkins, and twice in simultaneous breaking of long silence with cross-purposed remarks, Faye rose and took Gordon's plate to the sink. Motion made her a little dizzy, and carried with it, its own momentum.

"Gordon," she said.

"Uh huh?"

She looked back at him, upright at the kitchen table like a sentry. She could not, had never managed to, square his military good looks with his evident devotion to her own lanky intellectuality. "You know," she said at last. "I jus' cannot afford to get pregnant."

Gordon blushed. "Well, sure, Honey."

"No, I mean it. You know how I feel about you, and you ought to know that I like ... well, you know. Kissing and all. Surely you do know that. You've been very kind and patient. I know you want to go to bed, and we're in a perfect place for it. I'm just going to ask you to keep on ..." She threw him a bashful look. "Well, you know. Being patient."

He smiled, and rose to put his hands on her waist from behind. "All right."

"Really?" Turning then to look at him closely "You mean that?"

"Sure. Yes, I do, Faye. I want for you to be happy."

Faye wiped her hands on a dishtowel, her eyes stinging. This would be so much easier to figure out if he wouldn't be so damn nice. "All right, then. I think there's some ice cream in that freezer. I'll get some rum out of the panty – the pantry to put on it. Then let's go see if there's anything on television."

There was a ball game, the Senators against the St. Louis Browns, out of a Raleigh station. They ate ice cream and held hands, Gordon scoffing in turn at the Senators and Brownies, the two worst teams in the American League. Faye paid little attention to the gray midgets romping in a snow-struck fishbowl, using the time and what she had left of thought, in trying to compare the dizziness of rum and the deep agony of writing, to the dizzy agony of love. Or, she admitted somewhere around the third inning, of sex. Love seemed to be a manageable enough proposition by comparison, composed as it seemed to be of kindness, solidity, awkward letters, and a certain kind of smile.

She had made no great progress when Gordon took a break during a commercial at the end of the fourth, with the Senators up, 2-1. When he returned, it seemed to Faye a good enough idea to lean against the arm of the couch and put her legs, chaste in pedal-pushers, across his. Gordon laid a hand on her thigh, and left it to wander as it would. Kissing began in the bottom of the 6th, and was urgent by time the Senators squeezed home an insurance run in the 7th.

The Browns tied it with a pair in the top of the 8th. Some time in the 9th, with runners at the corners - but no one there could have told you whose they were - the rum, the champagne, the patience, and the gradual, irreversible building of lust had Faye flushed and trembling on Gordon's lap, knowing that there could only be two endings to this, wanting neither of them.

"Oh, heck," she sighed, helping Gordon with a button. "What the heck, I can't stand the suspense. Let's do it and get it over with, OK? Just please be ... be nice."

Gordon paled, whuffled, and started on the pedal-pushers.

"Wait," Faye said, tossing her head at the TV set. "Not here. Upstairs, one of the- " She gestured over Gordon's head.

Without answering, Gordon grabbed her and dashed to the hall with Faye held to his shoulder like a Torah scroll. He took the steps three at a time, and dropped her on a four-poster in the first room they came to. Faye recognized the pink bedding; but they stripped frantically and, within two minutes of her speaking, Faye felt herself penetrated in a bleak epiphany of pain. She drew a long breath, tasting the flowery staleness of the room and the sweat of Gordon's naked shoulder. *There it goes.* And, later, *Maybe I can write while the baby's sleeping.*

They made love twice more during the next 33 hours. The second, at dawn on Sunday, was initiated by Faye, whose body chemistry drifted already toward languor and heedlessness, the witchery of skin and the lunar sway of fertility.

Courtenay and Calvin returned also on Sunday morning, but late enough that Faye had bathed and put herself and the house somewhat in order. Still Courtenay, guided apparently by her own witchcraft, beelined to the library and found the ice cream bowls and rum. Faye supposed that she looked about like Forde Morgan, and turned her head to keep Courtenay from detecting the heat. Courtenay winked at Fay while she turned off the hissing TV.

"I usually remember to shut this silly thing off," she drawled. "Unless I get really distracted. Where's the lug?"

"Gordon? I think he's getting dressed." Trying not to look as if she really knew.

"Naw, I'm here," Gordon said, coming around the corner doing up his olive-drab tie. "Folks back?"

Courtenay beamed at him. "There you are, Luggo. Did you have breakfast yet?"

Gordon shrugged, not sure. Courtenay twinkled, danced into him in her little ballet slippers and planted a pretty solid kiss on his cheek. "Thanks for taking care of my house," she breathed, peeling off a little slowly. A shiny spot on Gordon's cheek put Faye, unfondly, in mind of the ear kiss that had ended the Bristol Cream evening. "And my friend. You can do it any time."

In Calvin's daddy's car on the way to the bus station, Gordon wiped his cheek and turned to Faye. "Who was that again?"

15.

T HE GUILT and disorientation that followed Gordon's first visit was nothing to what now invaded Faye. She felt an odd tingling in her blood and belly; her breasts felt suddenly heavy. Fallen, debauched, pregnant: the first three words in Sister Penitentia's crimson litany of consequences plastered the walls of her soul like circus posters. She had yielded to sin, and she was no better off than the loosest dropout that ever flunked Health.

In another week, she passed the 29th day since the last small red dot on her calendar, and knew that she was doomed. She prayed nevertheless that the cup of pregnancy be taken from her, thumbing through a compendium of saints at the Public Library. Reasoning that the Blessed Virgin, having triumphed through the opposite experience, might not be receptive to the prayer of a non-virgin that she not conceive, Faye looked for a lesser saint who specialized in girls in trouble. There seemed to be no such entry, so she settled for St. Anne, patroness of pregnant women. She found a quiet corner of the reading room, bowed her head to the table, and asked humbly, passionately, to be dropped from the saint's list of women in need.

Leaving the book at the reference desk, she realized that she felt not the slightest comfort, or the least hope that anything would come of it. She wondered whether this meant that she was losing her faith – in fact, she had not been to Mass since coming to Charlotte – or just that she was so far gone in sin that she no longer heard its voice.

Because in fact Faye could not make herself wish Gordon gone from her soul. Even during her deflowering she had felt loved and protected; and the sex she herself had originated on Sunday morning had been ecstatic, revelatory; she blushed and felt herself soften at the memory of it. She hoped, dreaded, knew, that it would happen again on Gordon's next visit. She stopped writing home because she feared that Mama would read the awful news through her lightest reference to Gordon, to weekends, to the humidity; even to Alma Brackett, somehow.

Her night vision crammed with the bristled side of Gordon's head, his naked shoulder, and the canopy of Courtenay Weston's four-poster. She dreamed of children, articulate at a month old, explaining Faye's dementia to choirs of older women, all of whom had felt and done exactly as Faye had, and rued the day. When her defenses were at their very lowest, at three and four in the morning, she did not know which she more wanted with her in the lumpy cot, Gordon at her breast or a blade at her wrist. Sister Penitentiary, transformed to a jail matron, chased the corpse of Horatio Haney from her nightmares, slammed the gate, and turned to Faye, eyes narrowed.

Convinced more by the calendar and by the heaviness in her body than by the stony silence that greeted her prayers, Faye figured numbly that she had maybe two months, given her skinny frame, before she started to show. Not much time to save the hope with which she'd begun this summer. And really, not even that long, since her internship at the Star-Dispatch would finish in a month, and she would have to go back to Missouri, go through the motions of getting ready for school, and then have to face the fact that she was not going anywhere but the maternity ward. Some time in there, she would have to give Gordon the glad news, and he would slam her into a bridal gown. That would be the end of hope, the end of writing. Surely in this month that she had, she could summon the will and the brains to find a future that would outlive motherhood.

Sure, she thought at her desk one morning, I'll write for Stars and Stripes, how's that? "Mrs. Master Sergeant: Observations of an Army Wife." By Faye Simmons, winner of the Pulitzer Prize for reportage, back in 1947. There's probably half a million army wives that think they're gifted somehow, and half of them think they can write. Say, fifty thousand who really can, forty thousand of whose husbands would outrank Gordon, and maybe a thousand of those who could write better than Faye. That was still a lot of competition.

Still, "Faye Simmons" – though it sounded, sure enough, like a waitress or a checkout girl at the A&P – had a little more heft to it than "Faye Bynum," a name that had always sounded lame in her ears. Anything would be better than "Mrs. Gordon Simmons," which disappeared Faye Bynum from the universe and turned Gordon into a married woman. She wrote on the pad before her. Faye Simmons. Faye B. Simmons. Faye Bynum Simmons; Faye Bynum-Simmons, which sounded sort of European, but also sort of like something a cricket might creak outside her window. Faye B. Simmons, she wrote again, this time with a Hancockian flourish. Not too bad. The sort of name you might find on a woman in jodhpurs and a pith helmet, pushing aside vines in the Congo. _King Kong's Consort,_ starring John Wayne, Ray Milland and Faye B. Simmons. _What unnatural thing grows in her womb?_

"Lovely, dear," Alma Brackett said over her shoulder. Faye jumped, slapped a hand on the paper, and lost her hold on the pen, which bounced once on her dictionary and skittered down the line of desks to fetch up at Elaine Barnes' feet. Elaine glanced at the pen, flared a nostril, and returned to proofing with a little shake of her head.

Alma Brackett sighed. "I take it you are actively seeking to make a fool of me for saving your job. If Len Biggs has given you nothing better to do than to waste paper playing bridal games, I can use your feeble skills on the Society desk. What in the world has gotten into you? Stupid question. Exactly what it appears, I suppose."

Faye stood with her back to the paper, opened her mouth, lifted a shoulder, and sat down again, shaking her head. "Yes, you have found me out," she said. "I have got it bad, Miss Alma, ... Brackett, and there is no point in denying it. What can I do for you?"

"More to the point, what did you do to yourself?"

Faye shrugged. "Nothing."

"Nothing. And yet this Nothing that you did, has transformed you virtually overnight from a competent, arguably promising young woman into a vaporous, quasi-sluttish pre-Raphaelite whose ..." Alma Brackett glanced at Elaine Barnes, tucked the corner of her mouth back, and straightened. "I have an appointment to wheedle a few spare dollars out of one of my spoiled dimwits. Does a return to those ancient days appeal to you? I am not nearly so convincing when I play the bumpkin as you can be without half trying."

"How can I say no to that sort of wheedling?"

Alma Brackett nodded. "That's better. I will be at my car in fifteen minutes. Join me there, be so good."

"Vaporous slut, I think you said?"

"I did not. You'll never make a reporter if you can't remember the quote accurately after twenty minutes." Alma Brackett whacked the Packard into third and veered onto Romayne Boulevard.

"Thank you. There is no need to concern yourself."

"Evidently not, Mrs. Simmons. It is as clear as can be that you have compromised yourself, and that you have yet to feel anything but a happy glow about it, regardless of the risk to your career. Let me tell you, my girl, brighter women than you – "

"Compromised myself? What makes you think that?"

"Really, are you serious? One minute you blush, the next you're as pale as paper. You stretch and strut and yawn. You work furiously for five minutes, then you get up to sharpen your pencil, and you walk to the sharpener swishing your tail like a mare in heat. Do you think I can have followed the social lives of dimwits for forty years without recognizing the stigmata of lost virtue? It's so evident that even the sports writers have noticed. They are getting up a betting pool on who it was that "decked" you, as they put it. Right now, the money is evenly split between Len Biggs and Horatio Haney, with a small and hotly ridiculed minority favoring Forde Morgan. No one mentioned any Simmons."

"Now I know you exaggerate. Alma Brackett, please don't press me on this. I am the same person I have always been. I've been tired, is all."

"Oh, I see." Alma Brackett swerved the Packard into a beshrubbed drive. "Evidently, you are not ready to be addressed frankly. All right, here is the place. The girl's name is Felicity Jane Trotter. Try not to look too much like a Dock Street floozy while you lisp your line about 'Ever so gay an' sort of la-di-da,' will you please?"

Forty minutes later, Alma Brackett pulled two tens and a five from her wallet and placed them on the seat next to Faye. "That tiny simper when Felicity Jane's momma picked up the candlewood was just what the doctor ordered, and reminiscent of old times. Your carriage and decorum were exemplary. You have not lost your touch, my dear, whatever else you may have lost."

"All right," Faye said. "All right, all right."

"All right, what?"

Faye picked up the money and looked at it absently. "I was only saying that because I couldn't think of anything else."

"You _are_ in a bad way. For heaven's sake, Faye, snap out of it. Do you think all women are either wives or virgins?"

She called me by my actual name. "Do you think I haven't told myself that? I have exactly one month to do something I haven't managed to do in my life so far. To write something that people will remember."

Alma Brackett waved a dismissive hand. "Good heavens. You have years to do that, and very few achieve it in any case. Your work on the police beat has been quite competent – up to last week, at any rate. So, my dear. What changed that?"

"Well, for one thing, I don't know about all women, but I'm neither a wife nor a virgin. That's not all that bad, if you want to know. But – "

"Thank you for informing me, you presumptuous little piece. Nor am I, but you don't see me swanning around the office like Mata Hari, do you?"

"I can't even imagine it, but that's not the point. I think I'm - " She sighed. "I think I'm probably pregnant."

Alma Brackett rolled her eyes and waved a hand. "Oh, my. Thus, you will shortly have to get married. From there to maternity, to diapers, more babies, PTA, what have you. In any case, no more girl reporter, hey? And all of this to kick in at the end of this internship, because you don't want to be showing too obviously as you waddle down the aisle of Gabbro Presbyterian or some wretched little wedding chapel in Dillon, South Carolina. My warmest congratulations."

Faye sat upright, pale enough to see her own face, gibbous in the windshield. "You summed it up admirably," she said. "But you left out one thing. My future husband, assuming that he will marry me, is none of the candidates you mentioned, certainly not the one from Gabbro. He is a paratrooper stationed at Fort Bragg, where he makes something like ten dollars a week. I'll have to wait tables to buy the ... the..." She put her face in her hands and sobbed, pounded her knee with her fist; Alma Brackett, with a glance over her shoulder at the Trotter manse, started the engine.

"The diapers. Well, you poor little thing."

"Poor little idiot," Faye gritted. "The only thing I can think of is to hope maybe in six or seven years, I can go back to some kind of part time writing, for some Army base newspaper. Oh, God! Ow!" This last because a convulsive sob made her fist hit the dashboard instead of her knee.

Alma Brackett bit her lip. "Miss Bynum, please forgive me; I cannot but laugh. I'm sure this doesn't seem funny to you, but please bear with me. Ha, ha, ha. Very good, all done."

Faye managed a tearful laugh, nursing her bruised fist. "How good it is to amuse others so cheaply, at whatever cost to one's own dignity."

"Good, again. Now, for God's sake get hold of yourself. You want to write one memorable thing before you leave Charlotte. Well, what's stopping you?"

"You have to ask?"

"Yes. Enumerate your burdens, please."

"Fine. Pregnancy. Disgrace. Love. Distraction. Complete inability to think of anything else. Lack of motivation."

"Lack of what? What's wrong with self-pity? I thought I heard a great deal of that, wanting one ragged clipping to comfort yourself, while you wipe noses and sing lullabyes, that once you were a promising young woman, now you are a harried housewife."

Faye shrugged. "How kindly you put it."

"Have I not repeatedly asked you not to sulk in my presence? Let me remind you that all the horrors that await you are those of youth. Living youth at that. What happened to your indignation over Horatio Haney, for example?"

"Mr. Claiborne told me not to write about that."

"Oh, my, that's right. On pain of?"

Faye laughed. "A fate worse than death, I suppose. Already suffered that, didn't I? All right, suppose I turn what he called a girl detective. Do you think a mere woman has a chance of learning anything about that in this town?"

"I defended you before Harold Claiborne because I thought there was no "mere" to you. Don't tell me I was wrong."

Faye's head snapped around to glare at Alma Brackett. "Can we for two minutes skip this, this patronizing hoity-toity, for heaven's sake? If I'm such a disappointment, maybe you should find somebody else to help you grift petty cash from nitwits. I am doing my best to handle a situation that has me scared and ..." She shook her head and waved a hand. "I'm sorry."

Alma Brackett let in the clutch and the Packard exited the Trotter premises with a lowing of ancient gears. "Don't be. That was a reasonably complete telling-off, and I am glad to hear you still capable of it. But, my dear, why do you think I find you so amusingly typical of your sort? Never mind, I'll tell you. Because I am that sort also. You remind me almost unbearably of myself at your age."

Faye clutched her hair. "Marvelous. So, if all goes well, I can look forward to being yourself at *your* age, too."

When they returned to the Star-Dispatch, there was an envelope on Faye's desk; inside, a slip of newsprint about an inch high and seven inches long.

MISS FAYE BYNUM
CHIEF OLEROOD KNOWES MORE ABOUT HORATIO THEN HE IS LETTING ON.

Faye picked up her purse and took herself through the swinging door and down through the pressroom to the Ladies'. Passing Horatio's haunt, she saw that his books and papers were gone, though no one had bothered to collect his antique typewriter, abandoned and rusting on the splintered desk.

She locked herself in a stall, pulled out the note and bit her lip. Chief Olerud knows more about Horatio than he's letting on. Well, he'd be a damn poor cop if he didn't. Olerood, Olerud, OK, a mistake anyone could make. Christ, though, nobody at the Star-Dispatch would misspell "knows," surely?

Time and Chance

Well, yes. Almost anybody on the Sports desk might. But would Wil or Shanky – any of those guys – send her tips about Horatio? Faye doubted it so strongly that she recognized that it would be impossible to follow up with them; they would feign – no, they would display – ignorance, and snicker the second her back was turned, these sporting types who though it was a good bet that Len Biggs had been her lucky impregnator. She would kill herself before she would ask them anything, the – Faye raised an eyebrow and took a breath. She'd been about to think, *the stupid fuckers*. Jesus, Pope Pius, Mama, and Sister Penitentia sang 4-part chorales in her skull to save her from completing the wickedness.

Fine, but who, then? Or did it matter? She didn't have time to chase every piece of dubious information that landed on her desk. If she ignored it, either there would be no second tip, or the tipper, frustrated by her inaction, would speak more clearly. There was also, of course, Harold Claiborne's specific prohibition on it. Faye moodily ran off some toilet paper and blew her nose.

When she emerged from the Ladies, it was not to return to the newsroom. But, swinging down the street, she had time also to temper her impulse to march to Chief Olerud's office – assuming she could penetrate so far the fastnesses of the station– and ask flat-out what he knew about Horatio that he wasn't saying. But she didn't think of an alternate strategy until she passed the window of Miss Panama's Thrift Center. There, dangling a tag that read "Ask Us" was a cherry-red knee-length silk skirt.

It struck Faye that Chief Olerud might be like a lot of other men, under his blue serge, and that cherry-red silk might slippery his tongue a little, considering that this skirt would be doing well indeed to achieve knee length on Faye. She entered Miss Panama's, fingering the fiver she'd earned with Alma Brackett that morning. The skirt was on sale for 75¢ seeing, as Miss Panama remarked, that this spring's

New Look fashions had about wrung the neck of anything that stopped short of ankle length.

"But, land, Honey, I have to wonder a little if this number is going to fit you. It's not but a size 4."

"I've lost some weight," Faye said, choosing to misinterpret what Miss Panama was getting at.

"Well," Miss Panama said, and then dropped it. "You want to slip it on, the dressing room is yonder."

The skirt fit admirably, given Faye's current slenderness. It failed even to graze the tops of her knees, but Faye figured that would depend a bit on her attitude. "Well," said Miss Panama again. "If you won't fixin' to set down, you could get by. Be just 77 cent, with the tax. You got yourself a bargain, Honey, 'less you was the shy type."

"I am," Faye said. "But I will just have to get over that, won't I? I reckon I'll need about the shortest slip you have. Do you have any ballet slippers, size ten?"

Faye stopped tugging on the red skirt when she walked into police headquarters on Fourth Street. The walk from Miss Panama's had hardened her some to the kind of attention she figured to get here, but when the desk sergeant looked up at her and said, "You're early, Sweetheart," she wasn't sure what to say.

"For what? I didn't have an appointment."

The sergeant went back to his form-filling. "Don't need none. Vice, down the hall on your left. Doc won't be there for another hour, easy."

"Doc?"

"You here for your exam?"

"What exam?"

This time, he looked up, grinning. "Just teasing, Sweetheart. Man, though," he said. "Honest, you could make a million bucks in this town with that get-up. Let's start over again; Can I help you, Missy?"

"I'm here from the Star-Dispatch," Faye said, aware that she had been insulted, not sure what to do about it. "I've been writing the crime reports the last weeks."

"Uh huh. We send those over every week, you don't need to come here."

Faye wandered to a bench she guessed was provided for perpetrators and their dependents, sat down, and crossed her legs, trying for a little Dock Street and a minimum of vapor. She poised her notebook where the red silk ended, a mid-thigh latitude just beyond where she scarred herself with an X-Acto knife working on the Globe Theater diorama in the ninth grade. When the sergeant didn't say anything, she jiggled her ballet slipper to the end of her foot, wondering if "pre-Raphaelite" was in Mrs. Merrill's eight-inch Webster's.

"Ah was hoping to actually meet Chief Olerud, maybe get me a little more, you know, human interest this tahm?"

The sergeant polished his glasses. "He's out to lunch right this second. Seem human to you, does he, darlin'?"

Faye wasn't ready, but it had to start some time. She lowered her gaze and put her fingertips over her mouth. "Whah, Captain, I'm surprised at you. Ain't y'all human in here? I bet you are, now, plenty. You're just foolin' with me."

The glasses re-attached to the nose and bounced light at Faye's knee. "Darlin' you don't know the half. 'Fwe got any more human, we'd - "

The street door opened and a blocky, going-grey cop came in, his hat and jacket stiff with brass, holding the elbow of a plumpish woman. The sergeant's monologue cut off as if a door had slammed.

"Afternoon, Chief, Miz Olerud."

The plump woman ignored him. "Foley," the Chief nodded. "Hold my calls."

"Yessir. This here young lady – "

"Foley."

"Yessir. Visitors too, I reckon."

"Good work, Foley."

Olerud and his Missus disappeared through a door behind Foley's desk, and Foley turned to Faye.

"Not a good time, I reckon, darlin'. You got a card you wanted to leave?"

Faye had cut up some 3x5's, stamped them with MISS FAYE BYNUM and added the logo and switchboard number of the Star-Dispatch. She fished one of these from her wallet and wrote on the back, "Please call me in regard to recent crime statistics." While she was writing, she heard an alternation of voices from behind Chief Olerud's frosted-glass door; one steely as a seagull, the other rumbling the ominous patience of Mount Aetna. She rose to give the card to Sgt. Foley, holding a hand over her chest lest she seem wanton, and plucked the red silk skirt back into place. She figured one or the other ought to do something for Foley; she was gratified to see him lift his head a little to peer over the edge of the desk.

"You just leave that with me, Missy. I expect – "

He was interrupted by a substantial whack, a thump, and a choked-off cry of outrage from behind the frosted glass of Ivar Olerud's door. Something that might have been a bookend or a spittoon clanged to the floor. A shadow loomed against the frosted glass and Mrs. Olerud opened the door, pinning her hair into place.

"Sorry, sweetheart," she said to Faye. "The Chief won't be up to meeting his cupcakes for a little while. Run on home and wash your hair."

Faye stared. "Yes, Ma'am," she said.

Time and Chance

But when Faye was back at the <u>Star-Dispatch</u>, sorting through the crime reports and wondering Now what, the swinging door of the newsroom opened and Estelle the switchboard girl stuck her head in. "Faye Bynum? You got a call. I'll put it through to the pay phone."

And standing in the stairwell outside the pressroom, one hand clamped to her ear to shut out the roar of presses, Faye heard, as from Alpha Centauri, the distant rumble of Chief Ivar Olerud.

"... crime stats? What ... know?"

"Oh, thank you for calling, Chief - " Faye caught herself. "Chief, you are <u>so</u> sweet to call me back." *Little ol' me.* "Ah had some questions? About crahm and all? Look here, though, it's mighty hard to hear on this ol' pay phone they stuck you onto. You think you could see me in person some time?"

"You still got that red skirt on?"

Faye thought about the indistinct lump of progeny and woe inside the red skirt, tossed her head, and flung herself into her future. "Well, wouldn't you like to know, Mista policeman? Couldn't har'ly take it off at work though, could I?"

A beat of silence, then, "You know The Crappie Shack? Out on 74?"

"No." Faye panicked, thought furiously, coughed for time, and spoke again. "How far out?"

"Couple miles. Never mind. The Home Kitchen."

"I know the Home Kitchen, sure." It was the place Forde Morgan had taken her.

"I'll be there at half-past eight."

"Yes sir, Chief. Me too."

16.

F AYE LEFT the <u>Star-Dispatch</u> late and sprinted through gathering dusk to Mrs. Merrill's, past Junie ("Slow down, Darlin', ain't nobody chasin' I can see.") on the first landing. She gave Junie a bleak smile and went on, two stairs at a time to her domain under the roof. She put the red skirt on a hanger on the inside of the bathroom door and drew a tub of tepid water, hoping it would have enough steam to relax the skirt without parboiling her.

In that water, she slid down until it came to her chin, and laid an inquiring hand across the drowned mystery of her belly, wavering beneath the twin sea-cliffs of her thighs. Anybody home in there? Boy or girl? Or twins, wouldn't that be the ticket? From the open window by her bed, she heard the slap of today's <u>Star-Dispatch</u> on Mrs. Merrill's front porch, and the poop of air-brakes on a passing bus. A bus in the wrong city, going nowhere she wanted to be. She relaxed her knees and slid under the surface, hearing the subaqueous skid of her butt across the chipped tub. *Pregnant intern drowns self in bath while landlady reads newspaper.* Water invaded her nose; her hair lifted free and wavered like Ophelia's, in the scene you never see. *Full inches five thy mother lies ... something, something ... Nothing of her that doth fade but doth suffer a tub-change into something rich and strange.* Faye snorted a bubble and rose into humid twilight, reaching for the soap. One ought not leave the theater before the last act.

She arrived at the Home Kitchen at 8:25, trying to hurry without raising a sweat. Choosing a top to go with the red skirt had not been easy. Her wardrobe ran to dresses and jumpers, and the cupcakiest blouse she had was lime green, which, with the red skirt, might have gotten her arrested, committed, or elected Christmas Queen. She settled in the end for a ruffly white one that had lost a button in the laundry, rendering it unwearable at the Star-Dispatch. She solved that by moving the top button down, leaving her with a triangle of skin that, even with her recent sense of fullness, no one could call serious cleavage. It hit a tone of, she thought, openness. Willingness to listen. Also, it was a lot cooler than the fuzzy sweater that had been her only alternative. If she ever got a paying job, she was definitely going to buy some clothes.

At 8:45, Ivar Olerud had not arrived, and the waitress was starting to harass Faye about ordering something, or giving the table to somebody who would. At nine, Faye rose and headed for the sidewalk, where she was intercepted by a squat, gum-chewing guy with a smooth, cynical face and a raincoat over his arm. He smelled like cigars, Brylcreem, and breath mints .

"Faye Bynum?"

"Yes? Who are you?"

The guy flipped a badge open for a second and took Faye's elbow to steer her back into the Home Kitchen. The waitress rolled her eyes; Faye sat down again.

"Detective Lieutenant Larry Meyer. Chief Olerud sends his regards, and asks if you'll give him a rain check."

"Oh. Well, Ah reckon. Ah'm sure the Chief is very busy."

Detective Lieutenant Meyer flipped a chair around and straddled it, shrugging. "On the other hand, I got all night, like the fella says. Chief tells me you want a little more insight into crime and stuff, here in the Queen City. That right?"

Faye bent over and brushed a bit of paper napkin from the red skirt, giving the detective an opportunity to detect. She was a little reassured when he did, though not too crudely. Of course, why wouldn't he? Alma Brackett had told her plainly that she looked every inch the slut. "Ye- yayiss. Ah got a promotion at the Stah-Dispatch, to th' police beat. Ah thought maybe I could do a better job if I came to know some of the fellas on the fo'ce, how they do their jobs, what their problems are, and all. I don't expect our readers know much about all that."

"Who told you they want to? And by the way, turn off the phony magnoley baloney, will you? I came here from Denver with the Chief, and that crap turns my stomach. You don't do it all that good anyways."

Faye nodded. "Magnoley baloney, that's pretty good. Can I use that some time?"

Meyer grunted. "Be my guest, sweetheart. I like a girl that don't stand on her dignity. What did you want to know?"

Faye shook her head. "I see there is no point in beating around the bush here. One of my fellow interns at the <u>Star-Dispatch</u> was beaten to death by Klansmen. At least so he said before he died. The police say it was a traffic accident. Why?"

"Because the M.E. said it was, and we tend to believe him. Why would he lie?"

"Why would Horatio lie?"

"You'd be amazed, Honey. Anybody will lie about anything, including a guy on his deathbed. Let's say, he's out late, maybe fighting, shooting craps, wandering around drunk at four in the morning where he has no business. A car clips him and he crawls to the one place downtown he had some business being, the <u>Star</u> office, thinking he can get inside, clean himself up, who knows. He's hurt worse or drunker that he realizes, and he passes out. Next thing, there's an ambulance and a cop asking him questions. He's smart enough to know his career's over before it started if he tells the truth, so he makes up a thing about a bunch of Klan done it. We don't have Klan in Charlotte."

Faye sighed. "What would you say if I tell you I saw a bunch of rednecks in sheets on Mecklenburg Street last month? Their announced destination was, and I quote, 'Niggatown.'"

"I'd say you might want to be a little careful wandering around this town at night, slip of a thing like you. What would <u>you</u> say if I told you we took physical evidence from Mr. Haney's clothing the night he was hit, auto paint and glass chips from a headlight, and matched them up to a car that was taken to a repair shop that morning?"

"I would say, give me the name of the shop and let me interview the manager."

Meyer grinned. "Good for you, Honey. Not a chance."

"Oh, well, then." Faye looked across the table at Meyer. "You can make up any darn thing you want, can't you, and when I ask for corroboration, you tell me, Not a chance. Makes it pretty easy for you, doesn't it?"

"Some things, you got to make them easy, or they'll eat you alive. Why aren't you asking me about the owner of the car involved?"

"Because I don't believe in it. You'll tell me it was Horatio's anyhow, that he was so drunk he ran over himself."

Meyer smiled, snorted, and pulled a bulky olive-drab telephone out of his pocket and ran up an antenna a yard long. "See this? War surplus, slicker'n snot. Watch."

He thumbed a button, and the phone hissed and burbled. "Olerud."

"She don't believe nothing I tell her."

"I don't either, so good for her. Bring her out."

"Ten-four. C'mon, girlie."

"Just a minute. C'mon where?"

"Chief found an unexpected cancellation in his schedule. He can see you now, if that's convenient. He's just outside."

"Does anybody ever call you people on these fabricated, made-up double-dealing phony smoke screens of baloney <u>you</u> put up?"

Time and Chance

Meyer shook his head, weary but game. "All the time, sweetheart. Ask me where it gets 'em. Put these on, OK?"

Faye took off Larry Meyer's fedora and slipped his raincoat off her shoulders. Chief Olerud's car was sultry with cop-sweat and cigar smoke, but she was reluctant to squirm around on the seat trying to rid herself of it entirely.

"Is this a case of trying to fool the public about meeting a young woman in the back of your cruiser, sir? In any case, I don't think it would fool a baby, dressing me up like James Cagney."

"Not the whole public, no. Just a meatball over there in the entrance to the Mecklenburg Arms that my wife's got on my tail, and believe me, it'll be good enough. You always talk so smart to people you're trying to interview?"

"No, sir. I don't mean to offend you. I'm very interested in getting at the truth about Horatio Haney's death. I got an anonymous tip that you had more information to share about it." *An anonymous tip.* Faye allowed herself to be a little thrilled at that, and she pushed on. "In the interest of saving your valuable time, which I am truly grateful for, can we skip over the business about a car accident? Take that as said, and disbelieved? He had contusions and broken bones in every part of his body, he'd have had to be run over by a road grader. Which did not prevent him from telling me, under circumstances in which I could not doubt him, that it was the Klan, a bunch of white boys with baseball bats. Evidently, the police prefer not to acknowledge that. Why?"

Chief Olerud whistled. "You win some kind of debating award in junior high? I don't answer questions like that. Ask me something I can deal with."

Faye sat back and sighed. "Well ... all right, then. Let's see. Why is it easier to get away with forgery than with assault in this town?"

"Sometimes the guy assaulted does enough damage to mark the perpetrator. Ask me something hard."

"What purpose does it serve to deny the presence of Klan in Charlotte?"

"That's supposed to be a hard question? Christ, where'd you grow up, girlie? The purpose is to present an accurate picture of Charlotte."

"A flattering picture, more like."

"No difference, in this case."

"I see. Do you mind if I take notes?"

"Yes."

"How many pedestrian traffic deaths a year do you have in Charlotte?"

"I'd have to look it up. Not all that many."

"I did look it up. The last one was in February, during an ice storm."

"My. Bad break for Mr. Haney, huh?"

"There was no ice or snow, or even rain, the night he was injured."

"True. However, it is hard to see a jig at night."

"A ...?" Make him say it.

"A Darkie. A Negro. They don't reflect as much light as you and me, you see. Makes 'em tough to spot in the dark. Population of Charlotte is about a quarter Nigra, and they make up three quarters of the accidental deaths."

"Horatio's mother showed me the shirt he was wearing. It was white, except for the blood."

Olerud leaned forward. "Meyer."

"Chief?"

"Why don't we have a breeze in here? Could we get some motion on?"

"Sure thing. Any particular direction?"

"I need smokes. Let's run up north and show our hotshot reporter how the darker element gets through the night."

The cruiser pulled away from the curb; Olerud's arm rose against Faye's chest to push her back against the seat, and he leaned forward. In a panic, Faye pushed the arm off her breasts as a sudden light flared outside the car.

"Stop that! What do you think you're doing?"

Olerud leaned back. "Keeping your face out of that meatball PI's photographic memory, sweetheart. If you knew him, you'd thank me."

Faye was silent while Meyer drove them west past the Star-Dispatch office, then north away from Alma Brackett's warp and woof, into the Negro section. Faye recognized the corner of the Johnson C. Smith campus where she and Horatio trudged, wordless, looking for a safe place to converse. In five minutes, they were past the campus and into a part of Charlotte Faye had never seen. Two-and three-story brick crowded the sidewalk, offering Ribs, Bail Bonds, Holiness, and Girls. Chief Olerud grinned at Faye.

"How's this, Honey? Whole lot of folks hard to spot at night, ain't it?"

"Am I supposed to be scared?" In fact, she was.

"Why, no, Sweetheart. You're supposed to be filled with Christian love for these brothers and sisters of ours. Can't say I'd recommend you say a lot about it down here, though. They might take you up on it. Love and fear, funny thing. Sometimes it's hard to tell 'em apart, don't you find? This'll do, Meyer. Carton a Kools, and lay off the numbers while you're in there. Oh, an' pick up a Clarion for Miss Bynum. She'll pay you back."

And when Meyer had gone on his errand, Olerud turned to Faye. "That'll take him a good ten minutes. What kind of anonymous tip?"

The anonymous kind. "It was typed on plain paper. It said Chief Olerud knows more about Haney's death than he's letting on. Misspelled 'Olerud' and 'knows,' and used 'then' instead of 'than.' I have tried to think if that tells me anything, but sometimes I think nobody in the whole South can spell <u>cat</u>."

"Ain't it the truth? I don't know about you, I went to grade school in one room in Wheat Prairie, South Dakota. Nobody left that place not knowing how to spell, figure, and recite the Gettysburg Address. What the hell these dumbbells do in school all day down here?"

"I spent a week at the Wheat Prairie school when Daddy was barnstorming there. Miss Kern. No Gettysburg Address. They probably skip it down here, too. On the other hand, they can be very warm-hearted and helpful," Faye said, mostly to get back the initiative. "What were they talking about? This tipster?"

Olerud leaned back, pointing to a cluster of neon and pulsing light that had swallowed Meyer. Low-wattage bulbs, some of them dead, spelled out **Papa René's Northside Bar-B-Q**. "Some of the best jazz this side of Memphis goes on in that place, you know that? White folks come down here from all over town, slumming, 'digging,' I think they call it. The music, guy told me the other day it was 'crazy,' like that was something to be glad about."

Faye didn't say anything, just gave Olerud the level eyebrows. Olerud rubbed his chin.

"I don't know, maybe they were referring to the sound police technique of not spilling all you know about a crime. You can include this interview under that heading, too."

"So you consider it a crime? Not an unfortunate traffic accident?"

Olerud laughed. "I didn't say that. I was speaking generally. For the sake of continuing this conversation – because honestly, Sweetheart, you really are kind of fun to talk to, you know that?

Who'd think smart-aleck and skinny and pale would add up to sexy? Kind of like Margaret O'Brien sassing old What's-'is-Name in "Lassie" – Let's suppose it was an actual crime. Certain things we look for in a crime, as you probably know. We got your victim, we got opportunity. We got motive, if you figure maybe anybody'd resent a jig getting a leg up at a white paper. Thing is, you usually want to think about that stuff in connection with a particular guy. A suspect, we call him. Who's your suspect in this?

Faye didn't hesitate. "Everly ... Something? Basset?" Trying to make Olerud say it.

"Everett Bassler?" Olerud snorted. "That lunatic wouldn't have the guts and organization to put together a hymn sing."

"I heard he had the guts to murder a Negro lady and brag about it. But all right, then, who puts him together with a mob? Who is the man with the scratchy voice that calls him 'Ev'ett'?"

Olerud pulled back and gave Faye a look that was nothing out of "Lassie." "Honey," he said. "Oh, little Honey. You best go back and write another story about the circus getting its kitty swiped. I liked that little piece, half the reason I came out of my way to talk to you tonight. You got imagination and you got a sense of humor. But you stay with Unc – you stay with this topic, you are wading into deep water." He ducked his head and craned out the windshield. "Where's that dope Meyer got to?"

Faye shrugged. Under the amusement and the indulgence, overriding the creak of Chief Olerud's leather, she heard what she knew – because she had heard it from Forde Morgan and from Gordon – was the tight breath of fear. This block of authority beside her was scared; whether for her sake or his own she could not have said.

And in that moment, as if she had David Copperfield beside her on the seat, she saw the entirety of Chief of Police Ivar Olerud's life: the composite of the one-room Dakota school, of cop work in

Denver, the danger and boredom of it and the boredom and danger of marriage to a woman who would crown him with a spittoon (or a bookend, she supposed) for dallying with 'cupcakes.' Those dusty, aching dalliances, real or imagined, though Faye supposed that they were real enough, with girls who would later giggle to each other about his scratchy uniform and his Sen-Sen breath and his wife, his steel-and-brass Stalag keeperwife. The towhead, the earnest recruit, the appointee, the scarred and thickening man beside her who did not dare pronounce the name of a racist superthug who apparently ruled nighttime Charlotte as the Mayor and the cops ruled it by day. She opened her mouth to say, "Who is this 'Unc'." And she never got the words out. Detective Lieutenant Meyer rapped on Chief Olerud's window.

"About time, for crap's sake."

Meyer wiggled an eyebrow at Faye while he handed Olerud his smokes. "He also yells if I come back too soon, this situation," he said. "You folks ready to move along, then?"

"Where's the Clarion?"

Meyer blinked. "You were serious?"

"Am I ever not serious?"

"Two shakes, Chief."

Faye and Ivar Olerud sat in silence while Meyer jogged back into Papa René's. Olerud reached behind Faye and pulled Meyer's raincoat away from her. Faye tensed and held her skirt in place – it was a little too much like being undressed – and he snorted. "Don't worry, Honey. You're a little young for me, I think, whatever I might of said. Just, for the love of Christ, don't ask me about … what you were going to ask, OK? Let it go."

"Yes sir. Is that "Unc" with a C, or a K?"

Olerud turned to the window. "With a K, Honey. Three of 'em. But if you quote me on that, or anything like it, I'll call Hal Claiborne, and you'll be gone before he hangs up. Good, here comes goddamn Meyer. I want you to look at what he's got there, and see if that's the kind of journalism you want to spend your life on. Because that's what your life will come down to if you have one at all, you insist on this headstrong smart-aleck kind of reporting." He took a tabloid from Meyer and held it out to Faye. But Faye was looking past Meyer to the doorway of Papa René's, lurching across Olerud's lap now to press her face to the window.

"Oof! Hey," Olerud yelled. "Watch what you're leaning on, girlie."

Faye opened the street-side door and clambered over Olerud, all knees and shins and ballet slippers, the cherry-red silk up around her hips now. She stumbled onto the grit of Union Street gaping up at Courtenay Weston emerging in a bluesy swirl of smoke and saxophone from Papa René's Northside Bar-B-Cue. Courtenay oblivious to Faye, clutching the arm of her date, arching back to beam into his face the prideful beam of absolute ownership. And the face – stunned, shaved shiny, and spiffed to a fare-thee-well – was that of Corporal Gordon Simmons of the 82nd Airborne.

17.

F ROM THE Charlotte <u>Clarion</u> ("News of The African Community of Mecklenburg and York Counties") July 24 - 31, 1947:

Death of Charlotte Woman is Called "Suspicious" in Police Report

The body of a young Charlotte woman was recovered from the Catawba River on Saturday last. Eloise Jefferson, 20, of Freedom Street, was described by friends as recently despondent ...

Drug Developed at J.C. Smith for Military Finds Peacetime Use

Arthritis sufferers may find new hope of relief from the pain ...

Miss Melrose is Reading Teacher of the Year at Booker T. Washington

Miss Althea Melrose, long-time reading instructor at Booker T. Washington High School, was celebrated at the annual Charlotte Negro Achievement Awards banquet on Wednesday last, at the Northside Social Club. The normally retiring Miss Melrose betrayed ...

Time and Chance

Faye dropped the sodden <u>Clarion</u> on the floor and covered her eyes. Eloise Jefferson had nothing on her. God! Why hadn't she drowned herself? Could that have brought less pain than Gordon's betrayal? Or her disbelieving pursuit of the guilty pair through the streets of Charlotte until the reliable Thompson met them two blocks from Papa René's and ushered them into the whispering limousine? Thompson spotting Faye in the shadows and passing a remark that made Courtenay look over her shoulder with her fingers to her mouth and a spark of triumph in her eyes.

Faye then walking in her flimsy ballet slippers the two miles from the jazz-and-chitlins quarter through darkness, silence, wan streetlights and quickening chill until one of those Northern fronts Forde Morgan had told her about brought the rain that was her cold comforter for the final stretch to Mrs. Merrill's, wet red silk chafing her legs and clutching at her like a drowning child. Asking herself every squelching step of five blocks why she bothered, why she didn't curl up on the sidewalk and die. And finding in the end something in her that preferred life to wet concrete.

That something, still insignificant beside the pain and humiliation of carrying the barely-conceived child of a two-timer, was anger. Anger at Gordon, surely, for seducing her and then hooking up, however innocently, with Courtenay Weston. She could well believe that Gordon had been fancy-talked into escorting Courtenay on her darktown dive crawl, probably by some harmless 'joke,' or maybe a 'surprise' for Faye herself. *Gordon, you big lug, I just love you and Faye to <u>pieces</u>. I want to throw the two of you a surprise engagement party, but – Gee, this is awkward – I can't stand hotels and country clubs, I want to find someplace really special for you, but some of them, I'm scared to check out by myself.* Gordon would easily be dumb enough to buy that without a second thought.

Time and Chance

Anger at Courtenay, for if the innocent excursion from one party spot to another, a quick drink in each – *You never had a sloe gin fizz? Oh, you big innocent lug, you just have to try it. Here, take a sip of mine.* – even if it fell short of sexual liaison tonight, because even Gordon might not be that dumb, Courtenay had him in her sights, and it would be only a matter of time and patience. A matter of inexorable degrees like a soul's journey to the treacherous heart of hell, chauffeured and discreetly enabled by Thompson to a final betrayal; of that she had no doubt. Gordon was also not that self-denying.

But her heaviest load of fury was for herself. She had been right about Gordon from the start, knowing him for a galoot who would be nothing but dead weight to her spirit and death to her career. What a schoolgirl had she been, to be seduced long before they went to bed by the simplicity of his spirit, the animal solidity of his body, the earnest charm of his talk, and by her own sentimental sensuality. Really, Gordon's was just a run-of-the-mill infidelity, almost a reflex action that no one, least of all Faye, could have prevented, even if she'd seen it coming, if she'd been sitting in Thompson's limousine with them.

No; worst of all, Faye had let herself be seduced by Courtenay Weston, who had seen in Gordon the perfect means to get at her. The whole "fun girl," pink-sheets, twin-sisters, Bristol Cream business had been a deliberate project. Get Faye drunk, flatter her with cozy attention, probe for weapons and weaknesses. Bring the conversation by such imperceptible degrees to boy friends that Faye would not feel it turning under her reeling feet. And it had struck gold when Gordon was drunkenly revealed, giving Courtenay all the means she would need to humiliate Faye beyond recovery. And, of course! The traces she and Gordon had certainly left on Courtenay's very own pink sheets would have been all she had needed of further motivation. No doubt she would make sure to take Gordon onto those very same sheets, just for the elegance and completeness of the coup.

But why? What did Courtenay get out of it, beyond the doubtful charm of a spin with Gordon? Just an idle summer project by a bored princess to assay and consummate her superiority to a skinny, plain-faced hick? As she lay now in the stifling attic room, Faye's anger was minor compared to the hurt. But she knew that it was made of harder stuff, and would last as the pain faded. And when it had grown to dominate the pain, she would – well, she would see what could be done.

And she would see, too, what could be done to get rid of Gordon's child. She would bet that Junie would know of ways. As she formed this thought her sorrow quadrupled, and she realized that she had already begun to know the baby. That her tentative 'Anybody home in there?' this afternoon had been the first stirrings of maternal love that would be her undoing unless she could quickly divest herself of the pregnancy. *Murder your child*, Sister Penitentiary corrected her. Commit that damnable and un-fixable sin.

Fetal on the cot in her damp underwear, Faye pressed her face into the pillow, ground her fists against her temples, and wailed.

*

"Forde?"

"This is Forde Morgan." Forde jammed the receiver to his ear; the presses were starting up ten feet away.

"Yeah, this is Gordon."

"Who?"

"Gordon Simmons." Gordon stopped himself from saying "82nd Airborne," but not from adding, "Faye Bynum's fiancé."

Fiancé, is it now? "Oh, yeah. The soldier."

"That's right. I wondered if you knew where Faye is at."

"Where she is?" *Where she at, Bo?*

145

"That's right, where she's at. I been trying to call her for a week, and she's never in."

"Well, she's been out of the office for a couple of days too, I guess. I don't see her that much these days. Can I leave her a note?"

"Y … well, I guess. Thing is, I'm getting a little worried. Her landlady says she hasn't seen her neither. I don't guess you could drop by – you know where she lives at?"

"Yes. Yes, I do."

"You think you might drop by and talk to her landlady, you know, face to face? See if you can figure out what's going on?"

"You want me to call you back?"

"Huh uh. I can't take calls here. I'll call you this time tomorrow, OK?"

"I guess I could do that."

"Appreciate it. Thing is, I done used up about all the leave I got for the next month, or I'd come there myself. I don't hear from her, I'm like to go AWOL, and they don't take kindly to that around here."

Yeah, what a shame. "All right. Did you think about writing her a letter?"

"Yeah, I done that, but you can't tell if she got it or not, can you? Just from sending it."

"Nope, guess not. All right. About ten tomorrow morning, then? Listen, though, tell the switchboard girl to put it through to the sports desk."

"Gotcha. Appreciate it. Bye."

"Glad to help. Bye."

Forde Morgan glanced at Faye's table. Still empty. The note he had left under the corner of the blotter was still there; not exactly in the place he'd left it, but he was savvy enough by now to the ways of the Star-Dispatch that he'd kept the note businesslike and neutral. Gordon Simmons wasn't the only one who wondered where at Faye had got to. Forde asked Len Biggs once, got no satisfaction, and knew that a second query would never pass for casual.

When the day's edition was put to bed and the mercies of the pressroom boys, Forde made his way to Mrs. Merrill's Transients. It was a place he'd passed by often – sometimes going well out of his way to do so – but never visited. He mounted its steps now with a clear sense of foolishness and lack of entitlement. Junie answered the door, this being a Wednesday.

"He'p you, Sir?"

"Is F – is Miss Bynum in?"

"May I ask who wish to see her?"

"Well – yes, Forde Morgan."

"Please come in, Mr. Morgan. I will see if Miss Bynum at home."

Forde entered the hall, to be greeted by Butterball, whom Forde considered to be about the fattest, ugliest cat he'd likely see if he lived to ninety. "Hello, Kitty."

Butterball eyed him, read his mind, sniffed delicately at his pants cuff, and walked out. Forde, agitated and out of place, had all he could do not to give the pink aristocratic anus a good kick. While he gazed at prints above the tatty loveseat in the hall (*Love's Awakening; Autumn Splendour*) he heard Junie's descending steps.

"Miz Bynum regrets that she cannot receive company," Junie told Forde, looking regretful herself. "She say to tell you that she is indisposed at the present."

"Did you tell her who it was calling on her?"

"Yes. Did you have a hat?"

"No. Is Faye – is she OK?"

"She is indisposed."

"I see. Well, I guess I don't quite know what that means."

Junie smiled thinly at Forde. "It is a word ladies use sometimes when they are indisposed, Mr. Morgan. Good evening."

Time and Chance

"Yes. Well, good evening."
"Thank you, sir. And the same to you."

*

Faye huddled at that moment on a seat toward the front of a Greyhound, resting her forehead on the window, and shivering at the droplets of mist that trailed down the glass, fractions of an inch from her skin. She was cold, the bus was cold, and she had a griping pain in her belly, somewhere close to where her baby – if there was a baby, she told herself, knowing dark-whistling when she heard it – where the baby that she could not doubt, lay and grew and differentiated its way to irreversible personhood. Beyond the mist, in the grey of evening, the cotton fields of South Carolina passed her, showing white bolls that waited for black hands. Beyond each field lay a belt of woods; tangles of sumac and scrub oak, early darkness.

Hurtling herself into the core of that southward darkness, into a world of illiteracy and ignorance of all that she knew, and of knowledge of which she was more ignorant than a field hand at Harvard. In her pocket was the name and phone number of Junie's sister in Aiken County, South Carolina who in turn could bring her to someone who had done for Junie's niece, and for many another in Faye's situation, what Faye had steeled herself to ask Junie about. She would be grateful to Junie forever for the calm with which she heard Faye out, and the gentle hand she laid on Faye's head, while she talked of a sister a hundred miles south, who knew a root doctor who had helped other ladies - *ladies,* Faye marveled, *what a kind thing to call us sluttish pre-Raphaelites* - who had Faye's problem.

Behind Faye, a child fussed and kicked the back of Faye's seat. Faye started to protest, and heard the kid's mother smack it a good one, which doubled the kicking and grew the fussing into a howl. Faye turned to the window, catching in it a quick look at the family behind her. The child was lumpish, headed for bubba-hood; the mother looked as if she once might have been slender, with level black eyes now drilling into Faye's. Take a good look, they seemed to say.

The bus arrived in Winnsboro half an hour late, which seemed to be about on schedule. The driver announced a ten minute "rest stop" which Faye knew from childhood meant that if she wanted any rest, she would have to be about the first off the bus and into the country store and bus station.

"Rest room?"

"Ma'am?"

"Do you have a restroom I could use?"

"Out the back. Whites is on your right." The clerk pulled a yard of toilet paper from a roll under the counter and handed it to Faye.

The fluorescent light startled a pair of cockroaches into a footrace to the relative dimness of the stall. Faye considered how badly she needed it, and in the end used half her toilet paper to line the seat and peed as quickly and noncommittally as she could manage. It did little for the crampy pain in her belly, and less for her mood, which was too apathetic now to be suicidal. Rising, she tried with only middling luck to raise soap and hot water from the crusted washbowl. Faye looked around the little room, reflecting that, goodness, at least she was in the Whites. God knew what the Colored might have been like. Faye Bynum in that moment lapsed enough from her upbringing to bypass the Blessed Virgin and all the saints, and bring a prayer directly to God: *Get me out of this, please. Don't let me end up on a bus with a fussing baby and no money and a bitter heart. I swear that I will go and sin no more.*

By the time they started again, it was nearly dark.

The bus ran out of the rainy front in another half hour, and into a zone of stormy sunset and soft air. In Farnee, South Carolina, a girl of indeterminate late-teen years met the bus, holding a piece of cardboard bearing the crayoned message MISS FAYE.

"I'm Faye Bynum," Faye told her. "You're Junie's niece?"

"Yes'm." The girl looked taken aback, and was silent while Faye took the overnight case the driver handed her, silent still as they left the Pump House Café that served Farnee as a bus station. On the sidewalk, she shrugged, and turned to Faye. "How Aunt Junie been?"

"Fine, I think. It's awfully nice of you to meet me. I could have asked around."

"No sense. She told us you on this bus. Only one come through here anyways."

"Well, but … Well, it's nice, just the same. And I should be more truthful with you. Junie is not doing fine. She's really very upset about a boy in her neighborhood who was killed by a bunch of Klan thugs – "

The girl held up a hand. "You can call me Alice."

"All right, Alice." *You can call me Horace.*

"We go on by home, get you something to eat now."

"Oh, golly," Faye said. "I don't want you to put yourself out for me. Can we just go to the clinic?"

Alice tipped her head in a southeasterly direction and started walking. "Clinic? What clinic that?"

"Well, I meant where I can go for, for." Faye made a helpless gesture toward herself. Alice smiled and shook her head.

"Ain't no clinic for what you got, honey. We take you to Ol' Mista Graven, he fix you up. What were you saying, Junie upset over this boy?"

"Is it something I shouldn't have been talking about?" *I'm learning discretion. A useful skill for army wives, I bet.*

"Not back there at the Pump. You can talk now, you want to." They were walking through a section of middling commerce: a drugstore, sun-faded blue chintz in a mortuary-and-furniture emporium.

"Well." Faye said. "A smart young neighbor of Junie's, working at my newspaper got himself beat up and killed by a bunch of," Faye glanced behind her. "Of Klan…. What?" Alice blowing a little derisive puff of air, waving a hand as if at a fly.

Alice shrugged. "Nothing, Ma'am. We about there now."

Faye stopped. "OK, listen, Alice. Please. What did I say to make me go from 'honey' to 'Ma'am?' Did I say something wrong again?"

"No'm." Alice walked on, then stopped again. "Other hand, you the one in trouble this time, ain't you? Well, since you want to know, you don't need to butter me up, talking about no neighbor of Junie's work at your newspaper. Or what, he a real smart janitor?"

"No," Faye said. "He was an intern, like me."

"Intern."

"Yes. Tell me about Mr. Grave. Graven."

"Graven. Old fella out Spiveytown way, do root conjure. What interns do?"

"We're supposed to be learning the business. Working pretty much for free. What's root conjure?"

"Roots that work conjures, what it sound like? What business a color boy got, learning a white man's job?"

"Is that it? All kinds of business, I think. I don't think there's such a thing as a 'white man's job,' or I wouldn't be learning it either." Faye glanced at Alice, saw disbelief, and waved a hand. "OK, the Klan thought otherwise. I guess you agree."

Alice didn't answer. Faye didn't hear even the little puff of derision she'd drawn before. She stopped and put down her case.

"Oh, God, Alice, I'm sorry. I've got such a smart mouth. It gets me in trouble all the time."

Alice let that rest a little, then punched Faye's arm gently. "Not what got you in trouble this time, I think."

"No." Faye walked in silence for a time. "No, that was more dumb than smart. And it wasn't my mouth."

"That is the kind of dumb I owe something to, I guess. Mama didn't know Mist' Graven when she come down with me. Here we are."

Alice lived in a narrow shotgun house that faced an unpaved road. Under the porch light at Alice's house stood a woman in a flowered housedress, wiping her hands on her apron. As Faye approached, the woman stood upright and put her hands behind her back.

"Momma," Alice said. "This here is Miss Faye, that Aunt Junie call about."

"How do, Miss Faye," Alice's momma said. "I am Jane Dupree."

"How do," Faye said, feeling Southern. "Faye Bynum. It's very kind of you – "

"Come in the house," Alice's mother said. "We are pleased to help any friend of Junie's. She tells me that you were quite a help to a young neighbor of hers."

Faye slumped, climbing the porch steps. "Maybe so. Maybe I just helped get him killed."

"Junie says you helped him accomplish something no Negro had ever done, before he was killed. You helped him publish in the Charlotte Star-Dispatch. She also says he would likely have been killed in any case, sooner or later, since he seems to have been born without much common sense."

"Well," Faye said. "I would hate to think that might be true. He was a smart kid."

Jane Dupree said nothing to that, but motioned Faye into the kitchen, where frying chicken and fresh cornbread flavored the house-wide smell of kerosene. The kitchen, occupying a good half of the house, was evidently its heart and center. It had space for a generous pine table, a tin bathtub, a wood stove, and a sink with a hand pump, besides a collection of cabinetry.

"Would you like to wash up, Miss Bynum?" Jane Dupree asked.

"Oh," Faye said, and felt her eyes prickling. "Oh, this feels so much like home. I know that is presumptuous of me to say, but I can't imagine ever being lonesome in this house."

"Hm. I'll ask you about that come morning. You will be sleeping with Alice."

"Oh," Faye said. "I couldn't possibly impose like that. Can't we visit this ... this doctor this evening?"

"Old Graven is not – well, let's say he doesn't practice in the evening. We'll see him first thing in the morning. Now it is time for supper. You'll be wanting to wash up after your long trip. Alice will show you."

Alice picked up an oil lamp and inclined her head toward the back door. Faye, following, found herself in a fragrant darkness that the lamp pushed back, with middling success. From the far edge of its reach, a table with a basin and a pump appeared, and Alice led her that direction.

"You best scrub good," Alice said. "Momma is a plain fool for clean, and dirt show up on you pretty good, even at night."

Faye smiled and understood from that and from the cricket softness of the air, and from the bar of Fels-Naphtha that Alice handed her with the basin, that she was forgiven for being a smart-mouth stranger, white, and pregnant, and that this poor family was hers for this night. That they had taken her in and would stand with her and hurt with her. Her eyes stung, and she had work not to let a squeak of gratitude escape from her chest.

"Alice, God," she said. "You all are being so kind that I don't – I guess I just don't know what to say or how to thank you."

"Aw."

"No, really. I don't think anybody I know in Charlotte or back home would be this nice to a perfect stranger."

"No? Charlotte some tough place, all right. Where's home?"

"St. Louis."

"Land. Missouri? Why did you come all the way out here, get yourself in trouble? Do that quicker and cheaper back home, seems to me."

"I – I thought I was going to be a great writer."

"Like Horatio?"

"You knew Horatio?"

"Met him a couple times, years ago. Funny little yella kid with a big head an' a smart mouth, last I saw him. Took it kind of serious, having a fancy name like Horatio. Shame, him getting killed like that."

"He turned into a very promising young writer. He still had the big head."

In the kitchen, Alice's Momma had gathered the rest of the family – a lanky boy of growth-spurt age, and a worn man in bib overalls – and looked up at Alice and Faye from a massive Bible that she held open under her hand.

"Welcome back," she said. "Seem like long enough to get a couple of young ladies very clean."

"I was very dirty, Ma'am," Faye said, and Alice giggled.

"Mm. Let me introduce my husband, Mr. Dupree, and Alice's brother, Ishmael."

"How do you do, sir. Hi, Ishmael."

Ishmael shrugged and nodded. Mr. Dupree smiled and shook Faye's hand, without saying anything, and sat at the table. Jane

Dupree nodded at Ishmael and Alice, who sat in their turn. Faye guessed it was OK for her to sit, too. Mrs. Dupree opened the Bible.

"Dupree, I believe it is your turn to choose a passage."

Mr. Dupree raised his eyebrows, met Jane's severe glance, and nodded. "Yes," he said. "I believe it must be."

Not the Song of Solomon. Please, St. Anne?

"Suppose we just carry on from where we left off last time with The Preacher?"

"Very well."

Mr. Dupree opened the Bible at a ribbon marker and paged briefly. *"For to him,"* he rumbled at last, *"that is joined to all the living, there is hope, for a living dog is better than a dead lion. For the living know that they shall die, but the dead know not anything, neither have they any more a reward; for the memory of them is forgotten. Also, their love, and their hatred, and their envy is now perished; neither have they any more a portion for ever in any thing that is done under the sun.* Ishmael? "

Ishmael took the Bible with languid hand. *"Go thy way,"* he muttered. *"Eat thy bread with joy and drink thy wine with a merry heart; for God now accepteth thy works."* He shoved the Bible into his sister's place.

"Let thy garments – "

"Excuse me, Alice," said Mrs. Dupree. "Ishmael, that was the shortest, slackinest little bit of Scripture I believe ever came from a boy's lazy mouth. Just you take that Bible – "

"Huh uh, Momma. Bible tell me eat my bread and drink my wine with a merry heart, 'cause God <u>accepteth</u> my works. You want me to go against the Bible? Pass me the bread, an' where's my wine?"

Faye snorted and sent Ishmael a glance, and he grinned at her, a blazing transformation of his sulky face. Jane Dupree reached over and rapped his skull with a knuckle. "Smart-mouth boy, you find out you talked yourself into eternal fire and damnation one of these days. Very well, Alice. You may continue."

Time and Chance

Alice read about letting her garments be white and her head lack no ointment and, riding the coattails of Ishmael's indulgence, stopped after one verse and passed the Bible to her mother. "Next verse be best for you anyways, Momma."

Jane Dupree glared at her, and read, "*Live joyfully with the wife whom thou lovest all the days of thy vanity, which he hath given thee under the sun, all the days of thy vanity. For that is thy portion in this life, and in thy labor which thou takest under the sun.*"

"Heh," Mr. Dupree allowed, "Reckon so. Good thing I got me such a prize little wife. Don't get much else out there under the sun. Your turn, Miss Faye."

Faye took the Bible, following Jane's pointing finger to the place and read, "*Whatsoever thy hand findeth to do, do it with thy might; for there is no work, nor device, nor knowledge, nor wisdom in the grave, whither thou goest.*"

Faye glanced around the table, and saw polite encouragement. "*I returned, and saw under the sun that the race is not to the swift, nor the battle to the strong, neither yet bread to the wise, nor yet riches to men of understanding, nor yet favor to men of skill; but time and chance happeneth to them all.*"

Mr. Dupree shook his head. "A-men, don't they just? Lord, we thank you for the power of your holy word and for the bounty that I do believe is about to be served at this table."

18.

FULL OF chicken, corn bread, greens, and strawberry fool, Faye lay under a quilt at one edge of Alice's bed and watched Alice tying bits of white cloth into her hair by the light of a kerosene lamp. "Alice," she said.

"Mm-hm."

"You went to this Dr. Graven?"

"Mm-hm." Alice frowned a little in the mirror over her dresser.

"What was it like?"

"Hit was all right," Alice said. "He know a sight about roots. I don't think he is no kind of doctor, though."

"Is he ... you know. Safe?"

"I reckon. Never hurt me none."

"Well, what does he do?"

Alice shrugged. "Burn some ol' roots, make you breathe the smoke. Give you root medicine to take, taste like some kind of hot carrots."

"And it worked?"

"Work for me."

"Well.... will you go with me?"

Alice grinned at her in the mirror. "What you think, we point you the way an' give you a push? I got a married sister come here sometimes, share this bed that used to be hers anyways. She took care of me when I got in the baby way, cryin and upset, she calm me down, lie next to me, tell me hush, everything be all right. Be my job to take care of you just the same, then yours to take care of the next one. That's how it work best, seem to me."

Time and Chance

Faye felt her eyes clouding again, and she turned over without a word. When Alice slipped into the bed beside her, she lay still. Wouldn't it be fun to sleep over? We'd be like twin sisters. She felt Alice's hand, gentle on her back, rubbing away fear and, finally, wakefulness.

Horatio Haney came back into Faye's dreams, battered and speechless, staggering under the weight of a cheap picnic hamper. While Faye watched, terrified, Horatio opened it and pointed to a passage with a broken finger. *There is no device in the Graven.* Faye woke with a pounding heart to absolute blackness. For an instant, she believed that she was in the grave with Horatio, and then she heard the drip of rain from a window, along with a light so faint that she could see it only by looking away from it, at the ceiling. Beside her, Alice Dupree breathed. A faint smell of kerosene came from the hallway, or from the lamp on Alice's dresser. Around her, the narrow house full of people breathed and tossed in blackness and dreaming.

The sea of warmth and lonesomeness and fear was overwhelming. Faye realized that she needed to pee. Damn, why hadn't she figured that out before she got into bed? She folded back the quilt and slipped out of bed, occasioning a mutter and a cough from Alice. As long as she could feel the bed under her hand, she could stay oriented in the darkness. But memory instructed her that there was a matter of some six feet – two confident steps – between the corner of the bed and the door. She tried to remember whether Alice had shut the door, and guessed that she probably had. Confident steps were not a question. Shuffling, groping, she cast off from the doorward corner of the bed and dog-paddled into the vast lake of blackness. When she stubbed her toe on the chair she'd forgotten, to the right of the doorway, Alice woke.

"Who is that?"

"Alice, I'm sorry. It's me. It's Faye."

"Need to pee?"

"Yes."

"Down the hall, through the kitchen, to the right of the 'frigerator."

"Thank you. I'm sorry I woke you up."

"Hush, Paleface. I light up a lamp for you, or you end up in Georgia somewheres."

"All right. I hate what a pain in the neck I'm being."

Alice said nothing to that, but Faye heard the bed creak, and Alice's feet passing her in the dark. A match sparked and flared, and Alice was there, holding the kerosene lamp. She lit it and gave it to Faye.

"There, now. Cain't tell you how many times I done this, before I could do it in the dark. You run along, I wait up for you."

Faye made her way down the hallway, hearing snores and crickets and the tap of rain on the roof. The bathroom – an indoor privy with a pitcher of water and a basin – was where Alice said it would be. Faye seated herself and spent the next five minutes asking herself how she came to be in this humble place, months and miles from her home, pregnant, lonely, betrayed, half-broke, and friendless except for the charity of this family of strangers. And there was no answer to be seen in the ashy glow of the lamp. She rose, and took the lamp – some of the kerosene seemed to have slopped onto the handle; it was slippery, and Faye gripped it hard to keep from dropping it. When she got back to Alice's bedroom, Alice was asleep, but roused when the light struck her.

"Fine it all right?"

"Yes. Thank you, Alice. I'll try not to wake you up again."

"Mm." Alice's eye emerged to gleam in the lamplight. "Blow out the - land, what you got all over you?"

"Kerosene," Faye said. "It spilled somehow."

"Great day, girl, you want to go up like a fire chicken?" Alice sat up in bed. "Naw, what you talk? Ain't no coal oil. Look at yourself."

Faye looked. Something black had soaked into the front of her nightie, and her hand was black with it too. She made a noise of disgust and wiped her hand on the side of the nightie. The stuff was sticky, and smelly –

Faye collapsed to the floor. "Oh, my God. Oh, my God, Alice. It's my period. I got my period!" Faye began to cry, holding the sticky nightgown to her eyes, doubled over with a joy that was half sorrow; Goodbye, little baby that I dreaded and barely knew. Mommy is so glad you're gone.

Alice looked at Faye with big eyes in the glow of the lamp, and began to laugh. "Well, gracious. Don't they teach you nothin in them white schools? How long since your last time?"

"Today makes 49 days. Seven weeks."

Alice was gone, noiseless through the dark of the house. Faye heard a clink, and the splash of water. Faye got out of her nightgown and held it between her legs while she peeled back the quilt. Thank god, the sheets were unspotted. It had happened in the bathroom, or on the way, probably when she stood up. Alice reappeared, holding a washcloth and a bowl of water.

"Clean youself up a little. I got stuff in the dresser, you want to borrow it. Don't expect you brought nothing."

"Yes, I did. I thought I might need it afterwards."

"Well, I think that is what we got here, is afterwards. You maybe had a baby, something wrong with it, an' you lost it early. That kind of thing happen a lot."

"Alice, you must think I'm the stupidest girl that ever was."

"I think you are one lucky girl, what I think. Get yourself put together and come on back to bed."

And when the room was dark again, and they were again under the quilt in deep darkness, Faye said, shyly, "Alice?"

"Mm hm."

"Were you sad, or happy, after you, ... you lost your baby?"

Alice was silent, and Faye thought she was ignoring another dumb question from a dumb white girl. But she heard a rustle of covers, and felt Alice's knee against hers.

"Mostly happy. I sure didn't want no baby then, me fifteen years old and all. Since then, I see babies, I get a little sad sometimes. You feeling sad?"

"No! Happy ... mostly. I started to think about a baby starting out inside me, and I didn't want it, but I couldn't bring myself not to have some feelings for it. So I guess I'm sad, too."

Faye felt Alice's hand against her cheek, and put her own hand over Alice's. "Alice, you all are so kind to a stupid white - "

"Hush. Hold your hand up in the air. You see any white girl?"

Faye raised her hand, and Alice held on, their arms extended in the blackness like a winning fighter's. Faye had the illusion of two bars of perfect black against deeper blackness. She unclasped, and twined her arm around Alice's, reaching back to renew her grip on Alice's hand.

"You know what they say," Faye said. "All cats are grey in the dark."

"Uh huh. And all girls are reasonably good, when they had their period. G'on to sleep now, Faye. You a good girl."

"Yes." Yes, I am. I am a good girl. I will never be a virgin again, but I'm not pregnant. Thank you, God. Thank you, thank you, Saint Anne. Faye felt Alice's leg tangle in hers, and she scooted herself back against Alice's thighs. She had never been so warm; her belly hurt. She dreamed of water rising from caves, of deep rivers, and of landscapes under the sun.

19.

F AYE TRAVELED back to Charlotte in sunshine, and with Ecclesiastes steaming in her breast, chanting in the rhythmic slap of tires on the jointed concrete highway: Whatsoever thy hand findeth to do, do it with thy might. Write with thy might. Argue with thy might. Kick Elaine Barnes and Len Biggs and Courtenay Weston with thy might. (Do that with *all* thy might.)

Yes, and send Gordon Simmons packing and forget him with all thy might. And Forde Morgan and Alma Brackett might better stay out of her way, too, for there is no work, nor device, nor knowledge, nor wisdom in the grave, whither thou goest. Oh, little baby, now a spot on a wadded-up nightie in the belly of the bus, my baby, you had never even a day of thy vanity under the sun, and I am sorry for you and glad for myself, and that is vanity too, and a sin I am sure. But maybe I will see you again some day when I'm ready for you, and meanwhile, what I do with my might, I will do for you.

And while the cotton wheeled past her, still waiting for hands, the tears that sometimes spilled were neither tears of joy nor of despair – the two sources Faye Bynum had known in the childhood now past – but came of some third thing in which sorrow and gratitude and humility alloyed into a vision of herself moving across the face of the Southland under the sun. Seeing it now from the point of view of the sun: a woman among millions of women who were weaving the wilderness under the sun, holding their past with one hand and their future with the other, sometimes nearly torn apart by the burden and the hope.

*

Time and Chance

Faye arrived in Charlotte at sunset. When she reached Mrs. Merrill's Transients, Gordon Simmons was sitting on the porch steps in civilian clothes. Gordon, not trusting Forde Morgan's jumbled account of Faye's "indisposition," left Fort Bragg in civvies in the back of a supply truck without bothering to cover his tracks with a lie. Gordon also, with the sure instinct of the guilty, knew that Faye had somehow figured out that he'd spent an evening with Courtenay Weston. Just from how, when they got into her damn limousine, Courtenay had gone from friendly and flirty and flittery to hot, hot as a pistol, Christ. All over him, holding his face so he couldn't look out the window, rubbing against him, hand on his crotch so, Christ, what was he supposed to do? But Gordon, raised a Midwest Protestant, knew that these things did not happen without someone else, generally the worst possible one, knowing all about it through some punitive Divination.

"Faye ..."

"Hello, Gordon."

"Listen, Faye."

"Why, certainly."

"Listen, I ..."

Faye gave him time and a neutral, level look, but he sighed and threw up his hands.

"You what, Gordon?"

"Well, I can't say what I mean when you're looking at me like that."

Faye walked past Gordon and opened Mrs. Merrill's door. "If I never looked at you again, then you'd have a lot to say, I suppose. But then, what would be the point?"

Gordon brightened. "That's right, Honey. What would? So you're all right?"

"Not exactly all right, no. I am extremely tired, and I'm having my period just now, as I'm sure you'll be glad to know. I've just been on a long trip, and what with that and a lot of other things, I'm not fit for company. Particularly yours, I guess. So I'm going to excuse myself. Good night, Gordon."

"Faye, wait! You got to talk to me. I'm AWOL."

Faye put a hand on the door and disinterest on her face. "Really? Why ever did you do that? Won't they shoot you or something?"

"Let 'em. Naw, they'll stockade me, bust me a rank, I don't care. I got to talk to you, Faye."

Faye sagged against the door frame. "I have to warn you, Gordon, you could hardly have caught me at a worse time. However, since you may be shot before you get another chance, all right. I'm listening."

"Faye, I love you."

Faye said nothing to that, but gave Gordon the level eyebrows.

"Honey," he said. "Don't do that, OK?"

Faye rolled her eyes and looked at the skyline. "How's that? Now can I make a request? Is it my turn?"

"You bet, Honey. What is it?"

"Don't 'Honey' me. We're a long way from a 'Honey' basis."

Gordon looked contrite. "Sure, OK, H – OK, Faye. What's bothering you?"

"Oh ...Nothing."

Gordon perked up again. "Really?

Whatsoever thy hand findeth to do, do it with thy might. Faye straightened and faced Gordon squarely. "No, <u>not</u> really. I'm tired because I just took a long trip to get rid of the baby you and I made a few weeks ago, remember? It was extra hard because you can't help clenching up when you're crying your heart out for 48 hours straight. You end up sore all over."

"Baby?"

"Gordon, did you hear one word I just said?"

Gordon's face shone. "I heard that one, I heard 'baby.'"

Faye crumpled and spoke through tears she couldn't stop. "Gordon, look at me. There is no baby. I lost the baby. I guess there may have been something wrong with it, but I was on this trip to get rid of it in any case."

"Faye, why ever?"

"You have the effrontery to – " Faye realized that she sounded like Alma Brackett, but pushed on because she knew that she had only a certain time before she would be unable to speak at all – "to ask me why I didn't want a baby growing up with no father, why I was crying? Goodness, Gordon, you're as dumb as a stick, aren't you? Well, I'm too tired to drag this out. I'm crying because my supposed boyfriend, my fiancé and the father of the baby I was about to lose is two-timing me with Courtenay Weston, the Debutante of the Century. And don't dare bother to deny it, because I saw you. Good night."

Faye slammed the door, but, knowing it was a mistake, couldn't help opening it again, her face a stream of rage and sorrow. "And p - please don't hang around here and make a scene. I will ask Mrs. Merrill to call the police if you do. I never want to see you again, damn you. Just go on back to Fayetteville, and I hope they shoot you. Is that clear?"

This time, Gordon was quicker. He got a foot, and half his body, through the door before Faye could slam it. "You," he gritted. "You don't know what the hell you're talking about. You listen to me, you little ...Good evening, Ma'am."

"Good evening, Lieutenant," said Mrs. Merrill. "Faye, I thought I heard ... well, an altercation just now."

"You did," Faye said, wiping her eyes with her sleeve.

"Yes, Ma'am," Gordon said. "You surely did. Faye's very upset about a misunderstanding we had, and I don't blame her one bit. We're working it out, though."

"Well," Mrs. Merrill beamed. "The course of true love never did run straight, did it? I can't begin to tell you how many awful disagreements Merrill and I had before he passed, bless him. Are you all right, dear?"

"I'm fine, thank you, Mrs. Merrill. But I am quite tired, and I need rest. I'm hoping to persuade ex-Corporal Simmons to drop this painful conversation for now."

"Oh, honey," Mrs. Merrill said, raising her eyes to the transom. "How well I know that feeling! But do let me say just one thing, from long experience. Never, never let the sun set on a misunderstanding with your ... em, your beloved. You do look very tired. Suppose I just bring you each a nice glass of tea to buck you up? But I do so lovingly advise you not to part for the evening without making up. Believe me, Faye dear, I am thinking only of your happiness. You must know that I am quite fond of you or I would never dream of intervening like this."

Gordon made earnest little noises behind Faye, and Faye's resistance eroded. She turned to Gordon, saw hope and humility worthy of a Labrador retriever, and turned back to Mrs. Merrill.

"All right. Thank you for your concern, Mrs. Merrill. We'll pass on the tea, but perhaps if we could use the parlor ... or, no. I think we'll just walk around the block. May I leave my case in the parlor? Thank you. Come on, Gordon."

"Faye, Hon ... Faye, you got to believe me. Nothing happened with Courtenay. Nothing. And anyhow, she ain't wife material." Gordon snapped his fingers. "She means nothing to me."

"Really? That is not what I saw the other night."

"Well, where were you? Why didn't you say something?"

"Why didn't I say something? Let me see. I guess I was speechless. You've heard of that, I expect. People rendered speechless by a completely unexpected and shocking sight."

"Of course I have. And I don't blame you, if you thought there was something going on. I know I'd have been speechless if I ... Well, for example, if I saw that fella Forde with you."

"Forde Morgan? He means less than nothing to me. There's no comparison."

"Well, see? That's how I feel about Courtenay. And I don't even know _her_ last name."

"What were you doing with her?"

"Well ... where – " Gordon broke off.

"What does it matter where? If she's nothing to you, she's nothing wherever you were, seems to me."

Gordon thought about that while they turned the corner at the far diagonal of Mrs. Merrill's block. A streetlight threw shadows before them that lengthened faster than they could catch up. "Well," he said at last. "It don't matter. I was just wondering where you were, that's all. What were you, spying on me?"

"Oh, sure, Gordon. That's it. I had this premonition that you had come to Charlotte without telling me, and that you would be bar-hopping with Courtenay. Naturally, I gave up all other plans for the evening to spy on you, hoping against hope to catch you in a compromising situation, I think they call it."

Gordon snorted, and Faye knew she'd made him mad again, which was fine. "You little what?"

"Huh?"

"Right before Mrs. Merrill butted in, you said, 'Listen, you little.' You broke off before you got time or a chance to tell me what you really think of me."

"I didn't say that."

"Gordon, you clearly did, and you know you did."

Gordon shrugged and said nothing for six or eight paces, and then he said, clearly, "You little bitch."

"Oh, I see. My, that was honest. Well, of course, who could blame you? You get me pregnant after I specifically told you I couldn't afford that, and after you humbly and earnestly told me of course, you understand, and then you went right ahead – "

"You're the one that said, 'Let's do it.' You're the one woke me up Sunday morning fiddling with my dick. Sorry, but that's the way I remember it."

"Yes, after the damage was done, I agree, I admit. I decided that, what the hell, I'd given you what you wanted, and I might as well enjoy my new status as your mistress, fiancée. I heard no complaints from you about it, in any case. The point is, after you took me to bed and got me pregnant, then, behind my back, you date the hottest debutante in 500 counties while I'm trying to figure out how to have a life while I raise your children and darn your socks on ten dollars a month in some wretched, nasty army town. How bitchy of me to resent all that."

"What a shitty thing to say, Faye. What a shitty thing to think."

"What shitty behavior on your part, that led me to think it."

"Faye, I told you, she means nothing to me. It was just a sort of a ..." Gordon waved an arm, and brightened a little. "A situation, see."

"I'm sure it was. What, did Thompson tell you the Young Mistress wanted to consult you on a confidential matter? Or did she call you herself?"

Gordon was silent, shrugging, sulky. Then, "She sent that guy. Thompson."

"Of course."

"Of course, what? She wanted to ask me about a dress she'd picked out for you."

"Really. She wanted to consult you on ladies' fashion? How odd. But tell me about this dress. Did she model it for you?"

"It was ... Aw, Faye, now."

"No, go ahead. I'm intrigued."

"Well, it was sort of, I dunno. Pretty, I guess."

"You poor thing. Let me help. It was sort of a shimmery, metallic blue, wasn't it? With ruby highlights? Off the shoulder on one side – the left, as I recall, gathered under the bosom, very sophisticated and New Look. Tight-fitting on Courtenay above the waist, but a full skirt with the hemline at the ankle?"

"I guess, yeah."

"I remember it very well. So, let's try a little imaginary experiment, Gordon. Close your eyes, now, and imagine that we take that dress off Courtenay – I'm sure you can imagine that quite easily – and let's put it on me. What have we got?"

"I dunno."

"Don't go sullen on me, Gordon, be so good. What do you see?"

Gordon shrugged. "Be too big for you, you want to know. Courtenay's a big girl."

"Oh," Faye nodded. "Oh, isn't she just. Not fat of course, or even big-boned, but real tall. Long waisted, broad shouldered. Long legs, and a perfectly lovely fanny. Stacked, to boot. Whereas I'm average height, and kind of scrawny, really."

"So?"

"You don't disagree, I note. So, there was never the least intention of putting that dress on me. I'll give her credit for half a loaf, though. She had every intention of taking it off of herself, didn't she?"

Gordon flung out his arms as they reached Mecklenburg Street again. "Well, so what if she did? What was I supposed to do?"

Faye nodded, pierced again, the fresh wound a livid smear of fury from her heart to her belly. Slowly, she sank to the sidewalk, shaking her head. "Supposed," she whispered, barely able to breathe, "To do exactly what you did do, Gordon. You were *"supposed"* to screw her. And you did, didn't you? Good boy. God, what a fool I am."

Gordon stopped and stared down at her. "Faye ..."

"Shut up, Gordon. Just for a couple of minutes here, just shut up. I think that's done it. So thank you for coming out with it at last, so we can drop this stupid subject." Faye looked back down Mecklenburg Street. In the blackness, a pale shape wavered, and then another.

"Really," Faye said. "Already? It can't be more than nine or ten o'clock."

"Huh?"

Whatsoever thy hand findeth. "Want to have some fun, Gordon?"

"Huh? You OK now, Faye, Honey? You're not mad? Really, it didn't mean – "

Do it with thy might. "Oh, for God's sake, Gordon, look, forget about that, all right? Just shut up about it." The pale shapes were nearer now, their feet whispering on the pavement of Mecklenburg Street. "How'd you like to serve your country?"

"Huh? Well, sure. But listen, Faye – "

Do it. "Quiet. Here they come." *Do it with thy might.* Faye cupped her hands around her mouth and deepened her voice. "Hey there! Morons! Did Everett Bassler's mommy let him out tonight?"

The gaggle of white sheets came to a stop at the corner they'd just left, and Gordon yanked at Faye's arm. "Faye, for God's sake, you want to get killed? Shut up!"

"Shut up yourself, Gordon Simmons, you fucking cretin." Gordon blinked at the venom, and dropped her arm.

"Hey, Ev'ett," Faye yelled. "Whyn't you go back to the trailer court and molest some more parakeets?"

Two of the Klansmen broke away from the group with a gruff command, and came toward Faye and Gordon. One of them had a baseball bat. The other called out in the fluty, bubbling voice Faye remembered.

"You wonted talk with me, little girl? That what I hearn jus' now?"

"That's right, dimwit. You brave boys off to beat up some more Nigras? Fine night for it, I reckon."

Bassler pulled back his hood. He was broad-faced and pock-marked, with a dark crew cut. "Now," he said. "Excuse me, Ma'am. I don't believe I hearn exactly how you done address me just now. You call me dimwit? You must be tired of living."

Gordon swept Faye behind himself. "She didn't mean nothing, Sir," he began.

Faye pushed Gordon's restraining hand aside and stood beside him. "Yes, I did." Let them all chew on that.

"Faye, that's enough. She's upset just now, and that's my fault. We apologize, don't we, Faye?"

"No. These morons are racist murderers, Gordon. Don't try to butter them up. You ought to be treating them like the scum they are, except you might not want to waste the spit."

"Land," Everett Bassler said. He turned to the other Klansman, who stood hooded and silent, gripping his ball bat. "You remember anybody talk like that around us before?"

Apparently the question was rhetorical, because Bassler turned back to Gordon. "Son, you got three ways you can go. You gonna have to discipline this little bitch, right now, whiles we watch, or say you standing up for her, and you ready to make what she say stick; or else you gonna step aside while we teach her some manners ourselfs. What's it be?"

Gordon drove into Everett Bassler in a football tackle that slammed him back against the Klansman with the bat. The bat clattered to the sidewalk, and the three of them hit the ground. Bassler's shoulders landed at the edge of the curb, and his head snapped down into the gutter. Faye heard a crack and a rotten, heavy sound, and Everett Bassler heaved and lay still. The silent Klansman jumped to his feet and reached for the bat, but Gordon kicked his arm away and drove his fist into the man's shrouded face. He fell again and blood dribbled from the edge of the hood. He got his hands under himself, and heaved himself to his knees while Gordon yipped and shook his hand. Faye, knowing that her life was finished, knelt by the motionless Bassler and hammered on his ribs with doubled fists, getting no response. She began to suspect something horrible, when there was a yell from the street, and the rest of Klansmen charged.

Faye saw Gordon in the grip of a headless beast of sheets and scuffling boots that fell apart into a chaos of staggering, bleeding men in drunken orbit about him, and congealed again as someone jumped onto his back. Faye drew in a breath to scream; something white and rank with sweat cut off her vision, and she felt herself lifted, first to her feet and then higher, falling, caught over a shoulder, and carried by stumbling feet. The shoulder knocked the wind out of her; by the time she could scream again, the sounds of the fight were far away.

20.

F ORDE MORGAN found her at midnight. "Faye?" No reply.
Panicked, Forde bent to place an ear to her chest, heard rapid
thumping, and sat back blushing invisibly at the contact with a breast,
reassured but grieving still. Forde wasn't sure how Gordon had
caused the wreckage he saw before him now, but Forde blamed
himself in any case. He should have told the idiot bastard she was
down with a cold but basically OK; he'd have stayed at his damn
parachute base and not come to Charlotte. He never should have,
never, never should have left Gordon to wait for Faye. Just, there
wasn't any good reason for Forde to hang around, in the face of
Gordon's hostility.

Forde also had no idea what drove Gordon's berserk anxiety
over Faye's disappearance. But look what came of it: Faye
unconscious, bleeding, and – God knew, probably worse yet. Forde
looked down the alley toward Mrs. Merrill's house, wondering what
would happen if he knocked on the back door with Faye in his arms at
this hour.

"Nuh," Faye said. "Mnuh."

"Faye!" Forde took one of Faye's hands and chafed it,
knowing that this was something people did in cases like this, not sure
why it was supposed to help. Faye didn't seem sure herself; she
yanked the hand away and curled it against her face, a slender and
nonaggressive fist.

"Faye, it's OK. It's me, it's Forde. Faye?"

"What?" Peevish, unbelieving, unable or not wanting to wake.

"Faye, honey, wake up. It's OK now. They're gone."

"Who?" Then, scowling, "Who gone?"

"Well, whoever it was. There's nobody here but me."

"Gordon?"

"He's not here. Did he do this to you?"

"Nuh-uh. Do what?"

"Well, you got knocked out. Also you're bleeding. Plus… Geez, Faye."

" 'S OK," Faye told him. "Got my period."

Forde looked at the dark spatters on Faye's skirt, and blushed. "Is that all? Are you sure?"

Faye raised her head from the alley dirt. "I'm cold," she said. "Why's it so cold?" She dragged herself up on one arm, dazed and unfocused. She raised a hand to her cheek, passed it over her face to the back of her head, and gasped.

"Chris'," Faye said. "Jesus, Mary and Joseph. I'm, I'm …" She passed her hand over her skull, speechless.

"Yuh," Forde said. "Who did it?"

Faye sat up and held her head in both hands. There was a lump on the side, with a little crusted blood on it. Other than that, it was smooth, gleaming between her fingers like St. Peter's in moonlight. She started to giggle.

"They did a real nice job, didn't they? I don't feel any nicks or anything, except for where they conked me. That hurts."

"I guess. Listen, don't worry about it. We'll find you a wig or something till it grows back. The thing is, are you hurt?"

"Hurt? You're asking me if I'm hurt?" Faye's giggle darkened toward something that gave Forde a lurch of fear. "Christ, can't you see? I'm a wreck."

"No you're not, Faye. You look a little beat up, OK, but you look just the same as you always did to me. And you sound fine."

Faye levered herself to sit, folding her legs under her, covering her knees. Dizzy, and seeing for the first time the spots on her skirt. You sound jes fahn, "Yeah, great. Well, I'm not fine, by a long shot.

Nice of you to say so, though. You like your women bald and a little beat up, is that it?"

Forde put a hand on Faye's shoulder, and not a tentative one, either. "No. I like women who are brave and smart, and good looking. And … and come from the Midwest. St. Louis, if possible. Will you allow me to take you home? Can you stand up?"

Faye gathered her skinned legs under her, stood, swayed, and fell directly onto Forde.

"Oof. I got you."

"I could just as well have fallen the other way." Faye getting that on the record as quick as possible.

"Sure, Faye, I know. The question is, I could perfectly well carry you."

"Woo'n that be a tender sight? No, Forde, you don't have to carry me. But I guess I might hang on your arm. Christ, what will Alma Brackett say?"

Forde shook his head. Faye was still not making much sense, and she seemed to be all over the place. Forde started to worry about brain damage. "Who cares what Alma Brackett says?"

Faye stopped suddenly and clutched at Forde's arm. "Wait a minute. Where's Gordon?"

"I told you, Gordon's not here. Look, Faye, how did this happen, anyhow?"

"I … I don't know. Mrs. Merrill was going to bring us a glass of tea. Why am I out here? Where are we, anyhow?

"We're in the alley behind her house. Are you sure Gordon didn't do this to you? Is he in the Klan?"

"Klan …" Faye, for God's sake, you want to get us killed? Shut up. "No. It was onna sidewalk. I don't think I can think about it right now, Forde. Can you take me home? You mind?"

"I just offered … Of course I can, Faye. Let's get you home and into - into a safe place. Mrs. Merrill will help you clean up, I expect."

"No! No, don't make trouble for her. I'm all right. Just help me get to the door. Where's my hankie? Where's my wallet? Oh, God, no, where's my wallet?"

"Here," Gordon said, holding it out. "It was lying next to you. What's missing?"

"Let me see. Owoh, my head really hurts now. Nothing. Nothing's missing, I don't think. I had about forty dollars, still here. Hankie. Driver's license. It's all here."

"Where was it?"

"In the pocket of my skirt. Maybe it just fell out."

"Maybe whoever did this took it out and changed their mind. Or somebody came along."

"I can't think about it. Please take me home, Or – Forde. I'd appreciate that so much. I already appreciate how you're being here." Faye wrinkled her brow, and winced at the pain in her scalp. "Why are you here? What time is it?"

"Oh. Well, it's pretty late. I happened to know Gordon was in town. I knew he was upset. I guess I worried about it a little bit. I just thought I'd take a walk around your neighborhood and stuff. See if you were disposed."

"Disposed?" Faye started walking toward Mrs. Merrill's end of the alley. She looked like a lab project.

"Uh huh. Mrs. Merrill's maid told me you were indisposed the other day, when I came by. So if you were still indisposed, I would be worried, and if you weren't, then I guess you'd be disposed, wouldn't you?"

Faye couldn't help squeezing Forde's arm, threaded through hers to steady her. "I feel like hell, Forde. I just got beat up and my head shaved, and I can't remember anything about it. But I sure as heck am glad you're here. If that's disposed, then I guess I am. Least a little bit."

Time and Chance

Forde squeezed back, glad of the rationality of what she said, aware of the soft presence of Faye's left breast against his wrist. A little ashamed of it, under the circumstances, but aware all the same. "Faye," he said. "I know this is hard, but I have to ask. Are you sure that blood is ... well. Are you sure nobody, Gordon or whoever, you know." Forde looked away to keep his blush to himself.

"You mean, raped me?"

"Yes."

"Yes, I'm sure. I'd know." Faye was silent, assessing matters. "I guess it's possible that whoever it was started to, and found I was having my period, and let me alone. I can't be sure about that."

Forde took a breath and found himself trembling. "Damn it, Faye, it just makes my blood boil."

"Cliché." Faye laughed without using her face. "Shame on you. Still, it's comforting, Forde. If I knew for sure what happened, maybe my blood might boil too. So thank you."

They were at Mrs. Merrill's back gate. Faye turned to Forde, taking deep breaths that smelled to Forde of exhaustion and tears.

"I'm a bloody wreck, I ache all over, and I guess I must look like a billiard ball. If you hadn't come along, I'd still be lying out here. I owe you a lot, right there, and I don't have much to make that good. So, just ... thank you. Thank you, thank you, you dear, kind man." Faye crushed herself against Forde, burying her shiny head in the corner of his neck. *Why did I say that? He means less than nothing to me. There's no comparison. To what?*

Forde, heart banging and loins jumping, patted her shoulder, found leaves and dirt on it, and brushed at them. "There," he said. It was the first time anyone had ever referred to him as a man. "There, there. You're all right now, honey."

Faye stepped back. "Don't call me honey, OK, Forde?" *We're a long way from a "honey" basis.*

"OK."

Time and Chance

*

Harold Claiborne looked at Faye, looked back to the clean blotter on his desk, and folded his hands.

"I like your new hairdo," he said. "Very flattering, the way it, mm, it curls down your," He flickered a finger at Faye's chest. "Your front like that. Brings the eye to your bosom without being immodest. You do have a handsome little bosom, you know." He sighed. "Young thing like you."

"I'm glad you like it," Faye said. "It is on loan from my landlady's cleaning woman ... The hairdo."

"Yes. ... I beg your pardon?"

Faye swept aside Junie's Sunday wig to reveal her shaven head. "I borrowed it from a lady named Junie, who cleans my landlady's house for a dollar a day plus carfare, and who has been a steadfast friend through this entire summer." She raised an eyebrow at Claiborne. "I suppose you don't find my actual hairdo quite so fetching, do you?"

"Good God, girl, put the thing back on."

"It's rather prickly and hot, if it's all the same, particularly now that my own hair is starting to grow back. You'll just have to bring your eye where you wish, without help from a wig. I could undo a couple of buttons if that would help."

"Now, see here ..."

"Yes, sir. Would you like to know how I came to look like this?"

"Not particularly. You look like, like ..." Harold Claiborne shrugged. "Like hell."

Faye smiled. "When I saw myself for the first time, I couldn't help thinking of Elmer Fudd." *Saying 'Not pregnant.'* "In any case, the point is, I was accosted last week, kidnapped, knocked unconscious,

178

and had my head shaved by – " Faye narrowed her eyes at Claiborne. "I suppose you will say that it was done by a 1938 Chevy, driven by a drunken Negro. If so, I am like Horatio Haney, in my unreliable eyesight. It looked to me like a bunch of thugs in white sheets. However, I am observing the letter and spirit of your orders, that if I obtained the least inkling of Klan involvement in Horatio's death, I was to bring it to you. Well, here it is." And Faye, with a deferential little bow, laid a manuscript on Harold Claiborne's desk.

Claiborne looked at the papers without touching them. "That so? And how does this, this event – for which I have only your word, of course – how does it tell us anything about Haney's death?"

Faye shook her head, as if his obtuseness were beyond her. "Well, sir, one of the main arguments brought against Horatio's claim that the Klan killed him, is that there is no Klan in Charlotte. It absolutely baffles me how anyone can stick to that crazy idea, when they parade around in plain sight. Apparently, people are intimidated into silence. Well, I'm not. Again, sir: A bunch of thugs wearing white robes and white hoods accosted me and my fiancé on Mecklenburg Street last week. He fought them, but they snatched me away, knocked me out, and shaved my head while I was unconscious. If it was not the Ku Klux Klan, it was a very clever imitation. And, really, sir." Faye experienced a philosophical insight. "If a bunch of morons dress up like the Klan and act like the Klan, then it doesn't much matter if they really are or not, does it?"

"Mm. And your fiancé will testify to this as well?"

"Yes. I'm sure he will."

Claiborne nodded and looked out the window. "You know, Miss Bynum, in my experience, when people say they're sure so-and-so will happen, it's because they're not very sure."

"Yes, sir, of course. Sort of the way people say they're sure there is no Klan in Charlotte. But Gordon would have no reason not to testify to the truth." Faye tried not to look unsure. Gordon would have every reason, if testifying complicated his AWOL status with the Army. And besides -

"Well," Claiborne shrugged. "We'll see about that in due course. Temporarily, for the sake of continuing this conversation, which will only happen if you put that wig back on immediately, let's suppose that you did see some Klan last week. Why is that evidence that they killed young Haney?"

Faye looked at Harold Claiborne, and asked Horatio to be patient. She clapped the wig on her head, took bobby pins from her pocket, and confined all hanging curls to the back of her neck. Harold Claiborne didn't seem discouraged, eyeing the effect of her raised arms about as carefully as he had the line of curls.

"It may be," Faye said, still riding her philosophical rails, "that we will never know who killed Horatio, under cover of what kind of organization, or sheet. I am still far from clear, even now, on what happened to me, but it is coming into focus. My fiancé and I encountered a small contingent of men dressed in white robes and hoods on Thursday night. These men behaved very similarly to what Horatio described. They were armed with a baseball bat, and I could see at once that they were very dangerous. I ... there was a scuffle, and I believe one of the Klan, one of the white-robed men, was injured. The last I remember is that my fiancé attacked – was attacked by them, and that I myself was assaulted, carried away from the fight, and apparently knocked unconscious. When I came to, my head had been shaved. I made my way home."

Faye wondered briefly why she was leaving Forde Morgan out of the story, and decided that she didn't want him blushing and stammering all over it. He would inevitably say or do something that would make her path through this even more complicated than it already was. She opened a hand toward Claiborne, trying to look reliable and uncomplex.

Time and Chance

"I spent Friday and the weekend recuperating from this experience. That is why I did not report for work here on Friday. I also used the weekend to prepare a full description of the assault, which I have not yet given to the police, because of your order that I bring all such evidence to you first. However, if you think this material is too hot to publish, I guess I'll have to give it to the police."

Claiborne snorted. "You will 'have' to do nothing of the sort. Your position here, and your future employability, determine what you <u>have</u> to do, plain and simple. On the other hand, there is no such thing as news that is too hot for this newspaper. I will read your report closely, and you can expect to be examined on it in detail. I will assign you the story, if I decide it should run. But, tell me. Why did these men attack you?" He raised a hand. "No, wait, let me guess. You incited them, didn't you?"

Faye took a breath. "They may have taken exception to the fact that I didn't pretend not to see them, I suppose."

Claiborne's turn to shake his head in disbelief. "Odd, don't you think? You say they parade around in plain sight, yet they take offense at anyone seeing them. Are you sure there wasn't more to it than that? What did you yell at them?"

"Nothing that would justify assault with a deadly weapon."

"Do you think you will ever learn to keep your mouth shut?"

Faye shook her head, but said nothing.

But when she reached the door, Claiborne said, "Miss Bynum. Everett Bassler was found under the Mount Holly bridge in the early hours of Friday morning, with a broken neck and a fractured skull. The cop who found him, took him to County Hospital, where he died without recovering consciousness. If it had been anyone else... a Negro, a citizen of any value whatsoever, I would report what you just told me to Ivar Olerud, and he'd be down on you like the Inquisition, asking unfair and unfriendly questions. As it is, I expect Ivar will wrap it up as another traffic fatality – the third this year, no less – or as a suicide. What do you say? Shall I call Ivar?"

Faye strolled to the window in her turn, stalling. "Every child of God," she said to the window, "is infinitely valuable. That's what the nuns used to tell me. If you believe that, you should probably call him." She crossed the room, heading for the door, not looking at Claiborne.

Claiborne smiled. "You're quite the girl, you know that? I'm sorry for your, your misadventure. I expect it was pretty harrowing."

Faye turned halfway back to him, reaching behind her for the doorknob. For the first time in her life, she deliberately brought a breast into profile, possibly – she was unclear about her own motives here, as well as much else – as a reward for Claiborne's ability simultaneously to inform, comfort, and insult her.

"Thank you, Mr. Claiborne. Like everything else that has happened this summer, it was a valuable educational experience."

21.

A ND BESIDES. Where <u>was</u> Gordon? Her last sight of him, recovered painfully over the weekend from a jumble of bad memories, was of a massive figure swinging a baseball bat, surrounded by white sheets, scuffling boots, and cornpone profanity. Forde, who spent hours with her over the weekend comforting, sitting vigil while he stiff-armed Mrs. Merrill, listening, gently questioning, and once or twice touching her as one might touch the flimsiest of convalescents – Forde could tell her nothing about Gordon. Or, Faye admitted to herself, possibly <u>would</u> tell her nothing; there was about his ignorance such bafflement that Faye would have mistrusted him if it had not been so pathetic. Maybe Forde knew something, maybe he didn't; Faye was too intimidated by his kindness to press him on it.

As far as Faye could figure, Gordon must have gone back to Fort Bragg to face whatever music his unsanctioned absence might have occasioned. Or maybe he was still on the lam, drowning his sorrows in liquor and pathos in a York County juke joint. Or more likely yet, forgetting them in the lap of luxurious Courtenay. In any case, there was no way, and no motivation, for Faye to get in touch with him. His sudden absence bothered her sense of tidiness and fair play.

She did write him a letter late on Saturday night, having at last got Forde Morgan out the door, and realized after the fourth or fifth cross-out, crumpling, and start-over, that there was really nothing to say to Gordon beyond goodbye, good riddance, and go to hell. She crushed the last version into a wad and turned to a fresh page to start her account of Klan activity in the capital of slantways progressivism. But it did not come easily; her memory was still spotty, and she could not be sure what she remembered for herself, and what she agreed with Forde must have happened, must have been seen and suffered during her abduction.

And besides. Gordon refused to go to hell. Her last sight of him was of a defender, trying to protect her from men who, much as she hated Gordon with all her strength, were leagues below him in worth and deed. She was uncomfortably aware that she had taunted the Klan deliberately to put Gordon on the spot and, OK, probably did it to get him knocked around some. It came to her in a single image: the shuffle of Klansmen drawing on, Gordon sulkily hangdog beside her, the worn-down mother behind her on the bus, the triumph in Courtenay's body and face. And the lamp-lit permissive Holy Scripture, for don't time and chance happen to them all? You bet they do, easy as a finger-snap. The time was then, and who could say when the chance might return? Faye was ashamed of herself for it; but defiantly so, Gordon's twin in sulkiness before the irony of the All-Knowing. Faye sighed, and ran a hand over her head, feeling the prickle of a day's growth. Twelve o'clock shadow, she guessed they might call it. She laughed, and it turned so quickly to crying that she gave up on awareness, stripped, and turned off her light to lie on her cot in a twilit hybrid of sorrow and nightmare.

Sunday was better. Her head hurt less, she finished her detailed account of the Klan encounter and wrote out a fair copy to present to Harold Claiborne on Monday. She answered Mama's last letter – Daddy in jail overnight for doing 68 in a 20-mile-an-hour zone – with a neutral report of small news, just as if she had all her hair. By the end of the day, Mrs. Merrill had recruited Junie's wig, Forde Morgan had bought her a handsome and welcome supper at the Home Diner, and had walked her home, and bid her good night without trying to assert any kind of ownership or entitlement beyond telling her that she was a knockout in the wig, but not a patch on what she would be like when her own hair grew back. Really, Faye thought, she had badly underestimated Forde, and she was lucky he was around. She didn't know how she would have got through this mess without him.

*

Faye took off the wig as soon as she left Harold Claiborne's office. In fact, it was hot and prickly, and she wanted to see how the newsroom might take the near-nakedness of her skull – by Monday morning, her head was no longer shiny, but a stubbled thing like something sired by a porcupine on a tennis ball. She'd bet every one of them would stare, then pretend they hadn't, and not say a damn word. It would be like the moment Horatio Haney first walked in the place.

The scene never happened. Lounging outside the swinging doors was Detective Lieutenant Larry Meyer, chewing a toothpick and looking grave. When Faye approached, he flipped open a badge and said, "Miss Faye Bynum?"

"Of course. How good to see you again, Detective Meyer."

Meyer grunted. "That the clothes you had on, Thursday last?"

"Of course not. Do I look like the kind of person who wears clothes for four days straight?"

"Nope. Kind of lady that might do laundry over the weekend, though. Did you?"

"Y – What's this about?"

"Think you could take me over to Mrs. Merrill's?"

Faye felt a little chill. "I'm supposed to be working. Is this something that could wait until this evening?"

"Sure, go ahead and work. Just, this way'll save me getting a search warrant. Up to you, of course."

"A search warrant? For heaven's sake, what for?"

"Well. Are you planning to cooperate voluntarily, or involuntarily?"

"There's no such thing as involuntary cooperation."

Meyer shrugged. "You could be amazed. So you ain't cooperating voluntarily?"

"I didn't say that."

"Let's go, then."

They went. Meyer put a light hand on Faye's elbow on the way downstairs, just before they encountered Elaine Barnes emerging from the Ladies'. Faye knew it looked for all the world as if Meyer was arresting her. She felt unembarrassed; she thought she might have become unembarrassable. But when she took a couple of opportunities – at a narrow doorway, filtering through a little throng emerging from the break room – to slip away from the guiding hand, it didn't seem to slip. When they reached Meyer's car, double-parked outside the front steps, Faye stopped.

"Are you arresting me?"

"Why would I do that?"

"I don't know." Faye realized that she sounded like a sulky child. "Why would you?"

"Only if I had to. I'm asking you to accompany me to your place of lodging, and you are cooperating voluntarily with that request. I appreciate it."

Faye was silent on the way to Mrs. Merrill's. She put the wig on, hoping Mrs. Merrill would be away when they arrived, but of course she wasn't.

"My dear, home from work so early?"

"We're just here to pick up something I forgot. This is Detective Meyer. One of my, my contacts in the police."

"How do you do, Mr. Minor. Won't you have a seat in the lounge, while Faye fetches her … whatever it was. Would you like a cup of tea?"

"No, thank you, Ma'am. Let's go, cookie."

Faye turned toward the stairs, and Mrs. Merrill flared in alarm. "Oh, but Sergeant, I do not allow gentlemen visitors to my young ladies' rooms. Faye can bring whatever it is you need, of course. But I'm afraid I must insist that you wait here."

"Yes, Ma'am. Is this your cat?"

"Yes, this is little Butterball. She's – "

"Mm hm. Is that mange on her behind there? You serve food to your boarders?"

"Of course, don't I, Faye dear? But I don't see – "

"County Ordinance 46 - 0587, Ma'am. Diseased domestic animals to be surrendered or destroyed in any establishment that provides food for public consumption."

"But ..." Mrs. Merrill gathered Butterball to her bosom, and glared at Meyer. "This is some kind of crude shakedown, isn't it?"

"Yes, Ma'am. Do I have your permission to accompany Miss Bynum to her room?"

"It is of no conceivable concern to me, Mr. Wyer. It may well be your last official act before you return to walking a beat."

"Oh, my. Well, let's make the most of it then, hey, Miss Bynum?"

"Hey, Detective," Faye said faintly. They climbed the stairs.

When they reached Faye's domain on the third floor, she turned to Meyer. "So, is this a crude shakedown, or what they call a fishing expedition?"

Meyer snorted. "I kind of liked that, 'crude shakedown.' Get the feeling the lady listens to True Detective Mysteries."

"She does, top volume. Do you ever answer questions?"

"I ask 'em. F'r example, what were you wearing when this so-called assault happened?"

" 'So-called?' You think I knocked myself out and shaved my own head?"

"Hypotheses non fingo. That means – "

"I know what it means. Well?"

"Weirder things've happened. The reason I'm not fingoing no hypotheses here is, there's too many loose ends in this business. So, what were you wearing?"

"A corduroy jumper. What business?"

"Can I see it?"

"It's a mess, I haven't had a chance to wash it out. What business? I didn't ask for police intervention."

"I won't say they never do, but it's rare. You mean you left it wadded up somewhere?"

This was how her mother always described undone laundry, or any other chore for that matter. *I suppose your homework is wadded up in a wad in the bottom of your locker.* Faye placed her back to the wall and fought off guilt. However dark the mystery of Meyer, he was not her mother.

"I was too, too … I don't know. Stunned, for a while. I didn't even remember where I'd left it until yesterday. And then, I … I was reluctant to deal with it. It's in my laundry bag. Here."

Faye reached past Meyer and into a bag that hung by a drawstring inside the closet. She pushed aside some underwear and pulled out the wad of jumper. It smelled faintly of spoiled meat.

"It's a mess. You can have it. Why do you want it?"

Meyer took the jumper to the window. "This blood on it?"

"I'm afraid so. Menses, more accurately. I was having my period, and I expect the long period of unconsciousness led to some blood leaking onto my skirt."

Meyer grunted, and pulled a wax-paper bag from his pocket. "You mean it, I can have it?"

"Yes."

Meyer rolled the jumper and stuffed it into the bag, and looked around the room. "What about the underwear?"

"You mean the underwear I had on? I can assure you, it's bloody too. Could you – I know, you don't answer questions, but this is getting a little, I don't know. Pushy, I guess. What's going on?"

Meyer leaned against the wall and smiled at Faye. "Nothing that doesn't go on at least once a week around here, Charlotte, Meck County, York County. It's a rough place. Can I have the undies, please?

Faye sighed and reached into the laundry bag, then turned to Meyer. "Oh, no. I threw them out."

"How far out?"

"In the trash can in the alley. Trash is picked up on Fridays. They're gone."

"Uh huh. We're about done here, then. I'd like to ask you one more favor, though, if I could. You want to come downtown with me?"

"No. Would you count that as voluntary, or involuntary?"

"Up to you, cookie."

"Where are we going?"

"I got something I'd like you to see, give me an opinion."

Their way downtown was familiar to Faye, and ended at police headquarters. Faye tried not to sink into paranoia. Meyer entered an alley half a block past the entrance Faye had used, and parked in a courtyard full of police cars, some shiny, some prewar, battered and Keystoney. Meyer jerked to a stop next to a paddy wagon by a grated doorway that said NO ENTRANCE.

"Here we are." Matter-of-fact, cheery as a hospital orderly. The NO ENTRANCE opened, and a Negro man came out, supporting a weeping girl maybe Alice Dupree's age. Meyer stood back for them with brusque patience, and beckoned Faye when they were gone.

"Wait a second. What is this place?"

"A facility," Meyer said. "We use it sometimes. Let's go, Cookie. You want to get back to work some time today?"

"I want to get back to work right now. What is this place?"

"This'll only take a second. I'm not saying you gotta come in here, but it'll be a lot quicker if you just come along in now. I promise, you'll be back at work in twenty minutes, tops. Aren't you the one wanted to get more familiar with behind-the-scenes police procedures? Can't get no more behind the scenes than this."

Faye got out of the car. Her knees felt fluid, as if she could run all the way back to St. Louis. "All right," she said. "I hope to hell this isn't one of those cheap cop tricks, where they confront somebody with a suspect, and they're supposed to spill the beans."

"We wouldn't stoop to that kind of crude shakedown," Meyer said. "I just want your opinion on something."

"You're starting to repeat yourself, you know."

"Sign I'm running out of patience. You coming now?"

Faye shut the car door and brushed past Meyer into the NO ENTRANCE. He took the opportunity to apply the unslippable supportive touch to her elbow. They walked through dim-lit, green-painted corridors lined with numbered but unlabeled rooms. A faint antiseptic astringency reminded Faye of Mount St. Anne, though this place was silent as no high school ever is.

At the intersection of two corridors, Meyer turned left, and right at the next. Beyond the corner, a man in striped trousers and a numbered shirt leaned on a mop. Meyer ignored him. As they passed the first door in this new corridor, a brief scream came from behind it. Meyer turned, beckoned to the prisoner, and pointed at the door, snapping his fingers.

"Yassa, boss."

"Make it snappy."

Faye stopped. "Stop. Where are you taking me?"

"Right down here. C'mon, you're in Luke's way, standing like that."

"For the love of God, Meyer!"

"Montresor."

"Ha ha. All right, you've got seventeen minutes now to get me back to the Star-Dispatch. This better be worth it."

"I don't know what you'd consider worth it, Miss Bynum. Here we are."

The high-school stink was stronger here. Meyer opened a door with no number and stood aside for Faye to enter. The air that came out was chilly, and filled with the muted buzz of a ceiling full of fluorescents. There was a cold hush to the place, as if voices would expire before they reached any of the file cabinets that lined the walls. Mixed with the buzz and the glare and the hush was the smell of a biology lab. Faye thought about her frog, who had reduced her to tears by kicking when Sister Immaculata hooked a couple of wires to its long-dead leg.

Faye's scalp crawled, trying to get the stubble to stand on end. "Is this a morgue? What, you want me to identify Everett Bassler?"

"How'd you know about him?"

"Mr. Claiborne told me. Well, you've wasted your time and mine. I only saw him once, and it was at night."

"Oh, well. Naw, this wouldn't be ol' Ev'ett, I don't think." Meyer opened one of the file drawers and a puff of vapor accompanied a shrouded thing into the dead light. "It's ..." He shrugged. "Well, that's what I wanted your opinion on. You tell me." He gestured Faye to the head of the shrouded form, and pulled back a blood-spotted sheet.

Faye started to object, but all she heard was wind at the back of her throat, roaring in her ears like the breath of a frozen giant, echoing and murdered by the hush of this place. Paralyzed and unable to breathe out, much less scream, Faye looked into a dead eye and saw her own locked-open mouth; shoulders swaying and sinking, knees no longer able to hold her away from the bruised and asymmetrical remains of ex-Corporal Gordon Simmons.

22.

M EYER dropped Faye at the front door of the <u>Star-Dispatch</u>. She dragged herself up the steps where Horatio Haney was found – another one I killed – and into the downstairs lobby. There was a school group there, being shepherded by Elaine Barnes. Faye skirted them and went into the ladies' to look at herself in the mirror. There was a swollen welt on her chin, where she cracked it on Gordon's slab on her way to the floor. She straightened the wig and washed the smear of dried blood from her chin.

She looked guilty. Her eyes were haunted but dry, her mouth ragged and defiant. She thought she looked like the mug shot of a gun moll who egged men into killing each other for the fun of it. Nothing she could do with hanging curls would lead anyone's eye away from that. It was a truth that lay beneath her breastbone like stone, hardly letting her draw breath, and forbidding tears. Faye stuffed the wig into her pocket, wiped her face with a paper towel, and stepped forth into hell. Two or three of the school group gasped and giggled as she climbed the stairs. There was a note on her desk, dated the previous Friday:

Mr. Biggs will not be in today. Report either to Sports or Social News for assignment.

Faye glanced up at the sports desk, where Wil and Shanky were staring at her, eyes bugged and lips bitten to contain laughter.

"Faye?" Wil wondered at last.

"No, by God," Shanky said. "We got us a visitor from Mars. Take me to your leader, sweetheart."

"Dummy," Wil choked. "Don't you know a celebrity when you see him? How's life in the comics, Henry?"

Faye nodded – this was about what she could expect from now on – and walked to the sports desk. "I just got out of jail, boys. They deloused me." Her voice sounded hard and doomed in her own ears. "Come on, who wants to rub it for luck?"

They stared at her. "Girlie," Shanky said at last, "I rub it every Sunday, and I still don't get no luck."

Faye froze him with a look. "I understand Mr. Len was indisposed. Is he in today?"

"Not that I sawn," Wil said.

"Well, I'm supposed to report to either you or Alma Brackett. Guess I'll take my chances with her."

Alma Brackett was at her desk, not looking in Faye's direction, and apparently determined not to. "Go out and buy a wig," she said when Faye approached her. She kept her eyes on the window. "Come back when I can look at you without shock."

"I have a wig."

"Put it on."

"I don't care to, thank you. It's hot and prickly."

"Very well. You'll pardon me if I avoid looking at you, then."

"Alma Brackett, for heaven's sake. What is so shocking about somebody's head? You'd think I was running around naked. Come on, now, just one little peek. You'll get used to it if I can."

"Suppose I did? Why would I want to?"

"Because it tells you something. Didn't you tell me once that a good reporter keeps her eyes open?"

"I don't recall subjecting you to any such cliché. I do think I may have told you to keep your mouth shut. Now you see what happens."

"What makes you think this has anything to do with not keeping my mouth shut?"

Alma Brackett pursed her lips. "Like any good reporter, I have sources."

Faye walked around Alma Brackett's desk, following the swivel of her chair until Alma Brackett was cornered against her wastebasket, and could not avoid looking at her without contortion. "I'm intrigued to hear it, Ma'am. May we discuss those at an appropriate time? However, just now, I want you to look at me."

"Wig." Alma Brackett's hand waved at Faye's pocket.

"Oh, all right!" Faye put the wig on and looked at Alma Brackett through the tangle of curls. "Now look, if you can stand it. You are looking at a dead woman. A murderer."

"Murderess. We adhere to the niceties here." Alma Brackett glanced at Faye, and looked away. "Whom did you murder?"

"Gordon. My fiancé."

"Really. Well, more than half of the fiancés in this world certainly have it coming. Still, a slip of a girl – "

"If one more idiot calls me a slip of a girl again, I will scream." Faye clutched her head. "Oh, God, Alma Brackett. I didn't mean you."

Alma Brackett sat rigid for a moment, and smiled thinly. 'You did say, 'one more.' Let's assume you were warning me to cover my ears if any of the other idiots who frequent this room should happen to make that remark within your earshot. Noted, and warned."

Faye barked, meaning to laugh. "Thank you for not taking offense. I can't afford to upset people. Yes, a slip of a girl like me. I deliberately put him in a situation where I knew he would get into a fight, maybe get beaten up. I didn't expect him to get killed." Faye curved her wrist in a way that made her think of Courtenay, and said in a breathy, careless voice, "But he did, just the same."

"Was this to do with your pregnancy? How are you feeling, by the way?"

"Horrible. But I'm not pregnant. I lost the baby last week. So I guess that's another one I killed." Faye sighed, and collapsed into her old work chair, still parked by the card table. Talking, even to Alma Brackett, was giving her a reason to breathe, forcing air past the stone in her chest. "No, I was mad at Gordon for running around on me. I took advantage of the fact that a bunch of Klan goons were passing by, and I goaded them into threatening me. Of course, Gordon had no choice but to defend me, which is what I intended, coward that I am. I expected that the goons would beat him up. Not that they would kill him." Faye's face crumpled. "But they did."

Alma Brackett appeared unsurprised. "Running around? With someone here in Charlotte? Stupid me, how else would you know of it?"

"That's right. I think you know her. Sixteen hands at the withers, stunning face and figure, debutante of the epoch."

"Courtenay Weston? Good land."

"That's the one, her name slipped my mind. Gordon agreed with your description, apparently, particularly compared to his ..." Faye balled a fist against her forehead through the dangling curls. "His scrawny, pregnant little fiancée. What I hadn't counted on - and still can't believe, by the way - was that the Stunning One might in turn find Gordon attractive."

Alma Brackett leaned toward Faye briefly, and then sat back. "Will you be so good as to come with me for just a moment? I nearly indulged in a public gesture of motherliness just then, and I don't want the idiots to catch me in the least display of weakness."

Faye recoiled. "Don't waste your sympathy. For one thing, I have a mother of my own, though God knows what she will say to this. For another, this is another disaster I made on my own, and I will either get through it on my own, or ..."

Alma Brackett watched Faye shrug and blow her nose. "Or? And please feel free to take off that stupid wig, I suppose."

"Or ..." Faye took off the wig and sat up straight. "I won't."

Time and Chance

Alma Brackett glanced unwillingly at Faye's stubbled head, and nodded. "My analysis to a T. Well, then. I understand that your choice of an assignment for today is between myself and the Sports Desk. Have you decided?"

"Of course."

"Splendid. Come along."

Faye sighed. "All right. Who's the victim this time?"

Alma Brackett nodded, rose, and leaned close to Faye. "My mother. Bring your notebook."

Alma Brackett's mother Rose walked with the aid of two canes made of what seemed to be human leg bones set into carved ivory extensions. She looked old enough to have produced Alma Brackett when she herself was not young, and was now of an age that Faye did not expect to visit in this century, if ever. She fixed Faye with a faded blue eye.

"Do you know what it is to lose a baby?"

Faye blinked. "Yes, Ma'am."

"No you don't. Another damn fool called up about it this morning."

"Ma'am?"

"Her Pomeranian," Alma Brackett said. "It walked off a month ago, and Mother has been upset about it ever since." She shrugged. "Obnoxious little thing, we're well rid of it. Mother turns ninety this week. She doesn't hear well, you'll have to speak up."

"I hear well enough," Rose said. "Baby was feisty, certainly, but she was my baby. I got attached to her, which was my damn mistake."

"Eh," Alma Brackett said. "Here I thought I was your baby. Miss Bynum has been working with me this summer as an intern, and she is here to interview you on your ninetieth birthday." Alma

197

Brackett raised an eyebrow at Faye. "She's very bright, but she's had a few setbacks, and she needs a cup of something. If you'll excuse me?"

Rose Brackett nodded. "Come into the parlor, honey. Go on ahead, I move slow with these damnfool canes."

When they were seated she squinted at Faye. "How bright?"

"Not very," Faye said. She sat on a velvet love seat and crossed her hands. "Congratulations on your, your birthday. Let's see. I guess the traditional question is, to what do you attribute your long life?"

"Heh. Being born in 18 and 57, and not having had the presence of mind to die 25 years ago. Up to the age of 65, it was just one day after another. Since then, it's been the following very simple thing." She rapped the canes on the floor, left-right-left: "Not giving a damn."

Rose Brackett squinted over Faye's shoulder at the faint clinking sounds from the kitchen, and leaned forward, balancing herself on one of the bones. "If I've learned one thing in ninety years, it is that giving a damn is the stupidest thing God ever suckered Eve into. I spent the best part of my life caring about legs shot off at Sharpsburg, caring about Jim Crow, caring about cholera and the gold standard and Manifest Destiny and Kaiser Bill. The atom bomb. What good did it ever do? Caring, caring, caring. Say it over and over, and pretty soon it's just a noise, there's nothing to it. I got over caring when Alma's young man passed away, and I've never looked back. Have a peppermint?"

"Yes, Ma'am, thank you. I think you cared about your little dog, though."

"Yes, and see what I get? More sorrow. Damn fool called up this morning read my ad in the paper, which was another expense. Didn't know a Pomeranian from a poodle. What'd you do with your hair?"

Faye bit her lip. "It got shaved off by a bunch of Klan."

"H'm." Rose looked up at Alma Brackett, entering behind Faye with a tray of steaming teacups. "This little girl trying to straighten out the city, is she?"

"Just her corner of it."

"See what I told you?" Rose crowed. "Give a damn about anything at all, next thing you got your 'do shaved off. Drink your tea." She handed Faye a cup, which Alma Brackett intercepted.

"Uh-uh, Mother, that's the one with your saccharine." She took the cup from Faye. "Sorry. Mother's supposed to keep her sugar intake down."

"Damn nasty chemical crap, supposed to be the same thing as sugar. Well, 'tisn't. It's a fraud." Rose sipped her tea, and made a face. "So what, anyhow? I figure, I live to ninety, I get a pass on all this health business. What's left to protect?"

"Tell me about Baby," Faye said, diplomatically. "Did you have her for a long time?"

"Fourteen years and some," Rose said. "I got her from the pound on my way back from hearing Mr. Roozy-velt on the radio, the day he went into office. Only thing we had to fear was fear itself, he says, so I went ahead and got me a doggie."

Faye sipped tea and made a note. Nice touch, about Roosevelt. People would like it. Start with that. "Did you vote for President Roosevelt?"

"Me? I handed out flyers and song sheets in James A. Garfield's campaign, I voted for Warren G. Harding the first year I could vote, and I have voted Republican all the way down the line. I'll do it next year if I live that long. They're stupid and they're greedy, but they don't give a damn, and that's my ticket."

"I see," Faye said. Rose Brackett would get along fine with Faye's Daddy, who thought the New Deal was a plot to slow people down. She drank more tea – it was chamomile, sweet and not too hot, and it reminded her that she had not eaten since last night. "What would you say if a reporter wrote that you seem to give a quite a bit of a damn about a lot of things?"

"I'd snatch the hussy bald."

For an instant, a laugh rose in Faye's belly. But it clogged against the stone in her breast, and died.

Alma stirred, and straightened an already razorlike hem. "We were wondering if you might still have that wig you wore in 'Major Barbara'."

"Excuse me," Faye said. "I have a wig, and one is probably enough to get me through until my own hair grows back."

"You don't wear it because it itches, and when you do, you look like a fortune-teller. Indulge me in this, be so good. Mother?"

Rose nodded. "It's in the second hatbox down, upstairs hall closet. You'll have to fetch it yourself, Alma. These canes are no good, they slip on the stairs."

"You're holding them upside down, Mother. The rubber tips are supposed to go on the bottom, to keep them from slipping." Alma Brackett tossed a hand at the ceiling. "Honestly."

She headed for a back hallway, saying over her shoulder, "Just help her with that, will you, Faye? I'll be back in a jiffy."

When Alma Brackett's ascending footsteps sounded from the hall, Rose winked at Faye and spun the two canes like a gunslinger, catching them with the rubber-tipped ends down. The impact of the ball joints in her hands made her widen her eyes and stagger like a marionette. This time, the stone could not withstand the laughter that bubbled from Faye.

"Ma'am," she spluttered, hating herself. "Do take care."

Rose Brackett shook her head, and pointed one of the bones at Faye. "Why should I? If I break my hip, I'll die, and so what? I've already lived longer than almost anybody I know. I've buried all my friends except for Alma, and some days I'm terrified I'll outlive her."

Time and Chance

Faye looked at her notebook. It seemed unlikely to her that anyone would outlive Alma Brackett. Certainly not Faye herself. She felt dizzy, and she closed her eyes for a moment to stop the room from tilting.

"Here we are." Alma Brackett entered so suddenly that Faye suspected she must have tiptoed down the stairs and eavesdropped before entering. She was holding a hatbox, and she sat next to Faye and rustled tissue paper. "Now, don't say anything until you've tried this on. It will be as different as night and day from that Medusa business you were wearing. Come here."

Faye leaned toward Alma Brackett to peer into the box, and Alma Brackett brought out something shaggy and placed it on Faye's head, fussing at it while Faye frowned and tried to see what she was doing.

"Sit still, be so good ... there. Now take yourself to the hall mirror, kindly, and tell me you don't look stunning. Doesn't she look stunning, Mother?"

Rose Brackett clucked. "My stars and garters! Honey, you're me to the life."

"Mother wore this wig in the Chicago opening of 'Major Barbara' in 1906," Alma Brackett said. "The critics called her 'An American Sarah Bernhardt for the new century.' "

"Not that I gave a damn."

Faye walked to a pier glass in the front hall. Her legs felt as if they were part of Rose's canes. The wig was auburn, cut in a feathery bob that actually didn't look all that terrible, even after decades in a hatbox in a house with two cranky old women. The color was not so extreme as to contrast with her eyebrows, and it had bangs that could be adjusted to cover the new hair growing low on her forehead. Also, it was lined with something soft that did not itch or prickle. Faye touched it adjustingly once or twice, and snatched it off.

"No, but it is simply out of the question. I cannot parade around in a red wig while Gordon lies in a police morgue. It's obscene."

"Miss Bynum considers herself responsible for the death of her fiancé," Alma Brackett said.

Rose looked sharply at Faye. "Really? Good for you. Did this happen at the same time you got your new hairdo? And did he have it coming?"

"Mother!"

"Oh, shut up, Alma. At my age, you don't beat around the bush when you might be dead before you finish saying what you mean. Which is, did he trifle with your affections, Miss? Did he play the cad?"

"Yes," Faye said. She held the door jamb and leaned her head against it to steady things. "But that's not a death sentence."

"Is it not? Tell me, my girl, did you consider doing away with yourself when you learned of it? Even briefly?"

"Yes. Yes, I did. But – "

"But you didn't. Good for you. In my book, a man who makes a girl think of death is in the business, and he is asking for a taste of it himself."

Faye turned, meaning to excuse herself on the grounds of not feeling well, and to get out of this place, but she turned too quickly, and bumped into a knickknack table. A picture fell to the floor with a sorry jangle of breaking glass.

"Oh! I am so stupid and clumsy. I'm sorry, Ma'am, Alma Brackett. I just ..."

"You just need a rest, I think," Alma Brackett said. "Come with me, little girl."

Who is she calling "little girl?" "I'll be just fine, thank you. Just let me clean this up." Faye knelt and began to pick up broken glass. But her hands were thick and unreliable, and the next thing she was dripping blood on the hall floor and on the people in the picture. The impossible people, who could not be in that or any other photograph. Faye's heart pounded, pumping blood that dripped across the smiling faces of Alma Brackett, Gordon Simmons, and Faye Bynum herself, smiling with clenched eyes into a long shadow across the sand, the shadow of the unseen photographer, smiling against a frozen background of sand and curling waves.

Gordon, smiling ...

Her head sank to the soft sand before her, and she rolled onto her side to watch the clouds and the seagulls while the water washed and whispered at the shore.

Later, Faye remembered deciding to rest for a bit so she could finish the cleanup and think about this new horror, but then Alma Brackett was looming over her, and they were somehow flowing up the stairs, which is stupid because blood doesn't run uphill. *A high-water mark. Slowed to a trickle. Ooze ..* And there was stinging iodine and a band-aid and a pillow, and tossing waves, while Gordon and Alma Brackett watched her from the darkness of broken glass.

23.

FAINT daylight, a wet spot on the pillow. Cold feet. Faye despised improperly tucked covers, and resented their irresponsible feel on her ankles. She pulled her feet into safety. Breath, the dry side of the pillow, a sigh. The paralysis of complete relaxation. Madness.

Full sunlight, almost horizontal. Alma Brackett by the window, looking back at Faye. "I am sorry to disturb you, but I must go to the office. I'll tell anyone who asks that you are on an assignment, but I do very much hope to see you before midmorning. Mother will show you where the coffee and cornflakes are kept. Good morning."

"Good morning." But when Faye raised her head from the pillow, Alma Brackett was gone, and the sunlight was more oblique. She sat up, dizzy, remembering. She was still dressed, but barefoot. Her shoes and socks were on the floor by the bed. She put them on and stumbled out in search of a bathroom.

Rose Brackett sat at the kitchen table, reading the sports page of the Star-Dispatch. *Bullpen Blowup Sinks Hornets in Tenth.* She stubbed out a cigarette and tilted her head at the stove.

"Coffee's still fairly hot. Want some juice?"

"No … yes, thanks. Don't get up."

"I wasn't. That Mercer is a caution, he won't write an English sentence that doesn't call a baseball an aspirin or a spheroid, or call a base a bag, a sack, a pillow or – look at this, a 'port of call.' I don't think he knows the true and simple name of a single thing. I told Alma not to hire him."

"You told <u>Alma Brackett</u>? Not to hire him? Does she hire sportswriters?"

"She hires everybody that ain't union, honey."

"Really? Why … How …?"

Rose lifted her eyes from the paper. "Because, sweetheart, she owns sixty percent of the damn paper, don't she?. How'd you think she drives around in a Packard?" Rose snorted. "Nickel a word?"

"No, I …"

No, I thought it was picture frames. Faye sloshed coffee into a cup and returned the pot to the burner. The pot was lucky not to be glass.

"Spare the crockery, sweetheart."

Faye slammed herself into a chair across from Rose and covered Shanky's prose with a trembling hand. "No, but listen, Ma'am. Is anything in this town, or this newspaper, even a little bit like what it's supposed to be?"

Rose shrugged. "I suppose that depends on who is supposing, and what they suppose."

Faye took her coffee into the front hallway. The picture she'd broken was restored to its place, minus glass. She carried it back to the kitchen. It was apparent in better light, and with a clearer head, that the seaside frolickers did not, as she'd seen last night, include Gordon and herself. Still …

"Who are these people? Do you mind if I ask?"

"Course not. That's Alma and her young fella and me, down Myrtle Beach. Nineteen and – oh, I guess about seventeen. That's right, it was the month before Chet joined up and got shipped over to France."

Faye stared at the scene. Everyone looked pretty silly, in wool bathing suits down to their knees. Still, they seemed happy enough, Alma Brackett and Chet Bracken not looking at each other, but not at all ignoring each other. "She looks like you."

Rose took the picture. "Not hardly. That look like a ninety-year-old woman to you?"

"No, I mean, she looks now like you did then. And ..." Faye held her head, feeling the new growth a little softer now, a sixteenth of an inch long.

"And," Rose nodded. "She looked then like you do now, a little. That's why you looked like me in the wig. Though if I ever showed myself in public with no hair, I'd be laughed to oblivion."

"That hasn't changed," Faye said. "Oh, God. So that really is how I'll look when I'm middle aged."

Rose grinned. "Honey, it don't stop there. Want to see how you'll look when you're ninety?" She tongued an upper plate out of her mouth, flattened her lips against each other, and crossed her eyes. "Something to look forward to, don't you think? I'd give my right leg even to look like Alma does now. Back then, she was a knockout. Look here."

Rose reached to a sideboard and handed Faye a family-reunion sort of picture, with a line of faces grinning at the camera over vats of picnic food. "There at the end," Rose said.

Alma Brackett was in a serious mood, distancing herself from the grins and the corncobs. Her face looked thinner and finer-featured than in the beach picture. Her mouth was pensive, her eyes averted and shadowed.

"Oh," Faye said. The woman in this picture might have been Alma Brackett's estranged daughter, come to wartime grief in Budapest. "Is that after her fiancé died?"

"I don't believe so. No, that was the summer of '18, Chet was still all right. She looks like that because he was in France by then, and she was the only one in the family with any brains or talent, or any experience of suffering. To hear her tell it."

Faye smiled. Alma Brackett, sensitive soul. "The guy next to her looks familiar."

Rose peered at the picture. "Ought to. That's m'nephew Harold Claiborne, works down there at the paper."

"Harold Claiborne the <u>publisher</u>? He's related to Alma Brackett?"

"Honey, we're all related down here, didn't you learn that yet? We're as inbred as canned cockroaches. Here, look there. Know him?"

Faye sighed and looked at a bulky adolescent, grinning and aiming a drumstick at the camera like a knife-thrower. He looked like he was nursing a grievance behind the grin, and Faye didn't much like him, at sight.

"I don't think ... Oh, no. Len Biggs?"

"Little blister, he was then. He's straightened up some since. Went in the Army himself in '42, though he was old enough not to. Took him some while to settle down, after. Shell shock and all. That's when he picked up the mushmouth, for no other reason but that what he done and what he saw drove him a little crazy. He used to talk as clear as you and me; now he's scared to, or something. I forget what somebody said the connection was. He told me one time he saw a buddy get his head tore off by a hand grenade, and he saw that boy's soul rise up out of the mess like a fourth of July sparkler. There's a sight of boys came home like that."

Faye put down her coffee and held her forehead. Where was I when Gordon's soul rose up? Or did it seep out of his bloody mouth and straight down to Hell?

"Aw! Now look what I done, talking like that. There, now, honey. I ought to know better at my age, but I never had bat brains. Here, blow."

Faye took the offered paper napkin and blew her nose. "Don't apologize. I came here to interview you, and all I've done so far is break things and cry and sleep all night. I think Alma Brackett must have given up on me."

"Alma thinks you are the brightest prospect that has come past her in twenty years of newspapering. She told me so herself, weeks ago."

"Well, I've given her plenty of chance to reconsider since then."

"Well, she hasn't that I know of. Now, what else did you mean to ask me?"

Faye drew a breath. "Tell me about being an actress around the turn of the century."

Rose shrugged. "Not very glamorous, then or now. We traveled by train, and got there filthy. It was mostly hard, dirty work on not enough sleep. And of course the automatic assumption was that one was a woman of easy morals. The fact that it was true of most of us did not make life easier. One was never in a position to be easy with the right people at the right time. Mostly, it was fighting off directors and stage-door Johnnies, or else producers who thought they had something tangible coming for their money."

Faye raised an eyebrow. "How did you manage to deal with that?"

"Various of us in various ways. The great thing was not to get pregnant, that might be the end of you, and of course the technology for it was pretty primitive. Many a woman with more talent than I ever had would give you some kind of story about taking time off to study a new script, and you never saw them again. I won't claim I was virtuous, but I was lucky, except when Alma came along. I managed to last out the time as a wardrobe mistress, and I made arrangements for her and got back into the swing of things. Others..."

Rose looked out the kitchen window, and then consideringly at Faye. "I don't suppose the name of Lillian Sandbridge means anything to you."

Faye thought, shrugged. "Not really."

Time and Chance

"She was a successful actress in New York and London in the 18 and 60's, and she traveled in her own personal coach, wherever the rails would take her. She had a pretty little face, the kind that you can see is fragile, it's going to go fast when it starts, but up to that point, you didn't care, you just wanted to pinch her cheeks and take her home with you. Men, Lord, they worshipped her. And she loved them. Talk about easy morals, all she had to do was see an actress with a good looking actor, or a stagehand, for that matter, and she'd take him away just to keep in practice. Or like she was at the seashore, and he was a shell, got washed up just for her.

"That went on right through the '70's and '80's, but by the time I knew her she was definitely on the down side of the hill. Her voice and her nerve held out longer than her looks, though, so she made a life on stage in the bigger cities besides New York and Boston. Places like Cleveland, Cincinnati, Denver, even Memphis and Des Moines. I think it killed her that she wasn't young and brilliant any more, that she had begun to beg for roles that she would have turned up her nose at in her good years, and that the good-looking actors were swarming around the younger actresses. Including me, I admit.

"But she did everything she could think of to keep up the pretense that she was still a star, and that she took these roles in little out-of-the-way places as an act of noblesse oblige. I met her when I played Nora in "A Doll's House" and she was Mrs. Linde. I don't suppose you are familiar with that play."

Faye thought. *Henrik Ibsen, Collected Plays.* She remembered a fat volume rebound in orange, from her work as a library shelver, but she'd never read the thing. "No, Ma'am."

"Can't say I blame you. Talky damn thing. Mrs. Linde is a tired, desperate woman – it was good casting, putting Lillian in that role – and an old school friend of Nora's, though Lillian kept trying to make her a vamp of 25. She wore low-cut gowns and constantly upstaged all of us, certainly including me. She showed up late to

209

rehearsals, she kept trying to pump up the secondary role she had, and she treated me like some kind of Hollywood extra. She slept with every man that wasn't nailed down, including Helmer, my husband in the play, and a man I kind of enjoyed playing wife to, if you see what I mean. By the time we opened in New Haven, I was ready to strangle her the first chance I got.

"Well, like anything with any guts to it, 'A Doll's House' was banned in Boston, so during the summer of 1890 we did a production in Providence, Rhode Island, so Boston folks could see it if they wanted. I think the Boston and Maine ran special trains, and a lot of the Brahmins came by to have a look, and people like Mark Twain and George Bernard Shaw. And then, lo and behold, word came back from the box office one Saturday night that Henrik Ibsen himself was in the audience."

"Really?" Faye, wide-eyed, taking the chance to register that she had at least heard of the author.

Rose nodded. "I truly believe Lillian Sandbridge was ready to ascend bodily into heaven. She went back into her dressing room and did her makeup all over again, and damn near missed her first cue. She flung herself around the stage, she climbed the scenery, she stepped on everyone's lines, and she pulled the neckline of her dress about down to her belly button. After the last act, she looked up from her taking her bow, that was giving the whole audience about an acre of her matronly bosom to contemplate, and she stepped forward and held her hands up for silence.

" 'I understand,' she says in her fluty little-girl voice, 'that we are honored tonight by the presence of Mr. Henrik Ibsen. Perhaps he can be persuaded to take a bow.' And sure enough, a portly old fellow with a great bushy beard stands up in the back of the theater, and there's this great storm of applause, and Lillian asks him to come up and join the cast for a bow. Ibsen looks a bit taken aback, but Lillian beckons him down front like she won't take no for an answer.

Time and Chance

Thinking, I guess, she can salvage her career if she can get her hooks into Ibsen, who everyone knows is a womanizer, though he was over 60 by this time."

Rose Brackett smiled, remembering. "And sure enough, there is a woman with him, middle-aged herself, who's pulling at his sleeve and trying to get him to sit down. But he brushes her off, and down front he comes, the whole audience giving him a standing ovation, and up onto the stage, and sure enough, he can't get enough of Lillian's cleavage, it's like she'd put fishing lines on his eyeballs. I can't help noticing that he's a pretty disheveled old coot, with crumbs in his beard from the sandwiches people used to eat during the play, along with a chunk of what looked like lemon peel, or peach jam. Well, thinks I, so this is what genius looks like up close.

"But still, he's Henrik Ibsen for God's sake, and I'm about ready to rip Lillian's face off, because I hated her guts in the first place, and I'd done my best too, with the famous playwright out there watching. The play is about Nora after all, not some secondary character, and I thought I'd done her and Mr. Ibsen proud. So I snuggled up on the side of him that Nora wasn't occupying, though that was pretty much his back, because he was bending over Lillian's cleavage to kiss her hand, and she's simpering and blushing like a damn idiot. Finally, she throws her arms around him and gives the great man a kiss square on the mouth, and of course she also brings both barrels of the Sandbridge bosom to bear.

"This tears it for the woman Ibsen was with, and she gets out of her seat and comes trotting down the aisle, waving an umbrella, and yelling something I couldn't hear, because by this time the whole audience is whooping and whistling, and the house manager is starting to look nervous about getting the famous genius off the stage without offending him."

Faye scribbled on the margin of Rose's sports page. "This is great," she murmured. "Go on."

211

Time and Chance

Rose nodded. "And then Lillian gives a screech, and she jumps back and starts swatting at her bosom, and I can see there's a bee there, I guess disturbed from its picnic in Mr. Ibsen's beard. That's what I'd thought was the bit of lemon peel, don't you see. The uproar and the swats just made the bee anxious, so it walked over into the cleavage area and sat down to think things over, and I guess it decided to give Lillian something to screech about, because the next thing she's gone berserk, and I swear I lost a filling with the noise. Lillian would like to have fainted in Ibsen's arms, but she couldn't stand still, she's clutching at her breast and cracking the plaster with her yelling, and now Ibsen's lady friend is up on the stage, yelling, 'Henrik Ibsen, you come away from that stage hussy this instant,' and Ibsen's ignoring her completely, trying to figure out how to give Lillian a hand, so to speak, with what's bothering her.

"And then the wife, or girl friend, whichever, breaks her umbrella over his head and grabs his arm and she says to him – and mind you, I'm still standing right there, trying not to break a rib laughing at Lillian Sandbridge and her precious bee-stung titty, which is already starting to swell up a treat – the woman says, with this kind of low, menacing voice that I'm pretty sure Lillian and I were the only ones that heard, she says, 'Henry Morris Gibson, you wait till I get you home.'"

Rose smiled and patted Faye's hand. "Lillian Sandbridge never gave me a moment's trouble from that time on, and she retired for good at the end of the run."

Faye laughed, sipped coffee, scribbled, looked stunned for an instant; and then coffee erupted from her nose.

"Henry Gibson?" she choked.

Rose winked, and handed Faye a napkin. "Yes, Ma'am."

Faye giggled, mopped her face, shook her head, and began to write again. She grinned as the story unfolded itself in reverse in her memory. The great man. The furious wife, the desperate Courtenay –

no, *Lillian*. She looked up at Rose Brackett. And what she saw, in the wrinkles and the collapsed mouth and the faded eyes now so full of kindness, was the face of one who had done what her hand had just now found to do, and done it with all her might and with all her heart.

Faye shook her head, humbled by the magnanimity of an old, old woman. "You made that story up just now, didn't you? You made it up for me, to make me feel better."

"Of course not. Think I'm Jack Benny? I swear to the Lord, it happened, just ..." She thumped one of the legbones on the floor. "Well, so what?"

Faye detonated into laughter that felt exactly like what Sister Rose Penitentia kept trying to convince her bored and restless classes would be the helpless mirth of mortal, sinning man when enfolded at last in the overwhelming grace of God. Half-convinced, she let go all restraint and doubled onto the kitchen table, gasping and limp. Her howls of laughter were more than half tearful, a hybrid of emotions that rolled her defenseless tennis-ball head onto her arms, her face stretched into a mask of hilarity and woe. From time to time, she would get her breath, and seem to have herself enough in hand to sniffle and blow her nose on Rose Brackett's soggy napkin, and then be off again, as often toward laughter as tears, in no clear pattern.

After minutes of this, she rose, still ambivalently whuffling, and made her way to the roll of paper towels by the sink. She wet one, and passed it over her face. When the world and the poky little kitchen was shut out of her sight, she felt as if she were flying. She gripped the sink for grounding.

"Honey, are you all right?"

"Yes," Faye said. "I am pretty much all right. I'm so sorry that I've put you to all this trouble." *Some day, if I am very lucky, I will become a toothless old woman like this one.*

Rose Brackett pushed herself erect and put a hand on Faye's shoulder. "The world is a hell of a place, Faye."

Time and Chance

Faye turned and enfolded the old woman, fragile as a pharaoh, understanding that she held her own future in her arms. "So I am beginning to understand," she said. "Thank God you learned not to give a damn."

24.

R OSE BRACKETT *winked, and tapped the floor with her cane. "We found out later that the real Henrik Ibsen had left at the intermission, telling everybody he'd never seen such a travesty!"*

No longer as spry as she once was, Rose Brackett gets about on two canes made from ivory and human bone. Specifically, the ~~femurs~~ leg bones of her cousin and great-uncle, who lost them in ~~the Civil~~ the War Between the States, fighting respectively for the Confederacy and for the Union. The ivory is intricately carved with flowers and death's-heads. The combination of mortality and elegance expresses this aged Sybil to a T. "These bones," Mrs. Brackett told ~~this reporter~~ a visitor, "are my own flesh and blood. Anybody that doesn't like it, you can write down that I don't give a D---" , she added, using a word that will not be found in this newspaper.

"Oh, I think you could feel free to use that word," Alma Brackett said.

Faye looked up at her from under the Major Barbara wig.

"How liberating. And coming as it does from the – Who, by the way, for reasons that cannot possibly be put into ordinary rational English, concealed the fact – from the owner of this newspaper, it does carry a certain weight."

"She spilled the beans on that, did she?"

"Yes, Ma'am. Do you think you could formulate a simple explanation for why you concealed it from me, passing yourself off as a hand-to-mouth society editor, and do so without once using the words "dear" and "girl?" And if possible without commenting on how I remind you of yourself at my age?"

Alma Brackett gave her a frosty smile. "Easily. You came very highly recommended. I did not trust any of the other editorial staff to evaluate your potential fairly, since this apparent hot prospect was, unluckily, female. At the same time, I was afraid that if you knew you were working for the majority owner - still hand-to-mouth, by the way, don't imagine this is such a lucrative enterprise as all that - you would not feel free to be your true self. You might very well have been overly deferential to me, and by doing so, concealed your real talent. Such as it might be. Clearly, I needn't have worried about that last."

"I see. That even makes a certain amount of sense, once you grant the notion that an evaluation based on a whopping deception could have any validity. Well, now that I do know the truth, do you find me unduly deferential to you? The servile toady you feared? The, the - "

"Oh, for heaven's sake, dear girl. Really, you are myself to the life, before - "

"Ha! A triple killing, as Shanky would probably call it."

"Before, Faye, I learned the trick of forgiveness. I am sorry to see that you are upset, but I do not apologize for deceiving you. I had what I still consider sound reasons. If that piece is to make today's edition, it will need to be on Elaine Barnes' desk by noon. And if it does not make today's, well, what's the point of it? Mother's birthday was yesterday."

"It will be there. All the faster if - " Faye shook her head, and stood. "Alma Brackett, I apologize too. I don't know why I'm so, so …" Faye waved a hand. "So touchy, these days. I don't know about this trick you mentioned, but I do know one thing. You and your mother are probably the smartest, kindest, loveliest people I have ever known."

"Yes, well, you're young yet. Still, it is nice of you to say so."

"You know better than that. I'll have this done in plenty of time. Do you want to read it before I give it to Elaine?"

Alma Brackett smiled. "No, dear. It will just make me wish I were you. I'm sure it will be lovely, and it will thrill Mother."

Time and Chance

"Not that she'll give a damn."

The canes were made for her by an admirer whom Mrs. Brackett prefers not to identify, except to say that he was a young surgeon traveling with the Union army who treated both relatives after the battle of ~~Antietam~~ Sharpsburg, and who came to admire the glamorous actress in later years.

Rose Brackett, a successful actress during the latter part of the last century and well into the present one, did not lack for

"Miss Bynum?"

Faye glanced up. "Hold on, Jimmy Lee. I've about got this done."

admirers in her heyday.

She was the toast of

"No, but Miss Bynum?"

Faye glared at the copy boy, who was shifting from foot to foot by her desk. "What, then?"

Jimmy Lee gulped. "There's a fella says he needs to see you."

"Does he have a name, this fella?"

"Yes, Miss Bynum." Jimmy Lee concentrated. "Thomas? Tompkins?"

"Was it Thompson, by any chance?"

"Um ... I guess, yeah."

"Go back and find out."

"Yes'm."

the worlds of theatre and of

Faye scowled. 'Theatre,' that was a nice touch that probably wouldn't survive Elaine's copy editing. But how to name that other world Rose had described, a world of night clubs and hansom cabs, stage-door Johnnies and critics who would trade a good review for a good time? Faye had heard of the term "demi-monde," but wasn't confident she really knew what the hell it meant.

In any case, Rose had had a lot to say about that world, and about her survival as a single mother who used a besotted newspaper baron as a phony husband while she raised her out-of-wedlock daughter virtually single-handed. And who, as the price of silence when she caught him in a liaison with a German consular secretary on the eve of World War I, wrenched from him stock that in time amounted to majority ownership of the Star-Dispatch for her daughter. No word of all that would ever make the pages of the Star-Dispatch, of course, but –

"Yes, Miss Bynum, it's Mr. Thompson. He given me this for you."

Miss C. Weston is at home and wishes to speak with you.

"Tell Mr. Thompson that I am at work, and do not wish to speak to Miss C. Weston."

"Yes, Miss. He seemed ..."

"That's all, Jimmy Lee."

... and of social and artistic life from New York to Chicago, from St. Louis to Miami. "I believe I have seen the backstage of every theatre east of Kansas City," she told a visitor, "Not to mention the backstage of a good many prominent people, which was not always a handsome sight."

Faye pulled her chair closer to the desk, scowling. Here was the tricky part, making the transition without triggering a censor.

Time and Chance

"There were plenty of crooks, thieves, and roustabouts in the theatre in those days," Mrs. Brackett continued, "just like today. And not all of them were wearing work clothes, either. I could name you stage-door bankers that were nothing but small-scale grifters, so-called critics that couldn't write an English sentence, and lawyers that ramped around at night with the Klan."

When asked to comment on Charlotte's postwar prosperity and artistic renaissance, Mrs. Brackett nodded. "Charlotte is a right handsome town," she allowed. "I never saw such a truckload of nice new buildings to go up at one time. New theaters, concert halls, museums. It still isn't all that safe to move around at night, what with Klan and all." When a visitor reminded her that the police believe that the Ku Klux Klan is no longer active in Charlotte, Mrs. Brackett laughed. "Then who's the gang of morons that plays Halloween every week on Mecklenburg Street? They never asked me for candy."

She finished the article at five to noon, and put it on Elaine Barnes' desk ten seconds after that. Elaine didn't look up, which suited Faye. She left the newsroom and found a little knot of colleagues on the stairs, heading for lunch. Feeling the glow of accomplishment, Faye joined them.

On the street, puddles from a midmorning shower were taking their time evaporating in sunglare that found it uphill work, trying to coax yet more moisture into the saturated air. Faye slowed reflexively, shielding her eyes from the glare. At the curb, a familiar limousine idled, sheltering the reliable Thompson. As Faye passed, he slipped it into gear and idled along the curb beside her, driving with one hand and leaning across the front seat.

"Miss Bynum."

"Dear me. Didn't Jimmy Lee tell you I have nothing to say to your precious mistress?"

"She will find that difficult to accept, Miss. She is distraught at … at recent events, and wishes to know what she can do to help you."

"Help <u>me</u>? Not one thing, Mr. Thompson. Kindly go back and tell the useless girl to stop interrupting people while they are at work. You don't have to use that word with Courtenay, of course, it would only confuse her. But I'm sure you understand."

"Miss Bynum, you are making a mistake in not seeing her. Just a piece of advice."

"My land. Are you <u>threatening</u> me?"

Thompson grunted with annoyance, stopped the car and got out. Faye turned her back and walked on, but Thompson caught up with her in two steps, and took her arm. Faye yelled, mostly from surprise, but also because Thompson's hand was strong and roughly calloused. It didn't feel like the hand of a sedentary chauffeur. Faye yanked her arm away and backed into Wil Osborne, tripped, and teetered across his path. Wil steadied her with a hand on her waist and a pat to her rump.

"Whoa, Honey. Not right out here where folks can see us."

Faye, flustered and furious, and glared at Thompson. "You may tell Miss Weston that I <u>may</u> be available to speak to her here at the <u>Star-Dispatch</u> offices this afternoon after the close of business. That will be at about five o'clock. If I can find the time, I will await her until 5:15, after which I will no longer be available. Do you have that message clear, Mr. Thompson?"

Thompson eyed Wil, Shanky, and a gathering knot of <u>Star-Dispatch</u> staffers, and scowled at Faye. "Very well, Miss Bynum. I repeat, you are making a serious mistake in not welcoming Miss Weston's interest."

When he was gone, Faye adjusted the wig, which had slipped a little in the flurry. "Well," she said. "I do apologize for being the occasion of an interruption to our lunch hour. I am sure it will not happen again."

*

Courtenay Weston arrived at 5:16, and met Faye on the stairs.

"Sorry," Faye said. "I'm leaving."

"No, wait, Faye." Courtenay's eyes were shadowed, and she was dressed almost soberly: a modest summer frock and strappy pumps, a little clutch purse of green silk shaped like a half-moon. Her face looked thin, which startled Faye. How can you make your face thin and pathetic in a week?

"I'm really quite tired, Courtenay. I've been working."

"This won't take long. I wanted to talk to you about … about Gordon. I am so terribly sorry for what I did."

"Really."

Faye led Courtenay through the lobby and press room, taking the time to settle herself. She opened the door to the break room. At this hour, with the day's edition long since on the trucks, it was deserted. She led Courtenay to the booth next to the drink box, and sat across from her. Courtenay put a hand on Faye's.

"I mean it, Faye. It was not a kind thing to do, and I regret it."

"Gordon would be sorry to hear that, Courtenay. I'm sure he was hoping for further access to your favors."

Courtenay blinked, and a tear rolled through the shadow under her eye. Taking some of the shadow with it, Faye noticed. "Don't be mean, Faye. I said I was sorry. I was infatuated with Gordon, I admit. I only wish you both the very best." She opened her little purse and seemed to be looking for a tissue.

Faye smiled. "That's really very kind of you, Courtenay. Unfortunately, Gordon is no longer with us."

"What? No longer with who? You? You broke up? Oh, Faye that makes me – "

"Gordon is <u>dead</u>, Courtenay." Faye stopped herself from telling Courtenay she held herself responsible. Why give her that?

Courtenay stared at Faye. "That can't be true."

"Really? Why ever not? He wasn't immortal. He was beaten to death by a bunch of Klan thugs last week, in the middle of trying to explain to me why on earth he fucked you."

Faye thought she was probably more shocked at the word than Courtenay, but on thinking it over she couldn't imagine a better one. *Stet.* "Oh, for God's sake, Courtenay, stop blubbering. He didn't mean anything to you. It's beyond me why you even bothered."

Courtenay took her hand back, slammed it on the table, and glared at Faye. "Faye, I loved that guy. Even so, I came here to give him up to you." She blew her nose.

"You <u>loved</u> him? Amazing. You hardly knew him. Do you even know what you're talking about?"

"I probably know a thing or two about love that they left out of the health curriculum at St. Louis High School. But let's talk about you, dear. Do you think love means he'll never look at another woman?"

Faye laughed. "One thing I know it means, is that you don't cheat on the woman you just asked to marry you. And as for you, Miss Weston, you respect other people's engagements. What do you think this means?" She knuckled forward the ring Gordon had given her, still riding around on her left hand, reflecting more guilt and inertia in Faye, than loyalty to the doomed engagement.

Courtenay narrowed her eyes at the ring and smiled. "Yes. I saw that exact ring when I pawned the tacky gold picture frame you and bitch-face Brackett sold my mother. Sid's Pawn, Tryon Street, $12.50, two for twenty, ask us about bulk discounts. More than he should have spent, but Gordon told me he got a kick out of throwing money at the cheap little sluts who hang around Fort Bragg. Why should you be any different, you cheap little slut?"

"Ah." Faye pointed at Courtenay. "I get it. I can't believe this." She laughed a little. "It was the gold frame, was that it, behind all this? Here you were having such a grand time making fun of Alma

Brackett, and all I had to do was make you sound like the arrogant snot you are. Probably always were. Your friend Calvin says so, anyhow."

"You're a cheap little slut."

Faye rose from the booth. "Goodness, witty. Though it loses something in the repetition. Still, they must just worship you at Harvard. Stand up here, please, and try again."

Courtenay slammed her clutch on the table and stood. "I take it back. Whatever costs a man his life isn't cheap. The rest of it stands, you little slut. What, did he kill himself over you when you gave him a bitch fit about going out on a date with me? I mean, how stupid can a man get?"

"Don't call him stupid! Have a tiny speck of decency, you phony bitch."

"Listen, hick. Do you think I really gave a fat shit about your dumb-ass paratrooper? I wasn't finished with him yet, that's all." She kicked Faye's knee with her handsome little pump, making Faye gasp with the electric charge of pain.

Faye grabbed Courtenay's hair; Courtenay grabbed Faye's wig, and that gave Faye a momentary advantage that she didn't waste. She yanked Courtenay to the floor, pounced on her, and slapped her hard enough to leave a handprint on her cheek. Courtenay shrieked, kneed Faye in the back, and pummeled her with the Major Barbara wig. Faye got a handful of Courtenay's hair on each side of her skull, and pulled her face close. Courtenay stared at Faye, at the menace of a bald woman.

"Listen to me, stupid," Faye hissed, while she gently bumped the back of Courtenay's head on the floor grit. "You've noticed that I'm hard on people. Gosh, I never mean to be, but it just seems to happen, doesn't it? Maybe if I just bumped your head a little extra hard - like *this* - maybe I'd have another life on my hands, you think?

Not much of one, Gordon was worth twenty of you, but it's all you've got. Shall we *try*?"

Courtenay heaved and grabbed at Faye's wrists, but Faye dismounted, got a foot against Courtenay's hip, and shoved her under the booth. She sat back panting, while Courtenay yelled and gagged. Faye knelt to look in at Courtenay screwing her face away from the padding that leaked from the underside of the seat. She reached toward Faye, and Faye pinned her wrist against one of the legs of the booth.

"Ow! Stop it, you little freak, you're breaking my arm!"

"Lie still," Faye whispered. "Lie there and look up at the chewing gum and cigarette butts, whatever else is under there. Your trouble is, Courtenay, you only ever see the top side of things. Think for a minute about people who are beneath you, like Thompson, and Gordon, and slutty little me. People who once in a while might slip down below the surface. Then think way down past us to people who spend their whole lives down here with the chewing gum and the roach turds, so far down they don't even know you exist. Don't you think God made them too? Don't you know people love them, way more than anybody will ever love you? You're a fool, Courtenay, and time and chance will happen to you too. You'll waste your life being fucked by fools until you get to be middle aged, and find out they're finished with you. A long time after that, you'll die lonesome; but you're finished with my life right now. Stand up and get out of here."

Faye released the wrist, and Courtenay clawed her way from under the booth, scooting away from Faye with wide eyes. "You're goddamn completely fucking mad," she said.

Faye snorted. "You bet I'm mad. Can you blame me? Here, don't forget your little purse. Did you bring a little pearl-handled ladies' revolver in it?"

"No, but I should have. I brought a thousand dollars."

Faye laughed and bonked her forehead. "Silly me. Of course you would."

When Courtenay was gone, Faye sat down carefully in the booth and stared at her hands. One of Courtenay's honey-blonde hairs was caught under a fingernail. She pulled it out with shaking fingers and blew it onto the floor. It curled there, shining. Faye laughed, and felt welling up the same helpless half-laughter that convulsed her in Rose Brackett's kitchen. It held her in the booth for a quarter-hour, until one of the maintenance guys stuck his head in. Faye smiled at him, rose, and limped for the exit, her diaphragm still spasming. *If this keeps up, I may have to see somebody about it.*

When she opened the street door, Forde Morgan was sitting on the front steps.

"Courtenay Weston came past me a while ago with a piece of popcorn stuck to her butt," Forde said. "I didn't know anything stuck to her butt."

"There's not much that doesn't." Faye's eyes narrowed. "How do you know Courtenay Weston? Does she have her hooks into you too?"

"Hooks? Me? I read the Social News, so I won't miss things that you write. Anyways, who doesn't know the Deb of the Decade?"

Faye sat down next to Forde. "I'm sorry, Forde. I'm kind of frazzled just now." Her diaphragm spasmed, embarrassingly, making her gasp and croak.

"What is it, Faye? No, wait, look. I've got my uncle's car this week. Would you like to go somewhere where it's cool? Sit down and get supper, rest and catch me up? Is it the thing with the Klan?"

"That seems like a long time ago. Gordon's dead, Forde. I'm so upset, I just about killed Courtenay when she came weaseling around to apologize and give me a thousand dollars."

Time and Chance

"Apologize for what? She didn't kill Gordon. A thousand dollars?"

"No, I ..." Faye stared at Forde, and into an abyss, and recoiled. Forde was not surprised at all to hear that Gordon was dead.

"Look, Forde, honestly, I think your best move here would be to stand up right now and walk down the street. Tell people you never heard of me. I'm half-crazy, I can't stop this laughing and crying. I'm a menace and a jinx, everybody who touches me gets killed. Oh, and I'm a cheap little slut, by the way. A bald cheap little ... h-huhh ... little slut."

Forde stood and looked down the street, nodding. "Yeah, maybe." He reached a hand down to Faye. "But your hair's growing back. Maybe the rest of it will turn out OK, too. Come on."

Forde ushered her into his Uncle Harold's car, a grey DeSoto coupe with sun shields and a necker's knob, and drove her to a place called Mama's Eats, on 74 east of town. "They serve great Calabash here," he said. "And they're the cheapest place with an air conditioner this side of Raleigh. You want to split an oyster basket?"

"I don't know. I guess. I'm not very hungry."

"That's because you haven't smelled the oysters yet. If you need to go wash your hands, I'll order."

"Am I that grubby looking?"

"You know better than to ask me that. There is this little smudge on your cheek, though."

Forde was being diplomatic, Faye found, when she looked in the mirror of the Ladies'. The smudge on her cheek was part of a comprehensive mess that included streaks of dirt, a scratch on her forehead – from Courtenay's nails, she guessed – tear tracks, a blouse button undone, and skinned knuckles. She washed up, blew her nose, fixed the button, and retrieved the Major Barbara wig from her skirt pocket and combed it over the scratch. She still had the spastic

226

diaphragm, but all in all, she felt better when she got back to the table to find a towering glass of tea, a dozen shapeless deep-fried things that she guessed were the oysters, and a mound of hush puppies at her place. Forde was gone, but his plate held an equal abundance of aromatic brown stuff. Faye sat and sipped the tea. It was achingly sweet, with a lethal undercurrent of something Southerly to it. Forde reappeared, rubbing his hands on his pants.

"Scuse me, Miss, but – Jehoshaphat! Faye?"

"Oh, stop that, Forde Morgan."

"No, but the hair, my land! It's cuter'n a bug."

"It's Alma Brackett's mother's stage wig from 1906. I'm clean, too, for a change. Same … h-huhh … same girl under it though."

"Eat. You can tell me about it later, if you want to. I don't mean to pry."

Faye said nothing, but forked a bite from one of the oysters. "Oh, my Lord," she whispered, around the bite. "Oh, my Lord, that is … it's …." Faye stabbed the other half of the oyster and popped it in her mouth.

"Good, huh? That's Calabash style, and this is about the best place for it, this far from the coast."

Faye didn't bother cutting the next four or five oysters, but crunched them whole. And as she worked down through them, and sipped tea and ate hush puppies and corn bread and grazed at her slaw, once in a while looking up at Forde doing the same, the knotted, stony place in her chest that made her gasp began to melt. She breathed deeply for the first time in days. She drank off the tea, and felt a little dizzy. She could feel a flush spreading across her face, and some kind of forgiveness welling into her throat. Maybe the trick that Alma Brackett spoke of. She had been, she realized, starved, wound tight, and grieving. None of those seemed as acutely so, now. Certainly not the starving.

After a quarter-hour of silence, she sighed and leaned back. "My stars, Forde. If I ate like this all the time, I'd be as fat as Sarah ... Sanna Claus."

"Uh huh," Forde nodded. "Lots of folks do, and they are. I try to save it for a treat. When you're finished, we could drive on out in the country a little, if you wanted. Give you a change of scenery."

Faye staggered and grabbed Forde's shoulder when she stood up. "Dang, Forde, you sneak. D'you put something in that tea?"

"Yes, I did. About half an ounce of Southern Comfort," Forde said. "I thought maybe it'd help you relax a little."

"I ought to smack you, tryna get me drunk, up t'no good." Faye giggled. "I might, yet, you try anything."

"Naw, huh uh. That much Comfort wouldn't lose nobody their good judgment, just relax them a little. You want me to take you home?"

Faye sighed. "Maybe. Maybe that would be bes', Forde. You are so kind, you are a <u>kind</u> fella. You shouldn't be wasting your time on me."

"Uh huh, right. Whatever seems best to you."

But when they drove past the "Welcome to Charlotte, North Carolina, The Queen City" sign, Faye turned to Forde.

"Gosh, Forde, I just can't stand the thought of going back to Mrs. Merrill's right now. She'll be there with her poisonous cat and her snoopy questions. Is there someplace we could go and – just, you know, talk?"

*

Faye leaned back against a pine tree and looked downhill over the DeSoto, parked in a back-road pulloff, and beyond it to rolling hills washed in gold. The pine tree was a little sticky, but Faye didn't care. The air was cooling, and carried an evening hum of bugs tuning up, sending out feelers to the bug social world. *Maybe that's a demimonde.*

"And that's when she called me a cheap little slut," she said. "It's funny. I wasn't even mad by that time. I was ..." Faye tried to put a word to the circle of Hell from which she watched herself brawling with Courtenay Weston. "Well, I don't exactly know what I was. I was perfectly willing to crack her skull on the break room floor, I know that. But I wasn't mad at her. She was just something beautiful that had got dirty, and needed to be cleaned up."

Forde, at a right angle against the same pine, nodded. "I guess that's when the popcorn got stuck to her butt."

"No, that was probably when I shoved her under the booth."

Forde grinned, and Faye squinted at the sunset. She had told him everything: the pregnancy and its initiation - in discreet generalities - the miscarriage, the fight with Gordon, the Klan encounter with Gordon, Detective Meyer and the morgue, the interview with Rose Brackett, the knockdown with Courtenay Weston. He laughed, a little tentatively, at the Henry Gibson story, and otherwise said nothing but, "Yes ," and "Mm," and "Uh huh,"

Faye was puzzled. Nobody could be as tolerant of promiscuity, madness and proxy murder as Forde was letting on to be. Though she had, she realized, perhaps veiled her own part in setting up Gordon to be roughed up. She wondered how stupid it would be to ruin the perfection of this moment. All she had to do was keep her mouth shut. Hadn't she learned that lesson by now?

"Forde."

"Uh huh." He sounded expectant, even hopeful. Poor boy.

Faye sighed, plucked a blade pine grass, and twirled it in her fingers. "Oh, nothing. Thank you for listening, that's all."

"<u>You</u> listen. I am thrilled to be of any help at all. I do care about you, Faye."

"Yes. I know. I'm not ... what was that word? Arranged?"

"I don't know. You're not arranged?"

"Uh huh." Faye yawned. "What Junie said about me that time."

"Oh. You're indisposed?"

"That's it. I'm not disposed ... well, no, I guess I'm not exactly <u>arranged</u> to be cared about ... No, darn it, that's not what I mean either. Look, I guess I mean, I'm just not available to be cared about. I'm in over my head on a lot of things, I'm sad and guilty and full of grief and frustration. I don't feel like I can ..." Faye tossed the pine grass away. "I mean I'll have trouble being worth the trouble of caring about for a while, I guess that's it. So any caring you feel like undertaking will be lonesome work. Rose Brackett says she lived to be 90 because she learned not to care. Not give a damn, is what she really said."

"How about I give a damn anyhow, just on the chance?"

Faye snorted, suddenly furious. Forde's bland, numbskull devotion was trivializing the whole thing. "Look, Forde." She stopped, feeling a compulsion to rub this innocent's nose in blood and shame. She pictured herself lancing the boil of guilt within, and without warning, slipping the knife between Forde's ribs, biting and clawing, hammering him with a rock. *You ass. I am a killer, damn it!. A cowardly murderer.*

She drew a breath and said, carefully, "Forde, the truth is, I <u>wanted</u> Gordon dead. I hated him, so I ... " She hesitated, sighed, tossed a hand in the air. "I murdered him." She tasted the thought, found it satisfying in the way it hurt. "I <u>murdered</u> Gordon in a vicious, cowardly way, because I thought I loved him, and I let him get me pregnant, and then he turned around and ... and betrayed me. I threw him into a den of killers, hoping they would beat him up. I can never forgive myself for that." *So you have no business giving your damn.* "And before I did that, I teased and stirred them into a rage, to make it worse for Gordon. That's the kind of person you propose to give a damn about."

Forde drew a shaky breath. "Oh, Faye, now wait a - "

"No, Forde. Wait for what? Some kind of miracle? I'm a rotten person, and I ought to kill myself." Faye buried her face in her hands, shoving the Major Barbara wig out of register. "I'm not worth spitting on, oh, God, and I had such a wonderful opinion of myself. I wanted to show people a thing or two, like I was some kind of Wonder Woman, the smartest, best, super ... " Faye was astonished that shame could be this complete. She lunged at Forde, not knowing what she intended, and wound up with her arms around his neck, banging on his back with both fists, Major Barbara's hair tumbling down behind her. "I will never forgive myself," she wailed. "Never, ever. Somebody should murder me, I should die, Oh, Jesus..."

Forde recognizing himself inadequate to this, threw himself around her like a doomed hero throwing himself over a hand grenade. He pressed her head against his, sliding on the tears, crooning words that meant nothing in particular. "Faye, there," he said, and felt a fool. "There, there." He racked his brain for the right thing to say, and came up only with, "There, there," again. He repeated it, softening his voice, matching it to what he hoped would feel soothing and - he laughed at himself for this, but couldn't avoid seeing it - soothingly sexy in some way. "There, there." At least, he thought, there's nothing positively, affirmatively stupid about that.

Faye seemed to find "There, there" at least not infuriating. She pulled herself onto Forde's lap to cry at the stone of guilt in her chest, to recognize at last that Sister Penitentiary was exactly right: that she, Faye Bynum, in no way otherwise than the dumbest lout in Home Room who couldn't diagram a five-word sentence, stood helplessly in need of grace. Forde's simple-minded incoherence seemed to her then the very definition of it. Maybe Sister P. would claim that it wasn't

Forde Morgan saying *There, there*, over and over, but …. She pulled back and looked into Forde's eyes. "Are you …

"Huh?" Shameful hope stirred in Forde's lap, and nudged Faye's hip, embarrassingly.

Faye saw then that it could hardly be Jesus, who comforted Faye with his *"There, there"* stuff. Anyway, Sister generally reserved Jesus and the BVM for popes and heads of state, invoking lower-grade Beatifieds to deal with the trivial likes of Faye Bynum. Mary Magdalene? Out of the question. Possibly St. Andrew, of whom Sister spoke dismissively, since the Protestants had hijacked him.

"Are you a saint?"

"Huh? Not hardly."

Faye laughed. "Never mind." And, knowing that she would bear this load of self-knowledge all the rest of her life, steeling herself to fake brightness she would never again feel, "Well. Thank you for your comfort. It was amazing. Amazingly effective. I apologize for breaking down on you. Again, no less. You must think I'm a neurotic wreck." She retrieved the wig and settled against the tree, hanging onto Forde's arm still, to keep from sliding straight down through the pine needles into Hell. And when that didn't look like happening, she acknowledged herself a new recruit to the company of treacherous and compromised humans who got through life, carrying their guilty cargo as best they could.

She reached back and took Forde's hand. "I'm so sleepy. Would it bother you if I put my head in your lap?"

"Not hardly."

"Don't get your hopes up." *Fatal Faye, the Charlotte harlot.* When she had her head nestled on his thighs, chastely facing his knees, Forde put the wig in his pocket and smoothed Faye's own dark bristle. When she closed her eyes on the steady dribble of tears, she began again to drift upward; she put a hand on Forde's shin to steady herself.

25.

A SWEEP of headlights, the racket of night bugs, and one particular bug crawling up her ankle pulled Faye into a world of chill and darkness. Blending with the bugs, the rasp and sigh of Forde Morgan's breath above her; Faye opened her eyes and sat up.

"Forde!"

"Hm? Oh, golly."

"I'll say. What in the world time do you think it is?"

"I can't see my watch. Pretty late, I guess."

Faye stood, brushed off the climbing bug, and took Forde's hand to pull him up. "I need to get home. Mrs. Merrill will die of the snoops if she catches me coming in at this hour."

"Well, we don't exactly know what hour it is." Forde stumbled to his feet.

"Well, it feels late to me."

"Uh huh. Midnight, anyhow."

"At least."

They groped and stumbled, holding hands, down to the road. When Forde opened the door to the DeSoto, the dome light let him read his watch. He whistled.

"What?"

"Well, it's almost 3:30. I'm sorry, Faye."

Faye laughed. "Don't worry. It won't ruin your reputation, and I don't have any left. So no harm done."

"It's not too late."

"Turn that key and drive me home, smarty."

He did, while Faye tried to brush most of the bugs and wrinkles out of her skirt. When they got near Mecklenburg Street, she leaned forward.

"Forde, I don't want you to think I'm such an emotional wreck as … as … Oh, wonderful. There's some kind of commotion going on by Mrs. Merrill's. There goes my chance to sneak in while she's asleep."

"Gosh," Forde said. "Look there! I think it's a fire."

When they turned the corner, they saw a flare of orange, two fire trucks, a ruck of helmeted men, and, in Mrs. Merrill's driveway, an ambulance. Forde stopped at the peremptory hand of a policeman, while Faye squeaked with dismay.

"Forde, that is Mrs. Merrill's house. Oh, gosh, look, it's really burning!"

It was. Flames licked through Mrs. Merrill's roof in two places, and smoke poured from second-floor windows. Faye ran from the car and into the grasp of the cop.

"Hold it, girlie. Got a fire going here."

"That's my house! I live there!" Faye squirmed and tried to pull away.

"Just you hold on a second. Your name Faith?"

"Faye."

"That was it. Come on over here." The cop hung on to Faye and started yelling at the ambulance. "I got 'er, she's here with me, I got 'er!" He took Faye to a little knot of people standing by the ambulance. "This here's that Faye," he said, relishing the idea.

One of the ambulance drivers turned to Faye. "Faye Beinert?"

"Bynum," Faye said. "That's me."

The driver grunted and poked his head in the back of the ambulance. "We got her, Miz Merrill. She's right here."

Faye looked in the ambulance and saw Mrs. Merrill with a mask over her face. "Oh, golly. Is she all right?"

"Jes' got a little smoke," the man next to Mrs. Merrill said. "Hauled her down the steps, what was a'ready on fahr some." He was himself black with soot.

234

Mrs. Merrill raised her head. "Faye? Oh, thank the Lord!"

"She like to kilt herself tryin' to clomb them steps up to the third," the fireman said. "Sez we cain't leave you up there. Looks like you come through pretty good,. 'Cept your hair," he added. "That'll grow right back."

"Faye, dear, how ever did you escape? I gave you up for lost."

"Well," Faye said. "I … well, it's …." She shrugged.

"Trellis? You climbed down the trellis?" Mrs. Merrill tossed aside the oxygen mask and sat up beaming "Clever girl! One of those feats of superhuman strength we read about, when good people are faced with a crisis. Well, dear, the Lord was with you."

"But," Faye said. She teetered on an edge, and looked at Mrs. Merrill. She shook her head. "No, Ma'am," she said, clearly. "I was not in my room."

"You were not? At this hour? Why, <u>Faye</u>!" Mrs. Merrill swung her feet to the ambulance floor and pursed her lips. And smiled at Faye. "Why, then the Lord must have led you to, to." She raised a palm to the world at large. "To where you would be safe. The firemen were quite sure that you could never have escaped alive. Apparently, your room is in violation of some kind of fire code. I will have some renovation to do before it is legal to rent again. And you must remember this, dear, and strive to live up to His purpose in sparing you."

"But Mrs. Merrill, your beautiful house! All your things! And Butterball, where is Butterball?"

Mrs. Merrill shook her head. "Butterball can't abide an uproar," she said. "When I had the house painted, she took to the woods for days. She's off, and won't come back for a month, I don't misdoubt. But, Faye dear, I'm afraid your things will be a complete loss. I will speak to my sister in Rock Hill, her girl Tammy that went off to Flora Macdonald was much like you in size and figure. She may have some clothing that will fit. But your books, your work …"

"Absolutely nothing of any value. You are very sweet, but you must excuse me for just a moment."

"But Faye, dear. Where will you stay tonight?"

Faye looked at the sky. "I think the night's about over, Mrs. Merrill. That gives me the day to make some arrangement. What about you?"

"I will leave for Rock Hill the moment I am able."

Faye went back into the night. The firemen seemed to be getting things under control; there were no flames on the roof, and not so much smoke coming from the windows. But the cop told her it would be hours before anyone could be sure whether it was safe to go back into the house. She went back to Forde, slumped against the fender of the DeSoto.

"Well," she said. "Here's a fine howdy-do."

Forde yawned. "Yeah. What are you going to do?"

Faye hadn't thought that far. She shook her head, and tears sprang to her eyes. "Maybe I'll have to go home. I can't count on getting another place for just a couple of weeks. There goes my Pulitzer." She looked at Forde. "Oh, don't look so ... so stricken, Forde. I told you I was a doubtful proposition, and now God, no less, according to Mrs. Merrill, seems to be taking a hand in it, that's her version of my spending the night snoring in your lap instead of being trapped in the flames. But I can't stay in Charlotte if I don't have a place to live."

"Sure. Tell you what, though. You want to come to my place for a - well, a cleanup, maybe I can find some clothes you could borrow. You can't just head for the train station like that, and without going to work first."

Faye nodded. "I'm dying to see what kind of working-girl clothes you've got stashed away. Still, I worry about the size a little."

Forde grinned. "That's the spirit."

Faye shook her head. "No spirit to it. It just seems like one thing after another comes along, and I give up on keeping track of it. Whatever crazy thing happens, that seems to be God's latest idea of a good plan for Faye. So, I give up. Lead on."

Forde gallantly held the door of the DeSoto, but before she could get in, they heard a sharp voice behind them.

"Hold on, Missy." Faye turned, and saw the cop and the sooty fireman walking toward them. Faye looked at Forde, smiled, and whispered, "God again, see?" She turned to the cop.

"Yes, sir?"

The cop said nothing, but turned to the fireman, who scratched the back of his head. "Miss, did you use a kerosene lamp up'n that room?"

"No." *Kerosene, Alice Dupree, Gordon's lost baby. Gordon.*

The cop shifted his weight. "Sure about that? Seem like you had second thoughts there for a second."

Faye turned to the cop. "No, sir. I'm just a little tired."

"Mm. No kerosene in the bathroom, closet, anything like that?"

"Not in the bathroom. I guess I couldn't guarantee about the closet, but ... No, there was no kerosene up there. I'm sure of it. Why?"

The fireman shrugged. "Pretty strong smell of it up them steps. Could have been something else, maybe. Get that when a fire gets set on purpose, though, see."

Faye sagged against the door of the DeSoto. "Well, you can get that right out of your head. I don't set fires."

"Nobody said that," the cop said. "You away from that room all night quite a bit?" He glanced at Forde, not respectfully.

"Never. I was with Mr. Morgan here, and we were out quite late, yes. But – "

"Miss Bynum and I were visiting my parents in Gabbro," Forde said. "Dinner ran late, and we didn't get on the road until after ten."

"Your folks'd back that up, of course. Gabbro's maybe three hours from here," the cop said. "Run outa gas, did you? Get a flat?"

Faye said, "Hold on, Forde. We're not going to ask your folks to back up anything. Sir, we were late getting back to Charlotte because we stopped to watch the sunset just east of town, and we both fell asleep. I can take you to the very spot, and you could probably detect the grass bent over where we were leaning on a pine tree. Separately. Let's see … why, yes, see this sticky spot on my jacket? Pine sap, go ahead, give it a sniff. Take it into the lab, why don't you?"

"Easy does it, Missy. You find somebody rents a room someplace, the place burns, maybe the fire was set, and lo an' behold, they weren't in their room that night, first time ever, to hear her tell it. Be a pretty lazy cop that didn't ask a couple questions."

Faye sighed. "OK, I see that. But why on earth would I burn down the place where I rent a room, burn up all my clothes and books, and ruin a nice old lady who, you must have seen, I am on very good terms with?"

The cop smiled. "Hard for me to figure, too, but you would be amazed at the stupid things a cop sees in thirty years. I expect we're woofing about nothing here, anyways. Don't go anywhere for a while, though, OK? Where can we reach you?"

"At the Star-Dispatch, care of Mr. Len Biggs. I'll be there until the first of September. I hope."

The cop jotted it down. "OK, honey. Go get yourself some sleep."

When they were a block away from the uproar, Faye turned to Forde. " 'Dinner with my parents ran quite late?' What kind of silly idea was that?"

Forde shrugged. "Pretty silly, I guess. I just wasn't ready to say, well, Miss Bynum and I spent all night in the woods."

Faye looked out the windshield. "So you let me say it. And the world went on turning."

Forde said nothing, drove meekly. Faye sighed. "Why don't I ever shut up, Forde? Can you figure it out?"

"No'm."

"Well, I can't blame you. God, what next?"

"Do you think somebody set that fire?"

"Oh, sure, absolutely. Somebody who hates cats. Or Mrs. Merrill set it herself, for the insurance. I know *I* didn't."

"Well, obviously. Unless you snuck off my lap, stole the keys, drove into town, set the fire, drove back, snuck the keys back into my pocket, and then woke me up. Gosh knows, you had time to."

Faye fell back against the seat, and Forde tooled Uncle Harold's DeSoto to the curb outside a rumpled and paint-peeling place called "Evening Star Transients."

"This is where you live?"

"Yup."

"Well, goodness. You mean there was one thing about your entire setup for this summer that wasn't worlds better than mine? I am stunned."

"Don't be fooled by appearances. Good ol' Evening Star is a doggone palace inside."

It wasn't. But Forde's little studio was clean and picked up, and it did have a decent bathroom. Faye was impressed. Forde produced a clean towel and a new bar of soap, as neutral and correct in this domestic setting as an undersecretary of protocol.

At eight o'clock, Faye was seated at her Star-Dispatch desk. She was clean, breakfasted courtesy of the Home Kitchen, and dressed Gibson-girlishly in one of Forde's Chinese laundered, ceramically starched white shirts and a 20-year-old skirt that Alma Brackett dug out when circumstances were explained. The rest of her outfit consisted, alas, of yesterday's underwear and socks. She figured to drop by Miss Panama's Thrift Shop over lunch. The swinging door opened to admit Alma Brackett with a manuscript in her hand.

"Where did you learn to write, Faye? You can't tell me that the high schools of St. Louis, Missouri did it."

"Not really. Those years I was out of school following Daddy's barnstorming around the Great Plains, I did nothing but sell tickets and read books."

"You sold tickets. Did he dress you up as a little aviatrix, with goggles and all?"

"Of course."

"And while Daddy scared the pants off the rubes at $5 a ride, you read books. It would be hard to imagine Harvard putting together a better writing curriculum. I certainly see echoes of Will Rogers and Dorothy Parker in this piece." Alma Brackett dropped the manuscript on Faye's desk and sighed. "Well, all that is by way of softening the blow. Elaine, Harold, and Len Biggs have outvoted me on the Ibsen story and the reference to the Klan."

"They outvoted you? I thought you owned this place."

"I am the majority stockholder, and I suppose I could enforce my wishes by bringing the matter to a formal vote at a duly called meeting of all stockholders. That would take no less than sixty days."

"Well – " Faye was sure Alma Brackett was bluffing, but she couldn't see why.

"There are other considerations. A victory on this matter would come at the price of prevailing on other questions that are, frankly, of greater moment. The rest of the piece is charming, and will certainly run above the fold, with a byline. Your first, I believe."

"The Ibsen story shows something very important about your mother, that she is kind and quick-witted at her age. She invented it out of bits and pieces, just to make me feel better about Courtenay Weston."

"Yes. I have already congratulated her on it. But it hinges on sexual matters in general, and a bosom in particular. Also, 98 percent of the readership will miss the joke entirely."

"Well, it's their loss. But why cut out the Klan reference? Is this more heads-in-the-sand about Charlotte's dirty secret?"

"Yes, if you want to put it that way. But where does it get us for you to do so?"

Faye fumed, gestured, sat back down. "Wouldn't we be doing a service to the community by exposing this ... this festering blight?" Faye looked past Alma Brackett at the door to the outer hall swinging shut behind a familiar figure. "This boil that so badly needs lancing? This cancer – "

"Miss Faye Bynum?"

It was Detective Lieutenant Meyer, holding Faye's eyes and flashing a badge.

"Oh, for heaven's sake, Meyer. Yes, I am still Faye Bynum, as far as I know. Can we make it snappy? I'm in a conference here. May I introduce Mrs. Alma Brackett?"

"Too late," Meyer said. "I known Alma Brackett for years. How do, Ma'am?"

"How do you do, Lieutenant. How can we help you?"

"You can let me take Miss Bynum downtown without a struggle."

Alma Brackett nodded. "Don't struggle, will you, Faye? I understand there was quite a dust-up in the break room the other day."

Faye looked from Alma Brackett to Meyer. "Wait a minute. Now what?"

Meyer leaned in and lowered his voice. "Had some developments in your friend's death, and Chief'd like to ask you about them."

Faye narrowed her eyes. "All right. I hope this is not another of your little tricks, Meyer. I still haven't got over the last one, and I'm already worried, you just gave me what seemed like a direct answer to a question."

"Give you all you want, just ask."

Faye snorted. "What kind of developments?"

Meyer leaned back and took a pack of cigarettes out of his pocket. "The blood on that dress ain't yours. Should we continue this in a quieter place, you think?"

26.

T HE ROOM was painted lemon yellow. It had a naked overhead bulb, a mirror on one wall, three chairs, and a table. Faye sat in one of the chairs, Meyer opposite her. He leaned on the table and tapped a pencil.

"Come on, Miss Bynum. You got your boy friend's blood on your skirt, you don't know nothing about how it got there?"

"I told you, no. As far as I know, that blood was from me."

"Wrong type. The late Corporal was O-positive, you're B-negative."

"I don't recall giving you a blood sample."

"You wouldn't. You were passed out on the floor of the morgue. I took the liberty of getting a swab from your chin after you cracked it on the slab." He shrugged. "Plus, that's what it says on your donor card. You must get a lot of calls for it."

"You went into my wallet, too?" Faye shrugged. "OK, I had O-positive blood on my skirt. That's the most common blood type."

"Yeah, and?"

"So it wasn't necessarily Gordon's."

"True, I guess. You kill somebody else that day too?"

"I didn't kill anybody, any day."

"Well, I'm glad to hear it. Though I gotta say, you don't sound real sure about it."

"I was – I had just lost a baby, and I'm still grieving about that. I feel terrible about Gordon being killed. I dream about killing people every night. All right, I'll even admit that I got him into a fight, hoping – no, knowing, that he would get beat up some. You don't think I could beat him up like that by myself, do you?"

Meyer shrugged. "Probably not, 'less you had some help. You were pregnant?"

"Not by the time Gordon was killed. I told you, I lost the baby. That's where all the blood came from."

"Not all of it. Too bad the panties disappeared, though. That'd lend a certain air of believability to all this other stuff. Tell me about these dreams."

"What other stuff? Why won't you believe me?"

A door opened and Chief Olerud came in. "Meyer, I warned you once about this kind of crap. She's just a young girl."

Meyer shrugged and snorted. "Yeah, so was Lizzie Borden."

Olerud sat down next to Meyer and patted Faye's elbow. "Listen, Hon, you gotta understand, Lieutenant Meyer hates when soldiers get killed, and he kind of loses perspective, I guess you'd call it. You want a Kleenex?" Holding one under Faye's eyes.

Faye nodded, and blew her nose.

"That's a girl. Now, really, just relax and think back. I know you want to get to the bottom of this as much as we do. You don't know how you got that blood on your skirt?"

Faye shook her head. "I thought it was mine, so it was embarrassing, of course, but it never occurred to me to wonder where it came from. I didn't even try to wash it out."

Meyer shuffled his feet. "That don't mean nothing, chief. She just never thought we'd suspect – "

Olerud turned on Meyer. "Meyer, don't try and tell me what to think, you got all you can do with your own head. Run out and get this little girl a sandwich and a coke, make yourself useful."

Meyer scraped his chair back and slammed out the door; Olerud shook his head. "Now, look, Miss Bynum," he said. "I knew right off you were a smart girl, and much too smart to get yourself into the kind of trouble Meyer keeps trying to put on you. You might be glad to know, by the way, I gave him a reprimand for that stunt he pulled on you with Simmons' corpse."

"Delighted," Faye said. "But isn't it obvious just from that, that I didn't have anything to do with Gordon's death? Anything direct, I mean." Faye subsided, leaning her forehead on her fist. *Nothing but cause it.* "He was beaten to death by Klan thugs," she whispered.

Ivar Olerud sighed. "Yes, miss. So you told us. Trouble is, see, Meyer don't believe that, and, honestly, between us, neither do I. I'd be the first to know if there was Klan activity in Charlotte, wouldn't I?"

Faye slumped in her chair. "Evidently not. Heavens, Chief, even one of the other interns at the Star-Dispatch had read up on it. What do you call it when a bunch of men dress up in white sheets and walk through the streets of your city, that you're supposed to be keeping order in, and beat people up?"

Olerud leaned back and looked at Faye for a full minute. Faye looked back, then away.

"What do you call it, Miss Bynum, when a couple of kids from somewhere nobody heard of, come here and see things nobody else ever said nothing about? A couple kids, what I understand, that spent the night in the woods last night. I call it not too surprising, when they seem to tell the same story, that nobody else can back up. You and this Morgan kid decide between you to get rid of Simmons, is that it?"

Faye gaped at Olerud, and started to laugh.

"That tickle your funnybone, Miss Bynum?"

"You think Forde Morgan was my secret lover, and he and I killed Gordon? That's not just funny, it's crazy. In the first place, Forde is a decent, gentle boy who wouldn't hurt – no, I take it back. Sometimes I think he might want to hurt a fly, but he'd have trouble. Gordon would have made mincemeat out of him."

"Not if Simmons was distracted by you, and Morgan sneaked up behind him with a ball bat. Had a murder in Rockingham last year worked just like that. Lady says to her hubby, 'Honey, put your head in my lap and get cozy,' and when the guy does, her boyfriend comes around the corner with a Louisville Slugger, stoves in the old man's skull. Coroner says the injuries to Simmons' skull are consistent with that."

"With what? 'Honey, get cozy?' or with a boyfriend around the corner? Your coroner must be a genius."

"You didn't say that to Simmons? What did you say?"

"I told him – "

There was a tap on the door, and Meyer entered with a paper-wrapped sandwich and a Grapette. "Sorry to interrupt, Chief. McKenzie says he's on duty, and do you need him to stay around?"

"Bring him in."

Meyer went out, and Olerud leaned close to Faye. "Think about this. We have a witness who says you admitted killing Simmons."

"What? That's crazy. Who?"

"Just think about it." The door opened, and Meyer returned with the fireman who'd asked her about kerosene last night. Or this morning, whenever. Faye yawned and goggled at the fireman. He still had streaks of soot on his face.

"Miss Bynum, this is Fireman Homer McKenzie, CFD," Olerud said. "He tells me it's likely that the unfortunate fire where you live was deliberately set. Arson."

Faye sighed. "So I understand. And, let me guess. You figure I set it to cover up my murder of Mrs. Merrill's cat."

"Somebody killed her cat? Why'd you do that?"

"Oh, I didn't, for Pete's sake," Faye said. "It's just the sort of stupid idea you'd come up with next."

Olerud raised his eyebrows and nodded. "I see. Well, of course, some of us were never child prodigies. Tell you what, Miss Bynum, how'd you like to spend the night here in a cell with us?"

Faye unwrapped the sandwich and took a bite. "That," she said around it, "would solve a big problem for me."

*

Alma Brackett looked up in annoyance. If that kid didn't stop mooning around her desk –

"You still didn't hear anything?"

"Mr. Morgan, you will be – well, no, not the first. You will be high on my list of those to inform, should I receive any communication whatsoever from Miss Bynum. Don't you have work you should be doing?"

"Yes'm." Forde turned away, and spun back as Alma Brackett's phone rang.

"Star-Dispatch, Alma Brackett speaking." Alma Brackett kept a neutral face as she listened to the voice on the line. It sounded faint and feminine to Forde Morgan, but he supposed that most of Alma Brackett's callers sounded about the same.

"I see," Alma Brackett said. "You're sure.... very well, yes. I think I can persuade someone to bring you some things." Here a look at Forde, a finger beckoning. "Do you wish to speak to him?"

Forde blinked, mouthed, "Me?"

"Of course, you," Alma Brackett said. "Make it snappy, she's calling from jail."

"From ... H – hello?"

"Forde, hi. All my clothes burned up, what I'm in is getting to need changing, and I'm in jail. Could you go down to Miss Panama's, on Tryon Street, and pick me up some new things?"

"But ... Um. I guess. Yeah, sure."

"Oh, you're a darling. Get Alma Brackett to give you the five dollars she owes me, and a shopping list, all right?"

"But ..."

"I have to go, OK? There's a big line for this phone."

"OK, but Faye ..."

"We'll talk when you get here. Thanks so much, Forde. I owe you a great big favor."

"Faye?" But the line was dead. Forde looked at Alma Brackett. "Jail? Why is she in jail?"

"I'm sure I don't know. It may have to do with her fiancé being deceased, do you think? I shouldn't be surprised. No matter, she didn't kill him, and any writer worth his salt spends some time in jail. Have you done time yet?"

Forde looked troubled. "No. She didn't kill ... She says you'll give me a shopping list and some money you owe her, and I'm supposed to buy her some clothes. Gosh, Miss Brackett, I can't shop for ladies' clothes."

"Can you not? Well, she'll just have to go dirty then. I certainly have no time for it, and you surely do not suggest Wil or Shanky, do you? Or Len Biggs?"

"No, I ... no."

"That's settled, then. Here, let's see. Shopping at Miss Panama's, I should think you could clothe her stunningly for three or four dollars."

"She says you owe her five."

"Hmf. Well, I won't put you into the middle of that. Here is five dollars. You can have her looking like Ginger Rogers for that. Of course, she'll need simple sturdy things that will wear well. And clean underwear, of course. Just a moment, I'll start from the most essential. Panties, three pairs. Brassieres – I don't suppose you know Faye's bra size, do you?"

Time and Chance

Ten minutes later, Forde Morgan left the offices of the Star-Dispatch and slunk three blocks across town to Miss Panama's Thrift Center, where, wordless and crimson, he laid a list and a five-dollar bill on the counter before Miss Panama.

*

Being in jail felt like freedom to Faye, like laying down for a while the burdens of propriety, of braininess and gender, and very nearly of sanity itself. What now about Gordon, about hope and virtue and career, about deadlines? Don't look at me, I'm in jail. They think I killed my fiancé, which is true, but not the way they think it is. And Olerud had gone over the ground with her again, at length, late in the afternoon, possibly hoping that sheer fatigue would produce a confession, if there was one to be had from her. Faye considered confessing to Gordon's murder, since in her, Sister Penitentia's, and God's eyes, it was the truth; but then realized that no prosecutor in the world would bring a case that relied entirely on a guilty conscience. Here was just another thing that, like the pre-Gordon days of the summer, would belong forever to Faye alone.

Her cell was long and narrow, done up in a palette of stains, with a porcelain horror on the back wall that made the Whites-Only Ladies' at the Winnsboro rest stop antiseptic in retrospect. There was a sink and a three-legged stool. The double bunk bore mattresses, stained and without linens, but Faye was provided with a sheet, a rough blanket, and a towel by the cellblock keeper, a matron called Queenie.

Faye vowed not to let the place intimidate or depress her. She recognized Olerud's claim of a witness to her admitting she killed Gordon as a bluff; she had never said any such thing to anyone but Alma and Rose Brackett, and both knew better than to believe her. She curled up on the lower bunk with her notebook and pencil, and began to plan a "jailhouse dispatch," something she knew the Star-Dispatch would never print, but might make a good essay for the journalism folks at Mizzou. She would ask Queenie about a typewriter and paper in the morning.

I write from a cell at the Charlotte-Mecklenburg County jail. My cell is Spartan and dark, with a single barred window in the door...

She woke in the middle of the night from a nightmare about an octopus, to find herself dragged onto the floor by a skinny woman with muscle and makeup who shot a thumb over her shoulder.

"Top bunk or floor, sweetheart. Bottom one's mine."

Faye, glad enough that it wasn't a real octopus, blinked and shrugged. "OK." She climbed into the top bunk, then hung her head over the side. "What about sheets?"

"What about 'em?" Not looking up, pulling off ragged nylons.

"Those are mine down there. Didn't they give you a packet of linens?"

There followed a silence, followed by the rustle of sheets and a sigh. "Nuh uh. Guess you lose out, huh?"

"No, but ..."

"Shut it, will ya, kiddo? I'm tryna sleep here." There was a further, and final-sounding, rustle, and a muttered, "*Linens*. Sheese."

The rest of the night passed slowly, and with some tears on Faye's part. Once she accepted that she would not sleep, she began to think about her jailhouse dispatch, but the notebook and pencil were still in the bottom bunk where she'd left them. She rolled onto her back and locked her hands under her head, to keep her nose and mouth as far as possible from the bare mattress, which looked like a museum of disease and fluid nastiness. Convinced that she would never sleep again, she fell into a doze and woke at dawn to find herself in a fetal curl against the night chill, her open mouth pressed against the mattress. Her stomach heaved, and she sat up. The woman in the bottom bunk was snoring, but there was a stir from the hall, and the rattle of some kind of cart. Voices rose around it, coughs and protests, words that were new to Faye, but that she recognized as vile. As the cart drew nearer, the voices trailed off. Faye concluded that she and her gruff cellmate were by themselves at the end of an empty stretch. The cart stopped outside their cell, and Queenie hollered through the barred window.

"Rise up and shine for Jesus, ladies. Gloriana, you got a court appearance at eight, you better shake your tail. Faye, some fella brang you a package a clothes."

"Oh," Faye said. "Oh, good. Thank heavens. Can I have them now?"

"Not 'less you lookin to arm-rassle Gloriana for 'em. I'll bring 'em by after she gone to her show-up. Glor, I thoughten I told you, move your cheap ass."

Gloriana turned on her bunk and blew a raspberry at the door. "Whyn't you stick it up your dyke nose, Queenie? What time's it?"

"Time for whores to hit the bricks, an' then some. Don't make me come in there swingin."

Gloriana muttered, "Don't come at all, what I care." But Faye heard a jangle of keys and the heavy lock snapped open. Queenie banged her cart through the door and brought out two tin plates heaped with grits. A wooden spoon stuck from the top of each, as if adorning a banana split. "Compliments a Meck County, from the heavenly kitchen of Miz Marvelle Olerud," she announced. "Don't let me see none of it go to waste."

When she was gone, Faye said, "It's a little after seven. Are you really a ... you know. What she called you?"

Gloriana snorted. "Crissake, kid, you got me wrong. I'm Dorothy Lamour, an' I'm in here 'cause they think I seduced Bing Crosby. I'll get off, though, the Pope's a buddy of mine."

Faye grinned. "You too?"

"Me too what? You a buddy of his? I never seen you around the palace."

"No. I meant you got a smart mouth that gets you into trouble. Me too."

"That so? Lemme look at you."

Gloriana's face rose above the bunk, and she and Faye surveyed each other, Faye spooning cold grits while she looked solemnly at Gloriana. Gloriana looked, Faye thought, maybe forty years old, though her mouth was full and vulnerable, the mouth of a much younger woman. She had the remains of a shiner, and her nose was a little off-center. Gloriana piffed a burst of morning breath at Faye.

"What happened to your hair?"

"Some Klan ..." Faye stopped. "It's a long story. How did you get to be a ... a prostitute?"

Gloriana shrugged. "Think you got a long story." She turned and braced herself over the toilet, her dress hiked around her waist. "You thinking of getting into the profession? Take my advice, scrub shithouses. It pays better, and the conditions are nicer."

"I bet. Do you have a heart of gold?"

Gloriana shook her head, standing pigeon-toed to pull up a pair of nylon panties. "Try me, next time you feel like a good cry. If I had a toenail of gold, Ivar Olerud would of yanked it out by now."

"Olerud? The chief?"

"We got more than one? Naw, he ain't my problem, though, I wrong the man. He's too high up. You got a hairbrush?"

"You think I give my hair a hundred strokes every morning to keep it shiny? You look OK."

"For a hooker?"

"For anybody. Don't you want to quit? Get a job, get married?"

"What's it to you?"

Faye shrugged, and said nothing.

"Well, let me tell you, cookie. This is a job you don't quit."

"Why not?"

Gloriana laughed. "Excuse me. I misspoke. There is a way to quit, which is to tell your pimp you quit. Then they find you under the bridge in a day or two, or maybe not. Do I make myself clear, here?"

Faye stared. "He'd kill you if you quit? Where does that get him?" Feeling fairly sophisticated here, not boggling at murder or pimpdom, making a hard-headed logical point.

Gloriana smiled. "Where's it get me, a'd be a better question. The Pee Dee River, after a while. I suppose some parts might float down far as the ocean. Where it gets him is, the other girls are less likely to act up, they see what happened to me." She sat on her bunk and fished under it for her shoes.

Faye scowled at the toilet, which was finishing a noisy job of flushing. "Can't you go to the police?"

Gloriana shook her head. "Honey, you gonna have me in stitches here. They'd be cutting off their own dicks, they bother him." She came over and leaned on Faye's upper bunk. "Who do you think the pimp pays, to keep his license? But, see, there's worse than cops, a mile worse."

"Who?"

Gloriana's mouth turned down. "Uh-uh, Cookie. The walls got ears. And besides ..."

"What?"

"Nothing. Never mind. You know what's good for you, keep your nose clean on this, hear? I gotta show up in court so's the judge can gimme a public lecture about decency."

"Well, what if you told him why you can't quit?"

"Think he don't know? Maybe I'll remind him next time, though. He's one of my Thursday regulars. 'Bye now."

Gloriana went to the door and banged her grits bowl on the bars. "Queenie, you mis'ble piece a chicken shit, lemme outa here."

Queenie appeared with suspicious promptness, stubbing a cigarette on the window bars. "You look like scrambled eggs yourself, Glor. I reckon we're even."

Gloriana blew her a razzberry. "Bye, kiddo. You watch your ass, hear? Don't end up giving me no competition." As they walked down the hall, Faye heard, "Next time, put me in with one a the queers. Kid like that could give you the willies."

Time and Chance

27.

M *Y STORY is tame and ordinary beside my cell-mate's, a ~~prostitute~~ streetwalker I'll call ~~Daisy~~ ~~Courtenay~~ Elaine.*

Faye was trying to think of an alias for Gloriana that would do her justice when Queenie clacked open the cell door.

"Hello, Queenie."

"Hello to you, little princess. I brang you the clothes."

"Oh, fine. Put them on the bunk, will you? I'll look at them in a minute. Do you think I could have a typewriter and some paper?"

Queenie snorted. "Why, Princess, your wish is my orders ta jump. Sure, I could buy you a typewriter downtown, you gimme a fi'tty percent commission for my trouble. How come you be so cool about jail? You think you cain't rot here for life?"

"Queenie, I expect I could do that, if I said the wrong thing to the wrong person. Just, for a little while, jail is kind of a relief compared to what was going on outside. Are you the wrong person to say that to?"

Queenie pursed out her lips, and smiled. "I am the wrong person to come all high horse to, that's a fact. Your horse ain't that high. Anyways, you be walkin out today some time. High type girls like you, somebody always writs 'em a alias corpus."

"I don't think I'm such a high type. I'm broke and I got nowhere to live, and my folks are broke, and my Daddy's a leadfoot drunk."

"OK, but you think you are cool and smart, and you will not be trifled with, ain't that so?"

Faye wandered to the bunk and took down the packet of clothing. "Maybe so. I'm the last one to ask about that. I am also ignorant about how things work in this town." She paused a moment.

"Any other town, come to think of it. This is just the first one where it made any difference." Faye opened the package of clothing and took out some worn-looking underwear. "Queenie, in your opinion, what is worse than a cop?"

"What's that, some kind of game? A robber."

"No. Gloriana told me she couldn't quit being a – a prostitute, because her… well, her pimp would kill her." Faye blushed at herself and thanked God her mother couldn't hear this. She gladly shucked out of such underwear as she could without stripping naked, and put on a pair of apparently clean cotton panties that faded from robin's egg blue at the waistband to a dubious foggy color at the business end. "But then she said, first of all, the cops are in cahoots with the pimps, and then that there's somebody worse than cops behind all that. 'A mile worse,' she said. If I'm supposed to figure out what's what, I guess I'd need to know what she's talking about."

Queenie pulled out a cigarette and lit it, shaking her head. "Honey, you don't need no such a thing. She's nuts. My advice to you is, don't you open your mouth to nobody else like you just done. You are a lucky girl you didn't blather this kind of junk to Chief, or …" She shook her head and looked Faye up and down. "Other folks. Try on that sailor blouse there. Might go pretty good with your hairdo."

"Wait a minute. You're saying there's somebody worse than pimps, worse than crooked cops and hypocrite judges, and I should just shut up about it? So you like it that way?"

"I didn't say no such thing. I didn't say nothing, which I recommend to you, if you're smart. Come on, get them clothes on, you got company."

"Forde?"

"Don't know no Forde. Change your clothes. Ain't nobody watching."

Faye finished stripping under Queenie's benevolent eye, and put on the sailor blouse and a patched blue skirt. When she was dressed, Queenie whistled to someone out of sight, and Faye heard footsteps in the corridor, a sauntering sh-clack of heel taps. Det. Lt. Larry Meyer came into view, chewing a toothpick.

"Paid your debt to society, little lady? Ready to re-enter the world of lawful pursuits outside?"

"It's been relaxing here, just not seeing you for a while," Faye said. "You can't think what a treat that's been."

Meyer scowled. "Don't be smart with me, Honey, will ya? I'd hate to have to make up more reasons to keep you. But I'll tell you, I got a million, and resisting arrest, insulting an officer, and suspicion of murder and arson don't begin to scratch the surface."

"I can imagine," Faye said, hating her own bravado.

"Yeah, well. Seems like they missed you enough around the paper that they blew some lawyer money on you. You're released into the recognizance of the Star-Dispatch. Your boss is on the way down to take custody."

"Alma Brackett?"

Meyer grinned. "Can you imagine? The lady passed up the chance. Naw, I believe it's ol' Len Biggs."

Len Biggs arrived after a tedious hour, toward the end of which Gloriana strutted down the line of cells, accompanied by whistles and suggestions, and stopped at Faye's cell.

"Crap," she said. "Dunno why Queenie thought I might snatch that little sailor suit from you. You see me in that, down on Tryon Street? Only business I'd get a'd be perverts."

"Glad you like it."

"Yeah, listen," Gloriana said, putting her head close to the bars. "Seem like I hearn you was working for the newspaper."

"That's right. What about it?"

Gloriana opened her mouth, closed it, and looked over her shoulder. She seemed to Faye to change her mind two or three times before she spoke; and then it was with a dismissive smirk. "Couple johns of mine work there is all. Wind up with ink on my ass every time. You watch yourself around them guys, hear? I told you there was worse than cops."

"What's that mean? Who? Olerud one time almost told me about somebody called 'Unk.' Who's that?"

Gloriana drew a sudden breath. "Jesus, Princess, that where you got that hairdo? Somebody's tryna get you assassinated, I think. Listen, forget it, it's more than I shouldn'ta said. Just watch your heinie, which I bet you already do, so why am I wasting my breath? So long, kid."

"Wait ... "

Gloriana jerked a thumb at the far end of the corridor. "Speak a the devil, there's my Sunday afternoon. So long, hon. Keep your legs crossed."

She headed for the exit, averting her face from the echo of approaching footsteps. Faye opened her mouth, shut it, and went to sit, legs crossed, on the rumpled lower bunk. Len Biggs was at the door with Queenie before Gloriana's heels had clicked through the door to the courtroom and freedom. Len seemed discomfited and grouchy about his assignment.

"There you are, Misch Bynum. Gather up your things, if you will, and we'll go."

Faye rose, and picked up the paper sack of clothing, pencil, and notebook.

"Why did she say that?"

"What?"

"Oh. Nothing. Mr. Biggs, you have a lot of experience with crime in Charlotte, don't you? Is there someone, something that's 'worse than the cops' here? Something above the law? Somebody called ... " *Jesus, Princess, just shut your mouth once, can't you?*

"A jailbird been singing to you? That everything?" Tipping his head at the bag.

"It's just a rumor, I guess."

"Probably. Ready to go?"

"Yes, sir."

Settled again at the <u>Star-Dispatch</u> behind a stack of crime-news assignments, Faye pulled out her jailhouse dispatch, recognized what she had as cliché, and stuffed it in her purse. She picked up a sheet of crime statistics, read down through the melancholy recital of burglaries, utterings of threats, assaults, and frauds, and put it down again, dizzy with exhaustion. She ran a sheet of copy paper into her typewriter.

The Queen is sick. She pretends otherwise, and no courtier dares to contradict her, but she is sick. Her color is off, and her appetite the same. Her hands tremble, and she is full of doubt, full of fears, and of enterprise dead a-borning. She has not had a new idea in decades, her crops are stunted, and her people wake reluctantly, drag through days of empty make-work, and go to bed early for lack of reason to stay awake. And while they sleep, the pale, malignant agents of her cancer roam at large, attacking, burning, destroying,

Faye looked up to see Alma Brackett leaning against Wil Osborne's desk..

"I haven't see keys pounded like that since V-J Day. On to something hot, are we?"

"Yes."

"Well, I won't detain you. Mother suggests that, in view of the difficulties with your former residence, you might wish to move in with us for the rest of the summer. We could put you in that spare room you used the other day. I would save on laundering your sheets for a few days. On the understanding, of course, that this would be a strictly short-term arrangement, and that you would try to stay out of prison while you are with us. When were you planning to return to the Middle West?"

"At the end of August."

"That will be in a bit over two weeks. We can put up with a guest for that length of time. Mother is quite fond of you."

"I would be reluctant to intrude."

Alma Brackett looked at the ceiling, and again at Faye, this time with a barely detectable curl to the left side of her mouth. "Very well. Let's suppose I am rather fond of you myself. Would that tip the scales sufficiently, relative to homelessness or incarceration?"

Faye nodded. "Yes, Ma'am. Thank you very much."

… undoing the best efforts of the Queen's healthy members.

'Healthy members,' for God's sake. Faye cringed and recognized that Allegory was not going to take her where she wanted to go, and that in any case, as Alma Brackett would have said, 98% of the readership would miss the point. She ripped the thing out of the typewriter and put in a fresh sheet.

The Ku Klux Klan roams at large in Charlotte, North Carolina on this day, terrifying, burning crosses, assaulting and killing with impunity.

"Misch Bynum?"

Faye looked up. "Yes, sir?"

Len Biggs stood at the swinging door. "Chief Olerud will be giving a conference on allegationsh of Klan activity in Charlotte at noon. Right up your alley, apparently. Can you cover it?"

Faye stared. "Yes, sir."

"Better get a move on, then."

Time and Chance

Faye glanced at the wall clock by the swinging doors, saw a quarter to twelve, and ran for the door.

The news conference in the police headquarters conference room was a whitewash that started a half hour late, and lasted ten minutes. Olerud read a statement that strung together a denial that there had ever been Klan activity in Charlotte, that it had ended for good in 1910, that the ringleaders were known to the police, and that arrests were imminent. He took a few baffled questions from radio reporters, ignoring Faye's waving hand, and exited through a back door. Faye left, fuming, picked up a BLT and a coke at Kress, and dawdled munching toward the Star-Dispatch offices. She was reluctant to go back into Len Biggs' presence, and without thinking about it, let her feet drift homeward. By the time she'd finished the sandwich, she was on Mrs. Merrill's block.

A lot of half-burned furnishings were scattered on the lawn; Faye recognized with a pang the frame and the torn canvas of "Autumn Splendour." The sign, "L. Merrill, Transients and Long-Term," was leaning under the weight of a charred window frame. Funny, Faye thought. I never did see any sign of a Long-Term. She walked across trampled grass toward the front door.

Deliberately set. Arson. Chief Olerud, the institutional liar. Having him say it was arson was pretty much a guarantee that it was accidental. The front door stood ajar, the latch broken, probably by a fireman. August heat and a stench of burn hung over the ruined house, silent except for the half-hearted jeer of a locust in the catalpas across the street. Faye considered whether Alma Brackett would have been so impressed by her article about Rose Brackett that she might consider one about Mrs. Merrill. It would certainly beat trying to make something sensible of Chief Olerud. Of course, Mrs. Merrill had not been forthcoming about her sister's address or phone number, and without an interview, it would be hard to come up with much except her own reminiscences of Mrs. Merrill's hairdo and her cat. She had never even told Faye what the "L." in "L. Merrill" stood for, or even if it were her initial in the first place, or that of the absent "Merrill" with whom Mrs. Merrill had so often wrangled and made up so heart-warmingly. Faye felt sweat on her forehead and a warning tickle below her heart. She stepped through the door.

The hall carpet was still wet, and smelled of cat urine. From overhead came a steady tapping, that Faye convinced herself was water dripping. Alarming, the thought that it had dripped like that for more than a day. Draining from the attic, Faye supposed, from insulation soaked by firehoses. She began to climb the stairs, the tickle in her belly growing at every step, until Faye had to acknowledge it as fear. It seemed to Faye that something very bad lay ahead, something that she could not turn and flee, but would have to accept.

The landing was blocked by a mound of trash: water-soaked clothing, newspapers, unidentifiable grey things with charred edges. Faye held her breath and stepped over it while it squished and tangled at her feet. Faye felt a crushing guilt at the sight and feel of it. *Another fine mess you've got us into.* Small, apologetic laughter burst from her lips. *This is not so bad. I can stand this, whatever it is that waits for me up here.* Faye smiled a little at her own stupid bravado.

The stairs ended at the second-floor hall. The smells here were worse, but they were lightened by a drift of fresh air whose origin was not clear. Faye passed the doorway to Mrs. Merrill's bedroom, and saw beyond it the puddle into which water from the attic tapped with melancholy regularity, keeping time to nothing. Beyond it, Faye saw the desk where Mrs. Merrill kept her accounts, like the receipted "Statement of Tenancy" she had presented to Faye every week, even though Faye had paid nothing until Daddy's two-month advance payment ran out at the beginning of August.

Faye opened the door to the attic stairs, and discovered the source of the fresh air. Half of the attic was gone, including the landing and the room she'd occupied – finished off, but very much a part of the attic furnace. The stairs led part way to a hole burned through the back of the roof, and to nothing else but a view of scorched oak branches against silver-blue sky. Faye stood at the foot of the steps and listened to the pounding of blood in her ears. The stairway and walls were black and peeling, ending in the weightless patterns of charred wood. So, easily, might her life have ended in the same emptiness.

Is this what I was dreading to see? It didn't feel that bad to Faye, though the tickle of dread remained below her heart, stronger now but not apparently related to the devastation before her. She put a tentative foot on the first step, and found it sturdy. Shunning the blistered and wobbly hand rail, she took another step, and another. At the fourth step, she could see the naked black rafters, like the bones of one burned beyond recognition. She heard an ashy creaking sound, and decided she'd gone far enough. A sweet, homelike note crept through the burnt smell of the stairway, something not quite strong enough to identify, but with overtones of coziness.

I am following the scent of my childhood, like a salmon returning to spawn. Faye shook her head, angry at its nonsense. She'd had quite enough of spawning this summer. She couldn't put a recollection to the sweet smell, overridden as it was by the stench of wet ash.

Faye leaned forward, pushing memory, trying to discount the smell of char. A night smell, deeper than anything in her childhood, the smell ... of kerosene. Ah. The flavor that saturated the Dupree house, and that Fireman Homer McKenzie claimed to have smelled here on the night of the fire, while he struggled up these same blazing stairs trying to rescue Faye in absentia. She retreated, and stood in the doorway.

Someone had poured kerosene here, lit it, and fled, hoping to incinerate Faye and caring nothing about Mrs. Merrill, immersed in the sleep of the deaf a few feet away. Faye knew she should be angry, but the indignation would not rise. What she felt instead was emptiness, as if someone had opened her to the vacuum of space, leaving a void where once there were talent, hopes, and plans.

Talent, yes. Faye turned and dragged her feet to the head of the second-floor landing. The emptiness she felt was all but unbearable. It was not because of the arson, or the emptiness at the top of the stairway. That only spoke to her of a deeper nothingness, of a life without family, without friends, without hope. Faye started to walk back down past the mess on the landing and out of this house.

As she waded over the mound of soggy debris on the landing, she saw the envelope of one of Gordon's letters, discarded weeks ago but saved from incineration by the tightness with which she had wadded it. She could not remember now whether it was the impatience of early summer or the wounded fury of betrayal that had powered her fist. The thing sprawled across one of Mrs. Merrill's floppy slippers, soaked open by water, pale as a corpse. Is that it? Is that the dread thing, that Gordon is gone and I killed him? I know that by heart, and I don't need poignant crap like you to remind me. Faye picked up the envelope and turned it over gently, so it wouldn't tear any more. The postmark was blurred and partly burned. She made out "-947." The year all hell broke loose.

Faye shook her head. She had seen what the house had to show her, and nothing in it – not the fire's devastation, nor her own brush with death, or the very real death of what life had been hers in June and July, before Horatio Haney and Gordon and Courtenay blundered and blasted through it with their so much greater needs – none of those measured up to the ache of desolation she felt, the load of dread under her heart. The smells, away from the sunned wreckage of the attic, were of dampness, of dusk and mildew. This house was crushing her, she could not get out of it fast enough. She stumbled down the stairs, feet splattering on the saturated stair runner, and stepped on something fanged and alive, something that sank needles into her leg.

Time and Chance

Faye screamed and yanked her leg away, and found herself in a dive, having barely time to think, This was what I dreaded; I will break my neck. Death or paralysis? She yelled as *Love's Awakening* wheeled across her vision; she ricocheted off it and banged against the railing on the outside of the stairs. The railing, already weakened by usage and rot, moaned and let her pass, crashing with her to the hallway below. Sprawling and headlong, Faye caught her left arm between two of the staves of the banister. As she and the banister plowed into Mrs. Merrill's telephone table, she felt a sudden numbness in the trapped arm. She crashed to the floor and lay there breathless and stunned. There was an instant of silence; then an inhuman moan rose from the ruined stairway above her. A ragged and spiky creature ran down the steps, hissing fury, and out the front door.

"For God's sake," Faye said to no one. "Butterball."

28.

F ORDE MORGAN looked up reluctantly from his typewriter. He considered himself graduated from Len Biggs, though Len did not, recruiting him time and again to run stupid errands, and then chivvying him about assignments not finished at deadline.

"Sir?"

"Where'd your girl friend get to?"

"Sir?"

"Brilliant, Morgan. Our jailbird geniusch. Bynum."

"I don't think she would consider herself my girl friend, sir."

"Irrelevant. Where the hell did she get to?"

Len Biggs had a couple of pieces of copy in his hand, and he looked mad. Forde settled on the unhelpful truth as the quickest way through this. "I haven't seen her since this morning, sir. Didn't you send her to a news conference downtown?"

"That was at noon. It's three goddamn thirty, practically. Damn kid. Go find her, Morgan. You oughta be able to handle that."

"Yes, sir." Forde rose and indicated the copy in his typewriter. "May I pass off this business about the library trustees to somebody?"

"You may not. You'll have Bynum back here before four, plenty of time to finish it, if you have to work on it all night. Get going."

"Yessir. Where was this news conference?"

"Mecklenburg jail. Get." Len clapped his hands as if shooing a cat; Forde got.

By the time he reached the street, Forde realized that Faye was almost certainly not still at the Mecklenburg County offices, unless she was in jail again. He stopped at Kress Drug and phoned Alma Brackett.

"Mr. Len sent me off to hunt down Faye," he said. "Have you seen her since lunchtime? Is she doing something for you?"

"I have not, and she is not." Alma Brackett sounded like she was scotching a rumor.

"Well, if she comes in, would you please tell her Mr. Len wants to see her pretty urgently, and I'm looking for her. I don't guess you have any idea where she would be?"

"She is going to move in with mother and me, since her prior residence burned. She may be there, or seeing how extensive the damage was at Mrs. Merrill's. I believe that she has only the clothes you bought her – congratulations on the middie blouse, by the way, it's perfect for her – beyond what she may be able to salvage. Kindly do not go and ring my doorbell. Mother generally naps at this hour."

"Yes, Ma'am."

The futility and delay gave Forde a chance to gather his wits. He caught a trolley to Evening Star Transients, sprinted up to his room for the keys, and took off again for Mecklenburg Street in Uncle Harold's DeSoto. When he fetched up at L. Merrill, Transients and Long-Term, Faye was sitting on the step, holding her arm against herself awkwardly.

"Faye! Are you all right?"

"No. As usual."

"What happened?"

"I tripped over stupid Butterball and fell down the stairs. I'm OK, I think. Basically. For somebody who manages to screw up everything she does, I'm about normal."

"What's wrong with your arm?"

"I wrenched it. Can you give me a lift somewhere?"

"That's what I'm supposed to be doing. Mr. Len was looking for you. He kind of had steam coming out of his collar."

"Me too. Mr. Len is just going to have to wait his turn. Do you know where Seven Lakes Lane is?"

On the way to Courtenay's house, Faye described lying on Mrs. Merrill's hall floor in a welter of scrap wood and dry rot, her head throbbing from its collision with Love's Awakening, and feeling that the blow had about knocked the foolishness out of her at last.

"Somebody did set that fire, Forde," Faye said. "I smelled the kerosene. Somebody wanted to kill me; or if they knew I wasn't there, they wanted to scare me, and they didn't care if they killed Mrs. Merrill by the way. I can only think of one person that mean in Charlotte, and that's Courtenay Weston. I'm going to go over there and make her admit it."

"Didn't you just say it knocked the foolishness out of you? Why aren't you going to the cops about this?"

"No proof. And anyhow, it would just be more foolishness. Chief Olerud thinks I'm a smart-aleck who's out to give him trouble. He wouldn't pay any more attention to my suspicions than a fly on his desk."

"But if she tried to kill you, what makes you think she'll sit still while you accuse her?"

Faye snorted. "She knows better than to cross me. I'll wipe the floor with her again."

"Come on, Faye. Can you see Courtenay Weston creeping up your stairs with a Molotov cocktail in her hand?"

"No," Faye admitted. "She'd send Thompson, her domestic ...." She waved her good hand. "Her cat's paw."

"And you can wipe the floor with this cat's paw, too? With a hurt arm?"

Faye was silent while Forde started the DeSoto's engine. "My arm's OK. I think it's just a sprain. If Thompson did it, it was at

Courtenay's orders. We don't have to involve him until we have proof that she ordered it."

Forde shook his head and pulled away from the curb. "The whole thing is just not Courtenay Weston's style, Faye. She may be silly and conceited and vain, but she's not a gangster."

"Really." Faye looked out the passenger window. "Gangster is as gangster does, seems to me."

"Faye, with all respect, I think maybe you're a little off-balance on – "

"Turn left here. Then it's the second street to the right. Look, Forde, you don't have to shoot people and need a shave to be a gangster. Courtenay Weston buys what she wants with money she didn't earn. She steals what she can't buy. She has sex with whoever she wants, when she wants, and nobody better get in her way. She has thugs to do her dirty work. Is Al Capone any different?"

"Well ..." Yes, it seemed to Forde, there was a difference, but he couldn't find the words.

"This is it. Right on Seven Lakes Lane."

Forde sighed and took the turn. The tone of things improved dramatically with every block; houses bigger, set farther back from the road, with longer stretches of lawn and woodland between them. No good, Forde thought, could ever come of taking on people who lived in this neighborhood.

"Look, Faye..."

"Yes, impressive, isn't it? See the stone gates up there on the left? Through there."

Forde slowed and turned to Faye. "Al Capone was known for getting away with murder, you know."

"He went to jail in the end."

"Which I'm sure was a big relief to all those dead folks."

"Don't be silly, Forde. Courtenay Weston isn't Al Capone."

"But you just – "

"Slow down, you'll wreck your fenders getting through the gate."

Faye was out of the DeSoto before it stopped, and at Courtenay's front door before Forde could pursue. There was no doorbell, but a brass knocker worthy of the Houses of Parliament. Faye exercised it.

"Geez, Faye."

"Hush. Get some backbone, Forde, or get in that car and drive yourself back to Uncle Harold."

The door opened to reveal a starchy-looking maid.

"Hi," Faye twinkled. "We're here for the sleepover. With Courtenay."

The maid looked troubled. It was her first week at this house, and nobody had told her about any sleepover. "I will see," she said. "If Miss Courtenay is expecting – "

"Expecting?" Faye shrieked. "Did you hear that, Fordey? I rahther think not!"

"I will see," the maid began again.

"Don't bother," Faye said. "We know the way. Come on, Fordey. You can bring the things in later."

Faye swept past the maid and skipped up the main stairway to the room that held Courtenay's massive four-poster. The place, Faye thought, where I lost my virginity, though not my stupidity. Courtenay was sitting at a dressing table, painting her nails. She saw Faye's entrance in the mirror before her and turned, one hand still holding the applicator and the other with the splayed rigor of one who tries not to smear fresh polish.

"Well," Courtenay said. "What a perfect goddamn pleasure. How did you get in here?"

"Your maid did her best not to let me in," Faye said. "But I was too quick for her. Where's Thompson?"

"Get out."

"Where's Thompson? I want him to tell me, to your face, that you sent him to burn Mrs. Merrill's house down with me in it."

"Get … What? I have not the least idea what you're babbling about, freak. Ella!"

Faye turned toward the sound of footsteps in the hall. It was not the maid or Thompson, but Forde, with a wicker basket on his shoulder. "I brought the stuff, Faye," he said. "Where should I put it?"

"Inside the door there, thanks, Forde. Courtenay, this is Mr. Forde Morgan of the Charlotte Star-Dispatch. Not from the society page this time, though. He's my cat's-paw. That basket has enough baseball bats and kerosene in it to send you up the river for the rest of your natural life. It'll go better on you if you own up right away."

Courtenay's eyes bugged. "I think Gordon must have given you some kind of disease that's spread from your ass to your brain," she said. "What passes for it. Probably something he got from the other little camp followers he bragged about screwing, back there at Fort Bragg. You never know, do you, dear?"

"Indeed. It's such a relief that he screwed you after he did me," Faye said. "God knows what I'd have caught, the other way around. Now, can we get back to business? Somebody set fire to the house I was staying in, trying to kill me. The only question is, was it you personally, which I can't imagine, or did Thompson do it for you?"

"I had nothing to do with that, nor did Thompson. Are you prepared to spend the rest of your life in jail for slander before witnesses? Because that's what's going to happen if I don't see your skinny butt on its way out my door in ten seconds."

Faye narrowed her eyes at Courtenay, and thought about stuffing her under another piece of furniture. She forbore, not sure she could do it again, and supposing that it would be dumb to give up the moral high ground. "Fine," she said. "If that's the way you want it. Let's go, Forde. Bring the evidence."

Courtenay caught up with them on the stairs.

"What evidence? Evidence of what?"

"Forget it," Fay said, still descending. "If you're innocent, it doesn't matter. As it is, you already know. We'll be going."

"Let me see in that basket. You have no evidence of anything."

Faye nodded. "I'd sure wish that, if I were you. Goodbye, Courtenay. Lock the basket in your trunk, Forde."

"Stop."

"No," Faye said. "I think not. I believe I saw Mrs. Merrill's missing cat out your window just now, and I know she would be comforted to have her kitty back. You'll be hearing from me."

"You crazy little thug. Come back here. Thompson! Ella!"

Faye waved Forde out the massive front door. "Kitty?" she sang. "Here, kitty kitty." And was stunned to see Butterball's face glower from behind a bush. She turned to Forde, keeping her back to Courtenay.

"How'd that cat get here?"

Forde juggled the picnic basket on his knee, fumbling with car keys. "I dunno. The way you had me drive, I couldn't help but notice, we wound up no more than a half mile from Miz Merrill's. There's that little crick that keeps you from driving straight here, but I expect there's ways for a animal to cross it."

"Or anybody else, like a bunch of Klan. We'll have to look into that, Forde, but for now, let's collect that cat and get out of here."

Forde followed her into the bushes, a few steps ahead of Courtenay. "When we do," he muttered, "could you give me some idea what you were thinking of, coming here like this?"

"Thinking wasn't in it. I just thought maybe we could shake something loose by charging in on her and pretending. I guess that only happens on the radio."

"Not any program I ever heard. Now we've got Courtenay and her maid on our case, chasing us through the woods and trespassing, I don't know what – "

"Trespassing, pooh, we knocked on the door like anybody else. Oh, gosh, now Thompson's after us, though. Kitty? Here, kitty-kitty-kitty."

"Who's Thompson?"

"Courtenay's cat's-paw." Faye waited while Thompson loped easily past Courtenay and Ella. "Good afternoon, Thompson. May I introduce Mr. Forde Morgan of the Star-Dispatch? You two will have a lot in common; Forde is my cat's-paw. Speaking of cats, though, please don't disturb yourself for us. We are here retrieving my landlady's much-loved pet, Butterball, who seems to have wandered into your woods. There she goes, into that bunch of bushes."

Thompson seemed to pay no attention to Faye, but pursued Butterball as if there were no other goal in the world. Faye may have been a skinny girl in many ways, but she was a good runner. She raced through deepening stands of pine and alder, and caught up with Thompson in time to see Butterball slink into a thicket of raspberry canes. Thompson swore.

Faye caught Thompson's sleeve and leaned on it, as much to immobilize him as to catch her breath. "What on Earth is happening, Thompson?"

Thompson didn't answer right away. He opened his mouth, and shut it as Forde Morgan came up. Forde was pale and sweating. "You can't guess who's fifty yards behind me," he puffed. "Mister Len Biggs, an' he's mad as a wet hen."

Faye snorted. "Ol' Mist' Len, mad as a hen," she sang. "What's he doing here?"

Thompson shrugged. "I called him when I saw you trespassing in the Weston's home," he said. "He was glad to get word of your whereabouts, young lady."

"I was on assignment," Faye said. "Len Biggs was perfectly well aware of that."

"And did that assignment include breaking and entering, uttering false threats, lying, and imposing your skinny fanny where it has no business being?" Courtenay had joined them at the raspberry thicket, running up like Diana on the hunt, not breaking a sweat at it.

"Real working women do what they have to do in pursuit of a story," Faye said. "There was no breaking about my entering, I knocked and your maid let me in. I said nothing that was not firmly based in fact and legitimate conjecture. What is it about my fanny that has you so bothered? Is yours getting a little saggy?"

Forde and Thompson winced and exchanged a glance. "Ladies ..." Thompson said.

"Faye, Honey ..." Forde hazarded.

"Faye Bynum," Len Biggs roared from upstage, stomping heavily through the bracken and leading a little band of runners-up that included the maid Ella and a bothered-looking silver-haired couple, the female half of which Faye recognized as Courtenay's mother Alice; the Maurice Chevalier guy must be Mr. Weston, owner of half of Mecklenberg county.

"I insist on an immediate explanation of your absence from your assigned post. What in the name of sense do you mean by submitting this libelous nonsense?" Len Biggs waved two or three half-crumpled sheets of copy paper.

"What libelous nons – " Faye blinked. "Why Mr. Len," she said. "You – " She shut up; none too soon, she realized.

Len Biggs thrust the rolls of copy paper under her nose. "Don't ask stupid questions, don't be evasive, and by God , don't you give me your sass, little lady." His voice sounded like the roll of artillery.

Faye's heart slammed, and she backed away from Len Biggs. Behind him, she could see Courtenay Weston, enjoying the show.

Courtenay twinkled at her. "What excellent advice," she said. "No wonder you've done so well this summer." She turned to the woods. "Why," she said. "There's your kitty now. And – oh, my – it looks like she has a gentleman friend. My, and another real horse, too."

Faye tore her eyes from Len Biggs. Butterball stood at the edge of the raspberry thicket; beside her a larger cat crouched. A handsome, tawny cat with walnut dapples, as elegant beside Butterball as Courtenay Weston was beside Faye, and as big as Gordon Simmons had been. The long ears were flattened against its head; it was hard, in the late-afternoon sunlight, splintered by the trees into a thousand lances of gold, to see the outlines of Butterball's friend - surely the AWOL ocelot - but it seemed clear to Faye that he was big, tough, and firmly attached to Butterball.

Apparently not so clear to Courtenay, though. She sauntered toward the cats, making little kissy sounds, and leaned down to pick up Butterball. "Well," she said. "Was this the dear little pussy that lived with the Girl Reporter? What a match you two do make. Come here, pussy-wussy."

She reached for Butterball. Faye, still in shock at Len Biggs, opened her mouth and tried to yell. As in a nightmare, no sound came but a faint hiss, more than matched by Butterball, and by her pal. Courtenay knelt and shook her head. "Bad kitty," she scolded. "What has your bitchy little chum taught you about manners? Come to Auntie."

Faye found her voice. "No," she yelled. "Don't – "

Butterball's buddy sprang from the shadows and wrapped himself around Courtenay's head, biting and clawing. Courtenay screamed and jumped back, tripping over her mother's foot and sprawling in the weeds and grass of the clearing. The ocelot, apparently satisfied with a quick victory, jumped off of Courtenay, grabbed Butterball by the back of the neck, and bounded into the forest. Faye stared after them.

"You know, Forde," she said, over screams and swearing from Courtenay. "I swear that's the happiest I ever saw Butterball look."

"Yeah," Forde nodded. "Not too happy over there, though."

Courtenay Weston was crouched in the weeds, her hands clutched to her face, screaming and sobbing while blood ran over her fingers. Faye snorted.

"Yeah, Miss Elegant got herself scratched up. Forde, we've got to get out of here, right now."

"No kidding," Forde said. "Come on."

But Len Biggs grabbed at Faye's arm. "Hold on a schecond, Bynum," he said.

"Yes sir. I'm on my way back to the office right now. Can we talk about it there? I think Miss Weston might need your help, sir. I'll have the news conference copy on your desk by the time you get back there. Forde will give me a lift. Thank you, sir."

She pulled out of Len Biggs' grasp and yanked Forde away. When they were in Uncle Harold's DeSoto, Forde turned to her with the key in his hand. "What – "

"Go," Faye said. "Go, go, go. Get us out of here. Now."

Forde did. When they were a block from the Star-Dispatch, he parked and turned to Faye. "Yes?"

"Yes? Didn't you hear him?"

"Who? Mr. Len? Of course I did. He got excited enough, he talked clear. Good for him."

"Not just clear, Forde. Think, for God's sake. Where did you hear that voice before?"

Forde stared at her. "Gee. I don't know."

Faye started to raise her arms to heaven, and bonked them on the roof of the little coupe. She grabbed Forde's head and pressed her mouth to his, not puckering, keeping her lips tucked in. But still, feeling the heat spring in his ears like somebody had turned on an iron, the dope. "That give you a hint, dope?" she mumbled.

When she pulled back, Forde was sweating and scarlet. "The ... oh, Jehoshaphat. The Klan!"

"That's right. We heard that voice weeks ago in June. He's the one, Forde. Everett Bassler the murderer takes his orders from Mr. Len Biggs, mild-mannered Sunday editor of the Charlotte Star-Dispatch. Took. Now, will you get us there so we can expose the heartless bastard for what he is?"

Forde shook his head. "No, wait a second. That's crazy."

"It's not, and you know it, Forde Morgan. Was that, or was it not the voice we heard running that little gang of thugs?"

Forde shrugged. "Well, it sounded like it, maybe. But." He lapsed.

"But what? And I'll tell you something else. All along, it's been like the Klan knew what was going on at the Star-Dispatch. How did they know we had a Negro intern? How did everybody at the paper, somehow, know right away that's why they killed Horatio? Same answer both times. They had a contact at the paper. Yes, and I'll tell you what else. What were they doing behind Mrs. Merrill's house the night Gordon was killed? They were coming over there to scare me off from writing about them, and when that backfired, they came back and set the house on fire. Who knew I had that bee in my bonnet? Len Biggs, that's who."

Forde snorted. "He was jealous of Gordon, I expect. Had a big crush on you I reckon, and – "

Faye felt a scorch of anger rise from her belly. "You! You talk down and mock when I see something you've been too stubborn and slow and too... too Southern to admit. Not that I was that quick about it myself, I admit. Christ, though. Sometimes I used to think Gordon was slow and stubborn –"

"He was, Faye." Forde, stung by Faye's anger, started saying things that had nothing to do with the subject, and that he knew he would regret. He didn't care. "Gordon was slow and stubborn, and he didn't care about anything but getting you into bed. He wasn't near good enough for you, Faye. I – "

Faye was not to be outshouted, however stupid the things she found to shout. "You! You couldn't wait to move in, could you? Christ, Gordon was hardly cold before you were … were …" *Before you were being sweet and attentive and humble and helpful.* Faye waved a hand, burst into tears and slammed herself out of the DeSoto.

Forde jumped out too, and left the engine running to scramble after Faye.

"Faye, listen …"

"No, you listen. I'm sick of being patronized and talked down to. I'm going back to the office, and I'm going to finish writing a story like you never saw in your life, and if nobody likes it, well, that's tough, I guess. Shut up. Don't follow me." She stamped her foot. "You can just drop <u>dead</u>, Forde Morgan."

Faye ran to the door of the <u>Star-Dispatch</u>, and into the Ladies – where I always run when I'm hysterical, she thought – to get herself in hand. She splashed her face with water, and when it was buried in the swath of roller towel, she swore. Why had she said those mean things to Forde? Well, she would have to apologize.

But when she came out of the Ladies, Forde was not to be seen. She pushed herself up the stairs to the newsroom. Christ, she was a bitch, and no wonder nobody loved her. When she opened the swinging door, Alma Brackett was waiting for her.

"This came for you, Faye. I'm terribly sorry."

"From Forde? Did he complain to you?" The little twerp. Good lord, whatever his faults, Gordon wouldn't have run to Mommy just because she yelled at him about something.

Alma Brackett didn't answer, but handed her a flimsy piece of yellow paper. Her face looked like a gravestone. Faye's knees dropped her against Alma Brackett's desk as she unfolded it.

Time and Chance

MISS FAYE BYNUM THE CHARLOTTE STAR-DISPATCH
MOTHER AND DADDY KILLED IN CAR WRECK STOP
FUNERAL FRIDAY STOP HURRY HOME STOP NANA

29.

M R. PORTER BARNSTABLE (known among Woolworth staff as "Portable," standing 4 feet 6, no more than 105 pounds) stubbed out a cigarette on his shoe and snapped, "Step it up, Bynum. Break's over in five." Faye took a shallow draw on her own smoke and nodded, not really hearing, since the cigarette, the heat of the break room and the apple jelly sandwich in her hand had transported her to the now nonexistent attic of *L. Merrill, Transients and Long-Term.*

The time is 8 or so in the dusk. The date, any day in those hermetic first weeks of the summer, in the era that was, Faye had then fancied, her own. The weeks when she had only herself to manage, only the distant demands of Gordon and Mizzou to worry about, only Alma Brackett to despise. That illusory peacetime before reality stormed in, killing and burning.

Faye looked over the bumpy, time-frozen shoulder of the rookie in the mirror and saw ... not even a stranger. Maybe some stranger's adolescent kid. Astonished, and finally depressed by the ignorance, by the narcissistic self-inventory, by a virginal brat who had never lost a baby, never even been pregnant, never manhandled by redneck killers, or jailed on suspicion of murder. Nor had she yet .... Faye drew a breath, astonished at the innocence of the waif that she, like Hamlet's daddy, now haunted. She'd had plenty of warning; it had rattled and hissed in her belly when she set up Gordon to be beaten up. Killed.

"When I killed Gordon. When I murdered my fiancé, Corporal Gordon Simmons." She made herself say it aloud to the empty room, the angry words ringing against the walls. I could prophesy, she thought; but not be heeded. What I can never do, what no one will ever do, is forgive me for killing Gordon. For murdering Gordon.

Time and Chance

When she left the break room and reentered the heat and clamor of the stock workspace, Portable shook his head, patted her butt, pointed at the clock - six minutes late from lunch break - and docked her pay a nickel.

*

"I can't hear you, Forde. Can you speak up a little?"

"Is this better? I said how are you doing?"

"Oh. OK, I guess. How ever did you get my number?"

"Oh, that. Well, they ain't but a couple dozen Bynums in St. Louis."

"You called every Bynum in St. Louis until you got down to me?" Daddy's phone-book name was William.

"Third or fourth one knew who I was looking for. A cousin of yours, or something."

"Cousin Del. Did he cuss at you for wasting his time?"

"A little bit, at first. But he was real nice, after he found out I was calling from North Carolina. Seems like he knew some folks here."

"He and Laney spent their honeymoon in Blowing Rock, and he won't shut up about it to this day. Forde, listen: I'm sorry."

"What for?"

"For saying those horrible, mean things to you. For leaving without telling you goodbye."

"Aw. You were upset. I was awful sorry to hear about your folks."

Faye was silent for a moment, and then said something that didn't survive the hiss and crackle of Long Distance.

"I didn't catch that."

"I said, I wasn't surprised, I knew it was coming. Daddy always drove too fast. The day he came home from the War, he took

281

Mama and me out in our old Chevy and like to scared us to death. Me, anyhow. Mama loved going fast. I think that's why she married him. She probably knew it was coming too."

Forde's turn for silence.

"This is kind of expensive, Forde."

"I know. I just wanted to, I don't know. See how you were. Anyways, the paper's paying. Don't worry."

"Oh, sure. I can just hear Mr. Len."

"Naw, I meant the *Intelligencer*. Daddy's paper. But either way, the other thing I called you for, Mr. Len ain't thinking about nickel-dime stuff. He's in jail."

"He's <u>what</u>? What for?" Len Biggs, eating grits with a wooden spoon and dealing with Queenie. And Gloriana, whose Sunday afternoon regular he was.

"That story you started? I finished it up, and that put him in the soup."

"Get along! He'd never let it see print."

"He didn't have a vote. I took it home and run off a thousand copies on the *Intelligencer* press, and had it put into the <u>Star-Dispatch</u> like it was a ad supplement. It went out with the Thursday bargains the same week, that thousand copies. Also, I give a copy to that *Clarion*, you know. The colored paper, they did a whole run. That helped out."

"You never!"

"Sure did. 'Course, Mist' Len was fit to be tied, but it was nothing he could do but fire me, which he done. But then a whole lot of Ni – of Negro folks come forward, turns out they knew all about him for a long time, just didn't dare say anything, for lack of proof, or any kind of support from white folks."

"And you supplied that. Forde, I am so proud of you."

"Naw, you supplied it, Faye. I just got it out into the open, which I should have done it long since."

"Oh. Golly, Forde."

"Uh huh. So Chief Olerud pretty much had to come over to the newsroom this morning and make a show of putting him in cuffs, Shanky told me. I was sorry to miss that. 'Course, he won't stay there. Harold Claiborne and Alma Brackett will bail him out. They're family, I guess you knew that."

"Yes, but ..." More silence.

"Uh huh. Well, it'll never come to a charge or a trial, nothing like that. Claiborne and Miz Alma Brackett tried to get him to stop that Klan business, and he wouldn't. But they covered up for him because of how, you know. The War, and all."

"'He Gave His All,' is that it?"

"I guess. Or blood is thicker'n water."

Faye slumped against the kitchen wall next to the phone. "And killing Horatio and Gordon is water?"

"Looks that way. I don't excuse it, Faye. I smartened up some this summer, most of it when I found you in that alley, knocked out and bald and bloody. I didn't know Gordon or Horatio, hardly, but I knew you. I never felt nothing like that in my life up to then. And, of course, what you said was the truth all along, wasn't it?"

"Well." Faye considered what she could say to that handsome somewhat apology. Of course Forde would have rehearsed it before he called, probably sweating all over the phone. "I guess. And I guess the blood on my skirt was maybe Mr. Len's, from when Gordon punched him in the nose. I hope it wasn't Gordon's, but I also hope I never find out." She laughed. "I'm getting to be a real Southerner, aren't I? The real truth about anything seems like the last thing that occurs to folks in Charlotte." But she remembered Forde's gallantry, and the hundreds of kindnesses that had seemed like the first thing that had occurred to Rose Brackett and Mrs. Merrill, and shook her head in resignation. "Not you, though. And not Alma Brackett. You were ... "

She gestured emptily at the kitchen window. "The world is a hell of a place, Forde."

"Looks like. But you know what else?"

"What?" *What now?*

"Remember how Courtenay Weston got her face scratched up by that wildcat thing?"

"The ocelot?"

"That was it. Well, I saw a piece in the Star-Dispatch, she's on her way to Switzerland."

"How lovely for her. She can seduce a yodeler."

"Nuh-uh. Our laundry girl has a cousin in Charlotte, that knows Ella, works for the Westons?"

"Yes?"

"Said that ossel – that thing, it tore something, a nerve like, in Miss Courtenay's face, so she looks awful. All ugly on one side, like she had a stroke. They was a lot of doctors come and go, and I mean from Harvard and Paris, the Mayo Clinic, what all, and they all said the same thing, no way to fix it. What she's going to Switzerland for, is psychology."

"Psychology?" Faye sat suddenly at the kitchen table, pushing aside her mother's box of letters.

"Psychology therapy. You know, Freud, all that. They're gonna to try to get her so she's OK with being ugly. Hate to put it that way. What our girl says, anyways. What do you reckon you'll do now?"

"About Courtenay?"

About Courtenay Weston as a player in her brief summer drama of hope, she would grieve, as she would have mourned the crippling of a beautiful, heedless animal. Of an ocelot, maybe, that you could admire, but had better not get too close to. The Courtenay who belonged to those first weeks of Faye's summer - the Deb of the Decade, the Courtenay of pink sheets and Bristol Cream - was gone, as dead as Gordon and Horatio. Another who would bear no portion of anything, like Gordon and Horatio and her own baby, their days of vanity under the sun unfairly short. And all for the difference between candlewood and gold; or out of simple boredom; or out of jealousy of a girl who, without money or breeding or, God knew, Courtenay's kind of looks, was making a life for herself out of her own materials. Or maybe, like Lillian Sandbridge, just to keep in practice.

"I'm sad, I guess ... I don't know why; she was a horrible person."

Faye was startled by the sadness she felt for Courtenay. Did it amount to some kind of forgiveness for Courtenay's arrogance and perfidy? Or some late-blooming guilt for humiliating Courtenay, banging her head on the break room floor? She wondered if this was Alma Brackett's "trick of forgiveness." Could you call something that worked this slowly a trick? More like a slow miracle. Something ... Faye had a vision of herself under the sun, her slow creep across the wilderness of her life, toward forgiveness. *Maybe the trick is to see it out there, years away under the sun, distant but waiting.*

"Naw, I meant about yourself. Are you going to live on your own? When do you leave for college?"

Faye laughed raggedly. "College. I had a talk with the probate folks this morning. After debts and funeral costs and all, I have enough for two mortgage payments on the house. Oh, and a bill from the wrecker to pay, yet. College didn't come into it. It is out of the question."

"Mm. Gosh, Faye. So you're going to work?"

Faye said nothing for a long time.

"Faye?"

"I'm here. I started at the Five and Dime this week."

"The Five and *Dime*?"

"Stock girl. I'm not out in public, where people would be offended because of my hair. I'm up to maybe half an inch or so, by the way. It looks like I had cooties last month, but hardly any skin shows through. I wore the Major Barbara wig to the interview. They say I can work myself up to ... to clerk, in time. Maybe I'll have enough hair for that by then."

"Well, but what about writing?"

Faye flared a little. "Well, what about it? I don't have a degree and I'm not going to get one. And they don't pay much for copy boys around here, which is all I could do without a degree. Writing is out, for me."

Another long silence. "Forde?"

"Yeah ..." Faye could hear, over hundreds of miles of copper wire, the quaver in the breath that Forde drew. "You know, Daddy's getting tired of the *Intelligencer*, and he keeps after me to start taking it over for him. I'm about ready to quit school and say Yes." Another silence, another shaky breath, then: "I guess that's what I mean to do."

Faye felt a pang, it was so unfair; and then took herself in hand. "Gosh, Forde, congratulations. That sounds so exciting. You're going to run a newspaper of your own."

"Naw, Daddy'll help a while, and sort of phase out, he called it. But I can hire some ... uh, some help. The business manager says I could offer maybe a dollar an hour, after Daddy's off the books. Probably along the end of October. That would sound pretty big to folks here."

"Uh huh." It sounded pretty big to Faye, too. Woolworth's was paying her 47 cents.

"Course, you'd get tired of working for a little country rag, but I expect you'd be moving up to F'etteville, Raleigh, before long."

"Raleigh ... Wait, me? You're offering <u>me</u> a job? Oh, nuh-uh, Forde. I'm no journalist." *And I'd rather die in the poorhouse than owe my career to a fella that everybody will say had a crush on me, or took pity on me.*

"I don't need 'journalists.' Doggone journalists and pressroom fellas we got can put this thing out with their eyes closed, which they do most of the time. I need a ..." Another shaky breath. "Well, a city editor, that won't believe every stupid thing somebody tells them. That has guts and brains."

Brightening, now: "And can already write like a pro, what Miss Alma Brackett told me. That story about her mother was just the nuts. I showed it to Daddy, and he says the same. So, you think it over, Faye. Don't say yes or no over the phone. Specially no. We'll write you a formal offer, you think it over, and write back. The whole thing don't need to cost us but six cent, if you say no. But I hope you won't."

Faye thought it over while she packed up Mama and Daddy's clothes for the Goodwill, and did a weekend yard sale on the small suite of useable garden tools and bric-a-brac. She thought it over while she talked to a real estate lady about the house. Sure, working for sweaty, red-face, redneck Forde Morgan, who'd already, not half way into September, gone back to his country way of talking, and probably of thinking, with his laundry "girl" and "they're family," like that excused murder and terror.

Sure, the "City" Editor of Gabbro, North Carolina, a title Forde had obviously invented on the fly. *Where's the city, Forde?* Writing up the school board meetings and the Jaycee light bulb drive for a little cotton town where sixty percent of the population couldn't read past fourth grade. Living and trying to make a writer of herself, in a place that valued "blood" above justice.

*

Faye found the letter under the mail slot, returning home exhausted and soggy after her second week in the stifling back rooms of Woolworth's. It looked nothing like Gordon's earnest penciling, but it was humble enough. Her address was typed with a ribbon that was well past its trade-in date, the envelope a little crumpled from postal handling. She slipped a finger under the flap, and felt the same warning tickle below her heart that had assailed her in Mrs. Merrill's burned-out house. She knew from that, what she would find in the letter: the same burned-out house of cards and ruin. It would be effusive, regretful, a little embarrassed that Forde's improvised "City Editor" notion had been vetoed by Daddy and the business manager; or that Forde had decided to go back to school, or tour the West for a year or two, before he did anything about the Gabbro *Intelligencer*, if he ever did; or that Faye might be taken on as a Midwest correspondent, a stringer, at three cents a word and subject to Forde's editing. At most, it would be the same "City Editor" nonsense that Faye had been deriding all week, a made-up job at a hick newspaper that would dead-end her for life in a small and stagnant pond without hope.

Faye felt dizzy and ill, and decided to take a shower before she opened the letter; she couldn't stomach the notion of reading whatever weaseling Forde Morgan had sent, with sweat and the smell of Woolworth's back rooms on her skin and the feel of Portable Barnstable's stubby hand on her butt, where he had begun to put it as often as they were in the same room together.

Twenty minutes later, Faye pushed aside the brittle and maculate shower curtain and emerged into the tiny bathroom in a cloud of steam. The tub gurgled out on a fading tenor note; silence and solitude returned to the house, punctuated by the tap of a last drop from the shower head. The half-steamed mirror over the sink showed a moving pink blur topped by a skullcap of dark wet hair, level eyebrows, and dark eyes that, for the first time in her life, anchored lines of strain and sorrow. *Wonderful. I'm twenty years old, and I'm already starting to look like Alma Brackett.*

Time and Chance

Faye dried herself, wrapped in the towel and went back to the living room. She drew the shades, and picked up the envelope. She inserted a finger, gritting her teeth against the warning tickle, against the competing disappointments of no job at all, or a job that would destroy her mind and soul. Faye considered a prayer, but it was impossible to decide to whom and towards what end it should be directed, unless maybe that whatever resulted would get her away from Woolworth's and Portable, not destroy her soul, and maybe pay a quarter of what Alma Brackett made. That would be $10 a week, a little over half what she was making at Woolworth's. Still, it might go far enough in a Southern country town, where things were likely to be cheap. *I will eat the pods that my boss's pigs discard.* And Forde Morgan wouldn't put his hand on her butt to save his life. She tore open the flap and pulled out four sheets of paper.

30.

The Gabbro Intelligencer
"Your Home-Town Paper"
Gabbro, N.C.   Ph. SAndhills 3573
September 17, 1947

Miss Faye Bynum
1148 Delmar Boulevard
St. Louis 11, Mo

Dear Miss Bynum:

This letter is to offer you the position of City Editor with this newspaper, at an initial wage of $.85 per hour, subject to a maximum limit of $36 per week, to commence on November 1, 1947, for an initial period of not less than one year. Your duties as City Editor will be subject to discussion, but will include leadership of this newspaper's coverage of events occurring within, or directly affecting, the city and county of Gabbro, North Carolina, and the production of no less than one editorial essay per week bearing on matters within your charge.

The Intelligencer offers its employees a modest package of fringe benefits, described in the attached ...

If you accept this offer, please so indicate by signing and returning the enclosed carbon copy, no later than ...

The editors and staff of the Gabbro Intelligencer look forward to ....

Sincerely,

Time and Chance

It was signed, prosaically, by a Custis Morgan, Managing Editor - Daddy's real name, she figured - with an added note: "Forde has shown me some of your writing, and it's what we want for the Intelligencer. Hope you'll consider our offer. He's added some thoughts on the next page but one."

Faye sank to the floor, clutching her head. She skipped over the carbon copy and deferred the page of retirement and health benefits, to maybe look at in a week, or forty years or so. She gave the instructions for signing and returning a glance and a promise, and braced herself to plow through whatever redneck "thoughts" Forde Morgan had managed to get down. She wondered whether they might include provisions for firing her if she should dare to mention the Klan in one of her weekly editorial essays. Probably.

"Dear Faye: The prospect taking over responsibility for the Intelligencer presents me with one of those crucial life tests that I would hesitate to take on without the collaboration of someone whom I know I can trust ex implicitly to ...

As Faye read, she sat up straighter, and tears - those ambivalent tears that had accompanied her on the bus from Jane and Alice Dupree's home, the tears of one whose journey under the sun was continuing in spite of everything - sprang to the corners of her eyes.

Forde spoke of his intention - his "vision," no less - to make a notable country newspaper of the *Intelligencer*, and thereby to make of Gabbro, North Carolina a small republic of literate readers and progressive thinkers in a wilderness of ignorant prejudice. It spoke of the need for articulate voices like Faye's, crying in a wilderness of slack-minded prejudice. *"I want your voice to cry in this wilderness,"* honest to God.

Time and Chance

Forde thought that he could, as prospective managing editor, set the tone, with some help from Faye: *"You always see things before I do, and see it more clear."* But of all people he knew or had heard of, only Faye Bynum had the eloquence and skill to make people sit up and read. *"I expect your weekly editorials to make the people of this community think, and to think new thoughts, that you and I might hope would result in a new Southern attitude of tolerance, civic virtue and pride. (But you need to know that if I think we need to go 'slantways' on something, I hope you will take my advice seriously)."*

In other words, Outrage the rednecks, but keep your mouth shut when I tell you. Well, we'll see about that. Forde's "thoughts" made up a mixed manifesto of daring and platitudes and impractical - impracticable - ideals, and a raw appeal for her help that made Faye yearn to see him again, to tease him about voices in the wilderness, and maybe to make him blush and sneeze with a kiss. To feel his gentle hand smoothing her hair. The whole thing was so crazy and earnest and laughable that Faye, cross-legged on the living room floor, almost cried in her own wilderness.

Well, she did cry. No one was there to hear it. What Forde wanted was something that she could do with her all her might, and would joy in the doing. The warning tickle returned to its seat below her heart, and this time she recognized it for what it was: the faint clamor of hope reborn, stubborn and irreducible. Faye rose, smiled goodbye to the hurtling ghosts of her Mama and Daddy, and walked into the kitchen. When she heard the distant ringing at SAndhills 3573, she stood and tucked the towel more firmly over the flutter in her breast.

"Forde?"

www.ingramcontent.com/pod-product-compliance
Lightning Source LLC
Chambersburg PA
CBHW030030180626
46810CB00001B/298